LIVING
AMONG THE DRAGONS

Living Among the Dragons

Delphine Hintz

Eclectic Collections

First Edition

Published 2024

ISBN (softcover): 979-8-9904-2612-2

ISBN (hardcover): 979-8-9904-2610-8

ISBN (e-book): 979-8-9904-2611-5

This book is dedicated in three ways.

To Evelyn, for listening and loving every story, including the ones she helped create.

To Bruce, for secret reasons.

To Sylvia, because Mom would be mad if I didn't include you, too.

The Island of Aradin

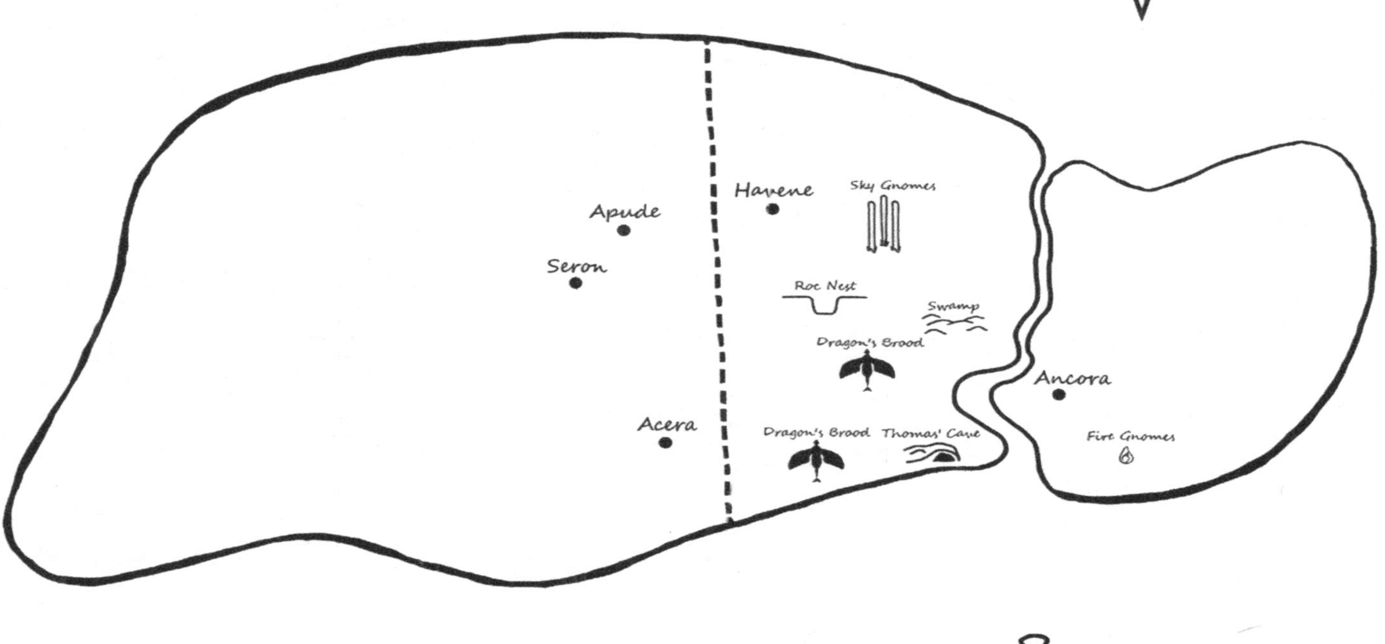

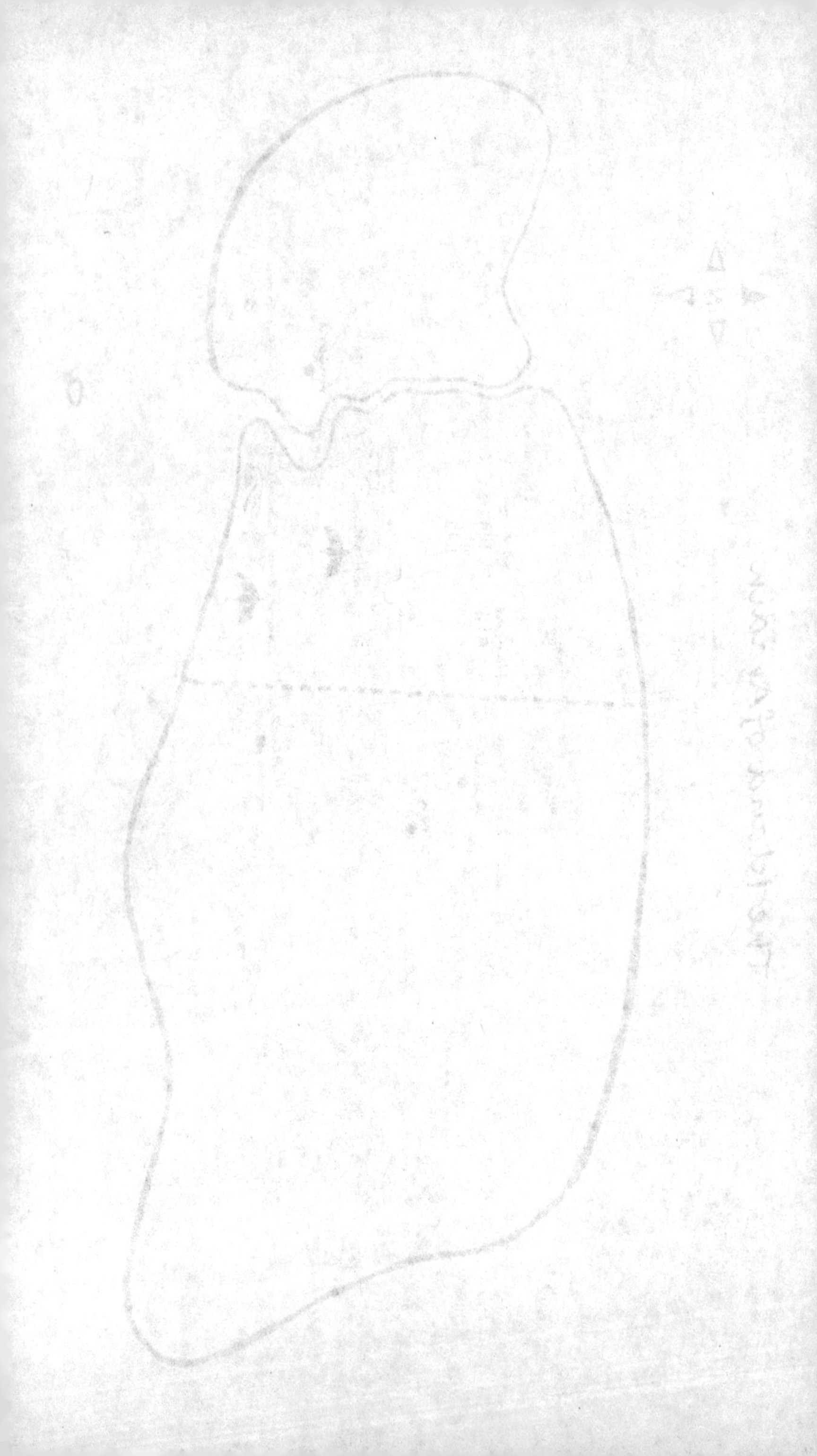

Contents

I

Where You Meet Many Characters but Only Need to Remember One (or Three)

Roars shook the timbers of their home.

"Quick," Timothy said. He snapped the wet potato sack, opening it further. Droplets flung to the ground. "Gabrielle, climb in."

The girl let go of Marie's skirts. When Timothy nodded, Gabrielle clambered over the edges of the sack and slid down.

"Gabrielle," he said, waiting until she looked at him. "Whatever happens, don't come out. No matter what you hear."

The girl bit her lip. She nodded.

Timothy kissed her forehead, lingering a second longer than normal.

He cinched the sack.

Another roar. Timothy glanced to Marie and tried to smile. Marie only nodded once, taking another step towards the door. Timothy picked up the sack, struggling slightly with the weight, then straightened completely.

He opened the door.

Heat prickled his skin. Timothy blinked his stinging eyes and jerked to the side, Marie's hand light upon his back. He continued onward, close to the burning house, close to whatever shadows were surviving the onslaught. Despite the time of the night, he could see the fields just beyond Kendrid's house. The sprouts had just come up last week.

They, too, burned.

A baby's wailing from the inn across the street cut through the air. Edith had borne her child less than two months ago, a cute little thing no bigger than a loaf of bread with tufts of hair that stuck out like a dandelion's beard.

A house-sized shadow whooshed past, the wind pushing Timothy and Marie further into the wall behind them. Another roar and more fire.

The crying stopped.

They continued.

Heavy smoke filled their lungs. Marie was coughing, chest shaking as she pressed her hand to her mouth. Timothy swallowed and swallowed, readjusting the load on his aching back.

The air cleared. Another field lay before them, but with only a few twisting fires. Marie pressed a trembling hand to

Timothy's back. She slipped her other one into the crook of his elbow and squeezed.

The wind gusted.

The dragon landed before them. It stood twice as tall as Timothy, its scales the color of water at night. Its black eyes glittered as it considered them.

The potato sack grew even heavier. Timothy swung the sack off his shoulder and threw it—and his daughter—a good five feet away.

The dragon took a breath.

Gabrielle felt when her father threw her. She whimpered as the ground jarred her bones and twisted her arm underneath her. She bit her lip, eyes squeezed shut. She couldn't hear her parents. She didn't feel her father's warmth. The dragons still roared.

She crawled out of the sack.

The dragon paused, head cocking at the sight of her.

"No!" Timothy yelled. He fell to the ground, hands scrabbling in the dirt. He found a rock and threw it. It skidded off the dragon's chest.

The dragon snorted, head whipping back to look at them. It turned, tail swiping, and knocked Timothy and Marie to the ground.

"No!" The word burst from Gabrielle.

The dragon's attention returned to her.

She began to gnaw on her lip. She stopped. Her hands clenched, and she straightened her back. "I won't let you hurt them."

The dragon bent down, his head less than a foot from Gabrielle's.

She trembled but did not move.

It grinned.

"Will you fight me, little one?"

Its voice was a deep rumble that was not unpleasant to hear. Made for roars.

Gabrielle glanced towards her parents. Her father was pulling her mother to her feet, pushing her mother in the direction of the field and woods beyond even as his eyes sought Gabrielle.

The dragon chuckled. "Ah. I see." Bitterness crept into his tone. He came an inch closer.

Gabrielle's eyes fluttered. She kept them open.

The fist-sized eyes of the dragon fixed themselves completely on her. He murmured, as if rocks could whisper, so only she could hear. "Do not be ashamed, little one. You harbor a potential few can even dream of."

He waited.

She did not respond.

His mouth quirked up in what could have been a smile.

He left, leaning away and wings opening and winds pushing Gabrielle nearly to the ground and . . . he was gone.

Another roar pierced the night. Timothy gathered Gabrielle up, setting her on her own feet. Marie brushed her down once with a hand.

Timothy considered Gabrielle as the dragon had.

Gabrielle trembled but did not move.

Marie brushed Gabrielle's clothes again and squeezed Timothy's arm. When he looked to her, Marie inclined her head towards the woods. "Let's go."

Timothy looked once more to Gabrielle.

She dropped her gaze.

"Let's go," Marie repeated, hands gentle and on both of them. Gabrielle felt her father leave, her mother starting to trail after him while holding Gabrielle's hand.

She followed.

But not before glancing at the sky, spying a small button of misplaced darkness flying towards dragon territory, away from the fray.

Then, only then, did she follow. She would always follow.

Until the day they came.

"Fill 'er all the way up this time!" he demanded. The cup he held swayed as if in a breeze.

"Twas all the way filled until you started drinking it, Adolphus," Gabrielle countered, but she plucked it from his stubby fingers anyway.

"Then why's it empty?"

Gabrielle pressed her lips together tightly, unsuccessfully holding back a smile as she wove her way towards the counter and away from the farmer. No matter the years she spent serving the folk of the tavern, she never quite got used to how befuddled their senses became. The traveling bards usually were even worse when one happened across their small village. Such entertainers were far from common in Seron, which suited Gabrielle fine.

Spying Antoinette, a merchant who dropped by the inn every few months or so, Gabrielle ducked under Thompson's arm and approached her, tray of glasses momentarily forgotten. Antoinette—Nettie, as Gabrielle called her—set down a quarter full cup, smiling with her unusually straight teeth. Her luscious brown hair gleamed in the candlelight.

"Hello, my dear," Nettie greeted.

"It's been too long, Nettie." Gabrielle gave her a half-hug, the tavern's noise fading for a moment.

"Don't let me distract you." Nettie gestured towards the tray. "I'll be in town for a day or so."

"Do you need a place to stay?"

Nettie laughed. "I've already paid for a room. Here, of course. If you have time later tonight, we can speak then. Otherwise, tomorrow will be soon enough."

Gabrielle nodded and smiled. Nettie rarely stayed longer than a night, carrying next to nothing with her. She always sold her wares before traveling thus far.

"Nonsense!" Richard bellowed, his drink thudding upon the table and slopping over the sides. Gabrielle kept her quiet sigh to herself, twisting around him and behind the counter. "The dragons started the war fifty years ago with the murder of the farming family!"

"That was the first war, you dunderhead!" Thaddeus spat back, his face its usual blotchy red. "We've been fighting them blasted snakes for decades!"

"For decades?" Roberts interjected. He tapped a calm, steady rhythm on his own mug, lips pursed upward.

Thaddeus glowered, his entire face now matching his tightly wound strands of red hair. "They stopped when I was a boy. Then they killed that village twenty years back and started the war, and they've been burning and killing ever since!"

"Are you sure they ever stopped, Thad?" Roberts again

questioned him calmly, a smile clear upon his lips. He was one of the few in the tavern who could always remember the way home though he only visited the village. He lived several hours' north of the village at one of the few secondary schools located outside of a city's limits, the same school Gabrielle's father had attended.

"Don't you go patronizing me, young man." Thaddeus turned to him completely.

"I am not patronizing you, just assuring myself of the evidence."

"What about the changelings?" Richard challenged. "They're an important part of the war."

Gabrielle's back stiffened.

"The changelings were nearly wiped out during the first war," Roberts said, a skip in his tapping rhythm the only indication of his irritation.

"Ah . . . best be careful, Robs," Thaddeus said. His sun-darkened arms flexed as he placed his elbows on the table, a thick layer of dirt further shading his skin. "Even though you may have never seen one, they're out there. Changelings are worse than dragons. That's the one good thing about a dragon. It can't sneak up on you. A changeling, though"—he shook his head warningly—"they can hide in plain sight."

"Do changings always come from changing families?" piped up Sandy May, Richard's youngest child. She was chewing at the end of her long, blond braid. With the purple ribbon sticking out the side of her mouth, she was not dissimilar from a wide-eyed calf chewing a flower stalk.

Richard looked displeased by the question, but Roberts

jumped in to explain as Gabrielle reentered the arena and began distributing drinks.

"Mostly, but there are flukes . . ."

Gabrielle went beyond the conversation's reach, sliding a drink next to Adolphus' head. She gave a bowl of root stew to the merchant Yvonne, skittered around the Leland twins, and caught another snippet.

". . . nothing has been proven."

"So, I could be a changing?" Sandy May asked.

"Don't say that!" Richard said.

Roberts just laughed, his fingers finally stilling.

"She's not!" Richard spat. "She's nothing of the kind. We're human, through and through!" He snatched Gabrielle's arm and gripped it tightly. "Mind if I take one of those?"

Gabrielle shook her head slightly and stilled while Richard lifted a cup up and chugged it. He set it back down on the platter rather forcefully. Gabrielle dipped and rapidly adjusted the plate to keep the rest from falling.

"Sorry, love," Richard said absentmindedly. He cleared his throat and rolled a shoulder back. "The king ought to kill them all. Save us a lot of sorry trouble."

Roberts pressed his lips together in another thin, up-turned line, eyes darting towards Gabrielle.

She gave him a tight smile, focusing on her tray. When she looked back up, he was glaring into his drink.

"It's too dangerous. Legends say there's a lot of funny things in the dragon lands," Richard explained, casting long looks over his companions.

They murmured and each took a drink.

Roberts, face sporting a sour expression, opened his mouth.

Gabrielle was hailed over to the other side of the room and had to drop the rag with which she was studiously washing the counter, grab a few tankards, and twist and turn her way through the lot.

Gerald, mouth open and face flushed, was still laughing as Gabrielle set down the four tankards at their table. Mildred, Gerald, Frank Sr., and Jillian stayed late and could afford multiple tankards per night, the amount depending on their conversation. Tonight they seemed to be discussing the increase in taxes the king had passed. There were sure to be many tankards.

"Gabrielle," Mildred interrupted Frank Sr.'s rant. Speaking over Gerald's continued snickers, she gestured towards the corner nearest them. "Mr. Henry needs a refill."

Gabrielle glanced at the man. Mr. Henry's eyes never strayed from the bottom of his cup, face both pinched and sagging as a hardened wineskin. She came to him and rested a hand on his shoulder.

The tavern's noise dropped. At the door, a rake of a man with wheat hair wore a fine set of armour that hung much too loose on his frame. His companion was of sturdier cloth, and darker in both hair and eyes, perhaps a farmer's fifth son sent to squire.

Gabrielle took a breath. She straightened, bundled her fear to the back of her mind, and picked her way over to them as the usual level of activity resumed.

"Welcome to Seron! What can I get for ye?" she smiled,

habit taking precedence. She clasped her hands tightly in front of her.

The wheat-haired man grinned at her. "Two drinks . . . and some information."

The brown-haired man glanced at the other.

The wheat-haired one grinned wider.

Gabrielle leaned towards them. Catching herself, she shifted back and gave a small smile, hoping her voice stayed steady. "What kind of information are ye looking for?"

"A guide—"

A shout from behind her interrupted the armored, wheat-haired man.

Gabrielle turned and saw Thaddeus grinning wickedly.

"Is that a knight of the king? Send him here, won't you?"

Gabrielle had no wish to break up that bar fight. She gave him her mother's stare. "I do not wish to scare off our guests by giving them over to ye."

"We would be happy to sit with them," the brown-haired visitor said. He grinned. "We don't scare that easily."

Gabrielle's attention snapped back to the two men. She forced herself to not take a step back. She glanced at them both before looking somewhere below their chins. "Their conversation in the past few minutes has not been very pleasant towards the knights and king."

The armored, wheat-haired one grinned wider than ever. "Then we'll most definitely have to sit with them."

"We're only serving our local 'shine and honeyed mead as a special, sir."

"We'll take the moonshine then," the wheat-haired one said, walking forward and coming much too close.

Gabrielle moved, taking a subtle breath as she stepped out of the way. Her eyes flicked up as they passed her.

Both of the visitors nodded to those at Thaddeus' table as they sat, and the men there quieted.

Gabrielle strode behind the counter and began carefully pouring the men's drinks.

The men of the village introduced themselves. The wheat-haired one responded in kind. "Drew, Sir Drew of Farfuh, and this is my squire, Davey."

"What brings a knight of the king to our neck of the woods? You are a knight of the king, not a wanderer?" Thaddeus grinned, folding his hands on the table. His thick fingers tightly wound themselves together in an act of mock politeness.

Gabrielle frowned, casting an eye towards where her father was serving a group of merchants in the far corner of the room. Frank and Mildred caught her eye. Frank nodded sternly, both of them focused on Thaddeus' table even as those around them talked. Some of Gabrielle's tension drained away.

"Indeed," Sir Drew answered. "I'm a knight of the king. We venture into dragon territory."

The table fell quiet. Sir Drew slightly cocked his head. "We had hoped to find a guide to get us to the edge."

"You'd be insane." Richard shook his head. His hand clenched around his drink. "Nobody's going to take you anywhere near dragon territory. Nearer. We're close enough as it is. Even if we don't see any dragons, the raiders in the area are enough to scare anyone off."

Roberts stretched his arms out over his portion of the

table, hands splayed. He brought them back to himself and straightened as he looked to Sir Drew and Davey. In a measured tone, he said, "You may not know this, sir, but since King Germaine has stopped the border patrol, raiding parties have cropped up all along the border. They are horribly common. Any person who dares to get too close is attacked."

The brown-haired squire Davey shifted uncomfortably but cut in, "We did not know, but we still must cross. Is there no chance of a guide? Time is critical. We cannot waste it going in the wrong direction."

"What's so important you are willing to die for it?" Roberts folded his arms, his back still a straight rake.

"We can't say," Sir Drew said, casting a glance at his squire.

A few of the men chuckled, lightening the mood.

Leaning back, Thaddeus told them, "You won't find anyone stupid enough to go with you, 'specially if you can't say what it's for."

"We seek the princess," Sir Drew announced.

Gabrielle looked up sharply at the easy admission.

The men fell silent.

Davey was glaring at Sir Drew, but Sir Drew continued, "She was kidnapped. We seek to bring her back."

"Kidnapped by whom?" Roberts asked, fingers slowly tracing his cup once more.

"Dragons," Sir Drew said. He glanced behind himself and noticed Gabrielle standing with two glasses. "Thank you." He took them gently and passed one to a scowling Davey as the men watched.

"Why did they take her?" Roberts said, back finally curved as the older men's were.

Sir Drew shrugged. "Bait, we guess. Get one, get the rest. Princess Danielle was taken while riding in the woods. According to Judith, her handmaiden, a dragon just appeared out of nowhere and snatched her." He gave a rakish grin. "They took the worst royal to anger if you ask me. They should've taken the easy bait of the prince instead." He shrugged and took a small sip.

The men shifted in their seats, eyes narrowing, and glanced at each other.

Thaddeus folded his arms. "You two are going to save the princess all by yourselves?"

Gabrielle winced at the disbelief, however merited, that was so evident in Thaddeus' tone.

"Yes."

"You won't find a guide here, sirs," Mildred spoke across the quiet crowd to them. "And we don't want any trouble."

Sir Drew and Davey took in the room, Sir Drew scanning with his eyes while Davey turned his head. At the absolute lack of support, Sir Drew wryly smiled. "I suppose a room for the night will have to do." He set his glass on the table and stood.

Davey followed, eyes flashing to Sir Drew's face several times.

Sir Drew ignored him. "Are there accommodations here?" the knight asked Gabrielle.

She nodded. "Would you like me to show you a room now?"

Sir Drew smiled more gently. "That would be much appreciated." He nudged the squire Davey.

Davey fumbled and pulled out a gold coin. He offered it, hand resting flat, to Gabrielle.

Gabrielle's eyes widened at the large amount. "I don't know if we have enough change, sir . . ." She *knew* they didn't have enough change, not with their bronze and single rose quartz.

Sir Drew rolled his eyes with a drawn-out snort, and Gabrielle jerked back in surprise. Sir Drew shook his head at his squire. He looked back to Gabrielle, eyebrows raised. "My squire doesn't know how to carry appropriate amounts of money apparently. Consider it a tip, for the wonderful 'shine.'"

Gabrielle looked to both of them, the squire now glaring at his knight. She carefully took the coin and slipped it into her pocket, ducking her head. The witnesses of the tavern could attest to the interaction if the coin brought trouble. "Thank you, sirs. Right this way." She led them towards the stairs, her father heading for the second floor right before them, no doubt to sit in one of the adjacent rooms "cleaning" till the knight and squire were settled.

The conversations behind them grew, but slowly. Very slowly. As they went up the stairs and to the second room on the right, the tavern continued to gain momentum, but the sounds were dampened by the floor and distance. Gabrielle opened the door and stood to the side.

"There is one blanket for each bed. The door locks from the inside. We provide a washbowl and water. Do you need your horses stabled or extra provisions?"

Davey answered, "That will be all, thank you."

Gabrielle fixed her face before her surprise showed. Many years had passed since she had seen a knight and squire, more than she recalled if Davey and Sir Drew continued in this manner. Regardless, she merely nodded and said, "If you need anything, we're right downstairs."

"Wait." Davey caught the door and held it open.

Sir Drew waited inside the room, watching them.

"What they said down there"—Davey jerked his chin towards the floor—"is that true? We will not find a guide to dragon territory? Not even if it is just to the border?"

Gabrielle's mouth dried, the image of the great dark dragon running through her mind. "The way is dangerous. As you know, the king has succeeded in pushing the dragons back to their original territory, but there are reports that they often wander across the border. The two villages that are closer than Seron, Apude and Acera, they have more sightings." Gabrielle cut off her rambling, pressing her lips together and worrying the edges of them.

"No guide would be willing to take us that far? Even to the next village?" Davey asked.

Gabrielle grimaced. Unseen tremors shook her. She hid her hands, tightened her muscles. "The quickest route to dragon territory is the direct one. Apude and Acera are not on that route."

"Can we find a guide?"

Gabrielle looked into Davey's eyes. Brown with flecks of blue. Human. Completely human.

"I may know a person . . ."

Davey's eyes lit up.

Sir Drew visibly responded as well, leaning closer, though still a few steps into the room.

"Who is he? Where do we find him?" Davey pressed.

Gabrielle's stomach squirmed as if she were sick but not feeling the sickness. "I do not know if . . . if he is willing."

"Will you ask him?"

She closed her eyes. Her toes curled. It was a knight of the king and his squire. *A knight of the king* and his squire, yet she could not imagine any better, relatively safe opportunity.

"Yes." She opened her eyes and forced herself not to fidget. "When will you be leaving?"

"Tomorrow morning," Davey responded immediately.

Despite the unsettlement Sir Drew's focused, alert eyes brought, Gabrielle continued in a steady tone, "If the person is willing to guide you, they'll be knocking at your door before daybreak." She swallowed and forced herself not to tremble. "If no one comes, you'll know the guide fell through."

Davey smiled fully.

Sir Drew's eyes narrowed.

Gabrielle's breath left her in a short rush. She could hear her heart. She twisted her fingers more tightly together, nails pressing into her palms, and tried for a steadying breath.

Davey, seemingly oblivious, reached out a hand and placed it formally on her shoulder. "Thank you."

Gabrielle nodded and gave a small smile, backing away. When the door was fully shut, she stopped and leaned against the wall, hand on her chest. She willed the racing to stop.

A door opened.

She jerked upright, but it was only her father. She relaxed.

He frowned and came to her, resting a hand on her shoulder. Quietly, he asked, "Are you all right?"

Heart fluttering, Gabrielle nodded and mustered a smile. "Just"—she waved a hand, eyes roving with it—"memories."

Her father's frown deepened. "I didn't think the knights had given you trouble before—"

"No!" Gabrielle glanced towards Davey and Sir Drew's door. She dropped her voice. "Not that, just from . . . from when they had to come before, to help clean up, and when they were fighting . . . memories from then."

Her father's face fell. "I'm sorry."

"It's not your fault." She swallowed and dropped her gaze, raising it to meet his after a moment. "The dragons attacked. The knights came to defend. I just can't . . . I can't see the knights without thinking of the attack."

Her father nodded knowingly, expression still forlorn.

Gabrielle hugged him, hiding her face in his shoulder.

She loathed lies.

Her father tried to pull away. When she held on tighter, he mumbled over her shoulder, "You said that you knew a guide?"

Gabrielle tensed. "Yes. A traveler. He's . . . shy, but I think he'll want to do it."

Her father didn't speak for a long moment. He tried to pull away again, and Gabrielle let him.

He peered at her, eyes scrunched, crow's feet deepened. "You'll tell me if you're ever hurt, or need help?"

Gabrielle knocked gently into his side, warmth filling her. "Of course."

Her father hummed. He nodded twice and sighed. "All

right then. Always know we love you very much." He pecked her on the forehead.

Gabrielle's smile softened. "I know."

He squeezed her hand, meeting her gaze. After a moment, he dropped her hand, and they walked back down, separating at the bottom of the stairs.

Despite speaking with her father, Gabrielle slipped into a daze, delivering drinks and greeting and doling out dishes and smiling and ducking all out of habit.

"Dear." Nettie caught her arm. She had been playing cards by herself, then conversing with Gabrielle's mother. "What's the matter?"

The past few hours slung up to Gabrielle like a slingshot. Suddenly, the dissonant laughing and clunking of tankards filled her ears. She smelled the sickly-sweet smell of drink, sweat, and her mother's cooking. The soft, tanned insides of her shoes rubbed softly against her soles. The thousands of miniature air currents swirled upon her skin. She shivered, the numbness receding with a quick douse of coolness that the warmth of the tavern overruled, the heat sinking into her skin, into her core.

"Just . . . a decision, one that I need to make," she said.

Nettie raised an eyebrow. "What kind of decision?"

Gabrielle hesitated.

Nettie grabbed both of Gabrielle's hands and looked into her eyes. Nettie had begun coming to their inn while they were still rebuilding. Gabrielle knew no other family than her parents, but when she was younger, she had pretended that Nettie was a long-lost aunt who lived only a village away. Gabrielle went to the woman when she feared what her mother would say. Nettie gave sound advice without begging for details.

"You don't know what to do," Nettie stated.

"I know what I want"—Gabrielle glanced over at her father, but he was preoccupied and her mother nowhere in sight—"I know what I want to do. I think. I'm really not sure."

"My dear, I often find that my decision is already made. I just have trouble committing to it." Nettie paused. She opened her mouth to say more, but then saw Gabrielle's expression. "You have already made yours, haven't you?"

Gabrielle hesitated. Her mind flew to Davey's eyes, so blue, so human.

Only human.

The resolve hardened in her. She smiled, truly smiled. "Yes." She reached forward and hugged Nettie.

Nettie gripped her tightly.

"Just be—"

"—careful and know I love you," Gabrielle finished for her, Nettie laughing as Gabrielle straightened. Gabrielle smiled. "I love you, too."

She turned as if to walk away, but then faced Nettie again. "Please do not tell my parents, but I don't believe that I shall be able to talk with you tomorrow."

Nettie's eyebrows rose again, but she only said, "All right, my dear. Then one more hug, perhaps."

"Perhaps." Gabrielle smiled.

They hugged once more.

Then Gabrielle swept off to finish her duties, Nettie glancing her way a bit more often.

The night began winding down, and in an hour, her

father was herding the last few customers out of the tavern. Gabrielle insisted on cleaning up for her parents. Her mother wished her good night, promising a big breakfast tomorrow. Her father argued for a minute or two, then just kissed her on the forehead and told her that he loved her. Another minute, and they were gone.

Gabrielle stopped bustling about and stood in the still room. Spills were on the floor, and one or two empty glasses had to be put away, five or ten washed. After that, she had to pack provisions and gather supplies and be up before daybreak.

She had decided. She had decided the moment she had said yes, but now she was committed.

An unknown reservoir of energy flooded her. Running through the list of things she wanted to be sure to pack, she began cleaning up the room. Tomorrow was a new day.

Tomorrow was going to be new indeed.

II

─────

Underestimating the Barmaid

Davey smirked. "I told you it wasn't going to be that bad."

"Not that bad!" Drew's fists clenched. He pushed himself forward on the narrow dirt road to glare at Davey, his face florid from exertion, eyes shadowed by a night spent sleeping on hard ground. "You almost died, you idiot! We barely made it out of there alive!"

"You pulled me through the swamp by yourself." Davey raised his chin as he spoke, an act he knew infuriated the other man. "Obviously, it isn't that dangerous."

Davey counted himself lucky for Drew's blessed five seconds of quiet.

Not that it lasted.

"And to think you're going to be king someday," Drew mocked.

Davey jerked his head forward. "Come on. You're slowing us down."

"Me? *I'm* slowing us down? Who just spent the last day *unconscious?*"

"Careful, Drew. If your voice goes any higher, we shall have to disguise you as a lady." Facing away from his servant, Davey allowed his smile to appear.

"Indeed, I have no doubt that I could pull off a lady, but that plan would never work because *you*, my *lord*, could never pull off a gentleman."

"By your standards perhaps, but not by those with actual class," Davey said, tilting his chin again.

Drew scowled at him, exaggerating the expression with a scrunched nose and shake of his head. He flicked an imaginary bug at Davey, one that Davey swore he could feel anyways.

He shook off the feeling, fleeting calm fading as the next fork came into view. Ruts ran deep on either side of the road. The deepest ones diverted to the left, probably leading to the village of Seron, which was closest to the eastern edge of the swamp. He angled himself to the right.

"Where are you going?"

Davey arched an eyebrow. "Are you sure I am the one who hit his head?"

"Tis almost night, Davey."

"But not quite."

Davey did not need to turn around to see Drew's own eye roll.

Drew sighed and said, "Seron's not far from here. We can spend a night in the inn and find a guide."

"For what do we need a guide?" Davey asked. He continued forward, the towering maples and oaks on either side a relief after the swamp's gnarled, stunted trees.

"Do you know the way to the border?"

"That way." Davey pointed to the right side of the trail but slightly more into the forest.

The steps behind Davey stopped. He turned to see Drew with both hands on his hips, the stance of a squire's irked wife. A flash of amusement, but then Davey scowled. "Stop wasting time."

Drew met his gaze squarely. "Either way, we'll be stopping for the night soon, and finding a guide would greatly make up for whatever little time we lose getting to the village."

"We know the way—"

"No." Drew's eyes flashed as he spoke.

Davey straightened.

Drew bowed his head slightly, bright eyes still meeting the prince's. "We got lucky in the swamp, sire. You're no use to her dead."

Davey's face hardened further. "I'm no use to her here."

"Yes." Drew grimaced, loosening his stance. The overly large plates of armor scraped together disconcertingly with his shifting. "You can help her later, though, if you stay alive and get to her quickly. Please, sire, I know you want to continue, but consider gathering your resources first."

Davey turned back to the fork.

The ruts ran deep to the left.

He closed his eyes and took a steady breath. He felt Drew's hand rest on his shoulder.

He shook it off.

"Fine," he bit out. "We'll get a guide. I need a drink anyway."

"Not while you're on duty," Drew scolded. He scurried with metallic clanks to catch up with Davey's sudden strides.

Davey rolled his shoulders back again. The tension stayed. "It always seems to escape your attention that I am the prince—"

"Not today! *I* am a knight, and *you* are my lowly, lazy, idiotic squire."

"I am not idiotic," Davey said, keeping up the quick pace as Drew fell farther behind.

Drew began to pant. "Just lowly and lazy then."

"Well, I cannot help it, can I, if you are the only model I have?"

"We would not want you to get too dependent now, would we?"

Drew's breaths became even more pronounced. Davey hid his laugh with a cough. "Tis called delegation. I delegate to you tasks that are below my taking."

"Above your ability more like it. Who was it that had to drag the other through the infamously dangerous swamp?"

"Hold your tongue, Drew."

"Of course . . . sire."

With cringe-worthy form, Drew made a dash past Davey, turning to send a smirk at Davey even as his face flushed.

Despite Davey's lent armor clanking, Drew faced forward and tried to go faster.

Davey shook his head with a grin. He broke into a jog. After a minute or so, he passed Drew, but continued at the new pace anyway.

The road soon spilled into a village comprising only of a few houses, a large tavern and inn, and several fields. Davey slowed to a halt at the edge of the village. Small puffs of dried dirt flew up around his feet, settling upon the leather shoes as he stilled. The buildings stood crooked and stooped. The straight edges of the two-storied tavern and inn—along with the establishment's size—distinguished the building from the others.

Huffs from behind him announced Drew's arrival. The thuds of the other man's footfalls stopped.

Davey strode forward.

"Davey!" Drew snapped. His breathing picked up once more as he jogged to pass Davey. Sweat dripping down his face, Drew barred the door to the inn with an arm. He dug through the solitary bag he was carrying and pulled out a cloth. Glaring at Davey the entire time, he wiped his face. Satisfied, he shook out the cloth and tucked it away. His shoulders dropped, and he glared. "I hate you."

"Mutual," Davey agreed lightly.

Drew finally opened the doors to the establishment. The noise in the main room dropped. Two dozen or more people were crowded into the room, their gazes ranging from curious to cold. A haze of resentment hung in the air although Davey could convince himself twas imagined. Many patrons had some sort of burn or disfigurement, more people than usual, but they were at a border village. It was to be expected.

A chair scraped, and the buzzing conversations swelled. Davey glanced at Drew. The other man, despite the unfamiliar armour, was handling the attention well.

A barmaid with a tightly bound brown braid wove her way through the tables to them. Her walk was somewhat stilted, as if she didn't really want to approach them.

The woman pasted on a smile. "Welcome to Seron! What can I get for ye?"

Drew grinned. "Two drinks . . . and some information."

Davey frowned.

Noticing Davey's caution, Drew grinned more broadly.

Surprisingly, the woman did not get them to a table to serve the drinks right away. Instead, she leaned closer and asked, "What kind of information are ye looking for?"

Davey sincerely hoped that not all of Drew's senses had left him.

"A guide—"

Someone shouted from behind the woman, and she turned to face him. The men were rough, farmers with perhaps one scholar among them. When they offered a seat, Davey gladly accepted, anything to sit and get out of people's attention, but the woman spoke again, trying to dissuade them.

She did not know Drew took such as encouragement.

Finally, they approached the men at the table, the barmaid slipping behind the counter to get their drinks at last while Drew and Davey took their seats.

Davey spent the next candle mark imagining creative ways to execute his servant.

Drew blatantly asked for a guide, which Davey accepted as necessary because that was the purpose of traveling to the tavern. However, at a half-hearted remark from a drunk farmer, the man laid out their entire mission and came as close as possible to revealing their identities without actually disclosing them.

Despite a continued absence of a guide, Davey was almost glad when Drew finally asked for a room. Almost.

Then the man—his *squire* for kingdom's sake—expected him to know how much a room for the night was worth when the barmaid had not even hinted at a price. Furthermore, he only ever carried a total amount of five gold coins on him, an entirely appropriate amount. He scowled because he hadn't *known* about any of this and how could he have known because he—

He was a squire. He was acting a squire now, so he should have known. Davey kept his mouth shut and fumed all the way to the room.

The realisation of wasted time hit him then. His desperation acted for him.

"Wait!" he called to the barmaid.

She turned towards him.

He calmed himself before speaking. "What they said down there, is that true? We will not find a guide to dragon territory? Not even if it is just to the border?"

The woman startled.

Davey took the time to look at her. Her face was clear of disfigurement and fairly pretty, he realised, like any market maiden's. There was an edge in her eyes although not malicious. Davey steadied himself further, hopes rising.

"The way is dangerous," she began, worrying the edges of her lips.

Davey let her speak fully before pressing, "No guide would be willing to take us that far? Even to the next village?"

Nervousness tightened the woman's face. "The quickest route to dragon territory is a straight shot. Stopping at a closer village would take you off track."

"Can we find a guide?"

She looked to him.

Davey held his breath.

Please.

He asked her.

Anyone. Please.

"I may know a person . . ."

Davey almost stepped forward. He held himself back by the door. "Who is he? Where do we find him?"

"I do not know if . . . if he is willing."

He would not give up now, not when there was the possibility of someone. "Will you ask him?"

The woman closed her eyes. The inane thought of comparing her to a statue flitted through Davey's head, no doubt a remnant of the poetry he had been forced to study upon a time. She was too real—floating loose hair strands, gently flexing arms—she was much too real for that.

Please.

"Yes. When will you be leaving?"

Davey held back a sigh, swallowing heavily once. He

replied, saying something, but he forgot the words as soon as he spoke them. The conversation blurred. Finally, *finally*, something was going right.

On impulse, he grabbed her shoulder and said with as much gratitude and respect as he could, "Thank you."

She nodded and smiled, eyes not fixing on either of them, and stepped away.

Davey shut the door and let out his sigh of relief.

Then he turned and saw Drew.

"Idiot. What happened to 'it has to be a secret'?"

Drew shrugged, tugging at the armor and straps. Twas clear that it was a bit of a struggle. "We needed a guide," he stated as if that solved everything.

Davey sent him another scowl. "Yet we still do not know if we have one or not."

Drew stopped, looking over at Davey. "She is asking. We may have one."

"Or we may not."

After a long moment, Drew returned to removing the armour.

Davey watched in silence. After the other man dropped a piece for the third time, Davey had pity and helped. To be fair, his armour was not made to be maintained by a single man.

They laid the armour out on a blanket, Drew obsessively brushing dirt from it. Davey wondered if the man would just give in and shine it before remembering that they hadn't brought any of the tools. As Drew continued fussing, Davey ran his fingers along his sword, as if he were sharpening the blade. The metal dulled further and further, Davey's eyes drifting closed every minute or so.

When he awoke, his sword was leaning against the wall next to the bed. He looked over to Drew, but the man was already up and putting the beginnings of the armour back on.

Davey groaned. "You just took it off."

"Now you know how I feel, your towering highness."

"Was that supposed to be an insult?" Davey peered at him from where his head lay on the lumpy pillow.

Drew paused, looking to him. His eyes flicked to Davey's hair, no doubt matted from sleep and sweat. His lips twitched.

Davey glowered. "Not a word."

"Of course, sire," Drew demurred. He smoothly slid back into action, picking up the pauldron.

Davey's scowl deepened. He did not respond but readied himself instead. They spoke in quiet voices after that, conscious of the thin walls. Just as they finished, someone knocked on the door.

Drew looked to Davey. "A bronze coin says it's the woman."

Davey snorted. "You're on, *Sir* Drew."

"It really bothers you, does it not, *Davey?*" Drew was grinning as Davey went for the door.

Davey rested his hand upon the plain, worn knob. He half-turned. The clean wooden planks and window light shone dully behind Drew, a morning mist without its dust surrounding him. The squire actually looked like a knight.

Davey's mood turned. His servant had not been trained for this. He was no knight.

Davey pushed the thoughts back and gave a wry smile. "The armour does not match your eyes."

Some sort of squeaking sound emanated from Drew, but Davey ignored him. He opened the door.

The woman from last night stood dressed in traveling clothes and with bags on her back, almost as if she were planning on being the guide. For a moment, her hair lightened and back straightened and stature shrunk. Bile rose in his throat. Another moment, and the image of his sister was gone. A fidgeting bar maiden eyed him, mouth poised to open and rush through her words as she had done the night prior. "Provisions are packed and ready downstairs. Are you ready or do you need a few minutes, perhaps?"

Davey's hand tightened on the door. "No."

She nodded several times. "Very well then."

"You are not coming."

"What he's trying to say is"—Drew elbowed him, forcing himself into the doorway as well—"are you planning on being our guide?"

Her muscles tightened. Her chin lifted. Again, his sister stood before him. Danielle in all her stubborn glory. "Yes."

"No." Davey repeated the word as the vomit rose. "You're not coming with."

"Do you no longer need a guide?" She shifted the bags further onto her back, too many for a woman—or a man—to carry.

"We'll find someone else."

She leaned forward. "There isn't anyone else. You heard them."

"No one else is stupid enough."

Her eyes flashed at his remark. Danielle certainly. "No, sir, just a solitary squire and his knight."

Drew's loud groan cut through the air. "How is it when I'm the knight I still belong to him?"

Startled, the woman looked with wide and then narrowed eyes at Drew. Her head tilted to the side.

An uncomfortable quietness descended. This had gone on far too long.

Davey cleared his throat. "We are trained—"

"I have lived here." She shot the words at him, eyes catching his once more. She swallowed but also tilted her chin.

Davey had to admit that Drew had a point. Tilting the chin was a bit presumptuous.

She continued in a stronger voice, "I will get you there quickly, and then what reason have I for continuing onward?"

"What reason have you for coming?" Davey leaned his arm on the doorframe.

The woman pressed her lips together.

Davey nearly tilted his own head, mirroring her earlier movements. "We haven't even discussed payment yet."

The woman shrugged, eyes roving to the doorframe, then the walls. "You paid enough last night, for the drinks, room, and guide."

"You'll be killed."

At Davey's flat voice, her eyes jumped back up to his, more open than before.

Drew elbowed Davey again, shouldering past him completely. "It's a suicide mission."

Davey straightened, his arm slipping off the doorframe. "Drew—"

"It is." Drew snapped with a glare. The man lightened his stance after just a moment and in a faux bright tone continued, "Our chance of success is miniscule, negligible, the size of a stunted midget—"

"Necessary," Davey interrupted. He inclined his head at Drew in acknowledgement, however.

"Oh, yes." Drew's mouth quirked up. "Completely necessary, according to my *squire*. We've always longed to die a painful, glorious, extremely painful, fiery death . . . that has lots of pain."

The ill-fitted armour on his servant's shoulders seemed to grow even larger while they were talking, the breastplate hanging heavily from the other man's frame. Eyes on his friend, Davey murmured, "As every knight desires."

Drew's voice gentled. "Perhaps not desires, but certainly accepts as a possibility, as I am sure even the squires do." His eyes lit up, and he turned back to the girl, gesturing broadly and cheerfully once more. "As a knight of a king, you are dedicated to serving the king, kingdom, and peoples in every possible way with all gentlemanly respect and integrity." He galloped through the oath. "Thus"—he inclined his head—"we die. Painfully. Gloriously. With lots of fire.

"Now." Drew clapped his hands for emphasis. "We have to do this. You, on the other hand, can live. I suggest living."

In the quiet that followed, the woman just stared for several moments.

She blinked and looked to Davey. "I'm coming."

Davey shook his head, chuckling darkly.

Drew clapped his hands together again. "Perfect. We'll be down in a skip."

"Very well," the woman said, bowing slightly, far from proper. "I'll wait for ye in the main room." She turned to depart.

"Wait," Drew restrainedly called out. Their conversation had been loud enough as it was. "What is your name?"

She startled again, but gave a small smile. "Gabrielle." She continued down the hall, and then her footsteps on the stairs sounded lightly for only a moment before fading entirely.

Davey kept his eyes forward.

Drew did not speak for a long moment.

Then . . .

"We need a guide. I would prefer, also, to take someone more experienced and less . . . female, but we do not have a choice, my liege. If you wish to rescue Danielle, time is of the essence, especially when considering that your father may have noticed our deception and sent out search parties. Besides, she will only take us to the edge, sire, and no further. Beyond that, she knows no more than we and will return home."

Davey's jaw tightened. "Alone?"

"There are other villages. She will not be in the forest the entire time." Drew's voice was light.

"There are raiders in the forest. She cannot just travel through villages. She is guiding us, so we don't *have* to go through villages."

A sigh. "I know, but in the end, we need a guide, and she's the only one willing. Do you see a better solution, sire?"

He turned to his servant at last, the smoldering anger flaring up in him. Despite its unfairness, he answered, "Yes. Not stopping here."

Drew did not reply.

They met Gabrielle in the unsettlingly empty tavern a short time later. She nodded when she saw them and slung the same bags over her shoulder, walking towards the door. The town dozed peacefully around them, dawn breaking over the horizon. Davey saw Drew run his hand over the morning dew glistening on the stalks of grain, water coating his fingers and falling to the ground. Forest overtook field. Plants increasingly encroached upon the road until Gabrielle left the path. They followed.

She was shy, it seemed, and admitted after a question from Drew that she was remembering the directions from maps and conversations. Davey's lip curled at that. When Drew turned to him for conversation, he replied curtly. Gabrielle caught on to the mood and shortened her responses as well. Drew soon gave up.

As the sun reached its zenith, Drew finally called for a break.

"All right, either you have all been possessed or are foolishly trying to see which of you can outlast the other in a mistimed competition of pride and strength." He flopped on the ground as best he could after stating the clearly rehearsed line. He evidently forgot that he had armor and clanged to the forest floor instead. "I, on the other hand, have no pride whatsoever and so will be enjoying a nice, well-needed rest. Either of you can join me if you desire. Preferably you, Gabrielle, because I do believe that you are carrying food."

Gabrielle smiled and sat across from Drew, looking grateful as the bags slipped off her shoulders.

"Actually, speaking of bags and food, especially food," Drew continued as Gabrielle opened a bag and began unwrapping some loaves, "I have been thinking that we should split up the bags more evenly. If we get separated, I would like to have a better chance of being with the bread."

Gabrielle's smile grew. She gently tossed a piece to him.

Davey watched her, mind thankfully blank. Although the trees grew thicker here, the shrubs were dense. They rustled and shifted unsettlingly. He chose to stand close to Gabrielle and Drew in the small clearing, but far enough away that he took a step forward to receive the bread she offered. "Thank you," he said, his other hand still resting on his sword.

"So, Gabrielle?" Drew began.

Davey bit into his bread.

Just five more bloody seconds of silence.

Gabrielle nodded, glancing at Davey before looking down at her own rations. "Yes, Sir Drew?"

"How long have you lived in your village?"

"My whole life, sir, though we spent a year camping on the outskirts." Gabrielle kept her eyes on the bread.

Davey had to admit, the food she had brought was a welcome change from the hard tack they had been eating before.

"Why?" Davey's eyes narrowed.

"My village was destroyed when I was eight. We had to rebuild everything," Gabrielle explained, looking up at Davey but once.

"Dragons?" he guessed.

Gabrielle nodded. Another glance at him. "Yes, sir."

"No need to call him sir," Drew interjected, grinning. "He's just a squire. Besides, when you are traveling to your doom, I always believe things should be a bit more informal. What do you say, Davey?"

"Of course," Davey said. He looked calmly at Drew.

Drew raised the bread up to his mouth and took a large, slow bite. Smirking on the inside, Davey sourly presumed.

Gabrielle looked uneasy. "I think there are people around us."

The bushes stopped rustling. Davey cursed his stupidity.

The raiders attacked.

III

First Blood

Gabrielle had heard shuffling where there should have been none. Even then, she was not prepared for the half dozen men charging from the brush.

Davey dropped the rest of the loaf to the ground and swiftly brought up his sword.

Drew stumbled to his feet, cursing the armor, his sword, and the bread he did not get to finish.

A burly bearded man with a scar running from his eye into his beard swung his mace at Gabrielle. Her heart jumped to her throat. She ducked instinctively, muscles remembering the many times she had done so in the tavern. He swung it back the other way, and she dodged again. Blood pounded in her head. The clashes and grunts of those around her blended into the harsh beat.

The scarred man brought up his mace yet again. More confidently this time, Gabrielle slid to the side, in between two bushes. She turned with the move, and she could see Sir Drew, who was only a few feet away.

Sir Drew ducked under the swing of a sword, dagger in hand. The raider stepped forward, and a prickly blackberry shrub latched onto the clothing. Drew slashed at a different stumbling raider and stabbed the one slowed by the tenacious bush.

Her momentary distraction cost her.

The scarred man grabbed her arm and drew her close. She pulled back. His grip only tightened.

The panic rose.

"Well, s—" he began.

Gabrielle's skin rippled.

"What—" He released her and backed away.

Drew spun and stabbed her assailant, the knight's cool eyes catching Gabrielle's before he turned to engage his next opponent.

Gabrielle crouched, sensing a man behind her.

He tripped over her and sprawled onto the ground.

She plucked a knife from his belt as the third man seized her arm and spun her towards him.

For a moment, her rushing blood drowned out all other noise. Gabrielle gripped the dagger tightly, angling it towards him.

It hit.

She gasped.

The man's grip on her loosened then faded completely as he slumped into her.

She snatched the dagger back and slid out of the way to

let him fall to the ground, twitching. She took a stuttering breath.

Someone gripped her shoulder. She spun with the knife in hand.

"Whoa." Davey put his hands up, stepping back.

Gabrielle swallowed convulsively. She realised her hands were shaking, white-knuckled around the dagger's hilt. Her entire body tingled. Her head felt light. She looked away.

The other men lay scattered around, dead or unconscious. It was a little more than a half-dozen, now that she counted. And recounted. She ignored her quivering muscles and counted a third time.

Sir Drew was gathering their bags. At least, he was gathering the rations from underneath one of the men.

"You did a decent job," Davey said. He reached out, taking her hand and carefully prying the dagger out of it. His eyes darkened.

Gabrielle clenched her hand and met his gaze.

He ducked his head. Barely, but he did. "It's always hard. The first time. You handled the ambush well, however."

"Well, thank you, sir. Perhaps next time I shall prepare for the surprise."

Sir Drew barked out a laugh, looking up from the man he was examining to grin at her. "I think I like you."

"I was just complimenting her," Davey groused. He crossed his arms and shifted, like a woman popping out her hip.

Gabrielle burst out with her own, breathy laugh at the thought. "I could, could tell from your . . . reluctance." Her laughter continued for an awkward moment, tears springing to her eyes. She looked anywhere but at them, struggling to calm herself and only succeeding in quieting to giggles.

Davey gestured sharply at her. "This is why I didn't want you to come."

Gabrielle took several large gasps. "That's a lie."

Davey turned away, running a hand through his hair.

Gabrielle put both her hands on her forehead, focusing on breathing.

Davey spun back. "You've never done this before!"

"And I suppose you were better! When you first did it!" Gabrielle's voice cracked. She clenched her fists and stared at him anyway.

Davey's face shuttered. "No. But that doesn't mean I think you should have to go through it."

Gabrielle shut her eyes for a few moments, breathing more regularly. She opened them. "I think that should be my choice."

Davey stared at her. His eyes glazed over, looking past her. Gabrielle distinctly felt he no longer saw her.

He shook his head. A smile flashed upon his face, gone before it existed. "You did well. Truly. I apologize for my surprise. You are of age and of good mind. It should be your choice." He floundered for a moment and nodded to cover it. "You did well."

Despite her tremors, a pleased warmth unfurled in her gut. She gave him her best attempt at a smile.

He stopped nodding, red creeping up his cheeks.

Gabrielle's smile came easier then, even as he turned away, clearing his throat and helping Drew find the rest of the supplies.

They left the bodies to rot. Gabrielle shivered when thinking of what the clearing would look like in a few days. She vowed to take a different way home.

Still, by the time they began walking, Gabrielle's heart had returned to normal, and the shaking was almost gone. Her mind stayed in a daze however.

They went for another half day before stopping and setting up camp for the night. Gabrielle had not camped nor traveled far from her home since it was burnt to the ground, so she was out of practice and unused to many of the trivial tasks. She was glad for the distraction.

It hadn't helped that conversation had been sparse. Sir Drew made several comments throughout the afternoon clearly meant to ease the tension and make them laugh. Gabrielle was also pretty sure he just liked to talk. He made frequent insults to his armor though he cared for it tenderly even after falling down at the midday break. He threatened Davey with making him clean it although, oddly enough, these threats seemed like jokes to both of the men, Davey taking more amusement out of them than Sir Drew.

The pair were odd. Increasingly so. A word from one was not easily rebuked by the other. Gabrielle found herself chewing on her lip as she considered it.

Once the thin bed rolls were out and Sir Drew's rabbit roasting over the fire, Gabrielle dug through the bags, checking supplies and looking for odd jobs that needed to be done. Sir Drew turned the rabbit, watching both it and Gabrielle closely. Davey leaned against a tree, running his sword through his hands, eyes drifting around the campsite and also coming to land on Gabrielle.

"Gabrielle," Davey said.

Gabrielle looked up from the bag she was searching through.

Davey smiled on one side of his face, a friendly smirk. "Are you looking for something in particular?"

Gabrielle thought about it for a second, shook her head, looked at Davey, looked back down, then began digging through the bag again.

Davey spoke anyway. "What are you doing?"

Gabrielle looked up again, not really wanting to face him, but knowing it was rude not to. "Looking."

"For what?"

"For . . . something to do."

"You're bored!" Davey said.

Gabrielle flushed though she didn't understand why. "I'm not bored."

"You're anxious," Sir Drew said.

Taken aback, Gabrielle did not contradict him.

"You're anxious?" Davey asked.

Gabrielle stopped herself from shifting. She couldn't lose this opportunity. "I'm glad to be here."

"Which means you're anxious," Davey concluded, eyes narrowing in challenge.

"Are you not?" Gabrielle ran her eyes over him. The red appeared in his cheeks again. Gabrielle realised what she had done and looked back at the bag.

"Of course I am." Davey cleared his throat, his frankness surprising. "I just don't show it by running around camp like a newly minted knight."

"Indeed, you'd rather play with your sword and prick yourself than do something useful."

"I *really* like you!" Sir Drew laughed.

Davey glared at him.

Gabrielle scrunched her face and ducked her head. These were not the village men nor peasant travelers. She needed to reign in her words better.

"Well, tis true," Sir Drew defended, cracking up again when Davey gave him an exasperated look.

Gabrielle shifted, squeezing her eyes shut for a moment. Finally, she opened them and asked in a conciliatory tone, "Do you wish to be a knight someday, Davey?"

At the lack of response, Gabrielle looked up.

Davey stared blankly at her, eyes unfocused. He blinked, noticing her gaze. He straightened. "I do not think I shall."

Gabrielle tore her attention away, back to the bag she had been rooting through. An extra shift, the only one she had brought, lay sprawled upon her lap. She ran her finger along the seam as she spoke. "Why not? The queen had once been a peasant. Cannot squires be knights?"

"Yes"—Davey's shrug was evident even in his voice, even with the wry tone he had taken—"but tis too much work. Too much pressure. Why be a knight when you could be a squire and just take directions? Fewer hard decisions. Less dangerous."

"Liar." Sir Drew frowned. "Squires go everywhere knights go and are the last people to get a sword except the ladies. It's very dangerous, especially when they have a master who seems to have a death wish. Secondly—"

"There was no firstly," Davey interrupted.

"Secondly," Sir Drew forged on ahead, "squires have to do all the work that the knights are too lazy to do. Catch the dinner, take care of the horses, clean the clothes, make the meals, fix the armor"—he hit his own armor, which he had taken off and laid to the side—"and, finally, the best squires are those that *do* think for themselves and do not allow their moronic masters to lead themselves to destruction. However, some masters are so thick-headed and has his head so full of rocks that even the best squire can find himself at wit's end trying to keep the both of them alive!"

Davey's face had lightened, a smile beginning to appear. "Please, don't hold back."

Gabrielle looked between the two men, not sure what to make of them.

The fire crackled, and a spark landed near Sir Drew. It blazed up for a minute, bright as a miniature bonfire, then went out completely.

The quiet sounds of the forest filled their camp.

"That was interesting," Sir Drew commented, unconcerned. No vigor remained in his speech. He checked the rabbit again and proclaimed it done.

Gabrielle took a breath, brushing the conversation away. Her job was to take them to dragon territory. They would separate from there.

They ate and got ready for the night. Gabrielle estimated and told them that dragon territory was just one more day away. Davey was exceedingly cheered by the news. As

Gabrielle fell asleep, she noticed that Davey was still up, and, when she awoke, Sir Drew had replaced him.

If Gabrielle was anxious that night, she was even more so in the morning. Her parents would not be able to come after her because of the inn and tavern, but they could have sent someone else to go looking for her. She wanted to get up and get going as quickly as possible in order to avoid confrontation. Luckily, the men seemed to want the same thing, for they packed with haste.

The morning passed much the same as the day before had though Gabrielle's stomach twisted itself tighter the closer they got to dragon territory. Decaying leaves turned to rusty needles beneath their feet. Gabrielle stretched her head back to see the tops of the pines. Undergrowth gradually encroached on the open undercover of the conifers. Maples, oaks, and birches grew thicker over their prospective trails.

Sir Drew cursed under his breath when a branch held a moment too short thwacked him in the face. "Traveling through the woods would be a whole lot easier if there were no trees."

"Then it would be a field," Davey told him.

"We should travel through more field."

Gabrielle felt a prickling on the back of her neck. She glanced sharply upwards.

"Dragon," Sir Drew whispered, spotting it the same time Gabrielle did. The dragon was the green of grass after a thunderstorm yet only the size of a large rat. It began descending, but not towards them. "I don't believe he has spotted us yet."

"We need to hide," Davey announced.

"Don't move!" Sir Drew hissed. "It'll be easier for him to spot you if you are moving."

"It'll be impossible for it to spot me if I'm under a tree."

"I'm serious. Don't move." Sir Drew's voice contained a steel that surprised Gabrielle.

Davey heard the tone. He stilled, staring unamused at Drew. "I better not die because of you."

"You'll live because of me." Sir Drew did not drop his gaze from Davey's.

Gabrielle lowered her head. A bramble patch began near her right foot. She shifted away from it, daring a glance up. Sir Drew had lowered his head, yet Davey was craning his neck to keep the dragon in his line of sight.

"Davey!" she whispered. "Keep your head down."

"If it sees us and comes closer, I need to know."

"We'll know if he comes closer."

"Why? If I can't see it, it can't see me? That's rubbish."

"It's the movement, actually," Drew said softly. "You'll move your eyes and head to follow it, and some dragons have keen enough sight that such movement alone is enough to draw their attention."

Davey grimaced and lowered his head.

Gabrielle sighed and looked to the ground as well, surveying but not truly seeing the twigs and leaves and mosses there. After a few tense minutes, the prickling stopped. She lifted her sore neck, Sir Drew doing the same. Davey noticed and joined them. All three looked to the skies, but no dragon was in sight.

"Did I mention how much I love trees?" Sir Drew asked.

"Now, if we had been in a field, we would have been dead meat."

Davey looked at Gabrielle and rolled his eyes again. She smiled. She suddenly wished that they were at the inn, she serving drinks, Sir Drew regaling the townsfolk with his jokes and tales, Davey sharing his imaginary exasperation with her and rolling his eyes.

They continued traveling, but had not gone far before Davey spoke this time. "What did you mean, 'we'd know if it came closer'?"

"Perhaps we would have heard the dragon, his breathing, his wings, if he had descended. He would not have approached silently." Gabrielle glanced away, fingers rubbing the rough edge of her shift. She could not explain the conviction herself.

Davey was quiet for a moment. "What if we had not?"

"You may have ears akin to those of a rock, but I have exceptionally good hearing," Sir Drew informed them. "Just the other day I was two corridors down from you and—uh, your lady—and could eavesdrop perfectly fine."

Gabrielle kept her face clear. It should have come as no surprise that, as a squire to a knight, Davey had a fiancé or the like.

"You fiend! You were eavesdropping!?"

"Yes, and I was quite disappointed with what I had to hear. If you're going to bother to send me away and make me eavesdrop from such a distance, you should make it worth my while."

"He sent you away?" Gabrielle asked.

"Indeed," Sir Drew answered nonchalantly, jumping up

on a fallen log. "Imagine that. My squire thinks he can send me away and then get mad when I eavesdrop. The injustice of it all."

"You do know that you will have to take off that armor eventually," Davey threatened.

Gabrielle raised her eyebrows.

"Indeed," Drew repeated, grinning, "and unfortunately the next poor sap who shall put it on wears it worse than me."

Davey just snorted.

Gabrielle did not understand the statement, but she was not inclined to ruin whatever amusement they had gotten from the joke. "Does your lady approve of you going on this quest?" she asked.

"Well," Davey said, "she is not my 'lady' as much as she is a friend who just happens to be a lady, or is becoming a lady . . . someday . . . hopefully."

"She will do fine, my . . . friend," Sir Drew paused peculiarly. He hurried onward, "she is young still—"

"Sixteen, Drew, she should know better by know."

"You're just cranky because she's usually not cranky."

"She has not learned that she has responsibilities and that she needs to fulfill them."

"Yes," Sir Drew agreed with him, "but that will come with time and a little more experience. You must be patient, sss . . . say! We have not asked about any of your friends." Sir Drew turned the conversation abruptly to Gabrielle.

"None, sir." Not wishing to go any deeper and having been wondering this anyway, Gabrielle asked, "What would have happened if the dragon had descended? I mean, how do you even kill a dragon?" She had always wanted to know this but had been frightened to ask her parents and the other villagers. Once, she had asked an unfamiliar merchant, but he had only laughed at her and ordered another drink.

Davey answered, "Dragons' scales are tough. You cannot break through them with ordinary weapons. However, a weapon made from dragons' claws will do the job."

"I cannot imagine those being too common," Gabrielle said.

"Indeed," Sir Drew added, "tis more common to find a modest prince than a weapon made from dragons' claws."

"However"—Davey stared at Sir Drew—"my sword is of dragon claw, as are two daggers Drew carries."

"Are there no other weapons that will break dragon scales?" Gabrielle asked.

"A sword forged with dragon's fire is best," Davey told her, "although it technically does not have to be a sword."

"Indeed," Sir Drew added again, "but tis more common to find a modest and *competent* prince than a weapon forged in dragon's fire."

"Anyway," Davey continued, huffing once, hand rubbing the hilt of his sword, "if you have neither available, which usually is the case, aim for the eyes."

"The eyes." Gabrielle could not stop her face from scrunching.

Davey smiled broadly, his face transforming into that of a little boy holding up a slug. "Yes, the eyes. That is the only part of a dragon that is penetrable by normal weapons."

"That's disgusting."

"Why did you want to get closer to dragon territory?" Davey asked.

Gabrielle ducked her head, trying to assuage the fear on her face at his question. She looked ahead again after only a second, her heart pounding. "Perhaps I wanted to see more of what is here, more of the land, the people."

"May I advise next time going to the city of Aradin to see more people?" Sir Drew waggled an eyebrow as he spoke.

A snort escaped her. Surprised, Gabrielle covered her mouth.

Sir Drew only grinned.

Davey, not paying attention to either of them, not so subtly stepped his leg over Sir Drew's path.

Sir Drew kicked at Davey's leg, but Davey only tightened his calf muscle, leg still in front of Sir Drew's next step.

The knight fell, almost immediately popping back up and nearly head-butting Davey's chin in an obvious and awkward retaliation attempt.

Davey glared.

Sir Drew grinned and continued seamlessly, "Not all of the people will be friendly, but they'll probably have less of a chance of killing you than a dragon would. Most of them, anyway."

"So you did come for some sight-seeing?" Davey's face tightened.

Gabrielle sighed. "No."

The deep pit in her stomach yawned. The perpetual dark knot of fear tightened. She wanted to see that she was not like them. She wanted to see that she was more human than dragon.

But she could not say that.

"It's . . . more . . . more than that . . . but I do not know how to explain it. It should not matter to you besides. Another few hours and we'll part ways." The hairs on her neck rose, and she instinctively looked upwards again, surveying the skies.

"I do not like to see people get hurt, especially . . ." Davey trailed off, glancing between her and Sir Drew, who was also looking skyward.

"Women?" Gabrielle asked, neck craning in all directions.

"Those who have done no wrong and mean no one ill." Gabrielle halted.

Davey also stuttered to a stop, a light flush invading his face. He raised his chin at her gaze, flush deepening.

Gabrielle swallowed her smile, nodding instead. "That was well put."

"I agree," a deep timbre of a voice sounded to the side of them. A ruddy brown dragon was tucked amongst the trees. At their thickest, his four limbs were the size of fifty-year maples, each leg tapering to four murky claws. His teeth hid in his closed snout, and ridged bone grew from his head as a crown. Despite his size, the trees grew far enough apart that he could walk among them.

The dragon stalked forward. Sir Drew and Davey both stepped forward as well, putting Gabrielle behind them. She took a step back anyway.

"A knight of the king, I presume? His brave squire at his side and . . . a woman. Interesting."

"We mean you no harm," Davey called to the dragon, clenching the sword tightly, eyes narrowed. "We are not even in your territory yet."

"The squire talks?" The dragon cocked his head in interest, but then shook it. "No matter."

Davey deepened his stance at the dragon's words.

The dragon took a deep breath.

Gabrielle took a step forward.

Sir Drew threw himself at her. The ground jarred her—as did his elbow. Fire roasted the air immediately above them. Gabrielle barely raised herself onto her forearms. Flames outlined Davey. His sword rose before them, the thin edge blocking an impossibly wide arc of fire. Gabrielle was tempted to raise her hand closer to it. Despite their proximity to the flame, she felt none of its heat.

"His sword also is enchanted to do that!" Sir Drew scrambled to his knees and motioned for her to do so as well. "Come on!"

He began running in a crouch away from the dragon. Gabrielle followed, glancing behind at Davey. The dragon quit breathing fire and raised a claw to strike him down.

"Hurry!" Sir Drew grabbed her hand and dragged her along.

Gabrielle struggled to keep up, tripping over branches and in holes. She took a moment to realise the hypocrisy of a knight's squire having an enchanted sword before she heard tremendous steps behind her and looked to see the dragon crashing through the trees, a cut along one side of his leg where Davey must have scratched him.

In one swift motion, Sir Drew pushed her to the side and behind a tree. Without losing stride, he pulled a knife from his belt and threw it. An anguished cry. Then a mighty roar.

She waited a moment, on edge, and then ducked out on the other side of the tree, behind the dragon as it followed Sir Drew.

Davey was not tailing the dragon.

Sparing a moment for a steadying breath, she ran back to where the dragon had attacked initially and scanned the area.

He lay about twenty feet from her. She ran to him and knelt down, fingers dipping into the blood pooled behind his head. His chest still moved. She slipped the bags off her shoulder, searching. As the town's makeshift physician, her father had drilled into her head to always carry the basics.

Another roar, not nearly as distant as she would have preferred, came from the forest.

For the moment, Davey was out of harm's way, though he would need help as soon as possible. Sir Drew had fewer effective weapons than Davey and needed immediate help. Hands shaking, Gabrielle ran a little farther into the wood until she came to a clearing in the trees. She surveyed the area and gripped her clothing.

Fear paralyzed her. Was she really going to do this? She had not changed for many years. She had kept her temper. She had not feared too much. She had kept everything under control. Was she going to end her time of peace?

Another roar echoed from the forest.

She had made her decision.

She undressed, nearly catching her arm in her haste, and bundled the clothes together.

She changed.

Her limbs grew, the pleasure of a good stretch filling them and urging them onward. Her shoulder blades ached as if she had slept wrong. They elongated. She arched her back, and wings burst forth. The sensation of soothing an itch rippled through her skin as mossy green scales formed. The ground fell away beneath her as she grew. The trees around her sharpened, veins on leaves coming into detail. The smell of herself, the ground, the sap from the broken trees, she could distinguish them from each other. The sound of cracking twigs and roars sharpened as if she had opened a door.

It stopped. She shook herself, body rippling as a snake's. She stretched out her neck, relishing in the extension and feeling.

Where the young lady had been now resided a dragon.

She took off. Unfortunately, she had overestimated the size of the clearing, having underestimated her own size, but she was still able to make it into the air, above the trees. Her eyes raked the ground for the brown dragon, and she was pleased when she spotted him as well as a still-standing Sir Drew almost immediately. She beat her wings. The wind streamed past her, smoother than water, more invigorating than a swim. She gloried in the feeling.

She hovered above the dragon, indecisive, then just dived. The resounding crash jarred them both. He tumbled to the ground, and she scrambled to her claws.

"What is this?" the dragon yelled.

Gabrielle took a deep breath on instinct and exhaled as hard as she could, feeling a warmth inside her grow hotter with the breath and spread upon her air on the exhale, dousing the brown dragon in fire.

A claw swiped Gabrielle's face. Sharp pain split her cheek. She swung sideways.

The other dragon thrust his head into her stomach.

Her back slammed into the unyielding trunk of an old oak. Her chest convulsed, lungs empty.

"What is the meaning of this?" the dragon seethed. He shook his snout and pounced.

Gabrielle was ready this time. She pulled herself out of the way with a tree trunk, then flew around the side of the tree, legs painfully whacking against the closest trees. She hit him on the side of his head that had a bloody eye.

He roared and took another swing at her.

She merely ducked before ramming her head upward to hit him soundly underneath the chin.

His head snapped back, and he stumbled into a tree.

Gabrielle tensed, ready to attack again. The cut on her face flared. Her legs and back ached from hitting the trees. Blunt, pounding pain radiated from her crown. She desperately hoped he would not rise.

He shook his head, blinking several times.

Gabrielle considered this good enough. She turned around, looking for the best place to get back into the air.

Sir Drew stood before her, dagger in his hand, eyes on her.

Her heart jumped to her throat. He held the dagger in his right hand, eyes trained on hers, waiting for the opportune moment to throw them. She wondered briefly and almost hysterically if blinking would help.

He bowed.

It was just a slight bend of his waist, but it was more than enough.

Gabrielle took flight, grabbing onto and nearly destroying a few trees in the process. She stayed low to the ground while searching for the clearing, wanting neither of the men to see where she landed nor for any other person to see a dragon and come after her. She descended into the clearing. So eager was she to resume human form that she toppled a few feet from the air unto the ground. She rushed to her pile of clothes and pulled them on, a feat considering her trembling hands.

Something wet ran down her face. She raised her hand to feel blood trickling from where the dragon had swiped her. In human form, she healed fast, but not so fast that Sir Drew would not see her wound. Breath quickening, she ran back into the woods. Wincing, she purposefully fell down several times, scuffing her clothing and her body more.

In a few minutes, Sir Drew and Davey were within view. Davey was miraculously standing although supported heavily by Sir Drew.

Trees rattled where they had left the dragon.

Sir Drew caught sight of Gabrielle, raised his finger to his lips, and then motioned for her to follow him. Sir Drew did not even bother to say anything to Davey, just moved the stumbling man along as quickly as possible.

They headed away from the quaking trees and roaring. Gabrielle kept trying to calm her breathing and still her shaking hands.

Sir Drew gestured again for her to follow him, and she nodded. He took another step with Davey.

The ground swallowed them.

She stopped.

Twigs, branches, and leaves lay strewn about as they were before, yet she had surely just seen the ground swallow the knight and his squire. She backed away slowly from where they had disappeared. The trees rattled and her neck began to prickle. Even in her draconic form, another encounter with the brown dragon could be deadly. Disappearing into the earth or certain death?

Gabrielle took another step forward and fell.

IV

The Secret Village

Gabrielle landed heavily and unsteadily on her knees, bags tumbling to the ground. Her back, legs, and sides groaned in unison, new bruises forming from the ledges she had hit on the way down.

Sir Drew was just a few steps ahead of her, still buttressing an unconscious Davey. Mud splatters covered both of them though less so than she would have expected, and they seemed to have been spared from hitting the sides of the hole.

They were in a pit about seven feet deep with a diameter of the same that had seemingly natural steps or ledges carved out of the sides. Looking up, she could see the leaves high above her. She should have seen the hole before she fell into it, yet it was almost as if it had not existed until they had taken their tumble.

Down here, they were easy trappings for the dragon.

"I have heard of places such as these," Sir Drew said.

She turned to him, inclining her head in question.

He explained, "Dragons are not the only people in dragon territory. There are rumors of magic-users living on the fringes of the territory. The entrances to their dwellings are supposedly underground. I believe that we are at the threshold of their homes. This hole was disguised by magic."

Gabrielle took another look around the hole, yet no branches appeared leading off somewhere. The only clear way forward was up. "Perhaps we should go back up. The way forward is unclear. These sorcerers may not be the friendliest sort."

Sir Drew shook his head. "We need to get Davey to safety. His injury is serious and needs more than herbs. We need to ask for help."

Gabrielle looked around again. "Is the second entrance also disguised by magic?"

"Most likely," Sir Drew confirmed, grunting and shifting Davey's arm higher on his shoulders. "Feel around the edges of this place. See if there are any rocks that are not there."

Understanding his odd request, Gabrielle complied, running her finger along the stone walls closest to her. The ground squelched under her feet, a thick layer of mud covering the floor despite the fact that it had not rained for several days. She supposed that this must be part of the magic as well, so none got even more injured while entering though the sorcerers may be able to see the hole in the first place and just descend the stairs.

When she reached nearly the other side of the hole, right before where the stairs were about a foot above her head, her fingers slipped through the stone, sinking into the rock as if it were air.

"That'd be it," Sir Drew grunted, almost slogging forward to get to the rock wall that was not a rock wall. Gabrielle moved her fingers to the side and, still feeling nothing, stepped straight into the rock.

A corridor lit with gently glowing, floating blue spheres stretched before her, hard and dry dirt beneath her feet. Glancing behind, she saw Sir Drew staggering closer to the entrance with Davey. She quickly moved farther into the chamber and off to the side. A moment later, Sir Drew entered the corridor as well. One could tell the instant that he crossed the barrier, for the emanating blue light was abruptly cut off where the irregular stone wall would be. Once he crossed into the hall, the light shone on him as well.

Sir Drew looked up and grinned. "Well, we are definitely on the right track. Would you lead the way, Gabrielle?" He nodded her onward.

She acquiesced, grateful for the compact floor after the near mud-pit of the hole.

"By the way"—Sir Drew panted as he stumbled along—"do you have a nickname?"

Gabrielle shook her head.

"Really?" he huffed.

Gabrielle nodded.

"How about Gabby?" He paused and took a deep breath before taking another step and opening his mouth again. "No, probably not."

Gabrielle allowed herself a smile. She briefly considered informing him that he may not have to huff and puff so much if he were not talking, but dismissed the idea because, though valid, it was hardly fitting to say to a knight of the king, even this knight of the king. In the quiet, the relative peace, she had the sense to still her tongue.

Now that her heart was no longer hammering as a new-born chick, she began to wonder why Davey had stayed behind, and Sir Drew ran with her. Sir Drew lasted with the dragon longer, and they both were level with each other, neither one closer to the dragon. Perhaps twas simply because Davey kept the sword made of dragon claw though this set-up by itself seemed peculiar. She opened her mouth to question . . .

but who was she to question?

She closed her mouth. It wasn't important. Besides, her questions would only encourage theirs. Despite the use of an enchanted sword, they were still of the king's company.

The corridor twisted a few times, but no branches appeared. Dutifully, they continued along the path until Gabrielle noticed that the bluish hue of the corridor was beginning to be overpowered by something close to sunlight. The line of blue orbs ended as they stepped out of the tunnel.

A village that looked quite like her own only quadruple the size sprawled before them. Fields were interspersed with wooden houses, smoke issuing from their chimneys. Bright rays of sun lit upon the people in the fields, the men coming out of the woods with fresh kills, the little children running down the streets, giggling and chasing each other. A river marked its way through the town, women washing clothes on its banks while more little ones splashed in the shallows.

Turning around, Gabrielle still saw the entrance to the

corridor although, from the village, it would be well concealed.

"Indeed, I believe the sorcerers are what we have stumbled upon," Sir Drew announced. He began making his way down to the town, Gabrielle following closely. Sir Drew was a practical sort, it appeared, and fearless as well.

As they drew nearer to the closest home, a woman with long blonde hair stepped out, wiping her hands on a cloth and striding to where they were.

"Pardon, m'lady!" Sir Drew called out. "Our group is weary with travel, and one is injured. We seek refuge here."

The woman stopped coming forward and nodded, her clear blue eyes taking in the details of their troupe. "Ye are welcome in my home. Come." She strode back to the house as quickly and determinedly as she had exited.

Sir Drew staggered the short way with Davey.

Gabrielle soaked up as much as she could about the town before entering the home.

Fire crackled in a hearth beneath a pot. A large wooden table dominated the space with more pots and pans, dishes and bowls placed around the edges on shelves and in cabinets.

"Bring him to the next room over," the woman instructed Sir Drew.

He followed readily into an adjoining chamber.

Gabrielle was on his heels until she noticed an elderly woman resting in a rocking chair, skin crinkled as an old wineskin. Her striking blue eyes inspected Gabrielle closely.

Sensing Sir Drew and Davey leaving the room, Gabrielle broke eye contact with the lady and continued forward into a modest bedroom. The room contained only a bed, dresser, candle, and small wooden table and chair.

Sir Drew lay Davey on the bed, his own shoulder covered in Davey's blood. The knight brought Davey's shirt up and off.

The woman began examining Davey, lifting and turning his head as well as inspecting the bruises on his chest. She looked at Sir Drew, then departed from the room, pace never slacking. The woman's eyes caught Gabrielle's as she passed.

Gabrielle turned to Sir Drew, but he was fastidiously folding Davey's shirt.

Just a moment later, the woman reentered the room with a thick book in her hands and an equally tall, blonde man at her side.

Gabrielle moved to the outskirts of the room as they entered.

The woman set the book down on the edge of Davey's bed while the man inspected Davey as well. He had circular glasses propped at the edge of his nose, a chain running from each edge of them and around his neck as if it were a long necklace.

"I believe this one shall do," the woman said, pausing and pointing at a page.

"Indeed," the man agreed, adjusting the glasses and scanning the page. "With this sort of head wound, that would be the safest bet."

The two clasped hands, the woman reaching out her other one to stretch it over Davey. Reading off the page, they recited the words, nearly unintelligible to Gabrielle and promptly forgotten though she caught the last words: sano percuro.

Wide-eyed, Gabrielle saw the bruises on Davey fade, as if many days had passed, until all were gone.

The two broke their linked hands, the woman raising Davey's head to feel the underside of it.

Satisfied, she smiled. "He is healed as much as possible."

"Thank you," Sir Drew told her gratefully, nodding as he did so.

Gabrielle folded her arms, barely breathing. Sir Drew's tolerance extended further than she expected.

"Let me help the young lady," the woman said, gesturing towards Gabrielle.

The man waved Sir Drew away from the bed and into the next room.

Gabrielle's head automatically followed the knight, and she took a step forward.

"No," the woman said.

Gabrielle's hand clenched, gripping her shift.

White was beginning to blossom from the roots of the woman's hair, and her face crinkled considerably as she smiled. "I will help you in here. My name is Jesalyn. What be yours?"

"Gabrielle."

"Have you seen magic before, Gabrielle?"

Gabrielle shook her head.

The woman nodded, more to herself than to Gabrielle, a serious expression on her face. Gabrielle's mother came to mind, and Gabrielle swallowed the lump that arose in her throat.

"Have no fear," Jesalyn said. "I mean you no harm. I wish only to heal your cuts and bruises. Will you allow me to do such?"

Gabrielle paused for a moment, considering. They had healed Davey easily, and to have the obvious wounds healed now would save her from having to explain when they healed quicker than normal anyway.

And everything hurt, so she was just generally amendable to healing.

"Yes, please."

Jesalyn came closer and actually placed a hand on Gabrielle's cheek. It was warm and calloused, a farmer's hand. Gabrielle was surprised she found this surprising, but then this place all seemed a little surreal. Feeling the woman's hand, her warmth and callouses, helped ground Gabrielle.

"This wound is from a dragon," Jesalyn stated.

Cold fear cut through the warmth.

"I— I tripped, m'lady. Twas no dragon who did this."

Jesalyn smiled. "The edges are slightly curled, my dear, in the way all wounds from a dragon's claw curls." Jesalyn's hand gentled further on Gabrielle's cheek. "Take heart. If it be your wish, I will not share this with your companions."

"Thank you, m'lady," Gabrielle said, the fear retreating slightly.

"Percura. Sana," Jesalyn muttered.

The stinging on Gabrielle's cheek faded. Gabrielle's eyes widened, and her hand fluttered over the place. She frowned, attention drifting to the many other parts of her that hurt.

She saw Jesalyn's eyes follow and flushed. "Thank you," Gabrielle said.

Jesalyn frowned in response. "Where else do you hurt?"

"It's not important—" Gabrielle took a step back, but Jesalyn caught her wrist.

"Please." Jesalyn's face softened, and she offered another smile. "I don't like to see others in pain. It costs me little to heal you. Let me help."

Gabrielle's eyes flicked between Jesalyn's hand and her face. Jerkily, she nodded.

Jesalyn's smile came out fully again.

Gabrielle gestured towards her legs.

Jesalyn raised an eyebrow and gestured towards the bed.

The flush returned, but Gabrielle slid onto the bed, wincing as her back twisted.

"So, back first," Jesalyn said in an amused tone.

Gabrielle smiled, shoulders relaxing. "Yes, please."

Quietly, Jesalyn moved behind her, keeping a steadying hand on Gabrielle the entire time. Jesalyn muttered a few different words this time, sana among them but not the only one. She moved onto Gabrielle's legs next, both the bruises on her calves and the scrapes on her knees. The aches dwindled and then disappeared.

At Jesalyn's questioning look, the woman's eyebrow itching to rise again no doubt, Gabrielle smiled and pointed to her sides.

"Bruise or cut?" Jesalyn asked.

"Bruise." Gabrielle nodded as if agreeing with herself, then looked away embarrassed. "Don't you have to . . ." She gestured at her shift.

"I didn't for your back," Jesalyn reminded her, resting her hand on Gabrielle's side and saying the healing spell. "So long as it's simple, and I know what it is, I don't have to necessarily see it."

Jesalyn stood and cocked her head, another silent question.

Gabrielle stretched out her legs and back. She marveled at the lack of pain. "Thank you. How—?"

"Magic." Jesalyn laughed gently, leaning towards Gabrielle as if they were both in on the joke. "You are ignorant of magic as well, I presume?"

Gabrielle nodded her affirmation shyly.

"Your friend will need to rest for the night, his wound being quite serious and needing time to finish healing. You are welcome to stay here," Jesalyn offered.

"Thank you," Gabrielle told her again. She thought of Sir Drew in the other room. "Sir Drew would like to know this as well, ma'am."

Jesalyn raised an eyebrow, a twinkle in her eye. "Indeed, let's inform Sir Drew, shall we?"

They went into the next room. Sir Drew was hovering near the pot, talking to the elderly lady and the man. He stopped when he saw Gabrielle, a grin breaking out across his face. "You are looking much better!"

The older lady hit him roughly, though weakly, on his leg. "Is that how you talk to all the ladies, young man?"

"No, ma'am. Sorry. I meant no harm." Sir Drew grinned at Gabrielle, bowed, and announced in a slightly stuffy tone, "I am well pleased to see that your wounds have healed, m'lady."

Gabrielle was surprised by her own laugh—and by its brashness. She ducked her head and tucked any loose strands of hair behind her ears, the world muting for a moment until her heartbeat calmed.

Jesalyn was informing Sir Drew of Davey's condition and offering them a place to stay. Sir Drew graciously accepted and then asked if lunch and dinner were included in her offer.

Gabrielle internally cringed. Was this how Davey had felt at the tavern?

Luckily, Jesalyn only snorted, called him a rogue, and told him to sit down, shut up, and eat.

Gabrielle had to admit, she was grateful for the stew Jesalyn served them. The dragon had attacked around midday, and while nothing caused hunger to be forgotten like nearly being killed, her stomach had begun to growl.

The man was named Jonathon and the older woman was his mother, Bernadette. Jonathon patiently explained that the village was named Havene and was accessible only via the tunnels though one could leave Havene simply by walking over three hundred feet into the forest. Turning around after passing the line would only reveal woods before, behind, and all around. This was ample protection from dragons and those who feared magic.

Despite her hunger, Gabrielle found herself listening more than eating though Sir Drew seemed not have the same problem since he had already shared the story of their journey here and was slurping down the potato stew as fast as Jesalyn put it in his dish.

"What else do you know of magic?" Sir Drew asked between bites.

"We know much of magic," Jonathon answered him, eating a hearty portion of the stew as well.

"What about changeling magic?" Sir Drew asked.

Gabrielle's back stiffened, and she woodenly took another bite of the now tasteless food.

Sir Drew continued, "You mentioned that dragons could not get in here. Could changelings?"

"Indeed," Jonathon asserted. "Changelings could walk in as anybody else. Do you know why changelings exist?"

"Please explain," Drew asked politely, "and may I possibly have some more of that delicious stew?"

Jesalyn gave him more as Jonathon expounded upon the topic. "Magic is very interesting," he talked more to Gabrielle as Sir Drew attacked his bowl again. "Magic is everywhere, in everything. Each one of us, yourself and Sir Drew included, has magic to varying degrees. Those with little magic do not even notice it, cannot truly tap into that magic and use it. As one gains more magic, they are more apt to sense and use this magic. Thus, you get sorcerers. However, one may be born with more magic than even this. Their magic is so great that they are able to change forms, to become a being metaphorically 'made' of magic."

"A dragon," Gabrielle said.

"Indeed, a dragon," Jonathon stared intently into her eyes. "Dragons are entirely made of magic and use that magic to live. Changelings have less magic than dragons, so they have the option of staying in human form and using their magic for something else."

"Like what you and Jesalyn did? Spells and such?" Gabrielle asked.

"Yes. Magic takes practice and concentration to work, but sometimes magic will occur unplanned and intuitively in the untrained, especially changelings because their magic is so great compared to the average sorcerer," Jonathon explained.

Gabrielle nodded, trying to comprehend.

Jonathon grinned.

"Let me try to explain it in a simpler way. We do not have specific amounts of how much magic one must have to be a sorcerer or changeling or dragon. I like to think of it as a continuum with a specific, undetermined point for changeling and a specific, undetermined point for dragon. At one end of the continuum are those with so little magic they think they have none. As you travel to the right, more magic is gained, making it more likely that the person is a sorcerer.

"Then you reach that first, undetermined point where a sorcerer becomes a changeling. Continue further to the right, and the changeling gains more magic until you reach the second, undetermined point and become a full-fledged dragon.

"At this point, you could keep going on that continuum, but it is unlikely that any dragon will possess enough magic beyond the amount it takes to be a dragon to do anything with that magic though it is rumored that some dragons in the past have been able to do simple spells. These are dragons of legend, though. Nothing you would expect to see on a daily, or even bicentennial, basis."

Gabrielle nodded again, but more confidently.

"Most people and dragons are in the middle of their respective spectrums," Jesalyn added, "meaning there are more average sorcerers and changelings than there are sorcerers that are almost changelings and changelings that are almost dragons though exceptions exist of course."

"So, dragons have the most magic?" Gabrielle asked.

"Yes," Jonathon confirmed.

"Then why can they not go to human form?"

"Human bodies are not meant to hold that much magic. They are incapable of such. Changelings can because they do not have that immense amount of magic."

"Does that make them not fully dragons?"

"There is a good chance that they are limited in some ways a dragon may not be," Jonathon conceded.

"Like what?"

"Their senses may not be as sharp, fire as hot, much like a dragon with weaker magic would hypothetically be, hypothetically for I have not had the pleasure of lining up multiple dragons, changelings, and sorcerers and measuring the various aspects and skills they possess," Jonathon said with enough genuine regret that Gabrielle had to hide a smile despite the topic.

Gabrielle nodded again. She stirred her soup, looking down at it in the quiet.

"This was absolutely delicious," Sir Drew stated.

"I would hope so considering you ate enough for three men," Jesalyn said.

"Tis hard work being a knight of the king," Sir Drew drawled.

The tension broke. Gabrielle managed to stop her eyes from rolling but could not help the slight flutter. She heard Jesalyn chuckle under her breath and figured that her exasperation had not gone unnoticed.

"Indeed, sir knight of the king, would you like to take a walk through the village with me?" Jonathon asked.

"That sounds very pleasurable," Sir Drew said agreeably, standing up with Jonathon.

Biting her lip, Gabrielle considered that these circumstances were most unusual. Anyone caught using magic or magical items was immediately executed, so to have a knight of the king so willingly see magic used to save his squire was unheard of. To walk the town of a hidden sorcerer village amiably? Inconceivable.

Then again, to take only yourself and a squire to dragon territory to rescue the princess was equally absurd.

"May I show you some of the herbs I have?" Jesalyn inquired of Gabrielle.

Gabrielle's stomach twisted in knots at the prospect of being without Sir Drew or Davey, but she agreed. Sir Drew and Jonathon left the house, already talking about some aspect of the village.

Jesalyn waited only a moment or two before sitting down across from Gabrielle, completely focused on her.

"You're a changeling."

V

Re-Growing the Ceiling

"Don't worry," Jesalyn continued before Gabrielle's sense could return. "There's nothing wrong with that."

Gabrielle studied the table, unable to meet the woman's gaze. "I don't know what you're talking about."

Jesalyn stood, walked next to Gabrielle, and sat down. She took one of Gabrielle's hands in her own.

Gabrielle finally lifted her head.

"You have not met anyone else with magic, have you? Including changelings?" Jesalyn asked.

Gabrielle affirmed this with a single nod.

"There is nothing to be ashamed of, my dear. As Jonathon said, magic is a part of everything. We all have at least a touch, you more than others. Tell me, have you tried spells or any other sorceries?"

Gabrielle shook her head.

"But you do change often?"

Gabrielle shook her head again and opened her mouth, then shut it firmly.

"Gabrielle," Jesalyn coaxed, "not I nor Bernadette will tell anyone anything you tell us if you wish us not to. I promise."

Gabrielle glanced at Bernadette, and the elder smiled and nodded once.

"None . . . none in my family are changelings." Gabrielle began.

Jesalyn nodded, not saying a word.

"I . . ." Gabrielle shook her head, eyes lowering until they rested on their joined hands. "Before today, I had only met a dragon once." She let out a disbelieving breath and looked up at Jesalyn with dry amusement. "He was destroying my village. The only reason he let my family and me live is because I think he somehow knew what I was."

"Your parents do not know?"

"No." Gabrielle hesitated. She took a deep breath and continued. "How can I tell them that their daughter is . . . *that?*"

"You are not a '*that*,' as you say," Jesalyn declared. "Having your amount of magic makes you unusual, special, but not inhuman. You have not changed often then?"

"No. I used to change by accident when I was younger. If my emotions got the best of me, I had no choice. I practiced keeping calm. I have not lost that control in a long time." Gabrielle grimaced. "Yesterday was the exception."

"Have you ever changed purposefully?"

Gabrielle smiled sadly. "Yes."

Jesalyn waited.

"When . . . when I younger, before my village burned down, I had a friend named Mackenzie. I think we got in an argument one day, and . . . I changed by accident. It's hard to remember because I was only three, almost four. Even then I thought for sure she was going to tell, and I was going to be killed."

Gabrielle mustered a fuzzy image of a girl with strawberry blonde hair—or had it been more like wheat, as Drew's was? She strived to add details. Hadn't Mackenzie had a hooked nose? There was a scar that ran along the bottom of her foot from stepping on a rake. Was it the right or left foot? The image didn't become any clearer. Gabrielle ducked her head, hot shame filling her. She couldn't remember.

She swallowed. At the very least, she could share Mackenzie's acceptance. "Mackenzie never told. We would battle and go for trips, too, at night. We'd fly over the fields and travel far away from our village. I would pretend that we would never go back, that we would just keep on flying forever, but hunger has a way of making a person return home."

Gabrielle forced a laugh.

Jesalyn squeezed her hands.

"I remember one time I flew up so high Mackenzie began shivering even though it was the middle of summer. I had to take her back down, but I went up again a few nights later. I wanted to see the whole world. Of course, I ended up seeing only our little island though now that I say that, seeing all of Aradin is an accomplishment."

"What did it look like?" Jesalyn asked, smiling as well.

"Like a bean with one tip of it cut off! There was another island, too, possibly, it was dark and small, hard to see."

"You were up very high!"

"I flew almost straight up and down, yet it took me the whole night. I still remember struggling to keep my eyes awake the following day. My mother knew I had stayed up, but could not figure out what I had been doing."

Jesalyn let out a huff off laughter, eyes wandering to the bedroom doors. The woman was old enough to be Gabrielle's mother and then some, the same with Jonathon. They had enough rooms in their home for children, more than enough really.

Gabrielle opened her mouth to ask, but Jesalyn's gaze was back to her, her eyes a steady and strong hazel. "Why did you stop changing?"

Once strawberry-blonde hair was ash. The skin on the body had shrunk, clinging to the small frame in crinkling folds.

"Mackenzie died." Gabrielle forced the words out.

When the dragons came, she had hidden in a trunk, the only one her family had owned.

The burning shame returned. Gabrielle remembered the piled dirt of the grave better than the girl.

Gabrielle glanced at Jesalyn, begging for distraction. The woman sat calmly, patiently. Gabrielle had heard that couples eventually began to look like each other, and she could see the beginnings of such in the curve of Jesalyn's back, in the gentle angle of her chin.

Gabrielle continued, making her own distraction, "The dragons were resurging. It became much more dangerous to change, even at night. Then we were attacked, and Mackenzie killed. I saw no more reason to change. The night before the dragons burnt my village was the last time I changed. Until today."

"When you were attacked?"

"Yes. Davey got hurt, and Sir Drew could not hold the dragon off forever. I feared we would all die if I did not act."

Jesalyn nodded. "Would you change again, to save them?"

". . . Yes."

"Then let me give you a bit of advice," Jesalyn spoke gently. "Change. Not just when it is life or death. Change regularly and practice maneuvering the best way you can. Because of the time you are living, you are especially unique."

"Most changeling families are dead."

"Indeed, which makes you so unique. I have little doubt that there are other changelings out there, but they are few and far between. I would be immensely surprised if there were even seven or more. Practice being in both forms. Agility, strength, and, yes, fighting skills, will help you whether you are human or dragon."

Gabrielle shifted and leaned away though she did not pull her hands from Jesalyn's grasp. "I have had little need to be able to fight."

"Ah"—Jesalyn smiled sardonically—"but you are in dragon territory now. I suppose you have come here to see other dragons?"

"Tis not sight-seeing," Gabrielle automatically answered. An unexpected surge of anger spiked in her.

"I should think not! Tis learning." Jesalyn shifted, leaning more towards Gabrielle. "Seeing as you have survived thus far, I believe I need not tell you that it is easier to talk yourself to your death than listen."

Gabrielle blushed from her quick anger though she could tell Jesalyn had not noticed it. She nodded much more than necessary to Jesalyn's implied question.

Jesalyn let a smile slide across her face for a moment. Solemnity returned quickly. "Gabrielle, whether you are in dragon territory or not, being able to defend and protect in either form is important. Answer me truthfully, will you improve your abilities in both forms?"

Gabrielle did not answer right away.

In her village, she had seen little need to learn the sword or even basic fighting skills. She didn't know how to fight in either form, and the past two days had required experience far beyond what she had. She had survived the ambush and dragon attack on instinct and luck. Being in dragon territory would necessitate that she sharpens her skills.

However, she was not planning on being in the territory long.

One day, though, whether on this journey or many years from now, she would be changing again. That was assured. Improving her abilities in both forms would make her ready for that day and every day until that one came. She would *need* to change someday in the future, even if she didn't know when.

"Yes," she committed.

Jesalyn studied her for a moment. "Good," she said at last, standing up. "Then I have a gift for you."

"A gift?"

"Yes." Jesalyn rummaged through one of the cupboards below a shelf with neatly stacked books. She withdrew one and walked back over to where Gabrielle sat, setting the tome on the table. Neatly bound, the book was old but well-kept. No title bedecked its tanned, dusty-colored cover, just swirling designs around the edges. Jesalyn motioned for Gabrielle to open it. Inside was a list of words on one side with descriptions coming off of them. Occasionally, a page or section would be devoted to a lengthy topic.

"Tis a spell book!" Gabrielle said.

"Indeed. Tis yours if you wish."

"Could I use it?"

Jesalyn laughed. "I assume you mean 'magic' by 'it'."

Gabrielle smiled, face heating. "Yes."

"You should be able to. Being a changeling almost guarantees that your magic will be strong."

"Almost?"

"You may have the natural inclination to do so, but without the right mindset nor practice nor will, you will accomplish little. A small test should indicate whether or not your magic will come easily to you. Remember the continuum although that is just one factor." Jesalyn sat down and pointed at Gabrielle's cup. "Focus your mind on this cup, imagine it flying up and hitting the ceiling. An over exaggeration often helps new sorcerers. Your true objective is simply to raise it up." Jesalyn smiled encouragingly. "Imagine it hitting the ceiling and say 'sursa'."

Gabrielle swallowed and stared at the cup. She took a steadying breath. If over exaggeration helped, then, in her mind, the cup crashed through the ceiling and went so high into the sky she could not see it anymore. She imagined it disappearing into the clouds. She concentrated, feeling a sudden welling of something that felt similar to confidence buzz in her stomach.

"Sursa."

The cup flew up so fast that the wooden roof barely slowed its ascent. There was a splintering of wood and a sprinkling of dust.

Gabrielle jumped to her feet, Jesalyn doing the same. Gazing through the newly created hole in the ceiling, Gabrielle watched the rapidly rising cup until it was nearly out of sight, dipping into a curve at the last moment. She turned to Jesalyn to see an equally shocked face.

Bernadette laughed, startling Gabrielle.

"Over exaggeration, indeed!" Bernadette belted out.

"Indeed," Jesalyn agreed, her voice a few pitches higher, still staring at the ceiling, then Gabrielle. "Well, I do believe it can be said that you have a very promising amount of accessible magic in you and a *very* determined will to use it. I suspect you not only lifted the cup but strengthened the wood of the cup as it burst through my ceiling."

Gabrielle could only nod.

Jesalyn raised her hands, and the roof regrew over the hole.

"You did not say a spell?" Gabrielle questioned, shifting and raising her shoulders.

"Once you are familiar with a spell or exceptionally experienced, you may not need to say a spell aloud or even know one. Also, some sorcerer—pardon, magic-users, are especially in-tune with the magic and nature around us, so natural elements are the easiest to manipulate. For instance, fixing the wooden roof is much easier than casting a curse."

Gabrielle considered this. She forced her shoulders down. If Jesalyn took this in stride, then so could she. Spying the door to Davey's room hanging slightly ajar, Gabrielle wondered if she could close it. She imagined it shutting and felt the buzz once more.

Bang!

They all jumped.

"Sorry!" she squeaked.

"Control seems to be your greatest challenge," Jesalyn mused, Bernadette renewing her laugh.

"Yes, ma'am."

Jesalyn shook her head, laughed once, and tapped the cover. "Use this book wisely."

Gabrielle agreed whole-heartedly.

"Would you like to try to lift up another cup?" Jesalyn asked.

Gabrielle was not eager to try in front of her though longing to practice magic. Unable to see any better opportunity, she undertook the challenge.

The next few hours were spent moving cups, bowls, saucers, and other dishes around the room, Gabrielle gaining confidence and control with every exercise. Eventually, Jesalyn began asking her to move several objects at once, then in opposite directions. Jesalyn then began moving objects around the room, too, instructing Gabrielle to keep her own objects moving while stopping any objects of Jesalyn's that were going to collide with an object of hers.

This challenged Gabrielle, but she felt her mind was well-equipped to succeed with her years spent serving the numerous tables at her parents' tavern, keeping track of their orders, the amount of drink they had left, and how many more they could manage before her father would have to walk them home. While different, the mental agility it required was reminiscent of such. Her father would say it was like counting beans like one counted potatoes. After several hours, Jesalyn stopped the exercises.

"Tis getting late, and the boys are almost home," she announced. "You have done exceptional."

Everything of Gabrielle's drifted back into place, Jesalyn's objects not returning to the shelves, but setting themselves properly upon the table.

"Thank you," Gabrielle murmured, eyes on the dishes as they settled into place. "Do you use magic for everything?"

Jesalyn shook her head. "All magic has a price. It's best not to use it for every little chore." She gave a sudden grin. "But they were already in the air, and who am I to deprive you of seeing more?"

Gabrielle smiled, and Bernadette chuckled.

"Have you not had any incidents of magic before?" Jesalyn asked, now throwing together another stew, though vegetable this time, without moving a muscle.

Gabrielle's eyes followed a knife chopping carrots as she answered, "Now that I consider it, I believe I have used it in the past to keep the things I am holding balanced, like the trays though I cannot think of any beyond that."

"The trays?" Jesalyn questioned.

"My parents own a tavern and inn. I serve there most nights," Gabrielle explained.

"They let you come on this journey?"

Gabrielle stayed silent. The cutting board lifted into the air, and the knife slid the carrots into the pot.

"I see. . . . Any other times you can think of yourself using magic?"

The fire eagerly jumped higher as the last of the vegetables plopped into the pot.

"I believed I was a changeling, not a sorcerer."

"You are a changeling, my dear. Tis just that changelings are usually able to do what sorcerers can. Your answer wasn't straight, though."

"What do you mean, ma'am?"

"Twas not a yes or no." Jesalyn raised an eyebrow. "I have raised three sons, Gabrielle, all three now grown and residing elsewhere. The youngest of these, when he was growing up, had a habit of answering my question by implying something different than the truth. When else did you use magic, my dear?"

"I used it in front of Mackenzie," Gabrielle confessed, rubbing her arms. Though she had glanced over at Jesalyn, she returned her attention to the stew. "I was not sure if I had actually done it at the time, but her reaction convinced me that I never wanted to do it again."

"How did she react?"

Gabrielle hesitated. She could remember the moment Mackenzie saw her use magic just as well as she remembered Mackenzie's grave, but neither was fair to the girl who had accepted her.

The woman's hand, warm and calloused, rested upon Gabrielle's arm.

Gabrielle settled with, "Not well."

Jesalyn's hand on Gabrielle's arm tightened. "This was the same girl who knew you were a changeling?"

"Yes," Gabrielle admitted. "Sorcery was a little too much, I guess."

"Indeed," Jesalyn muttered.

Jesalyn did not lift her hand. Gabrielle did not ask her to. She was grateful that neither Jesalyn nor Bernadette would tell Sir Drew of her magic. No matter Sir Drew's leniency with the sorcerers here, she did not know where he marked the line. She did not wish to find out.

As if summoned, Sir Drew burst through the door, guffawing with Jonathon, the both of them scuffed and dirty. At some point, Sir Drew had taken off his armor, which was for the best considering that his clothing was quite battered, even more so than after falling into the hole. Gabrielle frowned, wondering where in the village he had put the armour.

"What's for dinner, dear?" Jonathon spluttered out.

"My sentiment exactly," Sir Drew added, taking great breaths to calm himself down, red in the face from his excitement.

"Vegetable stew, but neither of you will be getting any of it until you are properly cleaned. Go. Ye are getting the ground dirty," Jesalyn rebuked.

They left the way they had come, laughing and bumping into each other.

Jesalyn looked to Bernadette and then Gabrielle, exasperation clear on her face. Gabrielle laughed once. Twice. She sniffled. Took a wavering breath.

"Oh, dear," Jesalyn sighed. She moved as if to hug Gabrielle, but paused, brow wrinkling. "Not to be rude, but . . .

". . . would you be willing to wash first as well?"

VI

Oh, Well, Guess She's Going Onward

Jesalyn led Gabrielle to another room and gave her some new clothes and a basin of water. She offered Gabrielle the chance to go to the river and wash as well, but Gabrielle was content with the change of clothes and basin.

After she had washed and changed, the men came back, and they began eating supper. Sir Drew and Jonathon again acted as if they had not eaten for days. Gabrielle could only watch on with awe and wonder if Davey got any food when the two of them traveled together. Jesalyn made most of the conversation, explaining and commenting on the herbs she had "shown" Gabrielle that afternoon.

Eventually, Sir Drew took a minute to breathe after inhaling stew for minutes on end. "Gabrielle, we met some men in the village who reported that the dragons were patrolling the edge of their territory. We must have crossed over some-time after the dragon attack and before falling into the hole. In order to get back to the land of Aradin, you would have to get past all of their guards. That is highly unlikely. I would prefer for you to wait until we could make the crossing with you. What are your thoughts?"

Despite the rush of pleasure from him asking, a new knot grew in her stomach.

"You are welcome to stay here if you wish," Jesalyn told her, nodding meaningfully.

Gabrielle considered her stew. Turning around now was not a viable option, not that she desired to do so anyway. Staying here was tempting. Twas peaceful, and the people kind. However, she could not ignore the fact that there were no changelings here, no dragons. In addition, if these two days had made her realise how ill prepared she was, it also made her realise how much help her little experience could be for Davey and Sir Drew. To stay here would be to abandon them to whatever else lay in dragon territory.

She straightened, readying for Sir Drew's denial. "I would like to journey with you."

"Very well." Sir Drew nodded. He turned to Jonathon. "Do you have any suggestions on where we should look for Princess Danielle?"

Gabrielle bit back her smile. Davey would have had a conniption on several counts, and Sir Drew was only on his second helping.

"The dragons would have taken her deep within their territory. I would suggest to continue heading southeast of here. There have been rumors that the old Ancora castle has had an enormous upgrade in guards over the past few days," Jonathon replied.

"There is a castle in dragon territory?" Gabrielle asked, surprised.

"Indeed," Jonathon answered. "There used to be a time when those with all different levels of magic got along well. During those days, dragon territory was human territory and human territory dragon. All coexisted mostly peacefully alongside each other. Since the two sides have been separated, evidence of this period of peace has declined precipitously. Nonetheless, the Ancora castle stands as a testament to those years."

"The magic protecting our village was put in place by a joint force of sorcerers and changelings," Jesalyn added. "Few remember, but relationships between humans and dragons broke down first, then changelings and sorcerers and humans."

"What happened?" Gabrielle asked.

Jonathon's mouth thinned. "Hurt happened on both sides and each blamed the other. There were some humans who would have liked to war with the dragons and some dragons who would have liked the same against the humans. By their efforts and the lack of dedication to peace by others, the war began and has continued in spurts since."

The crackling of the fire—and Drew's slurping—filled the brief quiet.

Gabrielle shifted forward, eyes on her soup as she spoke. "Your continuum implies that we are all . . ."

"The same?" Jonathon's soft voice finished.

Gabrielle looked to him and away. Had Jesalyn told him

about her? Regardless, she would not be able to address it currently, not with Sir Drew present.

Instead, she replied, "Essentially."

"That's because we are." At Jonathon's candid tone, she met his smiling gaze. His glasses were hanging from his neck, but a small indent decorated his nose. "You will meet many creatures in dragon territory that are not the same. They also contain magic, as everything does, but you will find that they lack sentiment. Although, kelpies tend to act like they have it. They're quite interesting, and I've heard that once domesticated—"

"Dear," Jesalyn interrupted, eyebrow raised.

Jonathon cleared his throat. "Yes, um. As I was saying. Some lack sentiment. They are not beings with a mind and will like dragons and humans. This sentiment, this will, does not exist in them, and they have no self-reflection in order to create it. They are what they are made. Neither good nor evil, just . . . there. Dragons and humans differ in this respect. Those with sentiment are much more alike than you think."

"What else will we encounter in dragon territory?" Sir Drew asked.

"Many creatures, primarily rocs, chimeras, white stags, goldhorns, Anansi, crocottas, penghous, karkadans, tigris—"

"When you say 'primarily', you need to give a shorter list," Jesalyn interrupted again, shaking her head.

"Yes, dear," Jonathon answered, grinning into his stew.

A few of the animals sounded faintly familiar to Gabrielle, as if she had heard them in a tale of a traveler, but most were completely new, and no images jumped to mind for any of them.

"These creatures exist here because the environment is different?" Gabrielle clarified.

"Indeed, much different." Jonathon stirred his stew, almost smirking. "There are fewer kings fearing magic here."

"Oh," Gabrielle stated dumbly, cheeks coloring.

Jonathon chuckled. "Don't be concerned. Dragons can be just as guilty about causing local extinction as humans are."

"What do you mean?" Gabrielle asked.

"Dragons are usually easier on the environment than humans are. However, there is a certain plant that dragons have been particular in singling out." Jonathon paused, sensing Gabrielle's piqued interest. "Have you ever heard of dragonsbane?"

Again, the name sounded almost familiar, but not nearly enough that Gabrielle could recall anything. "Yes, but I don't remember anything about it."

"I'm not surprised." Jonathon nodded. "Dragons have always been eager to rid the island of dragonsbane. While many plants that affect humans affect dragons likewise, it generally takes a much larger concentration. Dragonsbane is different in that it is completely harmless to humans, even edible. However, I suspect that as the amount of magic a person holds increases, the toxicity of dragonsbane does as well, for the plant is intoxicating to dragons, much like a large amount of alcohol is to humans."

"Then I should think dragons love dragonsbane!" Gabrielle exclaimed.

"You would think," Jonathon agreed, grinning. "Nevertheless, such intoxication leaves a dragon vulnerable, and the plant was often used against dragons to their detriment."

Jonathon took the last sip of his stew, showed the empty bowl to Jesalyn, and reached for the pot again. He winked at Gabrielle as he dished more up for himself. "That's why dragons have tried their best over the years to destroy dragonsbane. As far as practicality goes, they have succeeded wherever a dragon flies."

Rapid knocking at the door startled Gabrielle, her spoon falling noisily back into her soup.

"Mister Jonathon! Mister Jonathon!" a small voice called out, the knocking pausing only for those words before recommencing.

Jesalyn smiled while Jonathon stood up, stew forgotten, and opened the door.

"Mr. Felipe," Jonathon mimicked the little, picturesque boy kindly.

Mr. Felipe was not taller than Gabrielle's waist and stick-skinny. He had beautiful, wide eyes surrounded by an equally handsome face.

Upon the door opening and recognition of Jonathon, Felipe ran forward and threw his arms around Jonathon's legs. "Mr. Jonathon! Can I stay? Please? Just for a little while? Please?"

Jonathon looked at Felipe, then to Jesalyn. "What about your mother?"

"She said I could come! I asked her this time!"

"Indeed, and what should happen if your mother does not know?" Jonathon raised an eyebrow.

Felipe's mouth popped open. "I would be in trouble then, Mr. Jonathon! Mother said I needed to ask before coming over anymore. She said I was bothering you. I promise not to be bothering, Mr. Jonathon!"

"You are not a bother," Jonathon assured the boy, placing a hand upon his head, "but your mother does enjoy seeing you occasionally."

"Please let me stay, Mr. Jonathon!"

"Of course you can stay, as long as your mother approved of your visit."

Felipe nodded vigorously.

"Would you like some soup, Felipe?"

Felipe nodded more vigorously, smiling from ear to ear. He took an extra chair in the corner and pulled it up right beside Jonathon. Jesalyn poured some soup into a bowl for him, but Felipe scurried to a low-level cabinet, tugging out a large book he could barely carry. He dropped it onto the chair, then climbed up onto the book, now able to reach the table. Jonathon pushed him in, and Jesalyn handed him a spoon. Felipe dug in just as hungrily as Mister Jonathon had done. Their conversation resumed. However, they were almost done eating, and Felipe ate eagerly.

After dinner, Jonathon told a long winding tale about a roc, an oversized, black bird that usually did not distinguish between humans and white stags, its primary source of meat, until Jesalyn gently encouraged him to focus more on the route instead of the various food sources for the many creatures in the territory.

Jonathon suggested they head southeast until they hit the river, follow the river, and then turn directly east before reaching the open sea. He then went into even greater detail about certain landmarks, most of which Gabrielle forgot as soon as Jonathon mentioned them. Fortunately, Sir Drew seemed to be understanding and remembering most if not all of the information. Felipe also listened closely, taking in Mister Jonathon's every word and gesture.

Gabrielle caught Jesalyn off to the side and asked if she could leave the spell book with her until they made a return trip.

Jesalyn became grim, saying, "Keep your head on your shoulders, and you will survive just fine."

Gabrielle was not too sure about that and was relieved when Jesalyn agreed to keep the book at her house for the time being.

The plan was for them to head out of the village in the southeasterly direction the following morning, after breakfast at Sir Drew's request. Gabrielle was glad they had a plan in place and even more so that she would continue traveling with Sir Drew and Davey. She had always had it in her mind to continue on into dragon territory but had worried about the feasibility of simply surviving. With Sir Drew and Davey, she would not be able to move as freely, but she would not be alone.

Sir Drew kept vigil in Davey's room that night, Gabrielle in another room one of Jesalyn's three sons had lived in. She found that she awoke early naturally and aided Jesalyn in frying eggs and meat for breakfast.

"Did Felipe leave last night?" Gabrielle asked Jesalyn. She had not seen the little boy after going down the hall to her room.

"Indeed, he went back home." Jesalyn smiled at Gabrielle.

"Felipe's father died when he was just a baby. He has taken to Jonathon, something I am sure you noticed last night."

Gabrielle nodded, smiling and mirroring Jesalyn's amused expression.

"He tries to come over all the time. He wants to follow Jonathon everywhere he goes."

"Does he have any other siblings?" Gabrielle asked.

"No, but his mother is kept busy enough with her job. She is the best seamstress in town. She has no problems watching Felipe. He simply finds more amusement here than where she works. She also doesn't mind him over here, but she does want to know where he is."

"That smells wonderful," Davey remarked, startling Gabrielle as he stood disheveled right in front of the room he had slept in.

"Gabrielle has done most of the cooking," Jesalyn told him.

"Then Gabrielle makes things smell wonderful." His face twisted as he spoke.

Gabrielle tried for a laugh. "Has Sir Drew been rubbing off on you?"

"If he has, that would be another good reason to take a bath," Davey's face twisted more, and he rubbed the bridge of his nose.

Her cheeks unusually warm, Gabrielle moved farther away from the fire.

Davey dropped his hand, eyes searching for and finding Gabrielle. He turned to Jesalyn. "Is this your home?"

"Yes, sir," she replied.

"Thank you for taking us in. Was I unconscious yesterday?"

"You were," Gabrielle said, and she continued to speaking despite her desire to stop at that, "and you slept like a hog and left this poor lady, her husband, and I to deal with Sir Drew alone."

Davey grinned, his embarrassment forgotten in light of hers no doubt. "Oh, really? Tell me, Gabs, how does a hog sleep?"

"Gabs!" Sir Drew interrupted, coming into the room, looking as if he had barely slept a wink. "A nickname!"

"A nickname?" Jesalyn inquired.

"Indeed!" Sir Drew said excitedly, but he began yawning before the word was completely out, making the word sound more like "indee—ah".

"Did you not sleep at all last night?" Davey asked Sir Drew incredulously.

Sir Drew shook his head and answered while still yawning, unintelligible sounds issuing from his mouth.

Gabrielle pressed her lips together, but still could not stop her smile.

Breakfast was made and eaten quickly, Davey running down to the river for a quick wash before tucking in. Then their bags were packed and ready to go. Davey argued for a few minutes about Gabrielle not coming with. Gabrielle's confidence was bolstered by a knight's backing however, so Sir Drew and Gabrielle's staunchness left him no choice.

They were walking out the front door when Davey paused to ask Jesalyn if she had given him any herbs or tinctures because he had been expecting bruises and aches from his fall yesterday, but was feeling exceptionally well instead. Jesalyn only smiled and told Davey that she believed Sir Drew or Gabrielle could relate the full tale as they journeyed.

Just as they were about to set off into the woods, Jesalyn caught Gabrielle in a hug.

"I wish you luck, my dear, although I doubt you will need any."

"Thank you, ma'am," Gabrielle responded warmly.

"Jesalyn, just Jesalyn." Jesalyn bestowed upon her yet another tender smile.

Then they left, heading southeast into a forest that would cause Havene to disappear behind them as if it had never existed in the first place.

VII

What Happens When One Gets Kicked in the Chest by a Goat

Gabrielle noted despairingly that they were only about two-hundred feet into the forest when Davey asked again, "What did she give me? I don't have a sore bone in my body. This is extraordinary."

Sir Drew glanced at Davey, then Gabrielle. "They were sorcerers, mi—my friend."

Davey stopped. "Sorcerers?"

Sir Drew nodded and, observing Davey's sudden stop, asked, "Have your legs stopped working?"

"Why did you not tell me they were sorcerers?" Davey's voice had hardened. His jaw had tightened, and Gabrielle immediately cast her eyes to the forest floor, her back stiff and muscles tense.

Entirely too blasé, Sir Drew asked, "Was it relevant?"

Gabrielle winced.

"Magic is deadly."

Davey's voice had deepened. Some part of Gabrielle's brain rationalized that this had to be intentional, that he—like some boys in the village—played man or knight by simply dropping their voice. She silently begged Sir Drew to let it lie.

"I know—"

"Really?" Davey snapped his words like a whip.

Gabrielle dared to look up.

As if sensing the movement, Davey turned to her. His face was hard and closed, lacking any hint of friendliness. Anger sharpened its edges.

"Davey," Sir Drew stepped forward, drawing Davey's attention back. "You needed help. They were willing to give it. Without their aid, you'd be dead by now."

Davey and Sir Drew stared at each other, each uncompromising.

Gabrielle shifted.

Perhaps Sir Drew would defend her—

"The more magic one has, the less human they are."

—but twas clear Davey would not.

A weight fell on Gabrielle's chest.

"The more magic, the more dragon," Sir Drew finished somberly, eyes resting on Davey.

Then Sir Drew cocked his head.

Gabrielle silently cursed the man and his foolishness.

Predictably, Sir Drew opened his mouth anyway.

"Funny, how Jonathon's continuum would match that assumption, isn't it?"

Davey's face, so carefully set, frowned, and Gabrielle wondered at the fear that finally entered his eyes. "Watch your tongue. Wag it like that anywhere else and it'll cost you your head."

Sir Drew didn't reply.

Gabrielle wrapped her arms around herself as the silence stretched, wondering if thinking loud thoughts about walking would get them moving.

"Davey?" Sir Drew asked.

"Yes?"

"Jesalyn and Jonathon are sorcerers."

"Thanks, Drew, real timely you are."

Gabrielle breathed out a quiet sigh of relief as Davey turned and finally began walking again.

The rest of the morning passed without major interruption though Gabrielle kept her eyes open for any signs of wildlife on the forest floor, especially at first. Sir Drew explained more of the creatures that roamed dragon territory, having read about these creatures in books. Davey wondered aloud if he should start paying attention to what Sir Drew was reading, to which Sir Drew responded that was unlikely because he was unsure if Davey had ever even opened a book.

Sir Drew spoke more of the rocs, but also of chimeras, fearsome fire-breathing beasts with a lion's head, a goat's form, and a serpentine tail. He told of wolf-like creatures that prowled around in packs, but could laugh and cry like a human—crocottas. Going into great detail, he expounded upon karkadans, enormous river-dwelling brutes with tough, leathery skin, and a large horn protruding from their skull.

Gabrielle began jumping at the slightest twig until Davey pointed it out. She retorted better jumpy than dead, to which Sir Drew replied better full than jumpy, so they rested and ate lunch.

As Gabrielle took the last few bites of her bread, she heard rustling in the underbrush. She stilled and peered into the foliage.

"Have you found your chimera, Gabs?" Davey asked, grinning.

"Shush," she told him, unsettled enough not to respond further.

The leaves swished again.

After a tense moment, a furry animal about the size of three bread loaves hopped out from the brush, soft, velvet nose twitching and sniffing the air. If not for the fuzzy, light brown antlers issuing from the creature's head, it could have been a rabbit.

"A jackalope," Sir Drew stated, as if it were seen every day. "They are also called skvaders or, if you are my brother, wolpertingers."

"When has your brother seen a jackalope?" Davey asked, eyes glued to the creature.

"You really have not opened a book, have you?"

"I like to do things, Drew, not read about them."

"Indeed, well, it just so happens that learning about the dangers in the supremely dangerous place you are going before you get there is kind of helpful."

"In what way?" Davey asked, clearly rhetorically, as he broke off a bit of his bread to feed to the jackalope.

"In the way that I know that if you feed him, he will follow you around until killed, mimicking your voice and causing general havoc for all who wish to stay hidden."

Davey froze, hand still outstretched.

"You're kidding."

"No. I would suggest not feeding him."

Davey retracted his hand, but the skvader jumped closer to him anyway.

"Mimicking my voice?" Davey asked, placing the bread in his pocket, eyes still on the skvader.

"Indeed," Sir Drew replied. "If he likes you, he may even do it without you feeding him."

"'Tis a good thing Davey is not particularly likeable then," Gabrielle murmured, realizing a moment too late she was much too loud.

"Thin," the mouth of the jackalope twisted, somehow producing the word in a voice with the likeness of Gabrielle's.

Gabrielle looked to Sir Drew in alarm.

Sir Drew laughed.

"Not all of them will follow you if you feed them, and few will if you do not feed them. You have nothing to fear, Gabrielle."

They packed up quickly after that, the skvader sticking around for a few more minutes of investigation before scampering off when Davey shooed it away.

The afternoon passed as the morning had. When suppertime came, Sir Drew lamented that no jackalope visited them this time, for he figured that they could have had the jackalope feed them instead of them feeding it. "Just imagine. Gabrielle could have been eating the legs, I could have had the breast and ribs, and Davey could have gnawed on the antlers. Indeed, such a succulent meal we shan't taste today."

Instead, they ate more bread and some of the vegetables Jesalyn had packed for them. The following night, if everything was still going well, Gabrielle promised to make them her favorite dish with their remaining vegetables, her mother's potato and vegetable soup. Sir Drew proclaimed himself fasting until that meal in order to better enjoy it although he shortly thereafter announced that the fasting would take affect only while the moon was out.

Gabrielle, face hidden as she gathered wood for the fire, did not bother to hide her smile.

As the sun sank ever lower, Gabrielle insisted on taking a turn watching the camp, saying that she would prefer the middle or last shift. Davey argued with her for a few minutes, as Gabrielle had expected, but Sir Drew was unconcerned either way. At last, Davey gave in, but demanded that she take the last shift and he take the middle. Gabrielle thanked him tersely, but gave an embarrassed smile a moment later. Davey cleared his throat several times in the following minute.

Gabrielle did not particularly relish the opportunity to wake up early and watch over the camp, but she wanted the time alone to practice her magic. Though she did not have the book, she calculated that she would be able to improve upon what she already could do and experiment using magic without any spells. When her turn watching the camp finally came, she did such, finding little success in her new endeavors, perhaps partially because she was so fearful of waking Sir

Drew or Davey. However, she felt her ability of moving items with little movement of her own had grown. Gabrielle treasured her few solitary morning hours and decided to make the few hours of practice a habit. Upon the men awakening, she immediately suggested that they keep the arrangement.

They traveled another day in this state, spying a few more jackalopes and some distant dragons. Sir Drew or Gabrielle was always the first to spot a dragon, and it always undoubtedly led to several tense minutes of silence and stillness. To everyone's relief, none of the dragons noticed them, and they continued uncontested.

On the third day, it was blatantly obvious how bored Sir Drew was. Gabrielle often heard older patrons wish they had a child's energy, but Gabrielle wished that she could have the energy of Sir Drew's mouth. Eventually, Sir Drew roped Davey into a game where one of them would describe something that was in view, and the other person would have to guess it.

In the middle of this, the oddest creature Gabrielle had ever seen slunk out from behind a tree and some bushes in front of them. It had the muscular, trotting rear of a goat and a fierce lion head, teeth glinting as it growled. A serpent connected to it as a tail hissed and waved of its own accord. The entire beast was one and a half times the size of Sir Drew, armor included.

"Chimera," Sir Drew said. He flung the bags off his back and drew his sword. Davey did the same.

Gabrielle backed up slowly, the two of them taking precedence. Her mind immediately flew to her magic, but she chided herself. Not every emergency would require such drastic action. The less she used it, the less likely she was to be caught.

Davey and Sir Drew spread out to either side of the chimera, starting to bait it and withdraw suddenly. The beast snapped and swung at their swords, cuffing Sir Drew's once or twice. The men drew nearer, their swords coming ever closer, yet not reaching the beast.

"Careful, Davey," Sir Drew cautioned after Davey made a particularly close attack. "She is trying to bait us as much as we her. Remember, she breathes fire, yet she hasn't already."

On his next swing, Davey came even closer, and the monster blasted him with fire. Davey rolled out of the way, but the snake on the beast's tail struck.

Sir Drew rushed forward to distract it. He ducked a stream of fire.

In those moments, Davey smoothly slid to his feet, seemingly unhurt, and approached the creature from behind, his eyes almost transfixed by the writhing snake.

"Careful!" Sir Drew called out, opening his mouth to say more, but then the beast rushed him. Sir Drew maneuvered around and about it.

Davey took the opportunity to charge from the beast's rear, and a leg snapped out and hit him in the chest.

A crack rang out.

Davey stumbled back, gripping his chest, a stricken expression on his face.

Gabrielle's nails nearly cut into her flesh.

Sir Drew continued to evade the creature, occasionally landing a blow or two, but they barely scratched the chimera.

Davey, meanwhile, leaned on his sword to stand, the

sword sinking into the ground as he pressed more and more weight upon it.

The chimera whipped out at Sir Drew, pushing him to the ground.

Sir Drew brought up his sword, but the chimera flung itself to the side.

To Davey.

Davey snapped up his sword with sudden strength.

The quivering body fell to the ground. The lion head quietly thudded, tilted backwards as it rested at Davey's feet.

Gabrielle released her breath.

The forest was suddenly quiet and still, the wind the only disruption.

Abruptly, Sir Drew chuckled. "You were playing it."

Davey grinned wryly. "When the beast kicked me, I realized that it was smarter than it looked—"

"Looked pretty smart to me," Sir Drew interrupted. "After all, it had two more brains than you, one in the snake and one in the lion."

Davey made a face and shook his head. "Never miss an opportunity, do you?"

"Never."

"You were baiting it? Acting wounded on purpose?" Gabrielle questioned.

"Oh, he was wounded, all right," Sir Drew piped up.

Davey shot Sir Drew a withering look. Turning to Gabrielle, he explained, his expression becoming lighter and more energetic. "I could tell that the beast was smart, so, yes, I decided to bait it right back. I was injured, but merely a bite and broken rib, nothing that I could not work through."

"It did bite you, then?" Sir Drew asked, concerned.

"Yes," Davey affirmed, a smirk appearing on his face, "but other than the initial sting, it has done nothing."

"Indeed," Sir Drew commented, a grim expression on his face. "Keep an eye on the bite, though. The chimera's bite contains a deadly venom that does not pain its victim. It may not have injected the venom in you or it could have, but you will not feel the pain as the toxin works its way into your system."

Davey's smile faded. "How will we know?"

"If you're dead tomorrow morning, it injected the toxin."

Davey glared and opened his mouth.

A growl stopped him short. Another chimera, twice the size of the last one, prowled into view.

"They never travel in packs!" Sir Drew exclaimed.

"Is that what one of your books told you?" Davey asked bringing his sword back up and stepping nearer to Sir Drew until they were level.

"This one must have been her cub," Sir Drew concluded. A worried expression flew across his face. "The other parent or siblings may also be present."

Naturally, it was then that another three chimeras emerged from the forest, the smallest a little taller than the one they had killed.

"Well," Davey said, pressing his lips together. "This will get interesting."

Davey and Sir Drew split up again, but the chimeras did the same.

Gabrielle noticed that the two largest had leathery wings on them.

"What's with the wings?" Davey asked Sir Drew, perceiving them just as Gabrielle did.

"Only mature chimeras develop them. I should've known that the little one's family was present by the lack of wings on his back. I had forgotten that chimeras do not leave their parents' protection until they grow wings." Sir Drew huffed at himself. He backed up from the chimera prowling directly between Davey and he. The men exchanged tense glances.

"I do not believe that we should have split up," Davey observed.

"Indeed."

Instead of the men circling the chimeras, the chimeras circled them. For the moment, they ignored Gabrielle.

The chimeras were smart, very smart. Davey had remarked such and that was Gabrielle's main thought as the creatures tested the men, seeing how far they could reach with their swords, how hard they could swing, studying their balance and speed.

Then one pounced. The others followed suit and suddenly both men were ducking and rolling, twisting and diving, unseen scratches and bruises sapping their stamina.

With all this confusion, Gabrielle should be able to easily and unnoticeably use her magic. Committed, Gabrielle watched the fight with greater focus.

When Davey rolled under one of the chimeras as it swiped at him, she imagined his sword jerking upwards and into the creature's body. To her surprise, it worked, the sword sinking deep into the flesh.

Then Davey, gripping his side in pain, popped up on the other side of the yowling chimera—without his sword.

The injured chimera slowly turned to face him, but Davey dove under the creature and shoved his body upward, lifting the beast up as well. The other chimera took the opportunity to leap at Davey's exposed back.

In desperation, Gabrielle made the creature fly backwards, hoping to distance it by a few feet and give Davey enough time to recover his sword.

The chimera smacked with a sickening crack against the trunk of a nearby oak.

Gabrielle heard a commotion over by Sir Drew as well and risked a glance. Sir Drew had injured a chimera, the creature limping badly, but seemed to be holding his own.

Turning back to Davey, she saw him plunge the recovered sword into the chimera's back, the one that had taken a gut wound.

Gabrielle breathed another sigh of relief. They were down two and a half chimeras.

A roar thundered from above.

Three dragons soared above the treetops, two falling into dives.

Davey was there. He grabbed her arm and raised his sword. The fire split around them.

Sir Drew shouted.

The first dragon swooped back up as the second completed his dive, Gabrielle and Davey hitting the ground as claws swished above them.

Sir Drew stood by their sides a moment later as Davey pulled Gabrielle to her feet.

"We need to run," Sir Drew said, already halfway moving

away from the last two chimeras, his sword the only thing keeping them at bay as they tried to start circling again.

"No," Davey countered, hoisting his sword and gripping Gabrielle's hand tighter. "Let's retreat."

Sir Drew let out an annoyed snort and waved them on, eyes on the chimeras. "Go! Run that way with Gabrielle! I'll buy us a few minutes!"

"Only a minute!" Davey said, even as Sir Drew broke into a short jog.

Davey's face twisted, then his eyes landed on Gabrielle.

"We can stay." Gabrielle took a step forward.

Davey gripped her hand tighter. He turned and ran.

Gabrielle bit her lip, possibly causing it to bleed when she tripped. She stopped chewing and just concentrated on keeping pace.

He would be fine.

He would be *fine.*

She swallowed hard.

He would have to be fine.

Davey did not stop. He did not slow down. When a log came across their path, he finally let go of Gabrielle's hand but pushed her forward in order that he might follow her instead of lose her. Sometime during their running, Gabrielle realized that they were no longer heading southeast, but more south, perhaps even southwest.

Gabrielle's breath became more ragged. In the distance, she could hear the roars of the dragons though they were echoing across the land less often.

They still ran.

Gabrielle ached and could barely breathe, so she forced herself to think of it as if she were in a rhythm, a rhythm of burning lungs and seizing muscles, but a rhythm nonetheless.

Just as the cramps in her legs were about to stop the limbs from moving at all, an enormous ravine rose around them, the wooded forest at their backs.

Gabrielle craned her neck and spied birds' nests skillfully lodged on gigantic ledges in the cliff, only these nests were forty feet in diameter. She reeled to a stop, muscles clenching painfully and gut instinct setting off the equivalent of a bonfire. As Davey lurched to a stop beside her, her eyes scanned the nests, only the edges of which they could see.

"What . . . is it?" Davey gasped, leaning over onto his knees, clutching his sides.

"We . . . not safe," Gabrielle attempted a full sentence, but then just opted for the thought.

Not safe. Definitely not safe. She looked behind her, and seeing neither chimeras on the ground nor dragons in the sky, she led Davey back under the cover of the trees though they grew farther apart here and offered less protection.

Davey gripped his side tighter, leaning heavily against a tree, then just sliding down it until he reached the ground. His sword lay at his side, his hand still lightly wrapped around the hilt. Gabrielle had the worrying feeling that he was no longer exaggerating anything.

"Is it your chest?" she asked.

Davey nodded, grimacing. His breath caught. "I do not believe that you are supposed to run with a broken rib."

"I do not believe that you are supposed to fight and kill three chimeras with one either," Gabrielle added.

The comment cheered Davey enough that he smiled.

"Do you want me to wrap your side?" Gabrielle asked.

"Yes," Davey stopped breathing for a moment to swallow. "We can use my shirt."

They spent the next several minutes removing Davey's shirt and wrapping it tightly around his chest, trying to support and not further injure the rib.

Gabrielle privately noted that she could plainly see the bite mark of the snake on his back and the red circle that was growing around it. There was little they could do about that now, though.

Neither of them spoke of Sir Drew though Davey commented about an odd thing his sword had done, claiming that it had swung upwards into the chimera of its own accord and that he could not recall doing anything to make the second chimera fly against the tree.

Gabrielle suggested that fighting changes your perception of events.

Davey accepted this readily though he did admit that his perception usually was not that skewed.

After wrapping Davey's chest, Gabrielle began to collect firewood and a few edible plants. All they had were the two bags Gabrielle had carried. One had medicinal supplies and herbs in it, including bandages, but Davey insisted that they save those for when they really needed them because, according to him, he did not really need them. The other bag contained clothes for each of them. Everything else was lost.

By the time Gabrielle got the fire going, Davey was asleep, and night had begun to fall. Gabrielle stared into the fire, the flickering flames the same yet much kinder than those of the chimeras. Or of the dragons.

Unnatural noises drew her out of her reverie. Rising to her feet, she glanced at Davey's sword and Davey, then let both stay put. The rustling sounds increased, indicating that the beast was moving closer though it was still out of view.

She chided herself. It was probably just Sir Drew.

Remembering the dragons and the chimeras, Gabrielle grew sick with guilt. There was no way that it could be Sir Drew. She felt her face twist. With none to see, she let it.

Her nerves jangled. Her hands sweated. At that moment, it struck her that she had never even considered the other beasts in dragon territory when deciding to come. Oh, her stupidity. Or perhaps it was her ignorance? No, it was her stupidity at not realizing her ignorance.

The creature came into the light.

VIII

Rocks and . . . Rocs

Gabrielle could not believe her eyes.

"Drew!" she gasped, taking several quick steps toward him.

He held out his hands as if asking for a hug, and she complied.

"And here I thought that you two would have been celebrating getting rid of me." Sir Drew grinned.

Gabrielle took a step back, observing Sir Drew's blood-splattered, ripped clothing, his tired eyes, but his generally unscathed body. "How did you survive?" she wondered aloud, looking him over again and again.

He shrugged. "Believe it or not, I really am not half-bad with a sword, and I decided to ditch the armor."

Gabrielle lightly snorted. She grimaced when she realised the informality of the action. "That is incredible. With just your sword?" Disbelief crept into her tone. Her face twisted

114

again though twas true that even a knight of the king should not have survived three dragons and a chimera.

"That and a lot of, ahem, 'retreating'." Sir Drew offered a self-deprecating smile.

Gabrielle tried to return it.

Even a knight of the king shouldn't have survived.

Sir Drew straightened, authority sliding over his demeanor.

Gabrielle checked herself—for the moment. He was a knight of the king, one that let his squire use an enchanted sword and walked peacefully through a sorcerer's village. Perhaps he simply did not trust Gabrielle. Perhaps he trusted her as little as she trusted him.

"How is he doing?" Sir Drew asked, going to Davey.

Gabrielle relayed what Davey had told her as well as what she had noticed about the bite mark on his back.

Sir Drew nodded, taking items out of the medicinal bag and glancing at Davey as she spoke. "The red circle means that the toxin is spreading through his body."

"Is there anything you can do?" Gabrielle asked, hovering over the two of them.

Sir Drew stopped and fixed his gaze on her.

Gabrielle looked back.

He stared at her for several long moments, eyes never wavering, expression never changing.

Then he turned his attention back to Davey.

"Yes. I know a cure that may work."

"How do you know it?"

"Can it not be one of the books I have read?" Sir Drew asked jokingly.

"That's quite a specific read."

Sir Drew looked back at her.

Gabrielle refused to shrink back though she kept her face as expressionless as his.

Sir Drew looked down, smiling slightly, then returned his attention to Davey. "I must admit, twas a sorcerer who attacked the dragons, making time for escape. He knew how to stop the toxin from spreading although it may or may not require magic."

"There was a sorcerer there?"

"Indeed, one from Havene," Sir Drew asserted, his eyes downcast, but then he looked at her with his piercing gaze. "Yet I would prefer that Davey not know this, which is why I also initially did not inform you. If he asks directly, tell him. If not, then please refrain from mentioning it."

Gabrielle nodded, understanding after seeing how Davey reacted to hearing that Jesalyn and Jonathon were sorcerers, but then . . .

"Would it not help to have him know that a sorcerer was willing and did help us? I mean, would that not be a piece of evidence to help change his mind?"

"Davey has had plenty of help from sorcery," Sir Drew said flatly. "He still refuses to trust all magic."

She decided to press her luck. "Why?"

Sir Drew shook his head. "Tis how he grew up. His father fights dragons. They are considered evil in their house, and dragons are associated with magic. Thus, all magic is evil. That does not make it right, but that does make it what it is."

Sir Drew turned back to Davey and scanned the ingredients he had.

"Could you find some water? I'll need more."

Gabrielle complied, the skein of water coming from the supplies that Drew had brought with him. She had to search the woods only a little ways before finding a still pond. It would do.

Sir Drew spent the rest of the night fussing over Davey and explaining that the giant nests in the ravine nearby were roc nests, rocs being the enormous, carnivorous birds Sir Drew had mentioned earlier. The rocs were extremely dangerous, but very stupid, and capture by one may not lead to immediate death, just a trip to their nest although this was not assured by any means. Rocs were extremely territorial as well and traveled far from their nests only when food was scarce. Humans would qualify as food.

Gabrielle let out an unamused laugh at this again, especially since Sir Drew had unknowingly pointed them in this direction. Sir Drew countered by informing her that he had done that on purpose since rocs were large enough that even dragons tried to avoid them, and chimeras certainly did. Gabrielle's sense of humour disappeared abruptly.

Despite the danger, they would have to stay here for a night or two because Davey's wounds needed healing. There was the chance that they could have gone on even with him being injured before he had run so hard and fast, but now he certainly needed a few days to at least let the rib and injured tissue begin to heal.

Gabrielle offered to take first watch. Sir Drew did not argue and fell asleep almost immediately after lying down. Glad, Gabrielle practiced moving tree branches and rocks but focused on moving them subtly. Worried that her face might have given her away, she was lucky Davey had not pressed the issue of what his sword had done and that neither man had noticed one of the chimeras randomly flying backwards. In addition to subtlety, she concentrated on moving items predetermined distances at predetermined speeds, remembering Jesalyn's comment about control. She waited until the moon was a little past where it should have been, then woke Sir Drew.

Davey was already eating breakfast when Gabrielle awoke. Sir Drew had let her sleep in a little later than usual. She smiled.

"Morning." Davey raised a chunk of meet in greeting.

"Indeed it is," Gabrielle agreed, thinking that Sir Drew would have answered the same and smiling to herself.

Davey chuckled and gestured towards the fire. "Breakfast? Drew caught that jackalope he was pining over and made it up for breakfast."

"I thought I was supposed to have the legs," Gabrielle said, the lightness of lingering sleep soothing her as she stood and stretched.

"Yes, well, I made an executive decision that I would get the legs, you the ribs, and Drew the antlers."

"An executive decision? What did Sir Drew think about that?" Gabrielle asked.

Davey's expression had a quick fit of furtiveness flit across it.

"What's going on?"

"Well," Davey cleared his throat. "I did not actually ask if I could have the legs."

Gabrielle smiled.

"How was your night?" Davey asked.

"I slept like a rock."

"A rock?" Davey grinned. "So I sleep like a hog, and you sleep like a rock."

Gabrielle's smile softened. "My father uses that expression, but my mother always contradicts him, arguing that rocks do not snore."

"My father never uses any expressions," Davey told her, raising his eyebrows conspiratorially. "Everything he says is quite literal, and he takes everything everyone else says quite literally, too. One time, I remember my mother was telling me about this new knight that had come in, and she was complaining that he had no manners. My father came in halfway through and, after listening for a few moments, suggested that she just butcher him earlier than anticipated."

"What!?"

"My father heard mum say 'he's a pig'."

Gabrielle muffled her laugh with her hand. Davey's eyes crinkled pleasantly.

"I knew you were talking about me," Sir Drew wandered into their campsite carrying another jackalope. "Davey's always talking about me when he laughs."

Davey held up a hand and shrugged. "At least you admit it.".

"Indeed, I have known for a while that those who are jealous of others more successful than them often feel the need to make fun of those others to make up for their own inadequacies."

"What would I do without you?" Davey asked, shaking his head.

"Nothing, you would already be dead," Sir Drew stated nonchalantly. While he began roasting the other jackalope, Sir Drew explained their situation to Davey, stressing Davey's need to rest.

"I heal fast. I'm fine," Davey countered.

"You will be fine—finely ground, minced meat that gets sprinkled over the soups at cheap inns so they can claim it contains beef."

"I am—" Davey tried getting to his feet, then made a funny noise and halted, a worried expression on his face.

This time, it was Sir Drew who rolled his eyes.

"We will be here for another five days if you try to get up," Sir Drew walked over to him and helped him back down. "Indeed, glare at me," Sir Drew encouraged Davey, "since it is most definitely my fault that you got yourself kicked by a goat."

"A chimera," Davey spat.

"Which is a goat-like creature."

"With a lion's head," Davey argued.

"Did you get kicked by the leonine head?" Sir Drew asked. "No, you got hit by the goat hoof."

"This is why I need to tell others our adventures," Davey said, leaning his head against a tree. "You make it sound as if we walked across a barnyard and knitted our way to victory."

"Never underestimate a lady and her needles," Sir Drew winked at Gabrielle. "Those things can be sharp."

"I don't knit," Gabrielle said.

"Do you embroider? Crochet? Sew?" Sir Drew asked.

"Sew," Gabrielle replied.

"You only sew?" Davey sounded surprised. "Do you not do all those things?"

Gabrielle just shrugged. "They are not very useful. Knitting and crocheting perhaps, but sewing will yield quicker results with less effort. I see no reason to embroider."

"What do you do then?" Davey asked.

"There are many other things I am accomplished at." She managed not to put her hands on her hips. "I bake and cook with my mother and work in the fields when necessary and help my father when someone is ill. We try to read together, and my father spent much time teaching me when I was younger. Most of my evening time is spent keeping the inn and tavern clean and our customers happy."

"Is the tavern like that every night? I mean, when we came—" Davey struggled to coherently phrase the question.

"Yes," Gabrielle interrupted him, shoulders relaxing. "The tavern is busy most nights, and we usually only have one or two rooms open come morning." She smiled with pride. "We've always been busy. We were even busier when the patrols still went through, but we're still getting along just fine. My parents are fair innkeepers, and we strive to keep everything clean and orderly for the most part. Travelers come to the village just for our services."

"There was a little girl in the tavern," Sir Drew commented.

Gabrielle nodded. "Sandy May. She comes there with her father, Richard. The inn is rambunctious, but not dangerous. It is not unusual to have a few children or even a family present." She cocked her head, suddenly interested. "What do your parents do, Davey? Do they work with knights?"

"Yes." Davey nodded, eyes drifting towards the fire. "They work with many of the knights."

"What exactly do they do?"

He shrugged. "Well, Father . . . he organizes them. Mother tries to keep them in line for the most part."

"They supervise the knights?" Gabrielle clarified.

"Yes," Davey agreed. "That would be a good way to put it."

"What about your parents, Sir Drew?" Gabrielle asked, turning to him.

"Farmers." Sir Drew had picked up a stick from the fire and was twirling it in his hand, blowing on the end to make it glow red.

"The knight has farmers for parents and the squire supervisors," Gabrielle observed. Sensing the sudden quiet, she looked up, for she had been staring into the fire as well. "I did not mean that poorly," she began.

"Of course not," Sir Drew cut her off. "Tis odd, I agree. However, a knight of the king can be of any lineage. He just has to prove himself. Do you plan on taking over for your parents one day? Do you have any siblings?"

"No," Gabrielle told him. "I'm an only child."

"What about taking over the tavern and inn?" Sir Drew pressed.

Gabrielle paused and bit her lip. She had always assumed that was the plan. Her parents had encouraged such thoughts. Whoever she married was most likely to be a farmer, merchant, or some skilled artisan, and it was assumed that he would just take on the business with her.

However, as she sat by this fire with Davey and Sir Drew,

as she contemplated the journey they were on and the home she had left behind, dissatisfaction unfurled in her gut.

"Yes," she spoke after a moment's hesitation. "That is the plan."

"You are unsure," Sir Drew noted.

"Do we ever truly know where we will end up? Do we truly know that we will make it back from this journey?" Gabrielle smiled, trying for a lighter tone.

"Our destinies are already written," Davey spoke firmly, but surprisingly dispirited. "'Tis only our duty now to fulfill them."

"I disagree." Gabrielle frowned. "Perhaps for some there are destinies, but those destinies are only a result of our choices. What we decide today determines the destiny of tomorrow."

"Then we are still stuck with whatever path we are born on," Davey argued.

"No, we choose what path to take, it is just that our choices are already known."

"Then does that not take the choice out of it?"

"By no means, it just means that we are more predictable than we would like to think."

"You have thought much about destiny and choices?" Davey tried dropping it.

"I believe in free will," Gabrielle clarified. "Thus, I will bend to the idea of destinies, but only when destinies and free will are intertwined."

"The very ideas of free will and destinies are contradictory," Davey contended.

"Only because we have declared them such." Gabrielle

used her hands to gesture as she expounded upon her statement. "The idea of destiny really comes down to someone or something knowing your future, but knowing the future does not change the future any more than knowing that this plant is hemlock does not change the fact that this plant is hemlock. Free will may be what gets us to our destinies."

"We are destined to complete the path we choose," Sir Drew murmured.

"Yes," Gabrielle confirmed, pleased by the way he had summed it up.

Davey looked at her, still glum. "But do you not ever feel that you have no choice in the matter? That your destiny was decided for you, not by you?"

Gabrielle thought back to her hesitation in owning up to the fact that her taking over the inn and tavern had always been the plan, had been her privilege. "Perhaps, and the circumstances of our birth and lineage do play a role, but destiny is not a stone we cannot touch."

"What if that is not an option? Carving a different path?" Davey asked.

"There may be limited options," Gabrielle conceded, "but there are always some. Perhaps not pleasant. Perhaps not what we would choose, but then"—Gabrielle smiled—"that is why it is not our destiny."

"Indeed," Sir Drew said.

The talk subsided for a moment.

Then—"Indeed, this is wonderfully awkward."

Gabrielle giggled and caught Davey's exasperated look.

They continued talking throughout the day on much lighter topics, Sir Drew letting Gabrielle successfully insist on her stewing the rabbit in a pot Sir Drew had found hidden amongst their clothes, Sir Drew claiming that Davey must have packed that oddly organized bag.

Gabrielle, remembering Jesalyn's advice, asked that they teach her how to fight or at least defend herself. Initially, Davey was not particularly pleased about it, but, with Sir Drew's immediate and persistent support, they won him over to the idea. Sir Drew tried teaching her the basics of handling a knife as well as throwing it though Davey insisted on interrupting often enough.

Little disrupted the day. They saw no other animals save a few blue jays and a mockingbird though they heard rustling in the woods, an occasional swooping overheard, and a rare, far-off roar.

Sir Drew offered Davey first watch that night, but Davey predictably insisted on taking middle. Sir Drew gave Gabrielle a sly smile and wink.

Gabrielle offered Sir Drew his choice of watches. He hesitated for a moment, then chose last watch though he gave Gabrielle the option of switching shifts if she so desired.

She declined his generous offer. Even though she wanted the last third or half of the night because the boys tended to sleep more deeply, she knew that she would have trouble falling asleep earlier due to the laid-back day and her late morning. Besides, if Sir Drew preferred the last watch, then she could easily adjust. Gabrielle stayed up half the night again and then switched with him. She fell asleep quickly.

When she opened her eyes, slim, gray trees were interspersed throughout their campsite. Their branches only reached halfway up the other trees in the area, and Gabrielle's hands could fit around almost every trunk. Smaller trees were also present, saplings of every size, all in varying shades of gray.

"Penghou," Sir Drew stated, the pot over the fire already.

"Pain who?"

"No," Sir Drew chuckled. "Penghou as in the animal."

"The trees?" Gabrielle asked.

"Not trees, tree spirits. Penghous are tree spirits that can either take the form of a tree or a small black dog. They are scavengers, but will eat plants when necessary. They travel in large packs during the night. During the day, they stay in tree form for protection. There are fewer things that will eat them in this state than the other."

"You are very knowledgeable," Gabrielle complimented, examining one of the trees. "Will it turn into a dog while I am near it?"

"Usually not during the day and not unless it is desperate. Even at night, a penghou would have to be distressed to change in front of someone."

"Does it know I am here?"

"Not as you or I know, but, in some way, it does."

Gabrielle ran her hand along the bark and circled the tree. Other than the grey color and dwarf size, it looked like any other tree. "Are they dangerous?" she asked.

Sir Drew shook his head. "If you attack one, it will defend itself, but they are not out to hurt or eat you. Any harm that comes to you comes from you harassing them."

"Do they have teeth?" Gabrielle questioned, intrigued by the creatures but still wary.

"You can take a look for yourself." Sir Drew jerked a

thumb behind him. "There are two carcasses lying about thirty feet into the woods. I still need to go out there and bury them."

"Sir Drew . . ." Gabrielle eyed the pot. "What are you making for breakfast?"

Sir Drew glanced at her. "They may look like small dogs and, from what I hear, taste like small dogs, but they are not dogs."

"For some reason that does not make me feel any better."

"Will you want breakfast? That is what I planned to make for lunch as well." Sir Drew compressed his lips, his smile peeking through.

"Yes, I suppose. Tis no matter what it is. Tis food." Gabrielle sighed, promising herself that if they spent another day in this state that she would allocate some time to searching for edible flora.

Tramping through the woods behind Sir Drew, she found the two corpses. The penghous did look like small, black dogs with medium-length fur, a long tail, and canine teeth. She buried them for Sir Drew and returned to camp, finding Davey up and Sir Drew explaining the penghous again.

"You are incredibly odd," Davey informed Sir Drew.

"Odd?" Sir Drew exclaimed.

"Yes, odd. Who reads books that closely about places they never plan to go?"

Sir Drew sent Gabrielle an irked look.

Gabrielle returned his attention with a smile, and when her smile didn't stop growing, a small, muffled laugh.

"Gabs!" Davey greeted her. "Great! Are you ready to continue our journey today?"

"You should rest one more day," Sir Drew said.

"Come off it," Davey argued. "I'm fine. Healed and ready to go. We've wasted much time here, Drew. We need to get moving."

Sir Drew considered Davey. "I know you're anxious to continue onward, but we cannot afford to have you further injured. If you promise to take it slow, then . . . yes, we can resume."

"Great," Davey took a sip from the pot and put it to the side. With only a pot and no bowls, they were having to wait for their soups to cool before eating it from the very same dish it was cooked in. "I'm glad you agree because we were going to start with or without your consent."

"Really?" Sir Drew asked, surprised. "And just what direction were you going to take?"

Davey opened his mouth. He closed it.

"That way." Gabrielle pointed to the east. "Do we not need to reach the river?"

Sir Drew gave a startled nod.

Davey folded his arms. "You were saying?"

They ate breakfast and packed quickly, Sir Drew bustling around Davey in order to prevent him from straining too much, not that there was much to pack. Before long, they were traipsing through the penghou in an easterly direction.

"We'll reach the river, then head south until we are about one-hundred yards away from the sea. Then we go east again. There's the castle of Ancora," Drew explained.

"What will we do when we reach the castle?" Gabrielle asked. "Will it not be heavily guarded by dragons?"

Davey sighed and opened his mouth to reply.

A screech shattered the quiet. Four dragons flew above them. The two with differing shades of red had been in the group that attacked them two days ago.

"They were waiting for us," Sir Drew said, abruptly swinging back around and heading towards the rocs again.

Davey stood his ground.

"Davey!" Sir Drew halted when he noticed Davey was not following.

The dragons came nearer.

Davey gripped the hilt of his sword more tightly. "We need to get to Danielle."

"There is another way, one they will not expect. Come on."

Davey hesitated for a moment, then turned just as suddenly as Sir Drew had and raced towards the rocs. The tension Gabrielle felt released, and she followed their pounding footsteps. The dragons wheeled about, not pursuing.

Sir Drew slowed.

"They will expect us to return," he stated.

"Why?" Davey asked.

"Because the way we are going to go is very dangerous," Sir Drew said.

"Everywhere in dragon territory is dangerous," Davey countered.

"Indeed, but this way more so. We'll need to cross through roc territory and then try to squeeze between a swamp and a dragon's brood."

"A dragon's brood?" Gabrielle asked.

"Where they rear their young," Sir Drew explained. "'Tis also where many congregate when possible. Dragons generally have their individual caves or dwellings, but may meet in particular places or live with groups temporarily when deemed necessary. Tis necessary when raising very young children. Tis also possibly necessary when at war."

"What is in the swamp?" Davey asked.

"Many things that we do not wish to meet," was all Sir Drew said. Then he lowered his voice as the ravine came into view. "We should stay here for the day."

Davey opened his mouth to protest.

Drew continued, "Rocs feed primarily during the day. Once evening approaches, we have a better chance of getting through unscathed. We are no use to the princess dead."

They returned to their campsite and spent a restless day there. Gabrielle kept examining the penghou, which utterly captivated her, and the men continued to teach her basic defensive moves. As night began to fall, they set out again.

Sir Drew led them. He kept them on the edges of the ravine, walking right alongside the wall. Earlier in the day, he had explained that not all of roc territory in this area was located within the ravine, but the ravine acted as a good marker and as a hub of roc territory. The majority of the rocs in the area nested there because of the nice cliffs and ledges, only going into the forest for food.

Gabrielle was very glad that Sir Drew was leading. Paranoia crept along her skin. They walked as quietly as possible with only the sounds of Davey and Sir Drew accidentally kicking rocks accompanying them. The moon rose just as the sun sank completely. They moved to the middle of the ravine. It was impossible to track time. Gabrielle counted steps instead. When she reached a thousand, she silently sighed a few times.

Prodigious claws snapped Sir Drew up. He disappeared.

Gabrielle halted. Her clothes and hair whipped back with the strong gust of wind. Davey's sword hissed as he withdrew it.

A strong claw gripped Gabrielle's back. The ground left her.

The roc carrying her skimmed near the earth, but was rising quickly. They rose faster as the bird flapped twice. The few visible stars could no longer be seen and the ground blurred and became indistinguishable. Butterflies flooded Gabrielle's stomach though she did not feel sick. Should she change?

The claws released.

Gabrielle gasped, but then the ground jarred her. Something stabbed hard into her back, piercing her skin. She managed to strangle her cry into a sob. For a moment, she could see the moon and the branches, some as large as trees, twisted together around her, then a gigantic black blob blotted out her vision and settled partly on top of her. Rough feathers with enlarged, coarse hairs on them brushed against her. Luckily, the roc was not sitting directly on her, but was situated so that she was located in a slight, feather-filled cave. Trying not to whimper, she pulled herself off of the sharp stick she had fallen on with a sickeningly wet sound. She took a large, shaking breath.

Had Sir Drew been brought to this same nest? That seemed unlikely considering the speed at which the roc would have had to move to return and pick her up. Furthermore, it had not left to snatch Davey as well. Could there have been two rocs out for an evening stroll? Each possibility seemed equally unlikely. Regardless, staying here was no option. The nest was made of logs of varied sizes. The gaps caused by the larger logs may have enough room to allow her to slip through.

Hopefully.

Gabrielle reached into one particularly big gap and managed to slither her hand some ways in, but she would need to fit more than a hand to get out. She crawled about and investigated more spaces, finally finding one that she could easily slide into. Going feet first, she dropped down onto a lower branch. Unsteady but now really "in" the nest, she gripped branches on either side of her and lowered herself down even more. She continued this process, hoping that she would not reach a dead end where the logs and branches were too big and close to let her slip through. However, her fortune continued and she kept finding large enough gaps or gaps covered by only a few twigs that she could easily snap.

After descending perhaps five feet, Gabrielle's feet landed on something solid that was not circular as the logs had been. Looking down, she was relieved to see the rock of a ledge. At the bottom of the nest, feasibly well-hidden and secure from the roc, she began trying to maneuver her way to the edge of the cliff. The way was slow-going and difficult. Branches continuously blocked her way and the pressure from the wood and roc above made moving obstacles more difficult.

Gabrielle stepped forward again, forcing herself under some branches and gasping as her side twisted in another painful position. Her foot landed on thin air. She quickly reached upward and wove her arms and hands in with the branches.

She had reached the edge.

A slight breeze brushed her feet. Was now a good time to change? Sir Drew had said that the rocs were big enough to scare even the dragons away. She could climb down the side of the ravine, but with rocs on the loose and her inexperience, that would surely get her killed. As a dragon, she could at least fight back. Also, the chance of death by falling from a cliff was severely reduced. Gabrielle wavered between the options.

Someone shouted nearby. Whoever it was sounded close, perhaps the nest across the ravine. She saw an unbelievably large bird—a wingspan of one-hundred ten feet, a chord of six, its body perhaps twenty feet tall and five feet wide—peck at something in its nest. Dread coiled in her stomach.

A stream of light lit the sky and the roc on fire. Cawing, the bird flapped its enormous wings, which only made the flames blaze brighter. Darting in and amongst the flames, attacking the roc and retreating, a green dragon, almost emerald in the firelight, wore down the plodding bird. The roc was surprisingly sluggish even while on fire. The bird persistently screeched, but the dragon dominated the scene with more rapid maneuvers and jets of fire. Branches above Gabrielle creaked and groaned as the roc in her nest rose and then jumped and glided to help the other. Gabrielle saw the dragon dip once more into the nest, then rise and twist around both rocs, neatly slipping through a gap in their two sets of wings. The dragon flapped towards her, a small figure dangling from its claws.

Gabrielle suddenly felt exposed. She hastily tried to retreat into the nest, but the dragon was there. He plucked her from the nest with his other claw, smartly backed up, and plummeted into the ravine. Both rocs were still at the now-burning nest, squawking at each other, flapping their wings, and just generally making the situation worse for themselves.

They neared the ground, and Davey came into view, in a fighting stance with his sword drawn. The dragon flapped and hovered for a moment. It dropped them, then abruptly turned and flew back into the night, away from the cacophonous birds.

Davey's wide eyes gleamed in the darkness, as Gabrielle was sure hers and Sir Drew's were doing as well.

"Indeed," Sir Drew stated, a little out of breath, "we must be vigilant in roc territory."

Indeed, Gabrielle thought, we must.

IX

They're Redcaps, Sir

Davey managed to persuade the two of them that continuing forward was the best option though now all three kept their eyes to the skies as often as possible. They passed the rocs that had seized Gabrielle and Sir Drew, the first already dead due to the emerald dragon's fire by the time they reached it. The second roc, the one that had taken Gabrielle, was still living, but was also on fire. In an attempt to stop the flames, the bird doggedly flapped its wings and scraped them along the side of the cliff. Blood and grit rained down from its efforts, so their group put extra effort into watching for falling chunks of rock as they traversed beneath the frantic creature.

After that episode, they were all much on edge, both literally at the ravine's and internally. Gabrielle was not the only one jerking at the sound of swooping or sudden gusts of wind. Morning was a long time coming.

When at last daylight broke, Gabrielle was drained. They were not yet out of the ravine. However, the end could be spotted but a hundred yards from where they were. Stumbling, their group made the last three-hundred feet in a daze, nearly forgetting that they were still in roc territory. Upon reaching the woods, they all plopped down and promptly fell asleep, no one even thinking to take guard duty. Fortunately, when Gabrielle awoke in the late afternoon, Sir Drew and Davey were still present . . . and snoring. Gabrielle now understood why her mother argued with her father whenever he said he slept like a rock. Hog was much more appropriate.

The pain in her side and a grumble in her stomach re-oriented her. She went a few feet into the woods behind the men and checked the wound she had sustained last night first. Twisting pained her and revealed only crusted blood on her shirt. Hoping that she would heal the wound to the correct degree, she focused on the wound closing almost completely and breathed a sigh of relief when the pain went away. Gingerly, she contorted her arm so her hand could reach behind her back and feel where she had been stabbed. There was a scab over a smaller wound.

She paused, recalling her father's words about infection. She twisted and gingerly touched the area again, rubbing her fingers along the raised skin. She craned her head as best she could and the scar came into sight. Although the closed wound was not easy to see, she now knew that she could check for inflammation by herself, and at least then she would be aware of a growing infection as soon as possible, so long as she checked the area often.

Satisfied enough, though not entirely pleased with herself

for not cleaning the wound first, she switched her focus to Sir Drew's favorite subject, food.

She planned just to take plants, but upon spying another jackalope, she killed it by smashing it against a tree for Sir Drew. After she heard the resounding *thwack*, she realized that she could have tried just breaking the neck, thus testing her control, but it was a tad too late for that.

Sir Drew and Davey woke up and ate with her, deciding that they would camp for the night where they had fallen, since the day was already so far gone, and start fresh the next morning. Davey was not entirely pleased by the decision, but conceded without as much protest as before.

They gave Gabrielle first watch, but both stayed up with her through it. While Gabrielle was not able to practice more magic, Davey gave her pointers on using her knife once more. He had warmed up considerably to the idea of her learning to fight and was the one who suggested that she practice more. Eventually, Davey noticed the blood on her back, and Gabrielle explained that she had received an insignificant wound when the roc dropped her.

Gabrielle was the first to rise the next day. They skipped breakfast that morning, Davey eager enough to get going that he was willing to endure Sir Drew's remarks for a few hours.

"I feel faint," Sir Drew groaned.

"You *will* faint when I knock you out," Davey muttered.

The ground turned marshy, squishing with every step, and the trees grew shorter and denser. Gabrielle correctly identified a group of penghous, but their height was no longer relatively remarkable. More bugs whined around them, impossible to ignore, impossible to kill.

Answering Gabrielle's comment about it looking more like a swamp, Drew replied, "We're on the edges of it. I'm adjusting our course so as to stay away from the center while still as far as possible from the brood."

A flash of red caught Gabrielle's eye. She turned to the right, but saw nothing there that would cause such a color. Blaming imagination, she faced forward again, but then there was another flash, this time to her left. Her head veered to the other side, scanning the lush, green landscape for any hint of what she might have seen.

"What are you looking at?" Davey asked, only a few steps behind her.

Gabrielle shook her head. "I must be imagining it. I keep seeing flashes of red."

She bumped into Sir Drew's back as he halted.

"Flashes of red?" Sir Drew quietly asked.

"Yes," Gabrielle replied with equal quietness, her unease growing. "What is it?"

"Possibly redcaps," Sir Drew informed them, hand inching toward his sword. "They are quick, cruel, and murderous by nature. Don't underestimate them."

Sir Drew swiftly unsheathed his sword and something immediately flew at him from behind a bush.

Gabrielle heard Davey take out his own sword, and she brought up her knife.

They were surrounded, yet not. Gabrielle did not see a single redcap, but her eyes caught flashes of red all around her that she swung at wildly, still missing every single one.

High-pitched squealing issuing from around Sir Drew and Davey indicated that they were having more luck.

Gabrielle tripped over her own feet and fell to the ground, just missing her face with her knife. She felt the air in front of her move and immediately let out a burst of magic, desperately trying to stop whatever it was. As was becoming her apparent method of operation, the redcap flew backward and struck a tree.

Sharp stinging started on Gabrielle's legs. Looking back, she saw long gashes running along her calves. She saw more flashes and stumbled to her feet, waving her knife in front of her, hoping to hit something or at least ward the vicious buggers off.

"Gabs," Davey said.

Gabrielle paused, holding her knife still for a moment.

Davey and Sir Drew were looking at her, not moving.

Nothing stirred

Just as the redcaps had come, they were gone.

"So," Davey said, eyeing her knife warily. "First of all, the knife should always be pointed away from you. Remember?"

"Right," Gabrielle said, flipping it around, heat running to her face.

Sir Drew snorted. "Tis a good thing redcaps do not stay long or Davey or myself would be seriously injured by now."

"Drew," Davey warned.

"Right," Sir Drew agreed, "Gabrielle had as much a chance of cutting herself as cutting us. We were all in extreme danger."

"I . . . might have forgotten . . . a few things you told me about using my knife," Gabrielle admitted, face red as she realized how many of the simple rules she had broken in the last few minutes.

"They were quick little bastards," Davey defended, "not what you want to have your first knife fight with."

"I never knew 'fight' to be a relative word." Sir Drew grinned.

"Drew," Davey reprimanded him.

"No." Gabrielle held up a hand to stop him though she was a bit surprised that he was defending her so. "He's right. I did not . . . I did not do that well at all. As soon as they attacked, my mind flew, and I just started swinging. It was my bad . . . and twas very bad."

"No matter what it was, he doesn't have to be rude about it." Davey glowered at Sir Drew.

Sir Drew raised an eyebrow.

"Perhaps not, but then we would wonder what happened to Sir Drew." Gabrielle tried for humor, sending Sir Drew a weak smile and hoping he would take it for the joke that it was.

"Yeah, we would wonder who to thank for taking him and bringing us a considerate and gentlemanly fellow instead," Davey grouched.

"Blade away," Gabrielle began, nearly but not quite cutting Davey off, "and I use it primarily to defend and protect. Do not block with my arm unless absolutely necessary. Keep my knife in front of me, and do not overextend."

"Correct," Davey encouraged.

"Do not forget," Sir Drew piped up, "the sharp part can cut you."

"Drew!"

"Davey"—Gabrielle touched his arm—"tis really all right. I know he means well."

"He could mean better," Davey argued.

"I do not mind."

Before Davey could disagree, Sir Drew asked, "They harmed you?" He was looking at Gabrielle's leg.

Gabrielle tried to subtly shift the cuts further out of view. "Tis not bad. Do they have claws, Sir Drew?"

"Take a gander at the one you did kill," Sir Drew stated, gesturing towards that one had flown into the tree.

"See, she was not all bad. Gabs got one to our none," Davey reminded him.

Sir Drew only rolled his eyes.

They squelched their way to the body.

The redcap reminded Gabrielle of a boiled, sagging bean with an incredible number of white whiskers sprouting from its head like a mustache and beard. Its only covering was a red cap seemingly connected to its head, its bare feet curled and open to the elements. The creature was no more than two feet tall, closer to one, and carried a regular-sized sickle tinged with blood.

"Tis an ugly thing," Gabrielle commented.

"Yes, the creature let rust get all over it."

Gabrielle looked at Sir Drew, confused.

Davey shook his head, explaining, "He's talking about the sickle, not the redcap."

"Redcaps do not make their own weapons, but steal from others. This one they stole from a farmer some time ago, but obviously decided that upkeep was not important." Sir Drew sniffed. "Savage."

Gabrielle smiled and went back to examining the redcap. "Is the cap attached to its head?" she asked.

"Actually, tis not a hat at all," Sir Drew explained. "Redcaps have a protrusion of skin going over their heads that is naturally red and looks somewhat like a cap, but if you feel it, you'll notice that tis really just their skin."

Gabrielle did as he suggested and was surprised to find that the cap did feel like tough, leathery skin, not unlike a chicken's comb.

"Tis rumored that redcaps get their color from dipping their heads in the blood of the slain," Sir Drew continued.

"Is it true?" Gabrielle asked.

Sir Drew shrugged. "I have never had the opportunity to ask their slain."

"Is it usual for them to come and leave so quickly?"

"Indeed," Sir Drew affirmed. "Redcaps are wickedly fast, as you have just learned, but their energy gets spent quickly. Had they stayed any longer, we would have gotten the upper hand, save—"

"Stow it," was all Davey warned him with.

Sir Drew grinned.

"How are your legs, Gabs?" Davey turned to her, inspecting the damage the redcaps had done.

"Not bad," Gabrielle tried to surreptitiously move away from his prying gaze. "I recover quickly, so they should be looking pretty good soon enough."

Davey gave her a look, but did not argue.

Sir Drew had already bored of the conversation and was playing catch with himself using the sickle.

Davey turned, saw what he was doing, and swiped it from

the air. He raised it as if to strike Sir Drew, who just raised an eyebrow.

"I'll take it," Gabrielle suggested.

"No," both men said at once.

Davey held it as they walked along the outskirts of the swamp.

Deciding not to eat near where they had been attacked, they kept traveling although Gabrielle began collecting edible flora as they progressed. Eventually, it became evident that Davey was loathe to stop to the point where Gabrielle just passed out some of her gatherings to Sir Drew, who had taken to grumbling again. Gabrielle nibbled on just a few things herself, nerves on edge, stomach queasy, hair on her neck stretching as high as it could reach.

When night began to fall, twas as if Davey did not notice.

"Davey," Sir Drew said at last, "you promised to take it easy."

"I am," Davey stubbornly stated.

"Then let us make camp for the night, get some actual food, and sleep."

"It's been about a week."

Sir Drew was silent.

Gabrielle wondered if there was some deadline that they were not telling her about. Perhaps the dragons had given or left some kind of message. The message could explain how to get into the castle though then Sir Drew would not have had to ask where Jonathon thought Princess Danielle was being held. Perhaps the reference to the week had nothing to do with the Princess, but was referring to something going on back home to which Davey needed or wanted to return.

Whatever the case, Sir Drew seemed to have no comfort for Davey.

"You cannot help if dead, injured, or exhausted," Sir Drew said.

Davey stopped, gaze wandering to the sides of the path. Eventually, he nodded slowly. "Here?"

"A little to the west, s—" Sir Drew stopped. "Not southwest, just west. It will be closer to the brood, but we should not get sick from the cold, wet ground."

Gabrielle was perplexed by Davey's sorrow and worry.

A memory drifted back to her as they walked. Sir Drew, sitting at the table in the tavern, looking ill-fit in his armor, telling the place that Princess Danielle was taken in the hopes of drawing out the king or prince.

No.

Her mind rejected the thought.

This was Davey!

This was Davey, dejectedly following Drew, Drew who did not act like the knight he should be, pausing at odd times and stopping at odd syllables. This was Davey, standing up to the dragon first, carrying the enchanted sword, believing more firmly in the standards of the kingdom than Drew, emotionally invested more than a squire should be in the rescue of a princess.

This was Davey, whose name was awfully close to Prince David's.

Gabrielle took the last shift again that night. She struggled to fall asleep, and when Davey woke her for her watch and asked what the matter was, she firmly banished the disturbing thoughts from her mind and answered that all was well.

All was well.

She threw the sickle in the air and caught it, healing herself whenever she failed, careful to leave the cuts on her legs.

Indeed.

Indeed.

All was well.

X

Drowning

Perhaps Drew would not appreciate her effort, but Gabrielle spent the last part of her watch gathering "jackalope food" as he had begun to describe any edible plant. No more skvaders appeared although she did not want to clean and roast one anyway.

She didn't see any animals, in fact, yet every other minute, her eyes darted up and around, searching for the dragon she could feel but not see. Scratching her neck, remembering that she had been feeling this unsettled for a day or so now, Gabrielle wondered if general unease was unbalancing her senses.

Despite his eagerness yesterday, Davey was the last to wake up. Drew informed her that Davey had stayed awake through Drew's watch as well as his own. When Davey finally did awaken, he opted to eat while traveling, and they left.

The ground squelched under their feet after only a few

minutes. All three were more on the alert for redcaps, and a strong wind that was blowing through the area made the entire group jumpy and distracted. Drew still managed to talk, though, pointing out a scaly, grey lizard half the size of Gabrielle's hand, proclaiming it a swamp salamander and quite venomous and poisonous. He also took the breath to warn them of will-o'-wisps and sprites, will-o'-wisps possibly being gentle blobs of light. No one was definitive about this for any who approach are attacked by sprites and do not survive.

"There is another salamander to your left, Gabrielle," Drew informed her, barely glancing to the left but somehow spotting the creature.

Gabrielle did not stop as she had done the first time, Davey's impatience breathing upon her neck. She still managed to get a good look at the creature that appeared much like the first only slightly larger and with a few more dark spots.

Salamanders, will o' wisps, and sprites.

"You know a great deal about many animals," Gabrielle stated.

"Please," Davey interrupted, "he already has enough trouble fitting his head into his helmet. Which he lost," Davey interjected scathingly. "You need not make it worse."

"I was just wondering if you knew something about dragons to help us get into the castle," Gabrielle hedged.

"Nope," Sir Drew stated immediately and lightly.

"Do we have a plan for getting into the castle?"

"We do not . . ." Davey began. "You have astounded me," he said suddenly to Gabrielle. "Really, Gabs. We joke about your knife skills and paranoia, but . . . you have handled this all exceptionally well. I still . . . I don't want you to become vexed at me."

Gabrielle mustered a smile. "Admitting such just helped your case."

Davey smiled back, then frowned and continued. "I still don't like the idea of you going into the castle. Inside, we'll be safe, but getting in will be extremely dangerous. Deadly. I don't want you to get caught in the middle. This isn't your fight."

"Why is it yours?"

Davey hesitated.

Only for a moment, but he did.

"I swore to the princess that I would keep her safe. I fight for her safety." He stopped and turned to Gabrielle completely. "I will do what I can to keep you safe as well."

"Safe in dragon territory?" Gabrielle asked, ignoring the pang at his words. "Are we talking about the same dragon territory?"

"You have been a valuable traveling companion, but I wish you had not been inclined to travel this far," Davey frankly said.

Gabrielle glanced at him again. She understood the sentiment.

They resumed walking.

"What do *you* fight for?" she asked Sir Drew.

Sir Drew shrugged. He was silent for some time, for so long that Gabrielle had forgotten that he still had not fully answered.

Finally, "I fought for change."

After a moment of quiet, she asked, "Fought?"

He turned and gave her a bitter, grim look. "Change does not happen. You think it will. You hope it will. I fought so that it might. At times, you may even think it has occurred, but true change"—a cynical, mirthless smirk crept upon his face—"true change never occurs."

Gabrielle realized that they had stopped moving forward again, but Davey was not complaining.

Drew looked at the ground, jutting his chin out, then bringing it back in. His eyes went to hers again. "Be careful about what you hope to change. You may be sorely disappointed."

"Then what do you fight for now, my friend?" Davey gently asked.

Sir Drew's unflinching gaze went to him. Without hesitation, "For you."

"Indeed," Drew continued, examining the soggy ground once more, "I have given up on change"—he shook his head, a sardonic grin slipping upon his visage, his eyes going back to Davey's—"but for some vexatious reason I have not given up on you."

Sir Drew turned and commenced walking.

Davey and Gabrielle regarded each other, Davey appearing as unnerved as Gabrielle.

After the unsettling conversation, the day was monotonous for the most part, but occasionally one of them would stop, believing that they may have seen a redcap. Nothing ever materialized, which left Gabrielle plenty of time to mull over both men's answers. Try as she could, she found herself unable to reconcile their answers with who they claimed to be.

Nevertheless, there was always the small chance that they were telling the truth, that Davey and Drew were simply cocks in the hens' pen. She had difficulties either way she chose. Eventually, she just stopped deeply examining the issue at all, consciously repeating earlier thoughts without deciding.

The sound of running water reached her ears. After a few minutes more, it became definitive. Drew's pace quickened, and they reached a river. Water gurgled and sped at the same time, the river roughly forty feet across and looking re-markedly deep, sunlight glinting off the top and a few stones near the shore, but sucked into the depths round the middle.

"Do we cross here?" Davey warily asked.

"No," Drew replied. "To cross here is foolish. The water's deep. We need to go downstream a bit more. The river widens, and the water slows and becomes shallower."

Drew continued leading the way, the bank of the river pleasant to walk upon, especially with the wind instead of the trees brushing against them. A sense of enjoyment stole across Gabrielle, a lightness also coming upon Davey and Drew's steps although Drew's shoulders stayed tense and drawn.

He stopped.

A lovely young lady with lush, golden hair lounged upon an outcropping near the water, her toes dipping into the river. Her sky-blue eyes caught sight of them, and she laughed with joy, her voice as handsome as the rest of her. Her light blue shift rippled in the breeze. She slid off her rock and gracefully sashayed through the water toward them, her legs making smaller waves than one would have expected.

One of Drew's feet took a slow step back. His hand went up. "Wait," he said.

The woman stopped, head cocking, expression confused and bordering on hurt.

"What is it, Drew?" Davey asked, eyes on the woman as well, hand fingering the hilt of his sword.

"Hello?" the lady asked, her voice lilting with the breeze.

Drew visibly wavered, feet shifting, jaw clenching. Unsurety embodied him.

"Sir Drew?" Gabrielle asked.

Abruptly, he took a few steps towards the lady. "What is your trouble, madam?"

The woman lunged, body morphing to be longer, face shifting from nose to snout, head of hair to mane, the blue of the shift overriding her skin until her entire being was the color. Then the horse-like creature touched Sir Drew with a hoof, the animal's skin attaching to him more strongly than pitch and dragging Sir Drew down under the water with it. Both Drew and the creature disappeared into the depths, leaving only bubbles as proof of their dive.

A moment of stunned silence, of decreasing ripples.

Davey yanked off his belt, boots, and sword. He took out his knife and waded into the water, taking a deep breath and plunging in when it reached his chest.

Gabrielle stood on the shore, wavering just as Drew had done. Fewer and fewer bubbles appeared, the sinking sun reflecting off them.

She slipped off her clothes, throwing them hastily behind the nearest tree and changed.

She dove into the water, marveling at its startling depth for the relatively small width of the river. Her claws were terrible at swimming, and she did not see either man in the water's murky depths. She made her way to the surface, then shore, then took flight, only to turn over sharply and make a straight dive from sixty feet in the air.

The water and bubbles streamed past her as the river-bed approached, the scene below confusing and approaching quickly. She indiscriminately snatched what was before her. In another moment, she had hit the riverbed.

She leaned onto her back legs and heaved herself and the writhing mass in her claws skyward. The surface approached with stunning quickness, for which Gabrielle was glad. She could barely swim by herself in this form and certainly could not with whatever be in her claws. Her momentum carried her through the water and partway into the air. Without missing a beat, she stretched out her wings and flapped, hard.

The water around her went out in great ripples as she quickly flapped again and again, soaking the once-dry shore, but also raising herself and the beings in her claws out of the water. Steadying herself, she looked down to see the thrashing horse, which had hooves on its front half, a fish tail on its back, and an unconscious Drew still attached. Davey clung to Drew, both of them whipping back and forth with the horse's movement.

She landed on the shore, claws keeping a tight hold on the horse while ensuring she squished neither Davey nor Drew.

The creature thrashed even as she brought her claw along

its neck. A chicken, she told herself, just like a chicken. The animal convulsed a few times before becoming still. Gabrielle gradually released the corpse.

"Who are you?" Davey sat on the ground, no weapon, drenched and taking great gulps of air.

Still bold.

Gabrielle cocked her head. Was he not going to try to kill her or the like? Though she supposed that, having neither weapon nor backup, he might have assumed talking to be his only option.

"Do you fear me?" she asked instead.

Her anonymity made her equally bold.

Davey took another deep breath, swallowing hard. He met her gaze steadily. "I would be a fool not to."

Gabrielle stopped herself from smiling. No doubt it would have come out a smirk. "Could you also be a fool for doing so?"

"What do you mean?"

Gabrielle licked her lips.

Davey flinched slightly.

She internally grimaced, but tried to focus on the question.

Twas a good question because she wasn't quite sure either.

Her mouth opened without her permission anyway. "Perhaps you would be a fool for not fearing a dragon, but you can also be a fool for fearing a friend." Gabrielle kept her face blank, glad that her words, chosen in the moment and with unusual boldness, had not failed her. She crouched and leapt into the air.

She flew low and behind Davey on the same side of the river. She needed to get back to the river and her clothes before too much time had passed. Spotting a small clearing, she descended and changed.

Her hair was wet. Gabrielle panicked for a moment, then took a calming breath and focused. She saw the droplets of water cascading off and her hair becoming dry, returning to its normal state.

Nothing happened. Her hair stayed wet. Acidic panic nearly swamped her. She took a slow breath, imagining again.

It worked.

She let out a small sigh, patting down the fluffy strands. She shook herself and ran.

The river appeared shortly. Davey was carefully carving around Sir Drew's chest where the creature's hoof had touched him and still not let go. Being completely engrossed in the challenge, he did not look up as Gabrielle snuck to his right and stole her clothes from behind the tree. She put them on and ran out to Davey.

"Gabs!" he exclaimed. He dropped his sword and gave her a hug.

Gabrielle jolted at the cold, wet contact and proximity. Her earlier thoughts about knights and squires returned with a vengeance, and her gut twisted.

Davey withdrew, face pink assumedly from the chilled water. "Are you all right?"

"Yes," Gabrielle assured him, coming back to her feet. The lie came more easily to her lips, the sickness in her stomach growing as she said it. "The dragon told me to go into the woods a ways in case things got out of hand. Is Sir Drew all right?"

"Yes." Davey turned back to Sir Drew and picked up his

sword. He pushed against Drew's chest and swung the sword downwards, severing the creature and Drew once and for all. "He woke up, vomited, said 'that was stupid', and fell back asleep."

"What is that thing?" Gabrielle asked.

"No idea," Davey sighed, plopping down.

Gabrielle sat a few feet away. She held back a whimper as the impact jolted the bruises and aches she was just starting to feel.

"There's one thing." Davey faced Gabrielle, grim. "I think Drew knew what it was, or at least suspected."

Gabrielle agreed. "Why did he continue forward then? Why take the risk?"

Davey sighed again. "I don't know. After our conversation, everything was a little off."

"Does that happen often? Does he . . ." Gabrielle was not sure how to put it.

"Lose the smile?" Davey smirked. "I'll not say it to his face, but Drew is very smart, much more than a bag of laughs." His face grew serious. "But, yes, that happens at times."

Davey sent a glance her way, expression lightening. "'Tis only for a few subjects, and not often."

"He does not believe in change . . ." Gabrielle trailed off.

Davey gazed out across the relatively non-turbulent river. "When he says that, it makes me wonder what change he was fighting for. We've known each other for many years, since we were twelve or thirteen, I'd say. I knew Drew to stand up for what he believed was right, to let no one tell him otherwise. He still does that, but I think he's lost some of that fire, and his determination. Can I blame him?" Davey turned to her, honestly asking.

"Have you also? Lost . . . ?" Gabrielle asked. She clenched her shift, which had stuck to her still damp skin.

"Not as much, I think," Davey answered immediately, eyes going back to the water. "I know there are things and people that hurt and that they will always be there, but I also know that there are things and people that heal, that love and protect, and they will always be there. It is my privilege every day to choose which I shall do."

He looked to her again, a slight smile upon his lips even as he began shivering. "And how do you see the world, Gabs?"

Gabrielle contemplated the question.

"I do not believe that I have seen enough," Gabrielle decided.

Davey grinned. "In telling you how I saw the world, I told you what I believed it to be. Even if you don't feel comfortable describing the world as you see it yet, surely you must view it from a certain way?"

"From the vantage point of a villager?"

"From your perspective, as Gabs."

Gabrielle ducked her head, trying for a smile. "I have never had a nickname before."

Davey exaggerated puffing up his chest. "Well, then, I am quite honored to be the first to give you such."

A laugh, but twas neither Gabrielle's nor Davey's.

Lying on the beach not twenty feet to their left was another lady, this one with hair that blended with the darkening night, her laugh just as sweet, but a pitch higher, than the first lady's.

Gabrielle and Davey scrambled to their feet, Davey picking up his sword and holding it out in front of him.

"Swim? Hello. Swim!" The lady nearly pouted as Gabrielle tripped her way back to where they had dropped the two bags and water skein, slinging all onto her back as quickly as possible.

"What are you?" Davey boldly asked, standing his ground next to Drew.

"Come swim now," the lady cooed, a soft smile upon her lips. "Come. Swim."

"I have everything, Davey," Gabrielle breathed, coming up behind him.

"Good," Davey said, positioning himself at an angle to the lady. "Now take my sword and try not to look too surprised," he muttered.

Gabrielle did not argue but knew that a little shock skittered across her face.

Davey bent down and slung Drew over his shoulder with a grunt.

The lady stepped forward.

"Swim?" she asked.

"No," Gabrielle stated firmly, trying to hold the sword as if she were not terrified of dropping it on her foot. "Stay where you are."

"Please," the woman reached out a hand as Davey walked into the woods, Gabrielle covering him with her false bravado. "Hello? Swim?"

"We have already tried that." Gabrielle motioned towards the dead horse creature, feeling the words flow from her, nerves jangling so badly she could barely think.

Without further hesitation, the lady flung herself towards them, also changing as she did so, her scream somehow turning into an agitated neigh.

Gabrielle leapt backwards, keeping the sword in front and aimed at the creature, but they seemed to be too far from the water for the being to come after them, the horse-like animal stopping as soon as the grass outnumbered the stones, hooves stamping, tail flinging against the ground, a mere three feet from Gabrielle but unable to proceed. Gabrielle glanced back at Davey, who was eyeing the creature closely, ensuring that it could not come any nearer. Once satisfied that it could not, he continued deeper into the woods.

They set up camp less than fifty feet from the river, the ground being dry enough and the creature unable to reach them. Gabrielle was glad to return Davey's sword, even if he grinned upon seeing her relief.

Spying a regular rabbit just a moment later, Davey threw his sword at it in a quarter-hearted attempt to get it. Gabrielle, who was starting to agree with Drew's opinion that flora was jackalope food, saw that Davey was going to miss and helped his aim a little. Davey literally jumped in the air when he saw that the sword had hit the rabbit, turning to Gabrielle with an exultant expression on his face. Gabrielle laughed and congratulated him, glad that the little act had made him so pleased.

As they ate the rabbit, Davey asked again. "How *do* you see the world, Gabs? Not necessarily what you see it as, but how you see it. I guess I never really answered that question well, but . . . I still want to hear what you have to say."

Gabrielle looked to him, startled that he had remembered and that he cared enough to ask again. "Well, it does not matter how I see it," she began hesitantly. "That does not change what it is."

"But your perception changes how you see it, *determines* how you see it," Davey countered, "and we all must hold a view of the world that determines such. To say otherwise is contradictory."

The fire's heat caressed Gabrielle's skin, a slow, anticipatory warmth stirring within her. After a moment, she looked away from Davey's steady gaze. She cleared her throat as he coughed out a laugh that was a little too light to be only at her.

She nodded thoughtfully, purposefully avoiding looking at him. "Tis true," she conceded and, already unwilling to keep her eyes away, she met his gaze with a challenge in hers. "Perhaps I try to see it as it is then, however problematic that may be."

"What problems would you incur?" Davey questioned further, a slight smile upon his lips.

Gabrielle returned it.

Squire and philosopher. Her smile slightly faded.

"My biases could get in the way." She looked to the scar on his cheek instead. Scars on a squire. Sword calluses on the palms of a servant. "What I want to be true or not true impacts how I see the world." She paused and scrunched her face.

"What is it?" Davey asked, leaning forward, immediately concerned.

"Why . . ." Gabrielle hesitated, then plunged ahead anyway. "Why did he say that he fought for you?"

Davey let out a big breath and grinned, leaning back, then becoming more serious. "I think," he explained, "I think that . . . sometimes . . . tis hard to fight for . . . a kingdom, an idea. Not always." He smirked and shrugged. "Drew has accused me of such multiple times . . . but it gets hard. You find yourself fighting for the kingdom out of duty and habit and sometimes . . . sometimes you fight out of duty to a person, fighting for the kingdom only because you do not want to let the person down. I think that is what Drew is doing, knowing that he should fight for the kingdom, yet not finding enough motivation there, he has tied that to a person."

"To you," Gabrielle finished for him.

"Yes," Davey agreed.

"And you have tied it to Princess Danielle."

"Yes." Davey smiled to himself, caught up in his thoughts. Then his eyes, significantly clearer than they had been before, returned to Gabrielle. "Do you have any other questions?"

Gabrielle raised her eyebrows in surprise. Her mind raced to Sir Drew, and feeling suddenly and irrationally guilty for her questions, she instinctively closed her eyes and scrunched her face again.

"Gabs?"

"Why do you not call him Sir Drew?" Gabrielle let out in a rush, opening her eyes and unable to control her expression.

Davey sat back, shock racing across his face before he took control. "Well . . . like Sir Drew said, we like to be more informal—"

"That is true, but not why," Gabrielle stated immediately,

feeling as if her clothes were on fire, yet she was still insisting on letting them burn. "What are you not telling me?"

He looked to her, face tense and regretful.

"I . . ." He swallowed again, looking back to the fire, then to her. "We do not have permission from the king to be here."

Gabrielle blinked. "Why not?"

"He wanted to have a larger force assemble. Then he was going to lead a massive attack against the dragons. I thought a small group would be best. I convinced Drew of such. I have . . ." Davey moved his jaw. "I have little doubt that the king has either sent someone after us or is waiting for us on the other side of dragon territory."

Gabrielle's gaze drifted from him into the fire.

"At worst," Davey continued, "we'll be spending a night or two in the dungeons. At best, we will receive a verbal reprimand. The king is fair. You will not be indicted at any level."

Gabrielle saw in her peripheral vision that Davey was anxiously viewing her, awaiting a response. She nodded, completely taken aback.

Davey went to sleep shortly after that, Gabrielle having earlier won the battle for who would take first watch, debating fiercely for it because she suspected Davey would have tried to stay up the whole night. Her mind consumed with worries of the repercussions Davey and Sir Drew would face and with the possibility of her coming across the king, she still had not realized until he was sound asleep that Davey had never answered the question.

XI

═══════════════

The Castle of Ancora

"Gabrielle!"

Gabrielle awoke with a jerk, screeching accompanying the shout.

Davey was standing above her, wielding his sword against three small dragons who were circling above them, one mud brown, the other two a near identical pearl white.

The mud brown one landed at the edge of their campsite.

Drew was just beginning to wake up, eyes bleary and motions slow.

Gabrielle jumped to her feet but did not pull out her dagger.

"Stay back!" Davey warned her.

"They could mean us no harm," Gabrielle protested.

Jonathon said they were all the same. Why not a chance? Heart in her mouth, she approached.

The dragon hissed.

"Gabrielle!" Davey said.

"What is your name?" Gabrielle asked.

The mud brown dragon eyed her warily, head cocking, and the pearl dragons circling above stopped screeching.

Hope fluttered in Gabrielle's chest. Her resolve strengthened.

"Victoria," the mud brown dragon said suspiciously.

"I am Gabrielle." Gabrielle put a hand over her heart.

Davey readjusted his sword, and Victoria's eyes went to him.

"Do you live here?" Gabrielle asked, nervously attempting to draw Victoria's attention away from Davey.

Victoria did not answer, just stared at Gabrielle.

Gabrielle tried to smile and continued, "We don't. We're just traveling through the area. Gave us a scare the other day when we saw some redcaps for the first time!"

Victoria snorted.

Encouraged, Gabrielle continued, "That convinced us to stay farther out of the swamp. Any other places we should avoid?"

"You're here for the princess," Victoria said, quirking her face in an attitude that would have been sly had she been older.

"We want to take her home," Gabrielle stated simply.

"She does not belong there. *Humans* do not belong anywhere," Victoria said, eyes gleaming.

Davey took a step forward and to the side, partially hiding Gabrielle from Victoria's view.

The pearl dragons above screeched, and Victoria immediately belted out a weak stream of fire.

Davey held steady and then drew nearer to Victoria, blade raised, oblivious to the flames parting around him. One of the pearl dragons swooped towards him just as Victoria ran out of air.

Davey chopped upwards.

Gabrielle caused him to miss.

The pearl dragon was frightened enough to fly back into the sky for the moment, but further attack on Victoria could cause another suicide dive.

"Davey!" Gabrielle yelled, rushing forward and tugging on his arm.

"Gabrielle," Sir Drew said, suddenly awake and there and trying to drag her back.

She elbowed him in the gut.

Victoria backed up as Davey came less than four feet away.

Gabrielle grabbed Davey's elbow.

He glanced back at her, his frustration evident.

"She's but a child!" Gabrielle said. "Let her go!"

The other pearl dragon plummeted towards them.

Davey turned and quickly raised his sword.

Gabrielle saw Victoria getting ready to exhale. Thinking quickly and hoping greatly, she twisted around Davey to cover him, her body now blocking his from whatever hot air Victoria would exhale.

Victoria hesitated.

The other pearl dragon veered away, avoiding Davey's sword.

Gabrielle pushed Davey away from Victoria, or she tried to at least.

"What are you doing!" Davey snapped.

"We need to leave, Davey," Gabrielle told him, pushing to no avail as he planted his feet. "Do not fight them. They'll cause us no harm."

"Gabrielle! They are dragons—"

A bellowing roar cut him off.

Glinting in the rising sun, a silvery dragon, slightly smaller than the one Drew had injured with his dagger, rose in the sky.

"*That* is a dragon," Sir Drew murmured.

Davey did not resist Gabrielle's insistent hands and turned, hurriedly heading out of their campsite, Sir Drew already carrying the supplies.

Sir Drew led the way, hopping over logs and dodging around trees, bringing them to sections of the wood that grew thicker.

Gabrielle easily kept up, not being weighed down by bags, and they moved fairly quickly, the silvery dragon not giving a dedicated chase and quickly disappearing from view.

Suddenly, they burst out onto a shoreline, but not of a river. The sea.

With a resounding thud, the silvery dragon landed between the forest and them, blocking off their escape.

"You'll fight my little ones. Will you not also fight me?" she asked dangerously.

Davey hefted his sword again. Sir Drew took out his daggers.

Gabrielle scanned the shoreline for some means of escape or diversion.

Not far to their left, she noticed a cave with its mouth to the sea. Perhaps if the cave narrowed, they would be able to hide from the dragon.

If not . . . well . . . most caves got narrower.

The silvery dragon took a deep breath to breathe fire, and Gabrielle took the opportunity to dart around Sir Drew and Davey, running parallel to the sea, as of yet unnoticed by either man. Gabrielle was almost level with the mouth of the cave and turned to get in. She skittered to a stop right after entering, surveying the entire immediate entrance to make sure she did not miss an off branch or the like. Seeing no immediate solutions and unable to see if the cave narrowed or not, she started running forward again.

The dark rock of the cave rippled.

She froze.

The dragon's scales gleamed as the faint tricklings of sunlight hit him, the color identifiable closest to the shade of water at night.

"I told you we would meet again, little one," he rumbled.

Gabrielle's words deserted her, the sounds of Sir Drew and Davey fighting the dragon ringing across the beach but nearly muted by the cave's placement, the walls, and her memory, her mind many days' travel and ten years away.

The dragon tilted his head. "Your friends fight on the beach. Do you not think you should help them?"

"We seek shelter here," Gabrielle blurted out.

"Shelter? Here?" The dragon was amused.

"Yes, please. If the cave gets narrower, that is." Gabrielle straightened as she spoke. She felt recklessly audacious.

"This is a dragon's cave," he rumbled.

"Yes," Gabrielle agreed, "but cannot a dragon's cave get narrow?"

"Would not a dragon get in trouble for sheltering humans?" He grinned. "Besides, you need not me."

"Please," Gabrielle said. Her heart pounded in her ears, nearly drowning out the sounds from the beach.

"Your companions do not know," he said.

"Not for my sake, for the dragon you would have me fight."

"Marie," he told her.

Gabrielle startled at the familiar name, then shook off her surprise. "Marie. For Marie's sake."

"You think you could defeat Marie?" The question sounded almost like a test.

"I think both of us will be hurt," Gabrielle said.

A particularly loud roar made her glance back towards the beach though she could see neither Marie nor the men.

"There is a small tunnel about fifty feet into the cave. Do not speak of my involvement. Play along with what I say"— he leaned in closely—"and have some fun, little one." He jerked his head, urging her back to the beach, fearsome grin back in place.

Gabrielle ran.

Sir Drew dove and retrieved a dagger he must have dropped while Davey engaged Marie. Gabrielle ran up to him, Marie not even sparing a glance her way as Davey struggled to fight her in the sand.

"Needed to powder your face?" Sir Drew asked, flinging the sand off his dagger and hand.

"Go to the cave as quietly as possible. Do not fight the dragon there," she instructed him discreetly, ignoring the unusually venomous tone. She kept her eyes on Davey, struggling to think of a way to get the message to him.

Sir Drew did not move right away.

She looked at him.

He measured her up for an infinite moment.

Then, he inclined his head and began running.

Gabrielle focused on Davey. Hoping her plan would work, she dashed behind Davey as fast and safely as she could.

She concentrated on the wind. On her first try, a great gust redirected itself into the sand, flinging a great cloud of grit in front of the dragon. Gabrielle rushed forward and grabbed Davey's hand.

"Hurry!" she yelled, planning to explain most her actions and their luck with the wind later. Fortunately, Davey did not hesitate, but followed as she ran towards the cave.

Marie roared again, and Gabrielle tried to run faster. She could tell Davey was still slowing down for her. She waved him on.

Davey rolled his eyes, lucky he did not roll his ankle in the process.

Closing her eyes, having to reduce her speed to do so, Gabrielle manipulated the wind once more, sending a great burst of air against Marie again. Gabrielle picked up her speed as soon as she could, and both she and Davey rushed into the cave.

Davey stopped, spying the great dragon lying somewhat across the cavern floor, eyes closed as if sleeping.

A giant eye opened. The dragon's teeth gleamed. The eye closed.

Gabrielle snatched Davey's hand again and raced around the dragon and towards the tunnel. Gabrielle passed Sir Drew, and the knight followed her as she continued to half-drag Davey.

Marie roared at the mouth of the cave, her bellow echoing and reverberating through the enclosed space.

The great dragon roared back, rising slowly to his feet.

Their group of three continued deeper into the cave, Gabrielle searching for the tunnel the dragon had mentioned, Sir Drew searching with Gabrielle.

Marie spoke, "The humans! The humans are behind you! Move! You let them get past you, you, you—!"

"Marie! Is that how you address me?"

Gabrielle had the inappropriate urge to giggle at the great dragon's tone. He sounded like one of the grumpy old farmers being woken from a midday nap.

"Move! The humans are behind you!"

"What humans? I have seen no humans for many years."

"Will you move it, you—! They're right behind you!"

"I know who is and isn't in my own cave, Marie."

Gabrielle found the tunnel and turned into it, Davey following more readily now that he saw where they were headed. The voices of the large dragon and Marie faded as they journeyed deeper into the tunnel. Soon, the voices of the bickering dragons had faded into silence, and they heard nothing. Gabrielle doggedly continued forward as the tunnel, which had started about the size of a doorway, continued to shrink until she had to walk sideways.

"Where does this lead?" Drew asked at last.

"I don't know," Gabrielle confessed.

"Why did the dragon not kill us?" Davey said.

"I don't know," Gabrielle said again, but less truthfully.

"How did you know that he would not?" Davey pressed.

"I didn't," Gabrielle admitted. "I ran to the cave thinking that I could check to see if it narrowed. If it did, then we would be safe from Marie."

"Marie?" Davey asked.

"The silvery dragon. When I came into the cave, the other dragon saw me. We talked, and he told me of this tunnel. I do not know why he helped us, though." The deception still made her sick, but she saw little choice, especially after how Davey had reacted to the smaller dragons.

Davey seized her hand, or really, he tried to but missed.

"What is it, Davey?"

"How do we know that this is not a trap?"

"We are in a pitch black, cramped cave getting choked by our own breath with no clue where we are nor where we are going. How could you possibly think that this is a trap?" Drew piped up.

That had not occurred to Gabrielle. Regardless, "Would you like to go back and fight two dragons? Besides, what reason would he have for trapping us this way when he could have just killed us? And tis not pitch black."

"Tis easier. We are not prepared to fight, and I can't make out a single outline, Gabs. Tis as dark as I have ever seen," Davey countered.

"You call what you did out there fighting?" Sir Drew asked him. "You looked like a bumbling, rookie squire wielding a wooden spoon . . . with his pants on fire."

"I have never fought in sand," Davey said stiffly. "I did not see you doing any better. You missed your mark more times than I could count."

"Indeed, but that is not saying much. I could have missed as few as four times."

Davey took an angry breath, but then Drew continued, "The wind out there was terrible."

"But wonderful," Gabrielle interjected, not addressing the issue of Davey's and Drew's poor eyesight. "Did you see when it hit the sand just right? That was the perfect distraction for Davey and I to run to the cave."

"Indeed," Drew agreed again, "into the cave and then into the tunnel where we will meet our slow and painful deaths."

"We will not die here." Gabrielle realised she was gnawing on her lip and stopped.

"There is no light up ahead, Gabs. The exit to this is either far off or non-existent."

"Davey, I can still see," Gabrielle said. Twas dark, but she could make out the lines of every rock. She reached a wall and looked to the left and right, expecting to see another tunnel to the side.

Nothing.

Grimacing at what her immediate thought was, she scooted forward a little more, searching with her hands for another tunnel as well, the rock surrounding her on three sides, Davey finishing off her claustrophobic corner. She could not move forward anymore. There was no more tunnel. This was a dead end.

Suddenly, the tunnel seemed a whole lot tighter. Gabrielle took a steadying breath. She was not caught. Davey could easily move backwards, and Gabrielle could move with him.

"What is it? Why have we stopped?" Davey asked.

The air was so thick and hard to breathe.

"We have hit our dead end, haven't we?" Sir Drew presumed. "The 'dead' part being an apt description."

Gabrielle pushed against the rock.

"We have to go back to the dragons," Davey groaned.

Gabrielle's heart would have sunk had it not been so high in her throat. Had not the dragon said that the tunnel led out? She thought so, or maybe she had just assumed. Maybe he had wanted her to assume such. Had she actually led them into a trap? The dragon saving them for another day? For toying with them later? She pushed harder against the rock as the noise of Sir Drew and Davey starting to move back down the tunnel sounded. They were moving. She could back up. They were not trapped. The walls were tightening, but they were not because she could back up, all she had to do was back up. She pressed her hands against the wall in front of her in desperation, willing a way out.

With a tremendous crack, the wall in front of her fell forward, letting sunlight spill into the tunnel and upon their faces. The large rocks tumbled to the ground, along the shore of the river, which was considerably wider here. Stepping out and looking to her right, Gabrielle could barely see where the river met the sea.

"Well," Davey said, stepping out behind her, blinking in the sudden brightness. "That worked."

Gabrielle could only nod. Her breath came much easier. The sun comforted and warmed her skin.

She turned to view the rubble of the entrance to the tunnel. A slight cliff had risen along the side of the river. The rocks that had fallen looked like they might have once been piled to block the exit and then a small mudslide had covered them and cemented them together.

"Indeed," Sir Drew murmured, eyeing the situation.

Gabrielle rolled one of the rocks back in place.

"What are you doing?" Davey asked.

"It looks like the rocks were once piled here, blocking the entrance," Gabrielle explained. "I think we should put them back in place."

"Why?" Davey questioned.

"It would seem that they belong that way," Gabrielle stated simply, a little unsure herself.

"What if we need to get back in?" Davey wondered.

"Then we shall know that no one else has entered it," Gabrielle countered.

Davey halfway shrugged and helped her, Sir Drew joining in after commenting that the bags were badly scraped and would have to be repaired as soon as possible. That was before he realised that they had nothing with which to repair them. They finished the stacking the rocks fairly quickly, though poorly.

"How do you think he knew about the tunnel?" Davey asked as they placed the last rock in place.

"Like Jonathon and Jesalyn said, changelings and humans

and dragons all lived together peacefully. The tunnel could have been here long before it became his cave and was used by changelings and humans," Gabrielle reasoned.

"Dragons and humans lived together?" Davey asked incredulously.

"Well, yes, tis what Jonathon and Jesalyn said," Gabrielle informed him, surprised that he had not known that. Granted, neither had she.

"Tis true," Sir Drew agreed. "That is how the castle of Ancora was built."

"I guess that I never thought about that." Davey wrinkled his brow. "Are you sure we all lived together?"

"Together in the same area," Gabrielle clarified. "You are quite startled by that."

"Startled by the suggestion and the possible fact that no one ever told me such." Davey was frowning. "What do you think, Drew?"

"Jackalope?" Drew hopefully hinted.

Davey snorted and shook his head. "We are too close to stop. Do you know where the castle is from here?"

Drew sighed. "I'll tell you for a jackalope." At Davey's expression, he continued hastily, "Or I'll tell you for nothing at all. It should be right across the river and into the woods a bit."

"What was in the river yesterday?" Davey asked.

Sir Drew half grunted and sighed again. "Kelpies. I was a fool. First, I neglected to tell you about them. Second, I suspected what she was and did not care. C, there is an easy way to protect from such attacks, but I chose not to do so."

"First, second—" Gabrielle began questioningly before Davey stopped her.

"Don't ask. What are kelpies exactly?"

"Sea horses that may appear as humans. They lure their prey close before trying to touch them. Any part of you that touches a kelpie will be unable to separate from it. It touched my shirt, but shirts are not impermeable, so the creature adhered to me. After the bit of it left on me dries up completely, then it will fall off."

"Why did it try to drown you?" Gabrielle asked.

"Kelpies drown their victims, then eat them. They are carnivorous beasts. Nonetheless, some legends say that there are a few bridles that can reign in kelpies. Anyone who holds a bridle will not stick to their backs and once the bridle is in the kelpie's mouth, the kelpie is controlled."

"How?" Gabrielle could not imagine riding one of the kelpies.

Sir Drew shrugged. "Magic. The magic of the bridle is made to control the kelpie just as the magic of the kelpie is made to make them appear as humans and to have prey stick to them."

"You said there was a way to guard against them?" Davey questioned.

"Indeed," Sir Drew said and sighed another time, "and tis ridiculously easy. I must have temporarily had the rocks in your head transferred to mine."

Davey ignored the comment as Drew walked over to a group of plants that Gabrielle did not recognize.

"These are equon plants. Kelpies hate this. They are physically unable to come too close to it. Crushing the leaves or berries and putting them on yourself makes it impossible for them to approach you for days, even after the berries or leaves are washed off."

"That must have been what made it stop yesterday!" Gabrielle exclaimed. "Remember, Davey?"

Davey nodded. "Yes. I do not remember what was there, but that would make sense. Yesterday, the kelpie could not pursue us too far out of the water," he explained to Drew.

"Indeed," Drew agreed. "There could have been plants there, or it could have just been that the kelpie traveled too far from the water. They are tied to the river and cannot venture far from it. There are no kelpies in the sea. Tis highly unlikely that we will see any this far downstream as well."

Davey unfolded his arms and bent to pick the oval-shaped, many-veined leaves. "Regardless . . ."

Drew looked at him with wide eyes. "You do not want to go for another swim?"

"Careful, Drew, or I might be the one trying to drown you this time."

"Wait," Gabrielle paused, frowning as she looked up and down the river. "Does this river not continue all the way to the sea on the other side?"

"Yes!" Drew brightly grinned.

"Then why is it not salt?"

"Now, that"—Drew pointed at her, solemn expression in place—"is a very good question. Davey, take note."

Davey rolled his eyes.

Sir Drew broke into another smile and continued, "The water flows from the North Sea to the South Sea and should be salty. However, centuries upon centuries ago, changelings removed salt from the water as it flows over the riverbed. I assume they thought a fresh water river running through the island would be more useful than a salt one. At the top of the North Sea, after about ten feet of brackish water the river turns fresh."

"Where does the salt go?" Magic bent nature's laws, but certainly it could not break them?

"Gabrielle"—Drew placed a hand over his heart—"I think I'm in love with you. Davey, are you still taking notes?"

"Drew." Davey folded his arms and kicked at the knight.

Drew grinned. "Right at the entrance of the river at the North Sea are the salt flats. Coincidence? We think not."

Gabrielle nodded. "How does the magic work?"

"That is illegal." Davey looked at her, not warningly, more like he was alarmed and concerned for her.

"And unknown," Drew continued. "The knowledge of that magic was lost a long time ago. As the humans and dragons split to their own sides and magic began to be feared, even more knowledge was destroyed. Magic that could be done a few hundred years ago is now impossible because we simply don't know how."

"Enough," Davey commanded. "Let's just get the leaves and leave."

Drew raised an eyebrow at him but did not add anything.

They crushed and smeared the leaves over themselves, the smell of warm potatoes coating them. Drew moved many of the medicinal items to the clothes bag and the clothes to the medicinal bag, the medicinal bag being much more ripped than the clothes one. Davey carried one, Drew the other, and Gabrielle the water skein. As they crossed, the water never reached above Gabrielle's knees, the current weak and slow. The hardest part was not slipping on the rocks. Once on the other side, they continued forward immediately.

Gabrielle tensed, apprehension assaulting her.

"What is it?" Davey asked from behind.

"It seems she notices more than you."

Behind them, a dragon nearly as large as the one in the cave studied them, eyes glinting, her scales the green of grass at twilight.

Davey drew his sword.

The dragon chuckled.

"I am not here to kill you," she murmured.

"Then why are you here?" Davey gripped his sword tighter.

"To give you a warning."

"And what might that warning be?"

She grinned much like the dragon in the cave had. "You will not survive."

"That's helpful," Drew snorted.

"You have traveled far through dragon territory, farther than expected." Her eyes fell on Gabrielle, then went back to Davey's. "You have injured Decius, survived the swamp, and even found a way past the dragon's brood."

"You've been watching us," Gabrielle whispered.

The dragon's eyes slid to hers again. "For the most part. Ye have surprised the dragons here, but they'll not be moved. You'll die, whether or not ye turn back."

"Is that your point, to tell us of our impending deaths?" Davey asked, back straightening slightly as he spoke.

"No." The dragon smiled. "My point is to start the process."

Without warning, she shot her claw out and swiped

Davey to the side. She sprang forward and snatched Gabrielle, jumping and flying into the sky.

The dragon flapped higher and higher, heading out towards the sea. Gabrielle tried to swallow back her heart, it having jumped into her throat yet again. The ground raced beneath, and then the sea did. Once over the sea, the dragon went vertical and began climbing. Soon, Gabrielle began to shiver as the cold air whipped against her, the dragon's body blocking barely anything. At least the dragon was not digging her claws into Gabrielle. At last, after climbing hundreds of feet into the air, the dragon dropped her.

Gabrielle spun towards the sea, twisting in the air. Past the initial jerk, twas only like falling through very thin water. Gabrielle tried to intentionally turn herself, so she "stood" upright. She growled when she only flailed.

Growled!

She took as much of a breath as she could. The water sped closer . . . closer . . .

She changed.

Her wings burst out and hit the air hard. Her shoulder blades painfully snapped. She turned back over so she was facing the rapidly approaching sea and spread her wings out again, deciding that the jerk on her blades was better than her entire body slamming onto the water. After another jerk, she glided. Grimacing, Gabrielle swooped right near the surface of the water, creating thousands of ripples as she beat her wings. Directing her flight towards the shore, she landed and stretched, heart beating wildly and adrenaline still flooding her veins. She looked skywards, shoulders aching, but could not find the dragon. Regardless, what was done, was done.

Davey and Drew needed her.

Rising into the air again, she surveyed the land before her, looking only to the right of the river. She easily spotted the castle, a solitary structure enclosed by forest. There were few windows, which Gabrielle found interesting, but then the castle was also very built up and looked like it would have been well-fortified back in its prime. Dragons, including Decius and the one who had just dropped Gabrielle, sat right outside the castle conversing. At first, Gabrielle thought she should try to talk with them, but then realized that Decius had already seen her fight for the humans. Dropping in as either a human or dragon was likely to get her killed. Gabrielle flew so the dragons were no longer in sight.

"Who are you?" a familiar voice asked.

Gabrielle turned.

Victoria was flying towards her.

"You are a ways from home," Gabrielle commented, avoiding the question and startled to see the little dragon on this side of the river, especially after the incident with Davey and Drew.

Victoria did not come any closer, hovering a few feet from Gabrielle. "Mom is not too happy with me right now."

"Why's that?" Gabrielle asked, smiling. Victoria reminded her of Sandy May and the other young children at her village. Some seemed to have an inability to fear strangers, even if the strangers were truly strange.

"There were humans here. Did you see them?" Victoria asked excitedly.

"I cannot recall," Gabrielle said, cocking her head as if

embarrassed by the fact, to make sure Victoria did not think Gabrielle was mocking her.

"You can't recall?!" Victoria was shocked. "How can you not remember if you saw humans or not!? I and Heather and Ruby and me fought them!"

"Really?" Gabrielle tried to lift her eyebrows before remembering that she did not have any.

"Uh-huh! We fought them off, but they played dirty tricks on us."

"They were all really mean?" Gabrielle prodded, turning to fully face the young dragon.

"Well . . ." Victoria wrinkled her snout. "I don't really know. One of them seemed kind of nice. I don't know. She wasn't trying to kill us or anything."

"And your mom is mad because you attacked them?"

"Yeah," Victoria answered glumly, swinging her tail. "She says that humans are dangerous, and we need to stay away from them but did you hear that some dragons captured the princess!?" Victoria's excitement returned almost immediately.

"Did not *all* dragons capture the princess?"

"Of course not!" Victoria snorted. "Most dragons never go into human territory. Don't you know that?"

"Of course," Gabrielle bluffed. "I just was wondering who had captured the princess."

"Charlene," Victoria stated immediately. "She's like the leader of the dragons who go into human territory."

"I have never met Charlene. What does she look like?"

"Dark, dark green. Really dark green. Like her brother, but green."

Gabrielle nodded. That fit the description of the dragon who had dropped her well enough. "Does her brother help lead the dragons who go into human territory?"

Victoria shook her head. "He doesn't do much of anything. He's super old and boring. His name is Thomas."

"How old is Charlene?"

"Only kind of old."

"All right," Gabrielle calmly pressed on, "about how many years is that?"

"Thirty. Or forty. Something like that."

"How old is her brother?"

"Ancient, like fifty."

Gabrielle smiled again. She supposed that when she was younger, fifty seemed a long way off, too. It still seemed that way, but with her father pushing his late forties, "ancient" no longer seemed like a good description.

"Do your parents go into human territory?" Gabrielle inquired.

"No." Victoria did a flip. "Only Charlene and her group do, but if humans invaded dragon territory"—Victoria nodded her head emphatically—"*then* our parents would attack and totally be there and that's what happened today." Victoria sighed. "Ruby and Heather's mom saw us and came down and the humans ran away, and their mom went after them. She trapped them on the beach but I watched as they ran into Thomas' cave and escaped. Then their mom flew back to the brood and I knew she was going to tell my mom what we were doing, so I decided to go for a flight before I was grounded."

"Won't your mom be worried?" Gabrielle asked.

"What's going to hurt me?" Victoria replied boldly.

"Not all humans are threats, but your mom will worry about you being out and about with humans in dragon territory. Perhaps you should go home before you get into more trouble," Gabrielle gently suggested.

Victoria did a dramatic sigh, a little bit of smoke curling from her nostrils. "Why did they have to go and capture the stupid princess? I just want to be out having fun, and they have to invite humans to our territory? Life is so not fair."

"Would you like me to fly you home?" Gabrielle asked, grinning. She realised a moment after she said it that she really shouldn't have offered, not with Davey and Drew attempting to breach Ancora.

"No." Victoria peered at her, considering Gabrielle and her options. "Fine!" she sighed again. "Older dragons are such buzzkills," she muttered, flying back towards where Gabrielle knew the brood to be.

Gabrielle's smile only grew. Even though she was already flying, her body felt lighter.

Movement in the vicinity of the castle caught her attention. She flew closer to get a better view. Davey and Drew stood near the closed entrance to the castle, five dragons blocking any escape into the woods they may have attempted. Hesitating for only a moment, Gabrielle plunged towards them. She needed to help.

The dragons noticed her at the last second, glancing upwards as she righted herself just as she hit the ground, the dirt around her claws flying up slightly, her body between the men and the dragons.

"The humans' protector returns," Decius murmured, his injured eye closed and swelling.

"This is the one?" a grey dragon confirmed with Decius. When Decius nodded, the dragon snarled at her, "Would you fight us?"

"You would fight these humans," Gabrielle pointed out. "Let them take the princess and leave in peace."

"What's your name?" Decius growled.

"Valencia, I believe," Charlene interjected, eyeing Gabrielle.

Gabrielle startled. She pressed her lips together, debating the merits of correcting Charlene, but she could see little benefit to it except saving the real Valencia's reputation, and then Gabrielle would have to come up with her own name.

"I have heard of you," Charlene continued when Gabrielle hesitated. "Is that not your name?"

No, Gabrielle would not disagree. She neither knew nor cared who Charlene thought she was. It did not matter as long as the conversation continued down safer paths. "That is correct."

"You are the one who injured Decius in the wood, Valencia?" Charlene confirmed.

"Yes." Gabrielle thought it would not help to clarify that she had only dazed Decius. Drew had been the one to wound his eye.

"Did I not injure your cheek?" Decius questioned, glowering.

"Are we comparing wounds?" Gabrielle said, nerves

fluttering in her stomach. Ramble. She could ramble. "Perhaps we should consider that the greatest wounds are not physical ailments, but those of the heart, such as when one loses a daughter or a sister. The lady you keep in that castle is not of stone, but flesh and blood, belonging to the same. She has a family who misses her. Is not their wound more grievous than any of ours?"

"What of the wound of a loved one lost forever?" Charlene questioned, eyes glittering coldly. "My mother and father went to a village on peaceful terms, but the humans there killed them. They were murdered in cold blood. What then?"

Gabrielle narrowed her eyes but kept enough sense not to open her mouth. The war had started with the attack of Calumnia, not with any sort of peaceful venture. The initial draconic force had not wiped out the village, and the dragons had returned twice more. At least, that's what Gabrielle had garnered from the many stories she had heard.

She could not help herself entirely, though. "What village was it?" And then, when she realised how "human" that question sounded—"What were your parents' names?"

"Richard and Royale." The flick of Charlene's tail was the only display of possible unease or discomfort.

"They were upstanding Assembly members," Decius growled, "but the humans had no mercy."

The momentary bristling of Charlene's scales momentarily distracted Gabrielle, but Gabrielle shrugged off her surprise when the dragons shifted restlessly – and closer. "I cannot attest to what has happened in the past," Gabrielle spoke slowly and carefully, "though all death is unfortunate. Taking Princess Danielle, however, would not lead to the peaceful relations that would stop others from also losing their lives. Keeping her in dragon territory would only start a war."

"Continue the war," Charlene corrected, straightening to her full height.

Gabrielle forced herself not to back down.

Charlene coolly considered her. "Since the first deaths in King Germaine's rule, peace has never been declared."

Gabrielle kept her voice steady, hoping scales did not show trembling. "The action taken here is not a step towards that peace."

"No," Charlene agreed, an odd smile coming upon her face, "but that was never the purpose of kidnapping the princess."

Charlene's gaze appeared to soften.

That frightened Gabrielle almost more than anything else.

Charlene continued, "You're well-spoken and brave. I admire that. Don't fight us, and there won't be any repercussions."

Gabrielle successfully hid her surprise this time, Decius not succeeding as much. Gabrielle shifted uneasily. "And the humans?"

Charlene cocked her head. "They are in dragon territory."

"They are innocent!"

"They are far from it!" Charlene growled, her face contorting. She let out a breath of hot air, straightening slightly. "Step down, my dear. This is not your fight."

Gabrielle grimaced, eyes focusing on the ground for a moment. Not her fight?

She glared up at Charlene. "I don't want to fight at all! But I will protect those who—" She managed to bite her lip.

She straightened herself as Charlene had done, as if she had planned it, and stared the other dragon in the eye. "They have not wronged you, so I will protect them."

Decius opened his mouth to argue, but Charlene snapped, "They have! You cannot fight four dragons regardless!"

A retort burned Gabrielle's tongue, but she held it back.

Charlene glared. "Will you remove yourself?"

"No."

Charlene burst upward.

Gabrielle spun around, swiping Sir Drew and Davey into her claws as she did, and then lurched towards the dragons. Decius swiped his claw at her again, and she took a glancing blow by tucking her head downwards in order to charge. She almost plowed him down and used his body as a launching board into the sky. Charlene screeched, having wheeled around and was facing Gabrielle. Gabrielle ignored her for the moment and sling-shot Sir Drew and Davey into the castle, through the cloud of rising dragons, into Ancora through a window.

She grimaced. That must have bruised.

Charlene hit Gabrielle's back, forcing her downward. As she fell, Gabrielle saw Charlene reaching towards the castle, so she snatched wildly, just managing to snag the dragon and unsteady them both.

The other dragons had joined in. Gabrielle felt blows land on all sides, and she was too close to maneuver around them. She swung about with her claws out, flapping furiously, and made it into the air. The other dragons rose immediately, Charlene yelling after them to focus on finding the humans. Gabrielle employed the tactics she had used before, ducking and twisting out of the way, but the method garnered less success due to her unfamiliarity with her draconic form. She took many more hits than she would have liked. She needed to be done. Gabrielle journeyed a little higher, then dived, the speeding arrows of the other dragons whistling behind her.

Banking sharply, Gabrielle disappeared around the edge of the enormous castle. She aimed for a window and changed.

Her knee hit the ledge hard, and her balance wavered. For a moment, she was certain that she would fall and have to change back. With a small cry, she pulled herself into the castle, limbs knocking and bruising on the floor. She rolled against the outer wall with a whimper. Biting her lip to stop her cries, she listened.

Gigantic wings flapped furiously for one or two more beats, then continued, but at a slower pace. She heard their lumbering bodies pass the window, searching.

"Where did she go?" a new voice wondered.

"She must be here!" Decius said.

"She could not have disappeared." The voice, if possible, was deeper than even Decius' and right above her. Hot breath fell upon Gabrielle. She looked up. The sky-blue tip of a snout peered in through the window.

She tried not to breathe.

"What are you looking in there for?" Charlene sharply asked.

"Your Valencia could be a changeling," the dragon purred, still searching the corridor. "How did you know her name?"

"Changelings are extinct, Benjamin," Charlene snapped. "As for her name, I've heard of Valencia. She is foolish and young. Any dragon inane enough to challenge four others by herself qualifies as such. Have you any more comments or must you insist on sticking your snout where it does not belong?"

Benjamin puffed, unsatisfied, but left the window at last.

Gabrielle restrained her sigh of relief.

For several minutes, at least one dragon beat outside her window. Finally, Charlene called the chase a loss. "Tis no matter. We shall just have to get the humans when they exit." The sounds of the dragons faded, the prickling finally subsided, and Gabrielle began to breathe easier.

The consequences of the fight overcame her then.

Groaning, she sat up and leaned against the wall. Her body looked a mess, barely an unmarked space upon it. She closed her eyes and imagined it healing. After a moment, she peeked.

Nothing.

Casting back to the few spells she knew, she thought again of her wounds healing and murmured, "Sana." The hot buzz in gut grew more focused and direct. The pain began to diminish. She repeated the spell several times. The wounds were scars several weeks old.

With another sigh, she leaned against the wall, drained. Could she just sleep here? She shook the thought from her head.

Staggering to her feet, she used the wall to steady herself. She had entered through a lower window than Davey and Sir Drew. Typically, prisoners were kept in the dungeons. Nevertheless, she could not see how any of the dragons would have reached there to lock Princess Danielle up. Her immediate concern, though, was that Davey and Sir Drew would stumble upon her in this state. That would take more explanation and excuses than she could muster.

Gabrielle crept down the hallway, listening carefully, checking in the rooms she came across. In the third or fourth one, she found the musty, moth-ridden work clothes of a long-gone maid. Thinking that this maid would not have minded much, Gabrielle slipped the shift on and walked more confidently down the corridors.

The castle was as one would suspect an abandoned, decrepit castle to appear. Rusting armor lay scattered throughout the hallway, burn marks marred walls across from windows, dust covered everything in a layer so thick Gabrielle could have buttered Drew's non-existent bread with it. While the wind cheerfully rustled the leaves and the birds chattered outside, everything inside the castle walls was silent, cold. An enclosed tomb. Having to stay away from the windows, though few and far between, out of fear of the dragons did not assuage the grave-like feel. As soon as possible, Gabrielle moved towards the inner corridors.

After a while, she realized something was off. Understanding struck her. She threw herself against a wall, hair rising on the back of her neck. When nothing appeared, she crept closer.

In front of her was the inner courtyard, more expansive than she would have thought, the walls of the inner courtyard just as unassailable and defendable as the outer walls of the castle. In the middle of the courtyard sat the bright green dragon that had helped them with the rocs. Gabrielle watched the dragon, whose back, fortunately, was to her. He did nothing, just sat, patiently waiting for someone or something

Gabrielle could not see. Wondering if she should risk it, she peered around the courtyard, looking for an easy pathway to a place that would lend a wide but concealed viewing of what lay before the dragon.

The dragon's head lifted incrementally though it had not been bowed.

Gabrielle tensed, readying herself to turn and flee at the slightest hint that he had noticed her.

"I heard they call you Valencia." He spoke normally, as if she were before him.

Gabrielle stood paralyzed for a moment, then decided that the risk was worth it. She quickly lifted off the shift, not wanting to have to search for another one, and changed while coming out of the corridor.

"Tis what some say," she murmured.

He turned to face her, a grin spreading over his face.

"Valencia," he smiled. "A changeling."

Gabrielle paused mid-step. What kind of fool was she? How could she have gotten in here without him noticing if she was not a changeling?

She chuckled as best she could. "You believe the fool, Benjamin, then?" She hoped her bravado would save face. If she comported herself as Charlene had, perhaps. If not, a little offense would aid her. "You make me less than dragon? Perhaps you, like him, have forgotten that some need not be human to use magic."

His snout twitched. "You're sure about that statement?"

"Tis a rebuke. You jump to conclusions that show how little you think of me, how little you estimate others to have."

"Do you think so lowly of the changelings?" He questioned her, facing her fully.

Gabrielle considered the question. What would a dragon say? What would she say?

"Tis no matter." She'd try to distract again. "What are you doing lurking in the courtyard?"

"What are you doing?"

"I have made my position clear. I aid the humans. My purpose here is equally evident. Yours, on the other hand, is not."

"I have information," he stated, voice dropping slightly.

"Information?" Gabrielle challenged, tongue heavy in her mouth. She took a step forward. "Why not attack? Perhaps this is a trap. I see no other dragons in the sky over the castle. Are they not waiting in ambush?"

"They are," he confirmed, smirking. "They're in the bushes and trees to draw ye out, but there's a way out that they can't reach."

Gabrielle had not been moving, but she stilled even more. "And how do I know that way is not a trap? As it clearly is?"

The dragon snorted, shaking his head slightly. "Because it's the siege tunnels." The smirk grew. "Dragons can't reach the siege tunnels. Several come to the surface some distance from the castle." He shrugged. "They have no way of knowing which one you'll come out of or when. I don't think they even know they exist."

Gabrielle sat speechless for a moment. "Why would you tell me this?"

"Why do you help the humans?"

"I have my reasons." She tried to glare at him.

"And I mine. Look underneath the golden urn in the treasury."

Her suspicion grew. "This could still be an ambush. How do I know it's not?"

"You don't." Another infuriating smirk. "But you do know that dragons are right outside the castle."

"They must know you are here."

"They do. I am to watch for the humans inside the inner courtyard. Benjamin thinks you're a changeling. I was to draw you out, especially since I did not participate in the last fight." His eyes gleamed with no small measure of amusement and irony.

Gabrielle's stomach churned with dread and relief.

"He does not know you helped us earlier?" Gabrielle questioned, narrowing her eyes.

The dragon lifted his chin slightly, his eyes narrowing as well. "He does not."

"And what will you tell them?" The sick, churning stew grew in Gabrielle's stomach.

"Exactly what I saw." His tone was clipped. "Nothing."

"Your words would be true," Gabrielle hedged. A peculiarity struck her. "If so few dragons know about the tunnels, how do you? How do you even know where the location of the entrance is?"

He stared at her, arrogance gone. He straightened. "I just do. Good luck, Valencia."

Then he left, and Gabrielle stood in the courtyard alone.

Turning back to where she had come from, she surveyed the surrounding area to check for prying eyes. Seeing and sensing none, she changed and slid out of view as quickly as possible, snatching her shift and pulling it on.

Her mind was undecided about how valid his information was, her heart about his trustworthiness. Regardless, her first task was to find Davey, Princess Danielle, or Sir Drew. She set about exploring the castle again, checking rooms at a faster pace by simply softly calling Princess Danielle's name. Recognizing the blood smear underneath a window as her own, she realized that she had gone full circle, or square, around the castle on that floor and had checked all the inner chambers with the exception of one room. Before heading to the next level, she checked it as quickly as she had the others.

"Princess Danielle?" she whispered into the room, already closing the door.

"Yes?" a young voice answered.

Gabrielle opened the door fully to see a girl about sixteen bearing long, curly brown hair. She was dressed in clean trousers and gripped a cast-iron pot, a slight, hopeful smile upon her face.

"Are you Princess Danielle?" Gabrielle asked.

"Yes," Princess Danielle smiled broader and said excitedly, "and you are?"

"Gabrielle—"

"What a pretty name! Ours rhyme!" Princess Danielle strode closer to Gabrielle, eyes alight with delight. "Have the dragons captured you, too, or did you come with Davey and Drew?"

"I have come with Davey and Sir Drew," Gabrielle answered, startled by the Princess' demeanor.

"*Sir* Drew?" Danielle emphasized, then her eyes grew wider. "They didn't! Oh! I bet they did! Are they with you?"

"No, we got separated, but they are somewhere in the castle. What did they do?" Gabrielle's beaten-down suspicions reappeared in full force.

Danielle grinned mischievously. "Oh, no. Davey's going to have to explain to you himself. *Sir* Drew, I do say! He must be enjoying that!"

"He is not an actual knight, is he?" Gabrielle asked, folding her arms.

Danielle merely shrugged, eyes twinkling. "Shall we find them?"

Gabrielle declined to press her further, a new sick feeling spreading throughout her body, and just led the way down the hall. She explained that she thought she had heard the men on the upper level, also declining to explain how she had gotten into the castle, and they journeyed up a flight of stairs. Princess Danielle suggested splitting up in order to cover the ground faster and so there was less of a chance of them missing Davey and Drew. Gabrielle agreed after they decided not to move on to the next level until the two of them had reunited.

Gabrielle searched the inner rooms while Danielle stayed nearer to the outside of the castle. Coming into one of the inner corridors, Gabrielle turned a corner and ran into something that stumbled back as she did.

"Gabs!" Davey exclaimed, regaining his balance and jumping forward to give her a hug.

Gabrielle tensed but did not say anything.

He pulled back after a few seconds, hands still on her arms. "We thought you had died! How did you get in the castle?"

"Alive and well," Drew remarked, smiling, as he approached. "I told Davey it would be harder to get rid of you."

"You're worse," Davey told Drew, suitably distracted. "I've been trying to get rid of you for years, yet here you stand."

"I grow on people," Drew commented, "kind of like mold."

Davey rolled his eyes.

Before he could return to his original question, Gabrielle began speaking, "I found—"

"Davey!" Princess Danielle burst out in a semi-quiet manner, face lighting up as she swung around the corner from which Gabrielle had come.

"Dannie!" Davey greeted her, the two of them embracing.

The sick feeling in Gabrielle's stomach grew.

"Are you all right?" Prince David asked his sister, holding her at arm's length and examining her.

"I'm fine!" she laughed.

"What have you been eating?"

"Dust and mildew, what else?"

"Danielle."

"I've found enough. Do you not think I know my way around a castle yet?"

"Are you hurt anywhere?"

"I am *fine*," Princess Danielle asserted, trying to step away from him.

"You have been held prisoner, Danielle." Prince David's expression became stern.

"Really? Tell me more." Dannie rolled her eyes again. "Let

me just say that this castle was a lot more peaceful without you."

"Indeed," Drew agreed, scrunching up his nose, "Davey has a way of bringing chaos and mayhem with him."

"If you dislike it so much, then why are you still here?" Prince David asked him.

"Mold does not get to move by itself."

Princess Danielle gave Drew an odd but amused look and succeeded in tearing herself away from Prince David, enthusiastically hugging Drew. "I had hoped you would come. I knew it would be incredibly dangerous and that, under no circumstances, would Father let you out, but I still believed ye would come!"

"How have you managed to keep quiet for so long?" Prince David wondered, shushing her, for she had grown louder in her eagerness.

Princess Danielle rolled her eyes. "I have not had to stay quiet until you came and made all the racket outside with the dragons. Speaking of which, how are we going to get out of here? Oh! Wait! You need to tell Gabrielle!"

"Wh—what?" Prince David spluttered.

"Tis all right," Gabrielle interjected, cotton thick in her mouth. "Tis not necessary."

Drew eyed her closely. How many times had he lied to her?

Probably just as much as she had lied to him.

"You know?" Prince David shifted. His hand went to the hilt of his sword.

"Yes, sire."

Prince David let out a surprised burst of air. "I . . . you . . ."

"She didn't know for sure until she saw me," Princess

Danielle placed a hand on his shoulder, eyes searching Gabrielle. "Correct?"

"Yes, your highness."

"Pht." Princess Danielle waved her hand, grinning. "Once people travel along with these idiots to save me, they have *earned* the right to call me Dannie."

"Everyone calls you Dannie," Drew remarked.

"Everyone I know has to put up with you two." Princess Danielle brightly grinned.

"Gabrielle?" Davey slowly spoke.

Gabrielle swallowed. She had been such a fool. "Yes, sire?"

"Don't," he snapped. His hand tightened on the hilt. His face twisted.

Gabrielle looked down, unable to even glance at Drew and see his reaction, but he, most certainly, would have been wise enough to see this coming.

"Don't," the prince said.

Her jaw tightened. She had lied to save her life. What had they done it for?

For a minute, she imagined she could hear the blood rushing through her body, a dull roar that none else but dragons could hear. Her eyes prickled.

"How will we be leaving the castle?" Princess Danielle asked.

Prince David let out a long, hard breath. "Through the front doors. At night."

"And the dragons?" Princess Danielle folded her arms.

Prince David glared. "You have a better idea? Well?"

Princess Danielle rose up, eyes flashing.

"We're brainstorming." Drew waved his hand awkwardly between the two.

Princess Danielle suddenly smiled as brightly as before. "That requires a brain, you know, so tis not a job for Davey."

Then the princess turned to Gabrielle, still smiling. "Do you have any ideas?"

Gabrielle's throat was unbearably tight. What was she to say? Was she to tell them that another possible changeling had told her of siege tunnels? What would the son and daughter of a magic-hating king think of that?

But then the dragons would burn them all.

"Siege tunnels."

"Siege tunnels?" Prince David cleared his throat after the rough words.

Gabrielle kept her eyes on Princess Danielle as she spoke. "There are siege tunnels under the castle. I . . . I found them. That's how I entered. The dragon dropped me in the water, and I swam to shore. There was a tunnel there, and I followed it until I reached here. In the treasury."

"Where do they lead?" His voice was curt. Still grating though not nearly as much as a dragon's.

Sharp pain spiked from Gabrielle's lip when she tried biting it again. She stopped. "I don't know. I was confused when I came in. I can't recall."

"Do you remember where the treasury is? Do you at least remember if it's below us?" His voice became even colder.

"Davey," Drew warned.

"I do, your highness." She managed not to bite her lip again. Since when had lies become so easy?

After a moment, Prince David sharply turned and strode away.

They followed.

Luckily, the treasury was only a door or so down from one of the lower levels, Drew even spotting it for Gabrielle.

At the entrance to the treasury, Davey asked pointedly, "Let me guess, you don't remember where you came out of?"

Gabrielle fiddled with the edge of her dress. "Under the urn. It was large and golden."

He lightly snorted.

Princess Danielle whacked him on the arm. "Come on then!" She strode into the room. "Lest you are afraid of a little dust, *Davey*."

Drew went after her, Prince David lingering for a moment. Gabrielle eyed the chipped stone. He left.

With a light breath, she raised her head. Davey's back was tense. Prince David. And Drew . . . he appeared entirely unaffected. She looked away.

Large paintings leaned against walls. Intricately carved statues scattered themselves at the edges and near or on the walkway. Vases also lay about, each one worth as much as the tavern and inn. Few smaller trinkets, necklaces and such, were occasionally draped over other larger items.

"Found it!" Drew circled a large golden urn.

Gabrielle blinked several times. She hadn't taken a step yet.

Princess Danielle shouted happily and walked around it, scuffing the area around the urn more. The urn almost came up to the Princess' chest, the dull gold carved into twisting, textured dragons, a string of them biting each other's tails as they circled the urn. Flames superficially lit the area behind the dragons.

Prince David put a hand on the top of the urn and one halfway down, pushing. "How did you move this thing? *Why* did you?" He grunted as he let out a breath, arms shaking.

"To hide it. The entrance." Gabrielle gestured lamely. The pain shot through her lip again. She'd have to heal it later. "You're not doing it right."

Surprise stole across Davey's face.

Gabrielle ignored it. She was tired, in pain, and disappointed. She dropped to her knees and pushed at the very bottom of the urn, her magic trickling out to help her. The urn slid three feet to the side.

"Well," Prince David grunted once, rolling his shoulders back. "There's the entrance."

"Genius!" Princess Danielle said.

Davey squinted at her. "You could at least pretend to be glad to see us."

"I am glad to see you . . . well, Drew at least, and Gabrielle, too, of course! Although, we've not met before, so I didn't know she was coming. . . ."

Gabrielle pried the trapdoor open and dropped herself inside while Princess Danielle chattered.

Prince David came next, then the princess, and Drew last.

"Now tis just a guessing game," Prince David sighed.

"At least tis a game and not a massacre, which is what would have happened had we gone with your plan." Princess Danielle folded her arms again.

Gabrielle's heart lifted a little with the continued defense.

"Remind me that we need to de-barb your tongue when we get home."

Fortuitously for Gabrielle, the tunnels branched off in many directions. Prince David ran his finger along the wall, leading the way into one of those to their left. The tunnel was three to four times the size as the one in Thomas' cave, but Drew, Princess Danielle, and Davey kept to the side, each with a hand on the wall.

"We should've grabbed a torch," Princess Danielle announced to no one.

Prince David gave a long-suffering sigh. "We didn't see any, and we didn't have time."

The quiet returned.

Placing her own hand on the wall for a moment, Gabrielle glanced back at Drew. She could clearly make out his dimmed features. His eyes narrowed slightly when she turned, but his gaze remained unfocused.

Gabrielle bit back her sigh as her lip pained her again. Another nonverbal try at healing, and success soothed the ache. Tiredness weighed down Gabrielle's bones, and she belatedly remembered Jesalyn's passing remark about the price of magic.

No one spoke for the rest of the trip through the tunnels. They took only a few twists and turns, and at long last, they turned a final corner and reached a short set of steps. Sunlight weakly streamed down upon them between the jagged rock outcroppings crowding the egress. Davey hustled up the stairs, then turned around and motioned that the coast was clear.

Upon climbing out of the tunnel, Gabrielle saw that they were on the shore of the sea again, the sun beginning to set.

Princess Danielle plopped down on the sand, laughing. "It feels great to be out of that wretched castle!"

"If you're not careful, you won't be out for long." Prince David eyed the trees behind them and the skies above.

"If we don't eat, then none of us will be staying in this world for long," Drew commented.

"Do you want to look for your meat or shall I?" Davey rolled his eyes.

"I've got the meat," Drew volunteered immediately.

David was taken aback by his eagerness.

"You can make the fire." Grinning, Drew dropped his bag and dashed into the woods before Davey could argue.

Davey, Prince David, looked to Gabrielle with a face of mock irritation.

She turned away. She'd unpack the bag.

"Where are you from?" Princess Danielle asked.

Gabrielle glanced up. Prince David was gone.

Gabrielle flicked her eyes to the princess and away. "Seron, tis a little village near dragon territory."

"Why are you here?"

"What do you mean?" Gabrielle asked, deciding just to sit with the bag in her lap now that Drew and the prince were out of sight.

"I can't imagine Davey willingly letting you come along." Princess Danielle smiled knowingly at Gabrielle.

Gabrielle gently snorted. "Indeed," she said, unintentionally imitating Drew.

Princess Danielle laughed.

Gabrielle smiled, her sharp and belated embarrassment receding, and pressed her lips together after a moment. She explained how it had all started, Drew and Prince David needing a guide, her wanting to get out of the village, the first dragon, the sorcerers, the chimeras, the redcaps . . . Gabrielle began to feel quietly astounded by all they had done and seen in the past week or so. When Danielle pressed for details regarding the tavern, inn, and her family, Gabrielle gave them willingly and described her life in Seron in glowing terms.

"The little room at the back was your favourite place to go?" Dannie asked at one point.

"Among others," Gabrielle nodded, rubbing the sand between her fingers. "I loved to go many places in my village."

Dannie hummed for a moment. Then the questioning resumed.

They camped on the edge of the beach, somewhat covered by trees but still in a sandy area. Princess Danielle and Gabrielle did most of the talking that night, Gabrielle occasionally posing a question to Dannie, but asking more questions more boldly as the night wore on.

Danielle volunteered for first watch and immediately nominated Gabrielle for second. When the time came to switch watches, neither of them fell asleep, just talked more quietly, for Drew had complained that everyone would be up all night due to their cackling.

Gabrielle may have glared at him for that remark.

However, when Prince David's watch came, both men were fast asleep, and Dannie took great pleasure in dumping the water from the skein onto her brother to wake him up, Gabrielle acting as spectator and unsuccessfully trying to muffle her giggles.

Gabrielle and Danielle stayed up a little into Prince David's watch, mainly because Danielle insisted on fussing with the sand beneath her, trying to level out the ground where she would be sleeping but somehow also managing to hit Prince David with sand in the process. Gabrielle fell asleep grinning so hard her face hurt.

She awoke with a start.

The night was still upon them, the nearly dead fire sending a few weak embers into the air. Princess Danielle slumbered peacefully where she had fallen asleep, Drew where he had, and Prince David snored where he had sat down to take the watch. His earlier relentless drive was taking its toll. A slight breeze moved the leaves in the forest behind them, rustling and making the night come alive. Clouds covered the sky and blocked whatever extra light the moon could have provided. Gabrielle gripped the thick sand below her.

She rose to her feet. The dark forest. The dark skies. The dark seas. The dark forest. The dark skies. The dark seas . . . The wind ruffled the leaves, creating redcaps and dragons where there were none. It swept across Gabrielle's neck. She shivered, the night air sliding under her skin.

A snap.

She bent down next to Drew and slipped one of his normal daggers from his belt, having lost hers when Charlene dropped her. Her past few shifts had a concealed pocket where she had awkwardly hidden the knife, but this shift had none. She gently placed a few more branches on the fire, making as little noise as possible, then crept towards the woods.

Whispering surrounded her, swishing leaves and plants and . . . tails? Her hands trembled slightly, and she forcefully calmed her nerves yet was unable to stop them. She paused, searching for . . . for something. The buzz in her gut grew. Her body tingled. Without knowing why, she went deeper into the forest, the feeling growing.

Eventually, she realised she was going up an incline. Closer to the sky. She smiled slightly, then shook her head at the irrational thought.

Her eyes fell upon two rocks that were moving, elongated humps that rose and fell in a steady rhythm.

People.

Her senses told her that this was what she was looking for. Their campsite had little to it, just two breathing bodies lying on the ground, one sack filled with . . . food? Yes, bread and some potatoes. One of the bodies had a sword glinting on it. She leaned in closer, something strangely familiar.

Gabrielle gasped and took a step back, tripping over a root and falling on her bottom.

The man took a big, startled breath of air and sat up abruptly, tugging at his sword which got stuck on his belt, but eventually successfully pulling it out.

"Who's there?" he tried growling into the night, spotting Gabrielle. "Who are you?"

The woman beside him was awake now, too, sliding much more fluidly to her feet, though still stiffly.

"Dad? Mum?"

"Gabrielle," her father breathed, lowering his sword.

Gabrielle stumbled to her feet.

Then her father raised his sword again. "How can we be sure tis you?"

Gabrielle stood stunned, then remembered what they had to overcome to get this far into dragon territory. Without Drew, she knew she and Davey would have become very paranoid. Or, more likely, very dead.

"Ask me something, ask me something only I would know," she suggested.

Her father paused, seriously considering his options. Then, "What's the name of Gorlois' oldest sow?"

Gabrielle laughed lightly, her body relaxing further. "Pollyanne."

"Gabrielle," her father sighed, setting down his sword. He embraced her.

"Gabrielle?" her mother asked again.

"Yes," Gabrielle assured them, the prickling in her eyes overflowing as she hugged them.

"We've been so worried!" her mother exclaimed.

"I'm sorry." Gabrielle bit her tongue, face scrunched. "I'm sorry for making you worry."

Her father hugged her tightly again. Gabrielle almost worried that he would break her ribs, which was impressive considering that her father was not a built man. "But you are not sorry for leaving," he said.

"How are ye here?" Gabrielle took a small step away, avoiding the statement and wiping under her eyes.

"Frank Sr., Mildred, and their sons volunteered to take care of the inn and tavern while we went after you. Before we left, Mr. Henry even came up and said he was willing to serve tables until we returned." Her mother sadly smiled.

"You should not have left." Gabrielle cursed herself as soon as the words came out.

"*You* should not have left." Her mother straightened, eyes focused in Gabrielle's direction, but still with that slight glaze Drew had had in the tunnel. "What caused you to leave? You did leave willingly right? Or did that knight force you to come along?"

"No! No, Mom!" Guilt filled her. "Davey and Drew, um, they, they are fine. I came willingly."

"Davey and Drew?" Her mother raised an eyebrow. "What happened to the 'sir'?"

"I . . ." Gabrielle grimaced. "Drew, actually, is not . . . he's not a knight."

Her mother folded her arms. The steel in her eyes told of just how displeased she was. "They took you into dragon territory while neither of them was trained to fight."

"Well, tis not exactly true—"

A growling commenced.

Eyes dim, but two pinpricks still shining, a chimera prowled out from behind a few trees.

"Marie, take Gabrielle and go farther up the slope," her father murmured.

"Mom," Gabrielle argued.

"Come." Her mom gripped her arm tightly and quickly climbed up the slope with Gabrielle. There was little way to go, though, before they reached a wide-open space, the top of a cliff with the beach far below.

Her father swung the sword, the chimera batting it away and darting forward. He stumbled back, sword held out more like a shield. It happened again. And again. If chimeras could chuckle, this one would have. They backed closer and closer to the cliff.

The cloud cover broke for a mere moment, flooding the scene with moonlight, landing upon the chimera's skin, her father's sword, the roots twisting and curving upon the ground – on everything except the wind that played with Gabrielle's shift.

The beast struck in earnest.

Her father flung his sword at it. The weapon quietly fell to the ground feet away from the chimera.

Gabrielle thrust out her hand.

The sword jerked upward and into its body.

The creature fell.

Her father stared at the convulsing body.

"Timothy!" Her mother ran the few feet to him.

Gabrielle kept her eyes on the almost corpse, on her father staring at the almost corpse.

It didn't have wings.

"Mom! There're more!"

Another chimera dashed from the trees, much bigger than its fallen comrade.

Gabrielle raced to the fallen chimera, tugging the sword from its body.

Her mom pulled her father to his feet. They both tripped over another root that had stubbornly grown far out onto the cliff.

With a sickening slide, Gabrielle succeeded in drawing the sword out of the beast.

They tumbled over.

She dropped the sword and dove.

Wind whistled past. The falling bodies of her parents quickly approached. Her mother screamed. Gabrielle reached a little farther . . .

She got them.

She changed, wings snapping out even more painfully. Her mother's hair brushed the sand on the beach. Gabrielle flapped. Once, twice, and then they were flying.

They rose higher into the sky. She kept her eyes searching for a spot to land. Impulsively, she turned and swooped high above her own camp.

They were all gone.

XII

────────────

Firebugs and Fire pits

Blood roared in her ears. By the way the fire had died to nothing, Drew, Davey, and Danielle would not be just out of sight in the woods.

Her parents needed some place safe, or relatively safe.

Gabrielle banked, heading along the coast away from Ancora. She gently placed her parents down on their backs at the entrance to the cave, their expressions of shock unabating, then set down herself. She opened her mouth, eyes still above them.

She closed her mouth and walked in.

What was done was done.

Because she knew what to look for, she recognized the scales that rose, wavering in the darkness, as she approached.

"Back again?" he rumbled with slight amusement.

Gabrielle opened her mouth, but she still knew neither how to ask her question nor what question she wanted to ask.

"Why did you help us?" she settled on. Her claws impatiently twitched, but it had to be asked.

He huffed once, but with what Gabrielle thought was a smile that just looked like a smirk. "You need more help." His dark eyes gleamed, the moon staying out and stretching its light into the cave.

"Yes," Gabrielle confessed. "I left camp, and when I came back, everyone was gone. My . . . there are some people here that I found who need protecting, and—"

"Your parents," he interrupted.

Gabrielle hesitated for only a moment. Time could not be wasted. "Yes. I did not think it safe to bring them back to the campsite if everyone else had been taken."

"And what is it you ask of me?"

Gabrielle hesitated in earnest this time, glancing back at her parents who had made their way forward until they were close behind Gabrielle, their eyes wide but expressions somewhat more contained. "Can they stay here? Will you promise not to harm them?"

"In all matters, my involvement must—"

"Be kept secret," Gabrielle finished for him. "Yes, though I don't know your name, so I could hardly tell anyone even if I wanted to."

The dragon ignored the hint and grinned. "They may stay. No harm shall come to them. I promise, little one. Where shall you be flying off to?"

"I need to find out where the others went." Gabrielle began to turn around.

"There is an easier way to do so than flying out and searching the land."

She paused. "An easier way? Do you know where they went?"

"You can find out."

Gabrielle swallowed the unfamiliar urge to scowl. "How?"

"You are a changeling. Use magic," he spoke blithely.

Gabrielle's jaw tightened. "I don't know how."

"I will instruct you"—he leaned his head to one side—"if you wish."

Her claws curled towards the ground. "And how do you know how?"

He chuckled deeply. "I am not a changeling, but you are not the only one. There are very few, perhaps all from the same line, but there are a few."

Gabrielle opened her mouth. She winced. This was not the time. "How do I find them? My . . . traveling companions?"

The dragon stood taller. "You must be in human form to use your magic."

A breathy snort came from her. Sparks flew from her snout.

She lurched back, eyes wide.

The dragon laughed. Shaking his head and smiling, "Pick up a rock, little one."

Glaring, she did.

"Now change yourself and the rock at the same time. Need I elaborate?"

Gabrielle peered at him. "You are not a changeling?"

He shook his head, eyes glittering with amusement.

Gabrielle shifted, steadying herself on her claws. She squeezed her eyes and changed, focusing on the rock shifting as well. A simple shift.

The sand scattered upon the rocky ground prickled her feet. She crossed her arms over her chest. The rock in her hand was little more than a washcloth and the roughest one she had ever felt.

"Make it grow," he said.

Gabrielle restrained from snapping back. She closed her eyes again. Brute force wasn't an issue. Shifting from foot to foot, arms still wrapped around herself, she focused the magic, and refocused, and refocused.

It clicked, like the "a-ha" moment when untangling a fence.

The washcloth expanded in a rippling wave till it was the size of a child's blanket. She threw it around her shoulders, tucking it into itself as a wrap of sorts. She looked to the dragon, forcibly smoothing her face and straightening once more. Her chin jutted out. "Now what?"

Another chuckle. Perhaps he was helping just as a source of amusement, like the few oldest men in the village did when they had nothing better to do. Even now, the thought of this towering dragon being compared to a near-senile old man made her lips almost itch into a smile.

"Go to the pool of water to your left." His voice took on an instructional tone, not unlike Drew's.

Gabrielle readily complied, finding the large puddle rather quickly.

"You will be scrying. Those experienced and deft with their magic need little more than a reflective object for visual scrying, nothing if they simply use their senses. Still water is the next best scrying tool besides a mirror. Now I would suggest paying the cost of magic through a more direct route."

"The cost of magic?" Gabrielle asked.

"Magic does not come free, as no item nor action does. Even existing requires a price—time at the least. Magic usually takes energy. However, a quicker and more secure way of paying such is to drop blood onto the reflective item."

Gabrielle's eyes widened reflexively. "What else must I do?"

"Drop the blood in the water, then gaze past the water, focusing on the object or people you wish to see."

"Anything else?"

"No. You will know when it works."

Gabrielle nodded, then kicked a few rocks around on the ground. Finding one with a particularly sharp edge, she picked it up and scrunched her face, scraping the rock quickly along her arm. To her relief, she drew blood on the first try. She twisted her arm around and clenched her muscles, a few drops slowly dripping into the black water.

"Tis enough," he murmured.

She brought her arm down, closed her eyes, and took a deep breath. Opening her eyes, she stared at the water. The dragon had said past the water, though, not at it. Nerves jangling, she took another deep breath and tried to see "past" it. She played with the magic again, imagining it flowing through as a river, as a stream, as a stone, as an arrow.

Nothing.

Feeling like a fool and a failure, her shoulders slumped, and her eyes became unfixed, drifting towards each other. The feeling that had drawn her to her parents lit inside her chest once more. An unnerving calm quickly stole over the sudden nervous excitement. On instinct, she made her eyes more cross-eyed, eyelids beginning to flutter, mind focusing on Drew, his wry smile after a pointed remark, and Davey, defenseless and soaked as he spoke to his fear . . .

The two of them and Danielle, lying on the ground in the moonlight, eyes closed, smeared in dirt.

"I found them."

"Widen your gaze. See where they are."

The words were right next to her, but also seemed far off, echoing across a lake and beside her all at once. She imagined the scene getting smaller, as if she were flying away. They began to shrink and what was around came into view. Each was bound tightly with ropes at their wrists and ankles. Around them waddled little creatures who looked somewhat like redcaps, but their beards were smoother, they had less wrinkles, and their hats were pointier. None were taller than a foot, and they were considerably slower. Their faces were not twisted in ugly scowls but bright with cheerful grins. They chuckled and laughed, slapping each other on the back and occasionally tumbling to the ground with peals of amusement.

"There are little men with red hats, but they're not redcaps. They're grinning and laughing," Gabrielle reported.

"Describe their clothes," his calm voice continued.

Gabrielle focused on them more. "Their clothes are red, nearly identical to their hats."

She paused, trying to figure out how to say more, but the dragon spoke again. "Find where the creatures are. Get a broader view. Find your way here."

This time, the view Gabrielle had expanded much more quickly. She scrambled to stop the scene from growing too small and was relieved when her vision stabilized immediately. Cautiously, she expanded the vision at a slower pace, searching for landmarks she knew, a blazing bright fire near the creatures interesting, but not helping her locate where they were. Then . . .

"I see the castle of Ancora and the sea. They are between the two." With unexpected ease and confidence, she watched the view change as if she were flying, finding the dragon's cave just to be sure she knew where she was going. "I know how to get there." She opened her eyes fully and broke the connection.

"Those creatures are gnomes," the dragon told her as she faced him again. "The tribe you found are firebugs. They burn their live finds in a pit of fire." The dragon scowled. "They also have an infernal greed. Stole my golden horn years ago."

Gabrielle nodded. "Right." Because she could imagine him now with a golden horn coming out of his head. She began walking to the exit, ignoring her parents still. "I'd better . . ."

"Good luck, little one," he rumbled.

She broke into a run. At the opening to the cave, she changed and flapped rapidly, racing across the river to where she knew the gnomes to be. Her wings ached. She was not fully healed. She ignored this as well, for the fire had been large when she scried, large enough to be burning humans. The beacon appeared and grew larger. Danielle and Drew lay off to the side of the horde of creatures, but Davey . . .

A gaggle of gnomes approached the pit, a lump twisting and turning atop a sea of red. Gabrielle flapped harder. She tucked her wings and dove. Her form was made for this. She plummeted faster than she had before.

The wave of gnomes picked up the struggling Davey and tossed him with cheers into the fiery pit. Davey fell through the air, spinning slightly, the flames beginning to lick him, then Gabrielle snatched him with her claws.

She was too near the fire and too far in the pit to snap out her wings and glide away. She curled her body up like a caterpillar, wrapping her wings around herself and Davey, and hit the ground hard, dazing herself. A sharp crack came from her shoulder. A spike of pain. She roared.

She took a breath, collecting herself. The flames around her and the fuel beneath her continued to burn. However, it only felt slightly warm.

A memory drifted back to her.

It had been a chilly day, and Mackenzie's parents had been out of the house. In their usual fashion, the girls made light of Gabrielle's ability, and Gabrielle foolishly changed in Mackenzie's home. Due to the chill, the girls maintained the fire. Gabrielle got nearer and nearer to it until, to both girls' delight, she stepped right in without burning. After a while, she left the fire and wandered over to Mackenzie.

"You're glowing!" Mackenzie had exclaimed.

"Glowing?"

Mackenzie reached out. "Yes. It's so pretty—"

Then she shrieked, clutching a burnt hand.

Gabrielle's scales had acted as a horseshoe, absorbing the heat.

And now Davey was cocooned inside her wings as she rested on top of a giant blaze.

To get out, she had to use her wings or claws. Both required opening her wings. To open her wings would be to subject Davey to the heat and burn him to a crisp. To not open her wings and thus stay in the pit would roast Davey slowly. The question came down to whether she wanted him slow-cooked or fried.

The warmth increased. Perhaps she could blow the fire out. Gabrielle began puffing. The flames grew. Above, at the edges of the pit, a ring of red gnomes peered down at them.

The idea struck her.

It was insane. Absolutely insane.

Concentrating as fiercely as the fire blazed, she changed.

She thought of water seeping up from the ground, spilling over the wood piled in the pit, choking the fire within seconds, cooling her suddenly burning skin. She scrabbled with her magic, searching for the sweet spot before they both burned. The heat hit her in a wave. Blisters formed.

The water came.

She became dragon.

Davey had been angled away from her when they fell, and she had wrapped him facing away from her as well. He could not have seen her change. Relief flooded Gabrielle's senses as she snatched Davey back, hoping that he would not piece together what had happened. She more climbed with one wing and three claws than flew, her right shoulder blade searing, but dragons did *not* float. The water stopped rising when the pit was halfway full, so riding the wave to the top was impossible anyway.

They emerged from the hole. Davey's clothes were singed, and water soaked many places, but he had begun coughing and hacking and was oh so very clearly alive.

The gnomes booed. Some rushed forward.

Gabrielle fried them where they stood.

Gently, she leaned over Davey and cut his blackened ropes. He curled away, then rolled, eyes bright in his shiny and sweat-slicked face.

Gabrielle spread her wings to carry all of them away. Pain shot through her collarbone again. Her whimpering snorts expelled ember-laden smoke. Her stomach lurched.

She couldn't fly.

The gnomes cowered behind bushes and trees, leaving Danielle and Drew alone on the forest floor. Davey stood unsteadily.

Gabrielle strode past him, steps catching as her shoulder moved.

Drew rolled onto his stomach as she approached, and she cut his ropes. Danielle did the same, and Gabrielle cut hers as well.

Free, all of them looked to her. Her insides quivered. They could not know. They had to leave.

Gabrielle cleared her throat. She growled. "Go."

"Thank you . . . Valencia." Davey's eyes locked with hers.

Gabrielle paused. With a jerk, she nodded and blew a thin, long stream of fire in the direction of their campsite, clearing the path of gnomes.

Drew grabbed Danielle's hand. They began walking out, but Davey kept his eyes on her. "There was a fourth person in our camp, a woman named Gabrielle. Do you know where she is?" His hands hovered where the hilt of his sword used to be.

Gabrielle's heart clenched as she told yet another lie. "I

snatched her. Other humans in the area had asked for her. She is at the dragon's cave you escaped in."

Worry churned in her gut. He could not know.

"Now leave." She narrowed her eyes.

After a moment, he turned and walked down the trail, fire licking at its edges.

Just as he disappeared from view, little red hats dodged around trees and branches, following them. With another sparked huff, Gabrielle changed back to human form, pain lessening as she did. Biting her lip, she pressed her hand to the ground and called. The magic was working, if she had to guess, but nothing happened for several minutes. It was like talking to a rock.

She pushed the thought down and kept trying.

A small stone popped out of the ground, one with a golden sheen.

Then they were everywhere, most as small as pins but one the size of a brooch. Pieces of gold rose to the surface of the bubbling ground, and the gnomes came to them.

She stopped calling.

The creatures shoved the gold pieces into their hats, stealing from others when they had the chance. Some picked up regular stones and threw them at others to get the gold ones. Chaos ensued.

She sighed. A grimace. She turned her head away from her shoulder. "Sana," she muttered. The pain lessened incrementally. Repeating the spell several times served to dull it more, but when Gabrielle glanced at her right shoulder, she could see that it was still bent out of shape. Growling about what she knew she had to do, she procrastinated for another minute by putting out the few flames left on the edges of the path she had made. She changed back to dragon.

The pain worsened, both stabbing and throbbing at once. Now she truly growled, and a few of the gnomes that had wandered closer scurried away. Gabrielle changed back and repeated the spell a few times, made and awkwardly put on a blanket that looked a little more like a shift, and then began walking her way to the beach, at an angle from the path her friends had taken.

The way was slow, and she was not quite sure what she was going to do when she reached the beach and had to travel parallel to it in order to reach the dragon's cave, which is where she had told them she was. It was not like she could just wander back to camp leaving her parents with the dragon, with or without her broken collarbone.

She collapsed in the sand at the beach, breath coming in hard gasps. She closed her eyes and lied down completely, enjoying the slight breeze. Her breathing stabilized. The wind twisted the tendrils of her hair, brushing them gently against her skin. A sudden downward gust pressed the hair to her face or into the sand. Then there was another, rhythmic thump.

Why had she not paid attention to her senses?

She felt the emerald dragon carefully wrap his claws around her and lift her up off the ground. Her surprise and fear faded quickly as the reassuring beat of wings sounded. He had helped before, and she was, quite frankly, too hurt and too tired to worry much. Shortly, the dragon set her gently on her back on sand. She opened her eyes, surprised that she had closed them. The emerald green dragon immediately flew away.

"Gabrielle!" her mother exclaimed, getting down on her knees as Gabrielle slowly sat up, head spinning and senses dull.

"What happened?" Her father kneeled on her other side.

The moon seemed to be going under a cloud again, a thin but thickening veil of black falling over Gabrielle's eyes.

"Gabrielle?" her mother asked, but the words were dampened, as if Gabrielle were upstairs in one of the rooms in the inn while her mother was in the tavern.

The dragon rumbled something as the darkness deepened, his words indistinct and growing quieter.

Almost like a dream, Gabrielle felt her limbs go limp and her head and chest fall back against soft hands, feeling everything, but feeling it like everything had been wrapped in a thick, comfy quilt. Her senses quickly morphed, though, going from cushioned to non-existent, feeling like she was gliding without the wind. She realised dimly that this must be what going unconscious felt like.

Then the numbness reached her mind, and she thought no more.

There was warmth around her hand. A hand in hers. Gradually, it became more distinct, defined. Gabrielle shifted her head, perhaps trying to see it in the dim, flickering light.

"Gabrielle."

She was lying down, gritty sand and rock beneath her. Deep lines marred the hand holding hers.

"Gabrielle," her mother said even more eagerly.

Gabrielle opened her eyes, seeing the black rock of the cave ceiling above her and her mother's relief-filled face beside her. Nausea washed over her. Unable to stop them, hot tears ran down her cheeks.

Her mother sniffed, eyes also wet, and caressed Gabrielle's hair.

"I'm okay," Gabrielle choked out. She tried to sit up, but her mother pushed her back down.

"Let her up, Marie." Her father stood beside them.

"We'll compromise," her mother declared, wiping a few of the tears from her cheeks. She positioned herself behind Gabrielle, letting Gabrielle sit up only a tad so that her head rested in her mother's lap.

Gabrielle stole her mother's hand and pressed it tightly to her cheek, squeezing her eyes shut.

"What happened, Gabrielle?" her mother whispered into her ear after a few minutes.

Gabrielle shook her head and tried to sit up again, her mother letting her this time. The nausea and startling sadness departed.

Gabrielle stopped. She rolled her shoulder, but twas only stiff. She rubbed the shoulder, but there was only a bump where she knew it had been broken. With a look, she saw that the bone had not been properly set before healing. It had fused out of alignment.

"A man healed you," her father said.

Gabrielle looked up in wonder.

"We did not see his face," her father continued. "He appeared after the other dragon dropped you off."

"I told you that you were not alone." The dragon grinned.

Gabrielle was speechless. There was another like her.

"He did not set the bone properly before healing it," her father grumbled.

Gabrielle could not decide whether to laugh or cry.

"What happened, honey?" her mother asked again, resting a hand upon her, their knees touching as they faced each other.

Gabrielle took a deep breath. "I got there too late. They were throwing Davey into the fire. I could not pull up in time and dove in with him, shielding him from the heat and hitting the ground. I think I broke my collarbone."

"You did," her father assured her.

"You said the fire was in a pit?" her mother asked.

"Yes. I had to change back for a second to put the fire out, then climbed out of the pit the best I could. Davey was shaken up, but generally unhurt. They all walked back to camp."

"They do not know you are a changeling?" her mother asked.

"No."

"Did the gnomes not follow them?"

"Also no. I made gold appear on the ground to distract them. Those who had begun following Davey and the others came back to gather it."

Quiet fell, the only sound the waves on the beach, everyone sensing the dragon in the room.

Gabrielle asked the time and was told that it was the evening after the rescue had occurred. She had slept through the last watch of the night and the day. Her parents had leftover fish if she was hungry. She was not.

Gabrielle kept her eyes steady on her mother's hand, glad that neither she nor her mother had let go. Her parents knew.

They knew.

"Honey," her mother gently spoke at last, "I think we need to talk."

Gabrielle looked up in surprise, then fear.

"Nothing like that," her father finally drew nearer and sat down beside his wife and daughter, completing the triangle.

Gabrielle looked between the two, her father's stoic expression and her mother's regretful one.

"Many years ago, before you were born, your father and I were struggling to have a child," her mother began, clasping one of Gabrielle's hands in both of hers. "We were desperate, but having no luck. Finally, I conceived, but then . . ." her mother hesitated. "We lost the baby, about eight months in, but we could not bear to tell anyone right away." Her mother swallowed and looked down at their joined hands, the pit of worry in Gabrielle's stomach morphing, growing. "Shortly after we lost the child, your father was checking his snares one day when he heard a baby crying from the bushes."

Gabrielle closed her eyes.

"He picked up the child, who had nothing on her, and called for the parents. Nobody answered. He took the baby home, and we cared for her for a while, expecting the mother or father to come to town asking around for a child in a day or so, but . . ." Her mother sighed. "We did not tell anyone about the baby yet, half hoping that no one would come to claim you. After three days and no word from any parent, we told everyone that we had borne a child and claimed you as our own."

Her mother sighed and gripped Gabrielle's hand tighter. Gabrielle met her steady gaze, her sudden intensity. "We thought that you could have been abandoned by a desperate widow or unmarried mother, that perhaps your parents had died, or maybe there were just too many mouths to feed, but, Gabrielle"—her mother leaned in closer—"we always knew that there was the possibility that you were born to a dragon family, that you were a changeling that your mother could not bear to kill.

"Human or dragon, Gabrielle, we swore that we would love you. When you turned five, we started watching you closer, looking for any signs that you were a changeling, but noticed none."

Gabrielle swallowed, mind both numb and swirling. "I changed when I was three, almost four. By five, I was already used to changing."

Both her parents' eyebrows rose, a habit they had picked up from each other. "Did Mackenzie know?" her mother asked.

Gabrielle nodded.

"Why did you not tell us?"

Gabrielle raised her eyes to meet her mother's. "Why did you not tell me?"

Her mother was taken aback. "It would not be important if you were not a changeling. Your father and I loved you as our own child because that is what you became, dragon, human, or changeling."

"I did not know." A tear ran down Gabrielle's cheek. "I did not know that you would not care. You do not care?"

"Not a whit," her mother choked out and came forward, hugging Gabrielle fiercely, her father joining in.

Sniffling, Gabrielle finally withdrew.

"Is that why you came to dragon territory?" her father asked.

"I wanted . . . I wanted to learn." She was grateful that Jesalyn had summed it up so nicely for her.

"Have you learned enough?" her mother questioned. "Will you come home, now?"

Gabrielle opened her mouth to say yes but then paused. Cursing the pause, she took a breath to answer again. Finally, she just blurted out, "I need to make sure that they get back all right. Davey and Drew and Danielle, I mean."

"Danielle," her mother muttered, face lighting up with understanding. "Princess Danielle! Ye actually found the princess."

"Yes," Gabrielle assured her. "I want to make sure that they get back to human territory safely. How did ye even get here?"

Gabrielle's mother smiled. "Do you really think us that incapable?"

"Of course not," Gabrielle amended her words. "I just know how much trouble we had getting here."

"Perhaps twas because you were not traveling with a real knight," her mother suggested, mouth quirked in a disapproving frown.

"Actually"—Gabrielle winced—"Sir Drew is the prince's squire and Davey, Sir Drew's squire, is the prince."

"The knight is a squire," Gabrielle's mother said slowly.

Gabrielle nodded once.

"And the squire is the prince?"

Gabrielle quickly nodded one more time.

"Ah." Her mother's eyes glinted.

Gabrielle winced again, then tried for a smile. "What happened on your way here?"

Her parents spent the rest of the evening explaining their trip and listening to hers. Apparently, they had originally decided to let Gabrielle take the men to the edge of dragon territory and return by herself, trusting that she would be safe in their hands and on the return trip. However, a lady named Jesalyn had appeared at their doorstep a few days after Gabrielle had left, informing them that Gabrielle had ventured into dragon territory, convincing them of her veracity by accurately describing Gabrielle, Sir Drew, and Davey and by pointing out that Gabrielle would have returned already if just going to the edge of dragon territory. Her parents decided to take horses to the coast, then a boat into dragon territory on a tip from Jesalyn that Gabrielle and the men were heading towards the castle of Ancora. Her father shamelessly admitted that last night was their first night in dragon territory.

"Judging by last night's events, that was fortuitous," her father added.

Gabrielle ate some of the fish, a fantastic change from rabbit, jackalope, and flora, and told them about her journey, cleaning up almost the entire story, so it sounded more like Drew joked with the chimeras while Davey rolled his eyes. She did not leave out when she either became a dragon or used magic, poking much fun at her attempts. Her parents laughed at all the right parts, but Gabrielle saw knowing smiles, some sad and some amused, appear on each of them.

Her father asked a handful questions, but mainly about the animals and plants she had seen.

At the end of their stories, the great dragon, who they had all forgotten was in the cave, mentioned that Drew and the royal siblings would be at the cave by midday tomorrow. He asked that they leave before then to meet elsewhere. Everyone agreed and slept peacefully, none taking guard.

The next morning, Gabrielle was the last to rise, her father eating more fish, cooked, he stated with a serious face, by the great dragon. The smoldering embers and the dragon's snort made Gabrielle doubt this version of events.

Gabrielle flew to her parent's campsite right before they left the dragon's cave, gathering their items and spotting her friends trekking their way along the beach to the cave. She hurried back and reported what she had seen. Her parents had only three bags, so each of them took one. Gabrielle's parents started towards the cave's entrance, but Gabrielle turned to face the dragon one last time.

"Thank you," she told him.

He only gave her a calm look.

Gabrielle steadied herself and continued anyway. "May I ask you a question?"

"You may. I may not answer."

"Why are you helping us?"

The dragon was quiet for some time.

At last, he rumbled. "Why not?"

"Why not?" Gabrielle asked.

"Why not," he repeated, a small grin slipping upon his visage, but disappearing just as quickly. His face became more serious than it ever had been, a tremendous feat. "You are young still. You have the opportunity to make the difference I never did."

"What difference?"

"Change, little one. Change. I have seen much change over these years, but I also have seen little. I hope to see change by you."

"Change in what?" Gabrielle uneasily asked.

"In this kingdom. In minds, human and dragon. You have great potential."

Gabrielle did not like the sound of that, nor the pressure it created. "I don't know what you mean."

"Not yet."

Directly pressing clearly would get her nowhere.

She decided to continue trying anyway.

"What do you mean that you have failed to make change yourself? Have you not just made change by helping us?" she asked.

"I have facilitated the coming of change, not created it. I can no longer do such. My role is limited to simply aiding you in your ventures." His eyes wandered over to her parents.

Gabrielle ignored the nervousness the direction of his gaze immediately created. "What are these ventures?"

He grinned again. "You are on one of them, little one. Now leave, before the humans arrive."

Gabrielle turned, but then faced him again. "Thank you," she said, for she was grateful.

He nodded his reply.

She joined her parents, and they walked out of the cave.

Just as they were about to get out of the sight of the dragon, he called.

"Little one."

Gabrielle turned to him.

"My name is Thomas. Good luck."

He himself turned and swished his tail, disappearing deeper into the cave.

Gabrielle stood, stunned once more, then stiffly turned and started walking with her parents along the beach.

"What is it, honey?" her mother asked.

Gabrielle shook her head, wondering if the name was a coincidence, but the circumstances matched almost too well for that. "I am fairly confident that was Charlene's brother."

Gabrielle explained who Charlene was and her role in creating tension between dragons and humans as they approached the river, Davey and the others coming into view. Her mother was shocked and kept asking Gabrielle if she had her information right. Her father took it silently, like he took most things, but Gabrielle eventually thought she had them thoroughly convinced by the time they reached the river, which was fortunate because Davey, Drew, and Danielle were already crossing.

"Where's your boat?" Gabrielle asked suddenly, looking around on the beach as her friends neared them.

"Twas right . . ." Gabrielle's mother's voice trailed off, gesturing to their right.

Her father walked to the edge of the water and bent down, examining the sand, then he waded into the water a short distance, stuck his hand underwater, and pulled up a rope with an anchor attached.

Gabrielle's mother closed her eyes and smacked her forehead. "Timothy—"

"I have never sailed before, Marie."

"What happened? What does that mean?" Gabrielle asked.

"Your father did not tie the other end of the anchor to the boat."

Gabrielle snorted, unable to stop herself, hand reflexively reaching to cover her mouth.

"We have to travel through dragon territory to get out," her mother stated disbelievingly.

Gabrielle heard wet slaps for footsteps behind her and turned.

"Gabrielle." Prince David approached her.

Her stomach dropped.

"Sir."

"Gabrielle!" Danielle nearly shouted, greeting her in the same way she had greeted Prince David earlier. She ran up and hugged Gabrielle tightly. "When we saw you were gone, I started freaking out! Well, I mean, after I was already freaking out about being captured by little red men—"

"Gnomes," Drew interrupted, checking the bottom of the bag he was carrying for wetness and quickly hiding the bag behind his back, so Davey would not see that it was soaked—and still ripped from earlier, unfortunately.

"But then Davey told me that you were completely all right. Are these your parents?" Danielle asked, bounding up to Gabrielle's mom. "Hi! I'm Danielle! Are you Gabrielle's mother?"

"Yes, your high—" her mother began.

"That's all right," Danielle stopped her, looking to Prince David meaningfully. "We're dropping titles, right?"

"Are you and your parents all right?" Prince David asked Gabrielle, his back straight as a rod.

"Yes, sire. Are you?"

"Fine. We're going to make our way back to human territory."

". . . Okay."

"Drew suggests going along up the river and then branching off through where the sorcerers would be. We're not stopping, though."

". . . All right."

"Would you like to join us?"

". . . Yes. . . . Thank you."

After a long minute, Prince David started walking along the river. Danielle gestured for Gabrielle to follow after him. Gabrielle raised her eyebrows and widened her eyes meaningfully. Danielle gestured again for Gabrielle to follow after him, getting grander in her efforts. Deciding not to argue and draw more attention to it, Gabrielle took a deep breath and followed behind Prince David. She kept her eyes down when he glanced back to make sure everyone was following.

"So," Danielle began, questioning Gabrielle's parents, "Gabrielle tells me you run a tavern and inn. What do you like about that?"

Danielle continued the inquisition, Gabrielle interrupting only once to smear some equon on herself and her parents. Danielle also paused her questioning once right after they began, but only long enough to explain that they had been captured by gnomes. However, all of the supplies had still been at the campsite, the gnomes leaving the drab bags behind.

After that, the questions did not seem to have an end.

They were intriguing, Danielle asking Gabrielle's parents to share things even Gabrielle did not know. Gabrielle's mother responded in the same fashion Gabrielle had, answering all questions with expected poise and respect at first, but gradually asking her own questions until Gabrielle's mother was conversing with Danielle as she would with any other inquisitive sixteen-year-old.

"What is most important to you?" Danielle asked.

"Gabrielle," her mother answered without hesitation. "You?"

"Mm, my family in general. Except Davey of course, so I guess just my parents. If you could change one thing, any one thing, what would you change and why?"

"Oh, that's a good one," Marie commented appreciatively. "Are you reading these off of a list or something?"

"Mum made me a list of questions when I was younger to ask people at dinners and such. I detested those things—the dinners—but the questions made it easier to talk to people. Now I really like the questions, but Mum tells me I need to get away from them because they make me sound like a dungeon inquisitor. I love asking them, though. You get to learn so much about people that they normally would not tell you, and people are so interesting. Except Davey of course, but I'm not sure if he even counts as a person. So, what would you change and why?"

"May I think about that one?"

"Of course! Davey, you should pay attention, so you can see how it's done. You know, thinking."

"Really missed you, Dannie," Davey muttered, so quietly

Gabrielle was pretty sure he had not expected her to hear him.

After a couple minutes, Gabrielle's mother said, "I would—"

A throaty bellow from their left cut her words short, all in their group turning to face the animal.

Coming at Gabrielle from an angle was a giant, grey house. She felt hands grip her and wrench her out of the way. As the beast thundered past, too enormous to turn quickly, they saw that the creature was at least ten feet tall, about the same width, and about eighteen feet long. Davey gripped her tightly for a second more, then maneuvered around in front of her, drawing his sword as the beast slowed and tried to turn.

"Go! Go!" Drew yelled at her parents and Danielle, urging them forward, behind the creature as it turned.

Davey stepped forward as they rushed towards Gabrielle and him, but Drew discouraged him, "Our best bet is just to run, sire!"

Davey waited until Gabrielle's parents and Drew were past him, then turned himself.

Gabrielle had waited for him, anxious and not knowing if he would still attack the beast, which had almost completed the circle and was coming at them again. She turned as he did and began running.

"When he gets close enough, get to the side and let him go past!" Drew called back to them. "Don't be Davey, Davey!"

Gabrielle did not answer, presuming that Drew would figure out whether or not they had heard when they got trampled to death or not. The earth-rattling footsteps pounded nearer, and Gabrielle prepared herself to jump out of the way.

Just as she was about to hop to the left, Davey yanked her to the side again.

"You need to get to the side," he admonished her.

"I was about to before you grabbed me," she countered.

She grimaced after speaking and looked away.

Davey let go of her wrist and waist.

The beast was turning again. Drew directed everyone to proceed behind its back in such a way that the creature would turn heading downstream without realizing that their group had continued upstream. Davey and Gabrielle hastened towards them, following along with his idea. Their group began sprinting again, the bag Gabrielle carried smacking uncomfortably against her leg. They did the ploy trice more before the beast gave up the pursuit, bellowing just as bellicosely but with considerably less energy.

"So," Danielle gasped, clutching her side as they resumed walking, "what would you change, Marie?"

XIII

Scattered

Shortly after the attack, the sun got low enough to convince Drew to ask Davey to stop for the night. Danielle was the only other person who would have said anything to Davey about the time, but she was distracted by asking Gabrielle's mom more questions. Gabrielle had to wonder how long the list the queen had made Danielle was.

Gabrielle's mother had not answered Danielle's question about change right away, Drew interrupting to explain what the creature that had attacked them was—a karkadan.

Gabrielle vaguely recalled Drew speaking about them earlier, giant rhinoceros-like creatures with enormous horns that live along both edges of the entire river. Drew reiterated their slowness and how simply dodging at the last moment was the best plan of action to take every time.

When Gabrielle's father questioned him further, Drew also said that karkadans were solitary creatures, meeting only once or twice a year to mate, the mother taking care of the children for only one year. While karkadans were herbivores, they were prone to charging anything human-size or larger that moves, so once the person or animal died, the corpse would not get eaten.

To this, Danielle commented, "Great! Dead but not eaten! That makes all the difference!"

Gabrielle tried to hide her smile and agreement.

Drew was happy to oblige when Gabrielle's father asked for yet more information on the creatures. Her father reveled in talking about animals and plants, and his enjoyment in learning of the flora and fauna in dragon territory was clear— an enjoyment Drew only encouraged.

Danielle quickly stopped listening and drew closer to Gabrielle's mom, continuing their conversation.

Twas sometime later when Drew finally voiced the comment that made Prince David stop for the night. Davey had not been in a rush, but was clearly distracted. He did not reply to any of Drew's teasings nor Danielle's outright insults. All of which were, of course, soaked in sisterly love.

They slept on the edge of the river and forest, much like they had done on the beach. Everyone except Danielle insisted on taking a watch. Gabrielle and her mother took the first two watches like Danielle and Gabrielle had done a few nights ago. They whispered together about magic and changelings. Danielle tried staying up with them for a short while, but fell asleep by accident. All the men snored peacefully, though loudly, upon laying their heads down.

Drew caught fish the next morning, declaring the change

in food items good. Gabrielle noticed her parents exchanging exasperated smiles. The flaky meat delighted everyone else.

Timothy and Drew spent breakfast comparing and contrasting fire and swamp salamanders. Marie asked Danielle some questions, claiming them to be Danielle's reward for Danielle's intense inquisition the day before. David ate his fish in silence, as did Gabrielle, both commenting on either conversation only when strictly necessary.

When they were about to leave, everything already packed up, Gabrielle's father spotted and correctly identified one of the lizards they had been discussing and insisted on carefully collecting some samples, an act which Drew unhelpfully encouraged.

Finally, they set off again, Danielle much quieter than the day before, yawning often. Gabrielle's father and Drew made up the difference, though, conversing more about karkadans and also kelpies, then redcaps, eventually chimeras . . . Gabrielle doubted they would run out of creatures and information. Drew was like a well of dragon territory knowledge. Eventually, her father did not ask any other questions about the animals that he had not seen, just started to point to random plants and ask Drew for information. Drew never failed to comply.

"Dragon," Gabrielle interrupted their conversation.

The group shuffled back farther under the trees, the glittering gold still far enough away that they could take cover. They had seen six other groups of dragons throughout the day, Gabrielle being the first to spot each.

"The chicory plant does have the milky substance—"

"Dad!" Gabrielle whisper-shouted to him, incredulous that he would try to continue the conversation.

"Not the time," her father agreed.

"I would have expected to see more dragons," Danielle commented after the dragon disappeared, sounding surprisingly somewhat disappointed.

"They are probably still at Ancora. They never saw us leave, remember?" David voluntarily spoke for the first time that day.

"Not all of them were there. Not all of the dragons wanted to kidnap Danielle," Gabrielle spoke without thinking.

David gave her an odd look. "What do you mean?"

"Well, I was talking to the dragon in the cave, and he said that not all dragons, such as himself, thought that the princess should be captured. Not all want to war with humans," Gabrielle explained, forcing herself not to bite her lip.

"Not all humans want to war with dragons," David replied.

Gabrielle looked to him, startled by his answer.

He noticed and was just as startled. "Like my father, for instance, he would rather choose peace than continued warfare."

"But your father would kill all with magic if he had the chance," Gabrielle refuted, a strange feeling rising in her breast. It took her a minute to recognise it as indignation, perhaps with a tinge of hate. She tried to quell the feeling. It would do no good.

"My father acts only to protect," Prince David corrected, his facial expression betraying the assuredness in his tone.

They forged onward.

The ground became soggier as they reached the middle of

the stretch of swamp that lay by the river, the same swamp that they had walked the fringes of on their way to Ancora.

The rest of the day followed the morning's pattern. That night, a few hundred feet past the rough edge of the swamp, everyone took the same watches, Danielle managing to stay up further into Gabrielle and her mother's watches, but still falling asleep before the first watch was up. During the second watch, while everyone except she and her mother slept, Gabrielle practiced more of her magic, surprised at her own delight in watching her mother's eyes light up when Gabrielle made designs out of leaves in midair or called gold and other precious metals from the ground. There were significantly fewer stones that appeared, but Gabrielle did not know if there was less in the area or if she was calling fewer forth. She buried them afterwards.

The peacefulness of the night was nearly complete, encompassing all the surroundings. Gabrielle was relaxed, her mother beside her, her father and David sleeping not at all like rocks. Almost everything was still and if making a noise, whispering.

The wingbeats of something setting down less than fifty feet from camp were clear.

Uneasiness and prickling raced down Gabrielle's spine.

More wingbeats.

Gabrielle looked to her mother and saw anxious eyes. She motioned for her mother to quickly wake up those on one side of the fire and started to wake up those on the other side herself. Their noises boomed through the night like a blacksmith's forgings.

"Prince David," Gabrielle breathed, shaking his shoulder gently.

He awoke with a snort, eyes blinking rapidly and hand going to his sword.

She stopped him. "We are surrounded by dragons. Fighting is not going to be an option."

Gabrielle's mother was shaking Danielle awake, Danielle almost successfully sleeping through these efforts.

Drew motioned with his hands, but neither Gabrielle nor Prince David understood, so he scurried low and quick around the fire.

"This is why you should have played charades with me," Drew reprimanded Prince David.

"What is it?" the prince commanded.

"We should split up."

"Are you insane? They'll never make it!" Prince David barely kept his voice down.

"We have no other option, sire," Drew told him grimly. "To stand and fight is suicide, murder if we subject Gabrielle and her parents to the fool-brained plan. We must scatter and regroup later. In the dark with a few idiots screaming their heads off, the dragons may be sufficiently distracted, and the others can escape."

"Could we split into two groups?"

"They shall expect that. Dividing up completely is dangerous and insane, but tis the best option."

Prince David lightly sighed.

A stick cracked frighteningly close.

"All right. You and I will create confusion among the

dragons while the others escape. We'll meet up somewhere along the river later. Tell the others."

Gabrielle crept towards her parents and Danielle, who had finally awoken, catching Drew's parting words to Prince David—"I think you would do a much better job at screaming and being an idiot than me, sire. In fact, are you sure you even need me?"

Gabrielle quickly conveyed the plan to her parents and the princess, no more wingbeats breaking the night, only the ominous rustling of leaves. Their camp spread out in a loose ring around the fire, facing the forest. Danielle, Gabrielle, and her mother nervously glanced at each other. Her father stared straight into the trees, hand gripping a knife Drew had lent him. Drew muttered about the idiocy of the world's greatest idiot, and Prince David steeled himself for the words.

After a second's nervous hesitation . . . "Go!"

They went.

Fire lit the air, burning the undergrowth. It streaked in unexpected patterns. Amidst the blazes, Gabrielle could see a winding path deeper into the woods, away from the ambush. She ducked and twisted around trees, knowing that she had been spotted several times, but she did not stop, dashing around dragons, causing burning logs to fall where they normally would not and gusts of wind to feed the fire despite the still air. All the while, one could hear Prince David aggressively challenging the dragons.

Then there was Drew.

"Come on, ye old, rotten bag of scales and redcap droppings! Will-o'-wisps have more substance than you! You call that a blaze!? You should have seen what the firebugs can do, ye ugly salamanders with wooden claws and terrible breath!"

Gabrielle could no longer tell if she was heading away from the melee or into it. All was fire and smoke and confusion. She continued ducking and weaving, not sure if she was avoiding dragons or trees.

She ran into something hard as she swung around a tree, something hard and scaly that whipped around to meet her.

Gabrielle scurried around the tree again, recognizing Benjamin. She managed a stuttered, half-relieved breath before his claw gripped the tree and her, wrapping around her waist and the trunk together, cutting into her skin. A stifled cry fell from her lips.

Benjamin stepped around the tree, wrapped his other claw around just her, and picked her up, growling.

Gabrielle's body was slick with sweat from the inferno the dragons had created. In vain, she tugged at the claws holding her, but Benjamin only clutched tighter, causing her to gasp in pain.

His eyes narrowed, and he began crunching her in earnest.

Gabrielle felt the cuts in her skin dig a little deeper, but the pressure on her waist also increased, making it hard to breathe. She was choking at the waist, her ribs moving together and insides compressing in ways they should not. She could barely hear the crack amidst all the chaos, but Gabrielle felt it. The rib had snapped.

She became dragon.

Benjamin dropped her, unable to contain an entire dragon in his claws.

Valencia, he mouthed. Perhaps he had spoken it.

Gabrielle's side was burning, but she could breathe. She changed back to being human, counting on Benjamin's surprise to keep her safe for a few moments.

"Sana, sana, sana," she muttered, the pain almost disappearing entirely. She wished to feel her sides and inspect whether or not the rib had truly healed or needed more precise magic, but Benjamin's muscles tensed. She morphed back to dragon, his claw hitting her leg instead of her head.

"Changeling," he hissed.

She threw her hand up and at his throat, a defensive move Davey had taught her . . . only she had claws instead of hands.

The claw pierced underneath his jaw, through the back of his mouth.

He choked.

Blood gathered around the edges of the wound, his head heavy upon her claw. Her claw came out with a sickly, squelching slide. An inordinate amount of blood streamed for a few short seconds from his head.

He collapsed, convulsing on the ground.

With the roars, with the thundering, it was silent.

She backed away slowly, bumping into trees in the process.

A coppery dragon roared past her, glaring at Gabrielle in disapproval but not noticing the dragon dying, dying.

Dead.

A small figure darted across the space between Gabrielle and the corpse, noting the dead dragon and scampering past, then turning and catching sight of Gabrielle, stopping in her tracks.

Gabrielle lunged forward.

Danielle dove out of the way.

Gabrielle merely plucked Danielle from the ground and beat her wings, the fire swelling at the edges of the gusts she created. She flew higher into the air, unevenly, unused to the odd fusion of her collarbone. One of her sides ached. She had not healed her rib completely.

Eventually, she felt safe enough in her sky isolation to face the blazing pandemonium, find the river, and follow it several miles up before dipping lower and setting Danielle down. Or something close to setting. Perhaps it was a bit more like dropping from three feet in the air.

Gabrielle flew above the forest again, surveying the damage and continued attack. Davey and Drew no longer called. There was no sign of movement aside from the dragons.

One particular dragon caught her eye, a dark green one who was silently striding amongst the trees, not breathing fire, roaring, nor making other general racket.

Charlene turned a moment before Gabrielle reached the ground.

"Evening, Valencia," Charlene greeted her, eyes gleaming, her voice smooth and melodic like her brother's, but containing an edge.

"Evening?" Gabrielle asked. "With all this light from the fires one could almost believe it day."

Charlene laughed gently. "Your tongue is so silver, my dear, silver and sharp. Do not worry. We shall find the humans. By flame or by sunlight."

"Must you?"

"Must we not?"

Gabrielle paused, Charlene pausing with her. The two of them eyed each other.

"Why must you?" Gabrielle asked at last.

Charlene straightened. "The humans killed my—"

"And the dragons killed many of the humans." Gabrielle tensed her muscles as Charlene growled. Gabrielle continued anyway. "How is killing them going to stop the bloodshed? That's just going to continue the war."

"Only the magic-haters can end it, and they end it only once they die," Charlene challenged, raising her jaw.

Gabrielle lowered hers, an appeal. "'Tis not true, and you know it."

"'Tis only little girls and old men who believe that. We are neither. Leave here, Valencia. Leave this fight."

Gabrielle shook her head, jaw set. "This is my fight."

"Do not be foolish, my dear. I have instructed you little, letting you choose yourself, but don't be foolish. Leave."

"I will leave once you do."

Charlene stared at her, eyes dark and unyielding.

Gabrielle did not comply.

Dragons thundered past. One or two slunk.

The fires died down.

Coolness returned to the night air.

"You have distracted me long enough." With that, Charlene stretched her wings and went skyward, set in her ways for another night.

Gabrielle let out a sigh, breath puffing up in cool air. After a few minutes, she took to the sky as well.

"That was totally cool!"

She spun in the air.

Victoria and the same two pearl white dragons from before were flying towards her. All three were flapping furiously, eager and excited.

"Were you girls watching?" Gabrielle asked.

"Of course!" one of the lighter dragons jumped in. "We didn't want to miss the fun!"

"Mom wouldn't let us join, though," the other pearl dragon tried to speak glumly, but was much more out of breath than the other dragons and gasped the words instead.

"How long were you there?" Gabrielle asked.

Victoria shrugged. "I dunno. For a while. We knew they were going to attack because they told Vivian to tell everyone that they had gotten out of the castle but weren't supposed to be attacked because they were going to ambush them in the middle of the woods in the middle of the night and try to kill all the humans because they got the princess and Charlene thinks that the prince actually did come because Vivian saw him leading the way even though there were older humans there."

"We—they were spotted," Gabrielle sighed, eyes drifting close for a moment.

"Yeah, they were," Victoria rambled on, not noticing Gabrielle's slip. "Vivian told Benjamin because he is her husband and Benjamin told Charlene because Benjamin works with Charlene and doesn't like the humans, too, and then Charlene told Vivian to tell everyone to *back off* until the right time when they all attack together. That didn't work out so good, though, huh, because they heard them coming and split up like that, right? I don't think they expected that because they said it would be super, super dangerous, and everyone would end up super, super dead."

"Not every human," the pearl dragon who had not been out of breath pointed out.

Victoria turned to her, "Yeah, technically, but . . ."

Gabrielle stopped paying attention to the growing argument to take stock of her surroundings. Their group was far enough away from the former campsite and close enough to the sea to be out of the way for the dragons who were leaving the area. She wondered if a few dedicated dragons would stay even longer to try and find her friends and parents.

"I'm dying!" the other white dragon burst out in a breathy voice, interrupting all. "Can we please land?!"

"You have no air, Heather," the slightly larger pearl dragon rolled her eyes.

"We can show her our cave!" Victoria exclaimed excitedly.

"I do, too, have air!" Heather argued. She flew closer to the other pearl dragon and puffed in her face. pearl

The other dragon blew at Heather, sparks flying with the mini gust.

Heather was unprepared and stumbled backwards.

"Not fair!" Heather cried, voice rising in pitch due to lack of air and anger. "You know I don't like fire!"

"I didn't even use any flames," the other dragon rolled her eyes again. "You're such a wimp."

"I'm the same as you!"

"On the outside only."

"You have a head of *hot* air!"

"Better than an empty head."

"Come on!" Victoria interrupted them, jerking her head towards some cliffs alongside the sea's edge. She turned to Gabrielle. "Do you want to see our cave?"

Gabrielle sent another look towards the dark earth. She would be unlikely to find anyone tonight, not without scrying she supposed, and how could she give up this opportunity?

"I'd love to."

"Race you," the pearl dragon challenged Heather.

They were sisters, Gabrielle belatedly recalled from her conversation with Victoria outside the castle of Ancora. The pearl white dragons were sisters.

"I need a head start!"

"You really think that's going to help?"

The two dragons took off, Heather immediately behind her sister. Heather beat her wings faster and faster, but Gabrielle noticed that she did so awkwardly, not taking advantage of the wind currents. Heather's sister was much more adept, exerting considerably less energy to maintain a steady lead. Heather's sister could have increased her lead, but she chose to stay close though always well ahead.

Victoria hung back with Gabrielle, who followed the pair at a more leisurely pace. They headed towards the coast. The girls had traveled quite a distance over the past few days.

"Do you travel the entire island?" Gabrielle asked.

"We don't go to human territory," Victoria told her in a tone that it made it obvious that Gabrielle should have known this.

"I mean, do you travel across all of dragon territory?"

"Heather and Ruby and I usually stay on this side of the river but we go back and forth between the broods sometimes but not always because tis fun but we usually stay on this side of the island," Victoria explained.

"Where is your mother? Were other dragons watching?" Gabrielle asked.

"Mum's at home," Victoria informed her brightly. "Technically," she hesitated, "we didn't exactly specifically ask if we could come and watch."

"You did go home after we talked, right?" Gabrielle asked, surprised at her own concern.

"Yeah! It's just that we *just* got ungrounded and I really didn't want to get grounded again and I knew Mom would say no if I asked and so I didn't ask because then she couldn't tell me no."

"Was anybody else watching with you?"

"No. Everybody else said they didn't want to see it. They said it didn't matter and they didn't want any part in it but we weren't planning on doing anything, you know? And we didn't. We stayed back and didn't do anything and just watched, but, claw and talon! You did a lot of things! We saw you fly away with someone and were confused because we thought that you were going to kill them which didn't make sense because you didn't sound like you hated the humans but then you dropped it somewhere up there and then came back and we lost sight of you. But then we saw you by Charlene and you guys weren't talking or anything, just looking at each other really weirdly and we watched that for a while and then we realized that everyone else was watching you guys, too! Isn't that weird?! Everything was super weird."

While Victoria chattered, they drew nearer and nearer to

the cliffs, going past and out to sea, then swooping back to view the rock face. Caves and crevices covered the expansive wall. Gabrielle presumed Heather and Ruby had already disappeared into one of them.

"Is this part of the brood?" she asked Victoria.

"Yeah. This is one part of it. The other part of this brood is closer to the swamp and the rocs, but only older kids go by the rocs because the younger dragons get taken when they're not careful. Older dragons can, too, but the younger ones don't pay much attention and do really stupid stuff."

Victoria went nearer to the cliff and then tucked her wings and neatly flew into a smaller-sized hole, opening up her wings once she was inside. She dipped downwards and disappeared.

Gabrielle hovered outside a moment, sure she would shear off her wings if she tried that. Instead, she scrabbled for a hold on the ledge and crawled in, squeezing her wings close to herself. A few feet in, she could tell that the cave had widened, so she released some of the tension in her shoulders. The ground dropped from beneath her with her next step, and she fell through a hole in the cave. Sensing air around her, Gabrielle snapped her wings out, incrementally slowing her descent, but still heavily landing on the floor.

Victoria, Heather, and Ruby were dispersed throughout the room, but Gabrielle's attention was diverted as she caught sight of what was in the cavern.

Plows, boards, chairs, cups, saucers, tapestries, gold coins, statues, clothes, diamonds, emeralds, books, a glowing spherical object, mirrors, brushes, opals, pitchforks – the entire area was covered and filled with a wide variety of items, many of which were usually never seen together. A shop sign leaned up against a dusty throne. Books with strange lettering lay stacked atop an anvil. On the far side of the room, several statues were situated in a way that indicated they might have been played with, clothes draped over the stone. One figurine —possibly a long-gone king—had a stern expression, a bushy brow, a pink satin dress bunched around his neck like a scarf, and several blue and white shifts tied around his chest and legs. Another statue, this one of a queen, had socks on her delicately crafted hands and arms, a pair of working bibs tied around her neck and hanging in front of her like an apron, and a corn-husk doll strapped to her back with a few long, lacy curtains.

Next to the statues were a pile of blankets, more clothes, wall hangings, bed sheets, and the like, all mixed together and forming a sort of nest. Circling slowly, Gabrielle saw more mounds and stacks of the hodgepodge of items, some clearly used recently, other piles collecting dust. And there were books. Books everywhere.

"Do you like it?" Victoria eagerly asked, running up to Gabrielle as she finished surveying the room.

"Where did all this come from?" Gabrielle asked.

"We collected it," Heather piped up, sorting through a crate.

"Me and Victoria collected it," Ruby corrected.

"I helped, too!" Heather protested.

"Looking through our treasures afterwards does not count as helping." Ruby shot her down.

"I distracted Mom!" Heather argued.

"Like the time when you distracted her right to our location?"

"You guys never tell me when you're going out!"

"Yeah, cause you 'distract' Mom to wherever we're going, and we get in trouble."

"That's not how you use the word distract!" Heather yelled.

"That's how you do it!" her sister yelled back.

"Fiddlesticks!" Victoria shouted out.

"That's not going to work this time," Ruby snidely told Victoria.

"Jumping Jillies! Claustrophobic elephants!"

Heather snickered. "Claustrophobic elephants?"

"That's the best kind." Victoria nodded sagely.

"What do you mean?" Gabrielle was very, very confused.

Ruby rolled her eyes. "Victoria hates to argue, and she hates it when we argue. So now she just yells random words whenever we start to and tries to distract us. It's absolutely ridiculous."

"Then why does it work?" Victoria challenged.

"It doesn't," Ruby sassed. "I'm still mad at Heather."

"But you're not yelling at me," Heather pointed out.

"Give me two seconds. I'm catching my breath."

"Why'd you let it go?" Gabrielle asked cheekily, unable to help herself.

"What?" Heather looked at her.

"Nothing. Why did you guys collect all of this? From where did you gather it?"

Victoria shrugged. "Everywhere. We go to the old villages and stuff and get stuff from there. Sometimes we find stuff in the woods."

"One time, we stole some stuff from some redcaps." Ruby's eyes gleamed with pride.

"You ran across redcaps in the woods, refused to fly away, and Mum had to come and save you. She killed some of the redcaps, and you took two daggers and a curved knife thing that the dead redcaps had on them. You were all beaten up and had cuts all over you," Heather corrected her sister.

"Who asked you?" Ruby snapped.

"Truth. Truth and honesty and—" Heather began in a lofty voice before her sister pounced on her. The two rolled away shrieking and growling at each other.

Gabrielle raised her eyes in alarm and looked to Victoria, who seemed completely unconcerned.

"Do they normally do that?" Gabrielle asked.

"Of course. Don't you have any brothers or sisters?" Victoria looked at her in surprise.

"No," Gabrielle replied, "I'm an only child. Do you?"

"Yeah, but he's like three months old and doesn't understand *anything*. It's super annoying. The only nice thing is that I get away with more because Mom is so busy with him and the other babies."

"What about your dad?"

"He travels a whole lot," Victoria stated, trying to pick up a fork that had fallen in a small crack. Human hands would have easily been able to grasp it, but her claws posed a problem.

"Travels for what?"

"He's a Messenger."

"A messenger?"

"Don't you know anything?" Victoria questioned her, ignoring the fork and focusing on Gabrielle. "*Everybody* knows what a Messenger is."

"I am just interested to hear how you would explain it," Gabrielle clarified. She had to be more careful.

"He travels throughout the entire island delivering messages. You know, like if I wanted to tell Mum that Heather is dead because Ruby killed her but Mum was on the other side of the island and I didn't want to go, I could send a Messenger to tell her for me. Messengers get to hear *everything* that goes on and they go *everywhere*. I'm going to be one when I grow up."

Gabrielle was intrigued, not by the idea of the Messenger, but by the idea that dragons had this system. "What does your mom do?"

"She's a Caretaker," Victoria stated.

"How would you describe that in your own words?" Gabrielle asked, smiling.

Victoria laughed, but she was clearly enamored with Gabrielle's regard. "Mum takes care of the baby dragons. She takes the really little ones."

"What do the parents of those baby dragons do?"

"Something else," Victoria answered. "Some are Messengers, but there are Hunters, Protectors, Healers. . . ." She paused, eyes glittering. "There are Explorers, too. Did you hear about Geronimo?"

"I have not."

"What cave have you been in?" Victoria exclaimed.

"Geronimo is the Explorer who just returned from the eastern sea. He's said he's been to the Isle!"

"The isle?"

"Seriously? Do you ever get out?" She snickered. "You must be related to Thomas. *The Isle.* You know, the one and only isle that no one ever returns to?"

Gabrielle smiled and laughed. "Right, that isle, and Geronimo has returned from it."

"Yeah, which has, like, never happened before, so everyone's been asking what he saw but he hasn't told anyone anything yet. Where are you from?"

"I . . . live near the line between dragon and human territory. My family mostly keeps to themselves," if one didn't count running a tavern and inn, "and we don't travel much," which was entirely correct, especially when considering travel by sea.

"Yeah, I'm totally excited to learn what's on the Isle. You wanna see something cool?" Victoria abruptly changed subjects again.

"Of course!" Gabrielle exclaimed, imitating Victoria, who stayed oblivious.

Ruby and Heather had gotten distracted and quit tussling on the ground. They were rummaging through the crate Heather had been looking through before.

Victoria led Gabrielle over to the other side of the room, towards a small heap of books positioned on and around the anvil.

"These are all mine," Victoria gestured at the books.

"Oh." Gabrielle had not expected that. She leaned in closer

to examine the books. One or two looked like spell books, the ones on the anvil she could not read, but most were what one would expect: a child's tale, chronicles of the kings, medical books, books of herbs and other plants, and books regarding animals, some concerning magical creatures. There was a plethora of different sizes and subjects. "Do you read them?"

"Of course!" Victoria said indignantly. "It's kind of hard because of, you know, claws, but if you go real slow and real careful, you can read them. I haven't read all of them, but I've read most. This one's my favourite." She gently slid the books around, treating each with obvious reverence, pulling out one that she held up for Gabrielle to read.

"*The Personal Journals of Queen Galene*," Gabrielle read.

"Nobody else cares about those stupid books!" Ruby yelled from across the room, both sisters no longer digging through the crate and now out of view.

"You just say that because you can't read worth a scale!"

"There's no reason to read. It's useless."

Victoria stuck her tongue out at where Ruby's voice was coming from. "She can read!" Victoria shouted, indicating Gabrielle.

"Whatever," Ruby called back, not seeing Victoria's gesture but still seeming to understand to whom Victoria had been referring.

"Do other dragons read?" Gabrielle asked. Reading was a rare skill among villagers.

"Not really," Victoria told her, snout scrunched. "Their dad knows how to. I still think it's cool, though. Henry and Galene and Adelmar and Oliver and all these different people can tell me all these different things that I know nothing about and it's super interesting and cool and I don't even have to talk to anybody! It's like having a whole bunch of people telling you their story without ever having to go and meet them."

"I bet most of those humans are dead!" Ruby interjected from across the room.

"Imaginary infants!"

"Now she's mad," Heather commented.

"Make way, make way!" Ruby announced, stepping out from behind the piles she and Heather had been hiding behind. Ruby wore a bedsheet around her neck and a large bowl on her head. Her back claws were piercing too small boots, and her front claws carried a bucket of utensils and a long, wooden lance. She stood tall and proud, cleared her throat, and declared, "Your king comes!"

Getting out of the way, Ruby made room for Heather to step out.

Heather was even more oddly dressed with precious stones balanced precariously upon her head and horseshoes, washing racks, and other metal items dangling in front of her body. One of her claws grasped a rusty and dirt-encrusted sword.

"It's armor!" Gabrielle realized.

"Yes, professionally done," Ruby said proudly, patting a washing rack hanging on Heather.

"I'm the king," Heather intoned in a low voice, coughing because she went a little deeper than she was able. "Blah, blah, blah, kill the dragons!"

"Yes, your high-nice," Ruby replied, bowing so deeply that

her "hat", the bowl, started falling. Her hand and the bucket of utensils flew up to stop it. Forks and spoons got flung out of the bucket, a few hitting Heather who tried ducking out of the way.

Instead, Heather tripped over a crate and came clanging to the floor, armor completely disheveled.

Ruby's back snapped up straight. "It's the dragons' fault, your sigh-air!" She pointed at Victoria and Gabrielle, the bowl slipping over her eyes. She dropped the bucket and lance, yanked off the bowl, and charged towards them, the bedsheet flapping wildly behind her, the boots getting wedged further onto her claws.

Gabrielle backed up.

Victoria growled and rushed towards Ruby. The girls met each other near the middle of the room, colliding and getting twisted and rolled up in the bedsheet.

Heather was struggling to take off her armor, getting frustrated and starting to cry.

Gabrielle tried not to smile as she observed the chaos. She went over to Heather and began cutting the strings that had gotten twisted around her. It looked like the strings had simply connected two items that had hung over Heather's shoulder—one item in back, one item in front. However, during her fall and subsequent panic, the strings had gotten twisted under her wings and around her neck.

"Ruby doesn't like cutting them!" Heather sobbed, claws tugging at the strings around her neck. "It takes too long to redo them!"

"Well, Ruby does not have the strings around her neck," Gabrielle countered, not hesitating in the least to break them and the others wound around Heather, though Gabrielle looked for ways to avoid breaking them once the most uncomfortable strings were gone. They were so light that Gabrielle believed that the thought of the strings around herself frightened Heather more than the actual feeling.

"You're dead, king!" Victoria shouted, standing on top of Ruby.

"Dead! Dead! Dead and gone!" Ruby dramatically stretched out her limbs, then dropped them and let her head roll to one side, tongue lolling out of her mouth.

Victoria raised her head and breathed fire into the air, a dragon celebrating the death of the human beneath its claws.

Gabrielle's skin crawled.

"Victoria!" a voice shouted, coming from the entrance to the cave.

All three girls froze, looks of terror on their faces.

"I could hear you in there, Victoria! And ye, too, Ruby and Heather! Get out here this instant!"

The girls looked at each other, assessing the situation and desperately trying to think of a way out of confronting whoever's mother was out there.

"Hello?" the voice called.

"We're not here!" Heather said in a panicked voice.

"Gah!" Ruby yelled. "You don't answer, Heather! You don't answer!"

"Get out here now! I'm not going to be happy if I have to come in!"

Ruby made faces at Heather. "You go first, traitor."

"Technically, she's not a traitor because she didn't mean to give us up it's just that she didn't think and answered when she should've not said anything," Victoria commented.

"Now!"

Afraid to keep the mother waiting, Victoria flew up first while the other girls scrambled to take off their costumes.

"What is that clanging?" Gabrielle heard the dragon ask.

"What clanging?" Victoria answered.

Gabrielle shook with silent laughter as another washboard fell to the ground.

"Are you coming?" Heather asked, looking to Gabrielle.

Gabrielle hesitated. It would look more suspicious if she tried to hide in the girls' cavern than come out. Gabrielle nodded, then followed Ruby and Heather as they ascended and left the cave.

Squeezing through the tight entrance, Gabrielle fell a short ways before whipping out her wings and regaining her height. Before the entrance to the cave hovered Marie, the silvery dragon who had defended the girls from Davey and Drew.

"Hello," Marie said, pausing in the tirade she had been giving the girls.

"Hello." Gabrielle forced herself not to fidget.

"Marie, Caretaker, mother of Jakob, Ruby, Heather, Aeneas, and Stephan, wife of William, Rememberer," Marie listed off.

Gabrielle tried not to appear nervous as she answered, hesitating before she did, but then deciding to go with the name Charlene had dubbed her. "Valencia, daughter of Timothy and Marie . . . a different Marie," she added quickly. She stopped there, unable to recall the rest.

Marie almost squinted, but then she visibly relaxed her face. She sent a cool look towards Victoria, Ruby, and Heather. "I hope my girls were not bothering you."

"No, ma'am, not at all. They were just being very hospitable and showing me their cavern," Gabrielle hastily defended them.

At that, Marie did squint. "Do you live around here, Valencia?"

"No, ma'am."

"I didn't think so." Marie frowned. "You've made quite a few waves in the past few days, yet no one has heard anything about you before. I assume you are far from home. Would you like to stay in the brood for a night?"

Gabrielle's immediate reaction was to reject her offer, but then she considered it. Chances were she would not be able to find her friends and parents tonight. Perhaps if she scried she could, but the idea of spending a night in the company of dragons who were not trying to kill her was appealing. Besides, everyone should be fine for one night.

But what if it was a trap?

"There are some dragons who wish to kill me." She winced at her own bluntness.

"I am not one of them, and I let none kill my guests," Marie replied with a hint of a smile. "You shall have nothing to fear if you stay with us."

"It would be a pleasure, ma'am," Gabrielle accepted, heart beating faster.

"Follow me," Marie invited Gabrielle, sparing a moment to give a hard look to her children and Victoria. "Ye are coming home. This is not over."

Marie flew higher and parallel to the sea. The girls followed.

Gabrielle took a steadying breath. Anxious butterflies fluttered in her gut. She shook her head and joined them.

They went just a little farther along the cliff, perhaps half a mile or so, before Marie turned into a cave easily large enough for two dragons to fly in side by side. She dropped to the floor and began walking.

Gabrielle followed her model, walking right behind her, gazing in wonder at the walls. At first, only scorch marks appeared to mar them, but then Gabrielle saw the intricately designed patterns and shapes burned onto the stone with varying degrees of intensity, adding shading and depth. Mountains, roses, a map of the island, spears, swords, towns, fire, and—of course—dragons. Some of the scorches had been completed over carved rock that matched the image, adding relief and even greater perspective. One painstakingly carved relief of a dragon labeled with a large "A" to his side had individual scales etched onto his face, his body disappearing into the rock.

"I made that one," Victoria told her proudly, pointing at what Gabrielle assumed to be a self-portrait. "It's a firebreath of Hartburg."

"Is Hartburg your friend?"

Marie chuckled, and the three younger dragons laughed out loud.

Gabrielle smiled nervously.

"Oh, yeah!" Victoria said enthusiastically and sarcastically. "Him and I go on trips together *all* the time and have a totally awesome time and we talk about humans and such and it's great."

"And you and Hartburg and you eat humans!" Heather interjected.

"Hartburg never ate humans," Victoria corrected her.

"Yeah, he did," Ruby disagreed.

"Your dad says otherwise, and he says that the rumors are wrong, and Hartburg never even harmed a human," Victoria said.

"Well, Dad's wrong," Ruby stated flatly.

"Your dad is a Rememberer!" Victoria snapped. "He's not wrong!"

"Just cause he's a Rememberer doesn't make him always right."

"Of course you'd say that because you always disagree cause you're always wrong," Heather piped up.

"Girls!" Marie snapped. "That's enough!"

Gabrielle glanced behind to see Ruby puffing up her cheeks at Heather. Heather was grinding her teeth in frustration. Victoria seemed to be ignoring them both.

The tunnel suddenly widened into a large cavern, ten or eleven more tunnels splitting off around the edges and ceiling. Off to one side on the ground lay a pile of old dragon claws, scuffed and marked up, some of them with etchings twisting around them. In other crevices, smaller piles of claws resided, and carved chunks of wood and rock in addition to a wide variety of scales lay scattered about as well, some affixed to each other and other materials in elaborate contraptions that Gabrielle did not immediately understand the function of.

"I apologize about the mess," Marie told Gabrielle, sparing

a second to send another hard look at the girls. "A few fletch-lings were supposed to clean up after everyone before going to bed, but cried that they were tired and got out of it. Tired enough to avoid cleaning, but not tired enough to miss out on sneaking out."

"Mom—" Ruby began.

"No. I don't want to hear it. Go to the lower ledges, and I better not see scale or tooth of you before morning. Go. Now."

Ruby and Heather sighed.

"Sorry, Draconis Marie," Victoria apologized sweetly.

"Thank you. Now go to lower ledges."

The three of them stumbled their way to the third off-branching, one with a downward incline. All three made it seem as if the act of walking away was physically ailing them.

Heather mumbled, "Good night, Valencia," as she went past.

"Draconis Valencia," her mother corrected. "You need to show some respect, young flyer."

Marie waited until they were out of sight, then turned back to Gabrielle. "I am so sorry about that."

"'Tis all right. They were no bother."

"Do you need something to eat? Drink? Is there anything I can get you?" Marie offered Gabrielle.

"Thank you, but I am all right."

"I am afraid everyone else is already asleep or out, or I would introduce you. Valencia—" Marie cut herself off, smil-ing suddenly and awkwardly. "You are probably very tired after tonight's events. I apologize for keeping you. Would you like me to show you your cavern?"

"That would be wonderful, thank you." This was an odd reversal of nights at the inn.

"This way," Marie invited, stretching her wings and flying up to one of the exits in the ceiling.

Gabrielle followed after a brief hesitation. The exit did not lead to a single ledge, but became a shaft with multiple large crevices scooped out of the sides, each miniature cave around thirty to forty feet deep and twenty feet wide, inside some of which Gabrielle could make out large rising and falling mounds of rock—sleeping dragons. They passed ten or so lodgings before Marie landed in an empty cavern. Gabrielle set down beside her.

"Does this satisfy you?" Marie asked.

"Yes, thank you," Gabrielle replied immediately.

Marie smiled. "Don't worry. None here will harm you, and I will let none enter who would. You are safe. Do you need anything before you rest?"

"No, ma'am, thank you."

Marie cocked her head slightly, smile tightening the smallest amount. She nodded, then turned to depart. She stopped suddenly, facing Gabrielle again, a question upon her lips.

Gabrielle waited, not wishing Marie to feel uncomfortable, but not wishing the question even more.

After an awkward pause, Marie just smiled again and left.

Gabrielle breathed a sigh of relief, releasing tension she had not known she was holding. She rolled her aching shoulders, then stretched out her leg, remembering that Benjamin had hit her. A few the scales were chipped, and the area was sore in general. A sharp pain still thrummed in her chest as well.

She shook off the thoughts. It wouldn't help to dwell. Lifting her head, she examined the walls of the room. As before, she needed no light to make out her surroundings. Although they were undeniably dim, she could still see every rock and indent clearly. If she had one of Victoria's books, she probably could have read.

The walls of the room were less hodge-podge than the ones of the tunnel she, the girls, and Marie had used to enter the network of caves and caverns. Everywhere she looked, she saw kelpies or water-related scenes. A few beautiful women and men decked the walls as well, presumably kelpies in human form. Their long hair often flowed into a waterfall that ended with a pile of rocks on the floor or a river from which another kelpie sprang. The walls were also less crowded than the tunnels with plenty of open space for new firebreaths.

Gabrielle puffed a little smoke, contemplating trying to make some firebreaths, but now that she was alone, exhaustion tugged on her. Despite the fact that she had never slept as a dragon and that she had never slept on rock, both were looking like fairly desirable options.

Before she went to bed though, she wanted to check on her family and friends. She stared at the entrance to her own little cave for a minute, then changed. She had no mirror, she had no water, she had no even slightly reflective surface, yet she wanted to at least try to scry them. Gabrielle began looking for a rock in order to pay the price right away, but then realised that she would not know where to put the blood. Perhaps she would have to just pay with her energy as she scried, as Thomas implied that more experienced scryers did.

Closing her eyes, she thought of her mother. Both her mother and Danielle enjoyed each other's company considerably. Nevertheless, she had the feeling that Danielle enjoyed almost anyone's company—except Davey's of course. Danielle had insistently teased and prodded and poked her brother since being rescued, dumping water on him, making sly side comments concerning rocks purportedly in his head, throwing sand in his direction, and outright insulting him.

Gabrielle felt herself smile and nearly lost her balance as she swayed on her feet. She plopped down, eyes still closed.

Danielle loved Davey. Gabrielle felt a sudden, intense longing for a love such as that. Mackenzie had laughed and played with Gabrielle as if they were sisters, braiding each other's hair, eating at each other's houses. Keeping each other's secrets. After Seron had burnt to the ground, Gabrielle's family and Mr. Henry were the only ones to return among the few who had survived. More families eventually settled near them, building the village up as it was today. However, no girls Gabrielle's age had come. Gabrielle had devoted most of her energy to helping her parents, and the inn and tavern had consumed much of everybody's time.

Danielle was a reminder.

Mackenzie was braiding Gabrielle's hair, then Gabrielle Mackenzie's.

Danielle giggled beside them. She playfully pushed Mackenzie.

Gabrielle felt Mackenzie's hair slide through her fingers as Mackenzie picked up a large bucket of chicken feathers and threw them at Danielle, laughing with her mouth open, collapsing to the ground in giggles as some of the feathers flew in her own mouth.

Danielle unleashed another bucketful into the air.

Gabrielle grabbed her own bucket and added even more feathers into the melee. The girls fell to the ground, barely able to draw breaths between their shrieks of laughter, feathers sticking to their mouths.

Gabrielle drifted off to sleep, head upon a rock, mind full of feathers, smiling into the darkness.

XIV

How to Eat Raw Rabbit

A tremendous roar shook the ground.

Gabrielle bolted upright, hands scraping along rock. Before her towered a dragon with pointed scales and a small tear in his right wing. Her breath froze in its place. The dragon's back was turned to her, but all he had to do was twist his head a little to the side to spot her in her human form. Gabrielle dared not let the air around her stir.

"Benedict!" a dragon on the other side of the pointed-scale one yelled, sounding like she could be the one who had roared. "I told you never to wake me like that again!"

"I didn't wake you!" Benedict, the dragon in front of Gabrielle, protested.

Gabrielle thought about scooting deeper into the cave, but there were too many loose stones and pebbles scattered about, and he was too close for her to take the risk. She unwillingly let a thin, steady stream of air get sucked in through her nose, hoping that the noise was silent enough.

Benjamin shifted to the side, and the rocks underneath him grated slightly.

"You imbecile! You idiot! Yes, you did! You just wait till I tell Draconis Marie!"

"There is no need to tell me." A soft voice carried from the bottom of the shaft.

"Drac—"

"Benedict. Down here. Now. Same with you, Rebekah."

Gabrielle instinctively fell back as Benedict raised his wings and dropped down the shaft, giving Gabrielle a good look at Rebekah, who was in a cave across the shaft.

Rebekah was wound up enough she did not even notice the movement. Vexed, she plunged down after him, literally steaming.

Gabrielle let out a little breath of air, chest rising and falling rapidly for a few seconds as her heart beat wildly. Pausing only a second in surprise, she changed. Her breath came easier.

"We have a guest," Marie reprimanded the dragons.

"A guest? Is it a Messenger? An Explorer? A Protector?" Benedict said.

"A guest that you just awoke with your antics . . ." Marie's voice faded out of hearing as their group descended into the main cavern and away from the shaft's entrance.

Gabrielle looked around the cave, feeling much more refreshed after a night's rest . . . if it was morning. She could not tell in the cave. She blinked her eyes more out of habit than the need to awaken herself. Coming within a claw-swipe of death really revives one in the morning.

Gabrielle decided against trying to scry again. While she highly doubted that she would be tired enough to foolishly fall asleep in human form, the possibility of someone flying past and spotting her was present and the risk too high. Eyes scanning the kelpies singed on the wall one last time, she, too, flew out of the cave and down to the main chamber.

Gabrielle snapped her wings and hovered high in the air, right near the ceiling, upon entering the main cavern. What had been empty save a few toys the night before was now packed full of dragons. Most of them looked to be between eight and thirteen years old, if Gabrielle had to guess from what she estimated Victoria, Heather, and Ruby's ages to be, but older dragons bustled among the younger dragons, breaking up disputes and generally supervising. In total, Gabrielle would estimate that twenty-five dragons filled the room.

A fully grown male dragon with blood-red scales glided in through the main entrance, two chimeras dangling from his claws. The noise level in the cavern shot upward, the older dragons shushing the clamoring younger ones, many of whom were crying, "Dracon Michael! Dracon Michael!"

Dracon Michael did not even glance at the dragons, just dropped the chimeras and swooped back out without waiting to see the response.

The younger dragons pounced on the chimeras, but the older dragons pulled the younger ones back and somehow organized the chaos. Little rings of dragons situated themselves throughout the room, each group circling around a piece of the animals. Hums and crunches filled the cavern.

Off to the side, below Gabrielle, for she had unconsciously drifted nearer to a wall, Draconis Marie still berated Benedict and Rebekah.

Gabrielle kept her eyes on Draconis Marie, considering drawing nearer in order that Draconis Marie might see and direct her.

The noise quieted gradually, the crunches diminishing noticeably. Draconis Marie abruptly stopped rebuking the children and surveyed the cavern.

Gabrielle did the same.

Most eyes were on her. The dragons still talked but in whispers, most of the mutterings containing the name Charlene had christened her.

Gabrielle could now easily hear her own wingbeats.

"Good morning, Valencia," Draconis Marie called to her.

Gabrielle joined Marie on the ground, trying to ignore the ripples of whispering she made.

"Good morning," Gabrielle replied in a soft voice.

"Would you like some food? The Hunters are beginning to return," Draconis Marie offered.

"Do you want some of my chimera?" Heather asked from behind Gabrielle, her voice ringing out of the rising and falling murmurs.

Gabrielle turned, regretting that decision as soon as she did so.

Heather had a chimera leg in her claws. Broken tendons protruded. Silvery fat strips gleamed. Dark, red muscle canvased a half-hidden bone.

"Valencia can have some of my chimera!" an even younger male dragon with light brown scales spoke up, a long, thin strand of tendon tenaciously clinging from his mouth down his neck, moist meat sticking to scales. The fletchling noticed Gabrielle's gaze, stuck his tongue out of the side of his mouth, lodged his tongue underneath the trailing tissue, wrapped his tongue around the tissue, and sucked the tendon in with a loud, wet slurp. Then his blood-stained mouth curved into an eager, hopeful grin.

Her stomach churned.

"Where are your manners, Andrew? There was no need for that," Marie reprimanded him, then instructed them both. "Go back to your circles and quit bothering Draconis Valencia."

Andrew and Heather returned to their groups subdued, Gabrielle trying not to listen to the snaps and crunches and smacking anymore.

A golden dragon flew in, one obviously much older and one everyone loved even more than Dracon Michael.

As the cheers of greeting died down and the volume of the cavern resumed what Gabrielle assumed to be normal, the light gold dragon with scuffed, worn scales and three rabbits dangling from his claws flew to Gabrielle and Marie.

"Good morning, Dracon Liam," Marie greeted him warmly, eyes smiling.

"Good morning, Dracon Liam," Rebekah promptly added.

"Hey." Benedict nodded.

Marie glared at him.

"Sorry. Hey, Dracon Liam." Benedict nodded again.

Marie sighed.

"Good morning, Marie, Rebekah, Benedict, Valencia," Dracon Liam genially replied to their greetings.

"You may go and eat now," Marie dismissed Rebekah and Benedict.

Dracon Liam made to toss one of the rabbits at them as they passed, both of them looking up eagerly.

Draconis Marie shot them another look, but Dracon Liam pleaded for them, "Just one, Marie. Just one?"

Marie shook her head and sighed as Dracon Liam smiled, threw a rabbit at each of them, and then laughed over their delight.

"I thought you said one?" Marie unsuccessfully tried to frown.

"Yes, one each."

"Ah, Liam, you are too nice to them," Draconis Marie said, smiling all the while.

"They are good young flyers, Marie. You know, I remember when you were that age. Marie was a true spitfire," Dracon Liam told Gabrielle, eyes twinkling. "So much so that her actual nickname was Spitfire. She was a rabble-rouser, too! She'd stand outside caverns or around corners and tell people what to do as if she were someone else. Why, I remember this one time—"

"Dracon Liam, perhaps—" Draconis Marie began, but Dracon Liam interrupted her interruption.

"Oh, shush. Let me at least tell one story." He focused back on enthralling Gabrielle with his tale. "One time, she pretended to be Royale and told the Hunters to gather extra food for guests that night. There were no guests, but all the fletchlings had a feast!"

"If I recall, you did not complain," Marie reminded Dracon Liam.

"Twas food! What was there to complain about?"

Gabrielle laughed. She had found a draconic Drew.

"We have not yet even done introductions," Marie tsked. "I apologise, Valencia. Valencia, this is Liam, Hunter, son of Elijah and Charlotte. Liam, this is Valencia, daughter of Marie and . . ."

"Timothy," Gabrielle supplied, supposing it safer to go with what she had originally stated.

"Tis a pleasure to have your acquaintance, Valencia." Dracon Liam nodded.

"Tis the same for you, sir."

Dracon Liam's ears perked up.

Marie started speaking again, "May Valencia have one of your rabbits, Dracon?"

"Of course." Dracon Liam turned to Marie briefly, then back to Gabrielle. He slung the last rabbit in her direction and then said dramatically, "I must return to hunting! How will we ever collect enough food if I do not help?"

Marie snorted at this, sparks flying out of her nostrils.

Dracon Liam winked at Gabrielle. "Do you see why we used to call her Spitfire?"

"Dracon Liam," Marie protested.

"I shall be off in just a moment, Marie, and shall stop embarrassing you. Valencia, would you speak with me after hunting is complete?"

Gabrielle attempted to not appear nervous. "That would be wonderful, thank you," she stated, trying to inflect her words so they did not sound as unwieldy as they felt.

Dracon Liam did not notice – or he pretended not to – and left after another smile.

Since twas morning, Gabrielle knew that she should be heading back out to meet up with the others, yet she supposed another hour or so would not hurt. They were all split up anyway, so she could just pretend to have been utterly and completely lost . . . as she currently was.

"I shall leave you to eat your rabbit in peace," Marie said.

Gabrielle gave a panicked glance at the rabbit.

"Actually"—Gabrielle cleared her throat—"I really appreciate the rabbit, but I am not feeling particularly hungry this morning."

As she spoke, a score of hunters glided in, these giving their finds to the older dragons instead of simply dropping them. The older dragons began distributing the meat.

"Would you like something else?" Marie offered. "I believe I saw some chimera, perhaps a white stag—"

"No, really," Gabrielle interrupted her. "I'm not hungry."

"I insist," Draconis Marie insisted. "Is something else wrong? Are you sure you do not want a different animal?"

"No, nothing, really—"

"Jakob!" Marie called out to one of the dragons, a light grey one turning and coming towards Marie. "My son always knows what everyone brings back. He shall be able to tell you what we have here."

"Please, this is wonderful. I like rabbit. Thank you."

"Are you sure?"

Gabrielle nodded assuredly.

Marie gave her a slight smile just as Jakob set down. "Never mind," Marie told Jakob. "Thank you for coming."

"Like I had a choice," Jakob snorted.

"Jakob! What is this rudeness!" Marie was genuinely shocked.

Jakob glared at Gabrielle. "I see no guest. Only a murderer."

"Jakob . . ."

"Benjamin was killed last night." He stared coldly at Gabrielle. "A claw through his chin. He bled out in seconds."

This was news to Marie, who was silent.

Gabrielle gazed calmly back at Jakob. She felt sick. Should she try and defend herself to him? What could she say? She had no wounds to prove that he was going to kill her except for her broken scales and explaining to him that she had not meant to kill him would only cause more problems. Who aims for the neck with a sharp claw if they are not intending to kill?

"Well, regardless," Marie began, pausing after the words though her tone was the same as before, "Valencia is a guest."

"You house murderers in this brood then?" Jakob shot back immediately.

"Did anyone see it happen?" Marie questioned, regaining her composure.

"Who else would have done it? And I'm not hearing any protests from the murderer." His eyes flicked to his mother, but went back to Gabrielle.

Gabrielle's muscles were tense, her breathing short. "You were there."

"Twas I who found Benjamin," he growled at her.

Gabrielle could not help herself. "We met in the woods. He was trying to kill me. I had no choice."

"Really?" Jakob sneered. "No choice? There always is a choice."

Gabrielle longed to say that it was an accident, but again, too many questions came attached to that. Perhaps there had been a choice, but she had not wanted to die. "Twas my life or his."

"It should've been yours," he spat.

"That's enough. Thank you for your time," Marie dismissed him.

Jakob swayed almost imperceptibly on his claws, considering Gabrielle with loathing, his face twisting with disgust. Finally, he smirked without humour and shot at his mother, "Anytime."

He flew away.

Draconis Marie turned to Gabrielle, forcibly smiling. "Enjoy your rabbit, Valencia. If you are willing, I would love to speak further with you after your meal as well."

Gabrielle weakly smiled back, stomach further unsettled. If Jakob had to restrain from killing her in this setting, her insides churned at the thought of what other dragons would do to her if they found her in the woods.

Eyes wandering to the rabbit, Gabrielle's mind was snapped back to the present. She wondered how she was going to get out of eating the creature. As Draconis Marie began walking amongst the fletchlings, Gabrielle furtively glanced around her, searching for any spot to hide the rabbit or any dragon who would take it. However, the area around her was devoid of good food-stashing spaces, and the fletchlings were far enough away that to walk over to them would grab Draconis Marie's attention.

Gabrielle eyed the rabbit. If she did not think about eating it raw, she had no problem viewing it, gutting it, roasting it

. . . but it needed to be cooked. Thinking about eating it raw made her notice the way the skin was stretched where the neck lay twisted on its side and how its fur helped insulate the heat that was still radiating from it.

Drawing nearer despite her body's protest, Gabrielle leaned close to it, her mind running through what she was going to do. All she could think about was tugging with her teeth at the pliable skin, the smooth fur dampening and clumping together in her mouth as the flesh stretched from the bone and tendons, slowly pulling away, blood-soaked strings of tissue and slippery fat binding the skin and muscle together.

Then she would actually have to eat the raw meat and the organs inside. The lungs as globs of brownish tissue firmly attached to the sides. The heart nearby, filled with slick arteries and warm blood.

The intestines, stomach, and excretion system would be next. Slimy lumps of green, pink, and grey globs congealed together by thin, clear layers of fat. She could feel it. A slippery mess of connected organs sliding down her throat. Warm. Wet. Mucus-covered.

Then the end of one intestine would separate from the others, and a thin, slick small intestine would stretch from inside her throat to the back of her mouth. She would have to choke it down, the wretched insides of the intestine squeezing out into her mouth as she frantically swallowed the mucus-covered organ.

Gabrielle coughed and nearly began choking without even touching the animal. She squeezed her eyes shut, steeling her nerves, then opened them again, her eyes falling upon the head.

The dragons in the cavern ate the entire beast.

She winced as she heard a particularly loud crunch nearby, but perhaps she could deal with the bones.

But the head.

There would be a brain and fluid in it. Would it burst in her mouth as she bit into it? She surely could not swallow it whole.

Gabrielle glanced up and saw that Marie had not yet turned back to face this direction, but she was moments away from doing so. Internally crying, Gabrielle opened her jaws, closed her eyes, and gently fit the rabbit's head in her mouth. She tried not to think.

She snapped her jaws shut.

There was a decapitated rabbit's head inside her mouth.

The ears were smashed against the roof of her mouth, the stem of the brain against her tongue, the fur dampening and clumping just as she thought it would.

Still trying not to think, she chewed. Fluid squirted from places she had not thought fluid could squirt. The skull crunched between her teeth, and she felt one of the eyes get forced out and bump against the side of her cheek.

Gabrielle quickly turned away from the cave full of dragons, hiding her face from them. She tried to keep her shoulders from twitching as some slippery chunks of brain and fluid slid down her throat, and she swallowed automatically. Her jaws were moving faster than they ever had, yet it was not quick enough for her to not process every loud crunch and every slimy squirt and each warm, pulpy chunk of flesh that she swallowed on instinct.

With a gasp, she opened her mouth and breathed in the fresh, cave air.

It was over.

It was done.

Now there was the body.

Gabrielle held back a groan.

Surprisingly, the aftertaste of the rabbit's head was not particularly disgusting. In fact, as she ran her tongue along her teeth, searching for stray bits of brain, she realised that the taste had not been bad at all. It was somewhat like stewed rabbit, but sweeter. And warmer and pulpier and with a lot more bones. Considering the body, Gabrielle wondered if she would taste the same sweet, stewed rabbit.

Regardless, it was still raw rabbit, and her stomach heaved at the thought.

Swallowing her disgust, Gabrielle did not hesitate as long as she had with the head, grabbing the body and stuffing it into her mouth.

Gabrielle felt like a chipmunk. Blood dribbled from her snout, and she grimaced. This was terrible! Not only did she have the body of a raw rabbit inside her mouth and the head of the creature in her stomach, she had no choice but to choke or spit the thing out and eat it in pieces.

Whimpering quietly, she bent down and pretended to be tearing something apart when she really was forcing the moist corpse out of her mouth. Working quickly, she stuck half of it back in, snapped, and rapidly crunched the organs and bones into meaty pulp.

One of the legs got stuck in the back of her throat. She used her tongue to twist it around so she could chomp it into pieces. After a minute and a struggle involving her gag reflex, Gabrielle snapped up the last portion of rabbit and ate it, trying not to remember how she had seen the guts that were now inside her mouth spilling out of the half of the rabbit she had bitten.

Gabrielle sat back on her haunches with relief after the last swallow. She checked all parts and crevices of her mouth for any remains. The taste lingered, the body of the rabbit being a little less sweet than the head, but still sweeter than stewed rabbit.

Taking a deep breath, Gabrielle felt her panic, worry, and revulsion fade. A smile crept upon her face. It took her a few seconds to realise what was causing it. Pride. Gabrielle had just eaten her first raw rabbit. She could not stop the giggle from escaping as she tried to reconcile her horror with the act and her pride over it.

"If you want some advice, I would try not to make it look as painful next time," Dracon Liam noted behind her.

Gabrielle spun, surprised at Dracon Liam's quick return.

He was grinning playfully and held another rabbit in his claws. "Would you like a second?" he asked, eyes glinting with mischief.

"I'm satisfied, thank you." The words rushed out of her mouth.

Dracon Liam laughed. He slung the rabbit to the nearest group, who cheered with gratitude, then walked closer to Gabrielle.

"Word of advice . . . couple words, actually," he said. "First, come up with an excuse to avoid raw meat or get used to eating it. Also, do not call anyone 'ma'am' or 'sir'. Dragons don't do that. As a sign of respect, younger dragons will call older female dragons 'Draconis' and then their name or just Draconis. Same applies for the older, male dragons, but use Dracon instead. Do you understand?"

"Yes, sir." Gabrielle flinched. "Dracon Liam."

"Better. You are in a dragon's brood," Dracon Liam spoke firmly, confidently, and quickly. Gabrielle had little time to wonder about his reason for telling her this in her effort to keep up with him. "Brood refers both to the overall area where dragons are raised and each specific cave network in which each group of dragons lives. Caretakers of each brood include Nesters and a Healer or two. Protectors and Hunters are assigned to the entire brood, as in the entire area in which dragons are raised. There are three of these large areas scattered throughout dragon territory. There are multiple, shall we say, 'group broods', but each group brood has individual broods in it, such as this network of caves. Are you understanding?"

"Yes," Gabrielle replied. She was fairly certain she was. Well, perhaps only somewhat certain.

Dracon Liam seemed to know this and smiled more broadly.

"Each individual brood is also assigned a main Caretaker. Marie is the Caretaker and Healer of this brood. The dragons here range from ages six to twelve. Each dragon chooses a purpose at the age of fifteen. These purposes include Healer, Caretaker, Explorer, Singer, Hunter, Protector, Rememberer, and a few more, but no one would fault you for forgetting those. A dragon may change their purpose at any time or have none.

"Which reminds me, we dragons are run by each other. The Assembly is created with three dragons chosen from each of the three draconic regions to represent the dragons living within. The representatives must be fifteen, and all ages are allowed to weigh in on the matter of the representatives for their region. The Assembly coordinates the broods, supplies food for the elderly and injured, and organizes responses to humans although some dragons take that last duty into their own hands.

"There is much more I wish to tell you, but Marie is returning, is she not?"

Gabrielle glanced behind him and nodded.

"Do you have any questions?"

Her mind went blank.

"Do not worry, young flyer," Dracon Liam smiled softly, sensing her renewed panic. "You will be fine."

"Why are you telling me this?" Gabrielle blurted out, spying Marie just a few steps behind Dracon Liam.

"Because"—Dracon Liam leaned in close and winked—"any human-raised changeling who can consume a raw rabbit on her first try deserves some mighty respect and a well-roasted meal. Marie!"

Gabrielle's body froze as he faced Marie.

Dracon Liam boasted of the four rabbits he had brought in this time. He laughed after Marie's wry congratulations and insisted that his "rusty collection of scales" was still worth its weight in shriveled rabbit skins.

Marie laughed along with him, and Gabrielle managed a weak smile.

Then Dracon Liam dismissed himself, and Draconis Marie turned her full attention to Gabrielle.

"Was the rabbit to your liking?"

"Yes, ma-Draconis Marie. It was delicious, thank you."

"No trouble, Valencia. Would you be willing to speak with me? Preferably in a more secluded cavern?"

"Of course, m-Draconis Marie."

Draconis Marie led the way to the nearest exit. Gabrielle's heart, or perhaps it was the rabbit's, stayed firmly in her throat.

"Valencia," Draconis Marie began as they proceeded through a tunnel about level with the main area, "may I ask you a few questions? You must understand, we do not receive many visitors and even fewer of such . . . uniqueness."

"What do you mean?" Gabrielle snapped her mouth shut before she called Draconis Marie "ma'am" again.

Marie slowed until they both were walking level with each other, the sounds of the other dragons fading. "Few have caused such a stir as you have, and it's been many years since a dragon died at the hands of another."

Gabrielle glanced towards Marie and startled as she immediately met Marie's stare.

Draconis Marie seemed to realise her intensity and relaxed her gaze, casting a sweeping glance at the walls and looking forward. "It's just an observation. There's been a lot of excitement."

Draconis Marie halted, and they faced each other. Marie continued, "There's been relative peace between dragons and humans for the past five years. Just a few attacks. Most of that happens close to the border."

"Twas about twenty years ago when King Germaine decided that the dragons and their supporters were too dangerous to live," Gabrielle commented, more to herself than Marie.

"Twas about twenty years ago when Richard and Royale were slaughtered by humans!" Draconis Marie exclaimed. "They were the first to die in the king's plans to kill the dragons."

Gabrielle's brow scrunched. "The king acted in response to an attack on a village. The village Calumnia was attacked and many killed. They had no choice but to kill the dragons who were attacking."

Draconis Marie stared at her with wide eyes. "Where did you hear that?! You have it all wrong!"

"Twas . . . twas what I was taught," Gabrielle stuttered.

"Is that what your parents taught? You should have come to the brood to grow. We do not teach such nonsense here."

Her tone became rehearsed. "The dragons had been ignoring the humans except for a few fights here and there. They were not worth much notice. However, Richard and Royale, who were truly upstanding Assembly members, Richard also a Rememberer and Royale a Nester, decided that they wanted to have more interactions with humans. Why, no one knows. They had visited a particular village several times with no problems, but on one particular night, the humans brutally turned against them and killed them both. Were you taught this at least?"

"No, m—Draconis."

Marie shook her head, eyes narrowed.

Gabrielle grimaced. She should've said yes.

Marie continued. "Of course, the Assembly investigated and found that the king was gathering an army and this was only the first of many attacks to come, so the Assembly began doing the same in order to protect ourselves. For fifteen years, we fought the humans, the border shifting, naturally. We got it all the way up to the walls of Aradin at one time, but the line finally settled. The war continues. However, the king hasn't attacked again, and most dragons never wanted to war in the first place. So we come to a time when we are not at official peace, but the humans are once again below our notice or consideration. Not that Charlene and her followers think that way."

"I heard Charlene is . . . not an official voice of the dragons," Gabrielle hesitatingly stated.

"She's not," Draconis Marie agreed, "but while the Assembly does not wish to take action against humans, they don't necessarily disagree with Charlene's actions."

"Capturing the princess and murdering humans?" Gabrielle asked, a little stunned by her own brashness.

"Would you blame her for such action?" Marie asked. "After all, twas her parents who were killed. Charlene is Richard and Royale's daughter. Some dragons do not stop her because they agree, others because they do not care, but all understand why and do not blame her for her acts."

"Just," Gabrielle hesitated, but plunged ahead anyway, "we must still take responsibility for our actions. How can she justify the further loss of life? How would that make anything right?"

Draconis Marie eyed Gabrielle. "Yet you killed Benjamin."

Gabrielle tensed.

Marie pursed her lips. She inclined her head briefly, a silent acknowledgement, before continuing. "Why do you protect the humans?"

Gabrielle paused, but then remembered that Valencia had already established herself and reiterating those values could cause no harm. At least, no additional harm. "They have the right to live, just as we do. The princess was not bothering Charlene nor any of the dragons. She is but a girl of sixteen. The prince and . . . and the others came here only to get her home. They meant no harm to dragons. Besides, again, how is killing or hurting them any benefit to dragons?"

"It was not yet confirmed that the prince was in the group," Marie stated, eyes gleaming. "Tis true? He has come for the princess?"

"I can say neither one way nor the other," Gabrielle hastily added.

"Protection," Draconis Marie moved on with another incline of her head though she also sported a slightly amused, slightly sardonic smile. "We must kill the prince and the other humans in order to keep them from attacking."

"Kidnapping the princess only drew them here!" Gabrielle protested.

"Yes, which is why Charlene acted through her group and not the Assembly," Draconis Marie reminded her.

"Rub my scales!"

Gabrielle turned around at the new voice.

A black shadow came walking towards them.

Gabrielle's heart skipped a beat. This was darker than any shadow she had seen before, darker than any darkness.

"William." Draconis Marie smiled. "This is Valencia. Valencia, this is William, my husband."

Gabrielle's heartbeat gradually returned to normal as she realised that the darkness was a dragon.

"William gives a shock to most dragons who have not met him." Marie grinned at Gabrielle, spying her expression.

"I cannot even blend in with the night," William told her.

A few of his scales glinted, snatches of flinty silver, in the void that was himself. *Void.* Gabrielle finally understood the physicality of the word.

She shook off her surprise. Repeating the words several times in her mind before speaking them aloud, Gabrielle recited, perhaps still a bit stiltedly, "Tis a pleasure to meet you, Dracon William."

"Tis a pleasure to conduct myself before you as well," Dracon William informed her, eyes glinting with humour at a joke she could not see.

"We were speaking of your favourite subject, my love," Draconis Marie teased, head tilting.

"History! Oh—" William stopped and adopted a pathetic, wide-eyed look. "My words are too hastily spoken. I meant to say you. My favourite subject has always been and will always be you."

"Twas history."

"My other perpetually favorite subject." William smiled.

Gabrielle could not help her quiet snort, which was, unfortunately, noticeable in the even quieter tunnel.

Marie laughed, and William grinned as Gabrielle ducked her head in embarrassment.

"I am sorry, sir," Gabrielle hastily said.

"Tis reassuring to see that you retain a sense of amusement," Dracon William told her, not at all offended. "Do tell, why 'sir' and not 'dracon'?"

Gabrielle froze, then broke into a little bit of laughter. "I apologise for that as well! My family lives near to the border. We keep to ourselves. I forget that our sayings and habits are not the same as others."

"She said that the dragons started the last war by attacking the village!" Marie informed her husband indignantly.

"She's not wrong," William said.

Marie stopped. Her eyes lit up with understanding, and she sighed. "This debate again?"

"Marie, I do not understand why you do not trust—"

"I trust you, William. I just don't think what you believe happened is true."

"There is proof, Marie. I have studied the accounts and written records—"

"Everyone says differently, my love. Everyone else knows that the king was gathering an army, and Richard and Royale were the first to die."

"The timeline is skewed by that belief," William insisted. "King Germaine did not commence gathering an army until after Richard and Royale were killed at Calumnia. In addition, certain records indicate that Calumnia had been att—"

A great roar echoed from the main cavern. A high-pitched whistle sounded immediately, ringing out above the resounding melee.

William chuckled, and Marie shook her head, spreading

her wings and expertly skimming the ground in order to reach the main cavern faster.

Gabrielle looked to William, but he did not move.

He turned to Gabrielle and explained, "When a ruckus occurs, yet there is little chance of serious injury, a whistle is sounded in order to indicate a lack of an emergency, although Marie often still hastily departs, feeling utterly responsible for the brood as she does. Liam," Dracon William greeted Liam as he approached from where Marie had left.

"William," Dracon Liam nodded his greeting. "Valencia. I suppose William has been regaling you with his historic tales?"

"Why must everyone assume such?"

"Were you?"

"Possibly."

Liam chuckled. "You are a Rememberer, Will. Always were. There is no doubt about that."

William smiled again. "We were discussing Richard's and Royale's deaths."

"Ah," Liam nodded sagely. "Few but you find that a debate at all."

"Which is a true tragedy considering the repercussions of what is chosen to be believed."

"Could you explain further?" Liam inquired.

"Dracon Liam," William frowned, "we have covered this many—ah." His eyes fell on Gabrielle. "Of course. That shall be no trouble. Obviously, either way you bite it, Richard and Royale end up dead. However, there are two main interpretations of that event. The most widely accepted version states that King Germaine had already been gathering an army, and Richard and Royale were the first of many destined to die.

"The second version argues that Richard and Royale went to an antagonized village and were killed in the confusion. In response, King Germaine began creating an army.

"Historically speaking, either one is possible although the timeline suggests that the latter would be a more likely sequence of events. Nevertheless, the most widespread version is the former, where King Germaine was gathering an army before Richard and Royale were killed. This encourages enmity from dragons to humans and is a great rhetorical device that current dragons, such as Charlene, use as evidence that humans either need to be conquered or suppressed on a greater level."

Gabrielle blinked. Many times.

"William, what happened before Richard and Royale were killed? Before things were as they were then?" Dracon Liam questioned.

"Could you narrow your field of interest, perhaps? You have just asked for history almost in its entirety."

"Could you tell us about the time when the humans were in hiding and doing magic? Right before the humans, changelings and sorcerers rose up against the dragons?"

"Any human who does magic is considered a sorcerer." William shook his head.

"Do not all humans have some magic?" Gabrielle asked.

"Well, yes," William answered, taken aback. "Nonetheless, all humans do not use that magic. Any human who does use magic is no longer a human, but a sorcerer."

"Even if they do magic just once?"

"That is up for debate," William said. "Personally, I would define a sorcerer as any person who must stay in human form, yet has the knowledge and skill or the natural ability to perform magic."

This sounded like the same thing to Gabrielle. "So . . . they have to either know how to use magic and do it or just have usable magic?" she clarified.

"Yes," William agreed. "Sorcerers who have a noteworthy amount of magic but are not properly instructed may find themselves performing magic without the intent to do so. That is the kind of person I am referring to when I state that they have 'natural ability', not just ability, but enough that the magic is evident despite their lack of effort."

"Oh, I understand now," Gabrielle said, not quite sure if that was true or not.

"You desired more information concerning Bada's Rebellion?" Dracon William returned to Liam.

"I would appreciate it, yes," Liam stated.

Dracon William sat back on his haunches. "For about two decades after Adelmar slaughtered and frightened humans into concealment, the human population recovered and grew in strength. Many were forced to forge alliances with sorcerers and changelings, all three of the groups persecuted by the dragons. Striving for protection and eventual reclamation of their ability to live in the open, the majority of humans attempted to master magic. The human culture shifted to view magic as the solution to all ills. Anyone with magic once again became highly revered although sorcerers did not retain as much power simply because humans made up a lesser proportion of the population."

"Everyone was a sorcerer," Dracon Liam clarified.

"Not everyone," William corrected him.

"Right, I just want to make sure Valencia gets the general idea," Liam explained.

"Correct, but not everyone was a sorcerer. Tis just that a greater number of sorcerers existed compared to other eras and compared to humans due to almost all humans dedicating themselves to the study of magic and thus becoming sorcerers."

"Right," Liam agreed, grinning. "Please continue."

"Sorcery became a way of life, and due to close quarters and many close calls, changelings were viewed with both great suspicion and great respect. They were the best able to fight dragons, but also the closest in relation to them. Acceptance varied from community to community, but living with the dragons was impossible to those born among human families or who had resided with the humans for any duration of time. The dragons reluctantly allowed changelings to live, but changelings were considered less than true dragons. Attempts on changelings' lives dominated the draconic landscape regarding changelings although everything was done deep in the caves.

"After two decades, the humans, sorcerers, and changelings under the leadership of the sorcerer Bada struck back against the dragons. Ten years of bloody warfare followed during which both sides lost a tremendous amount of people. Adelmar, a dragon, retreated from the war midway, returning at the end of the tenth year to begin crusading for peace between the peoples. He faced fierce opposition from both sides and often weathered physical attacks, nearly departing from this life on numerous occasions. However, after Bada was killed, his daughter Galene became the leader of humans, sorcerers, and some changelings. She collaborated with Adelmar to bring an end to the bloody affair, but official peace was not declared until after Galene's son, Gasto, reigned on the throne. Galene, who was still alive, declared the day 'a beautiful sight to the blind'."

"What happened?" Gabrielle asked, for William had paused as if at an end. "How did we get here?"

William sighed regretfully. "For some time, peace descended upon the island. However, old suspicions grew and fears still flourished. Sorcerers and some changelings isolated themselves in a village created for those with magic, Havene, and interactions between humans and dragons increased in amount, then began declining. With the decrease, each population retreated to 'their side' of the island although no official border was declared for many years. Eventually, with all sorcerers concealed and magic repressed, sorcery faded from view and became part of human and draconic lore. Meanwhile, sporadic fights between dragons and humans increased until Richard and Royale were killed and the current war commenced. Any remaining known changelings were killed during that time."

"That is . . . astounding," Gabrielle breathed. Twas incredible to think that peace between all the peoples had once been in place. Just as Jesalyn had said. True, it had not been perfect peace and harmony by the sound of it, yet the relations between changelings and dragons and humans and sorcerers seemed to have been much more positive overall, at least, after Bada's Rebellion and the subsequent war. And changelings were once respected, to some extent.

"I am glad that you enjoyed listening to this history. Few dragons search and surrender the time for such practices." Dracon William did look very pleased. He cocked his head, listening.

Gabrielle did the same and suddenly became aware of Marie's voice. Gabrielle turned and saw Marie talking over her shoulder and drawing nearer to their group.

". . . warn him I'll rip off his limbs and chase him around with them if he goes within ten feet of her."

Marie faced them, still too far off for conversation, but this did not stop William who called out, "Do you need any help?"

Marie shook her head, visibly steaming. "Benedict cannot leave that poor girl alone. I told Rebekah off for screaming at him, but I can hardly blame her."

"How did the mischievous youngster amuse himself this time?" William asked, grinning.

"He chased her with a white stag's leg and hoof."

Liam and William roared with laughter.

"I am glad you two can see the humour in it!" Marie angrily spat.

Gabrielle tried to swallow her smile. She thought of the young dragon chasing Rebekah with an animal leg, got reminded of the rabbit she had just eaten, and suddenly had no trouble not smiling.

"He likes the girl, Marie!" Liam told her, exchanging amused looks with William.

"In what situation does chasing after a girl with a white

stag's hoof mean 'I love you'?" Marie questioned incredulously. "And even if so, that's hardly an appropriate response."

Liam shrugged, unconcerned.

William cleared his throat.

When they both looked at each other after less than a moment, smiles returning to their faces, Gabrielle was reminded of how even the eldest of villagers turned young in the midst of their peers.

"I apologize, Valencia," Marie spoke to Gabrielle.

"Tis fine . . . Draconis Marie," Gabrielle replied. She sounded like Drew trying not to call Davey "sire" or "milord".

Suddenly, she realised how much time she had spent in the tunnel, in the brood, how much time she had spent away from her friends and family while they wandered through dragon territory.

"Is something amiss?" Dracon William questioned her, concerned.

"I . . . had obligations today. I am afraid that I should be leaving," Gabrielle carefully chose her words.

"I will escort you out," Dracon Liam offered.

"Nonsense," Marie interjected. "I am Caretaker here and will escort Valencia." Marie stepped away from the center of the tunnel and nodded Gabrielle on, capping any discussion on the issue.

Gabrielle smiled and nodded at Marie. Turning to Liam and William, she said, "It was great to meet ye. Thank you."

"Twas our pleasure," Liam nodded, eyes glinting with amusement and knowledge.

Gabrielle had a moment of panic, thinking that he was going to tell Marie and William, but when she turned back to Marie and started walking out with her, Liam did not say anything. Gabrielle suddenly wished for a few moments alone with the dragon, but her worry over her friends stopped her from taking the desire further.

Marie walked Gabrielle out of the tunnel and through the main cavern, the noise level dropping again as Valencia walked by the young flyers.

"Valencia!"

Gabrielle started and turned a little later than she should have, but hoped none thought anything of it.

Heather was racing to Gabrielle from one of the sides of the brood, Victoria coming at about half Heather's pace, Ruby strolling towards them as if unconcerned if she would ever reach Gabrielle.

"Girls!" Marie rebuked them.

"Tis all right," Gabrielle assured her, crouching lower to meet a panting Heather eye-to-eye.

"Are you leaving already?" Heather asked, disappointment scrawled all over her face.

"Yes," Gabrielle told her, surprised at her own disappointment at the thought.

"Where will you be going?" Victoria questioned, catching up with Heather.

"Home," Gabrielle said. That was the safest bet.

"Will you be back?" Ruby asked loudly.

"Perhaps," Gabrielle nodded, then she smiled. "If I do return to this area, I shall look for you three. Just try to keep out of trouble until then."

"Yes, Draconis!" Heather readily agreed.

Gabrielle tried not to let her doubt at this statement be too evident.

"Have you said your goodbyes?" Draconis Marie asked them.

Ruby and Victoria nodded.

Heather ran closer to Gabrielle, then launched herself into Gabrielle's side. Heather's wings came out and fluttered around Gabrielle's waist, almost seeming to encircle her.

Startled, but thinking Heather's actions reminiscent of a hug, Gabrielle brought her own wings closer to Heather's body, nearly covering the smaller dragon completely.

"Please come back soon," Heather whispered.

Gabrielle tried to keep her face impassive, ducking her head closer to Heather's as her response. When Heather shifted, Gabrielle lifted her wings, and Heather backed away, smiling. Gabrielle nodded her head at the girls, them proudly returning her nod with their own, then Marie led Gabrielle the rest of the way out of the brood.

As they stood outside, Gabrielle about to depart, Marie opened her mouth.

She stopped.

Feeling more comfortable around her while also anxious to get going, Gabrielle asked, "What is it?"

Marie gathered herself and stared at Gabrielle for a long moment.

"Good luck," she said at last. Another momentary pause, then Marie simply walked back into the cavern.

Gabrielle stood by herself at the entrance to the brood.

Then she filed away the incident for later examination,

refocused on finding her friends, and flew off the cliff. She descended into the woods, creating an actual shift this time.

She picked up another rock and gradually morphed it into a thin sheet of obsidian, just like a necklace her father had bought her from a merchant many years ago. Deciding to try to scry without paying the price first, Gabrielle closed her eyes and concentrated. Within moments, she could tell it was working. Opening her eyes, she let them lay, unfocused, upon the rock.

The stone clattered to the ground.

XV

═══════════

Out of the Frying Pan

The night would have been peaceful, had not the dragons attacked.

Davey had stopped yelling a while ago, thinking that everyone else would have been able to get far away in the time he took to distract the dragons with Drew.

Well, that's *your problem. You started to think.*

Davey let out a short, heavy grunt, ignoring Drew's voice in his head. No matter where Drew was, Davey still couldn't get away from him.

Sweat made his clothes uncomfortably sticky, and despite the nice temperature of the night, he felt a few goosebumps pop up along his arms, not all due to temperature. He grasped his sword, the hilt slick. He opened and closed his hand a few times, readjusting his grip.

He leaned up against the tree behind him, waiting, listening. Roars built upon one another and bursts of fire lit the area near him. He was far enough away now that he had little fear of being discovered unless one of the dragons was wise enough to search quietly.

A slight gust of wind hit him straight on from above.

Startled by the unusual occurrence, he looked up, spotting a dark dragon flying above him, but low to the ground. It rose higher into the air, and Davey, guessing by a sudden, nerve-rackingly close burst of fire, realised that it was Valencia.

He kept his eyes on her as she flew away from him. If Drew or Gabs had been here, they would have noticed the dragon long before he did. Sometimes, he wondered if they had a trick to spotting the beasts, but he did not ask, for he knew what Drew would undoubtedly remark.

A trick? Indeed, it's called using your eyes, sire.

Davey turned away from the blazing area and snuck through the woods again, making much more noise than he wished he did. That was another thing Drew was pretty good at, being quiet when he wanted to.

The better to eavesdrop.

Davey rolled his eyes, then rolled his eyes at himself rolling his eyes. The amount of time he spent with Drew was clearly excessive.

The sounds of the ruckus faded. At last, he stopped, trying to quiet and slow his breathing. He was close enough to their earlier campsite that he still did not feel safe, but he did not wish to travel too far from the scene and away from the others. The following morning, he would journey back through the area—using his eyes to search for dragons—in order to make sure none in their party were killed.

Not that he would know if the dragons had just swallowed them whole.

He grimaced.

The night would have been peaceful.

He leaned against another tree trunk and slid down. His armor and all the provisions were still at the camp, whatever was left of it. Even if everyone else was dead—which they were not—he would still have to go back for supplies. With his sword, he could survive, but it would be a lot easier with a pot, some clothes, his armor, and a squire.

You could not last a day without me! Drew trumpeted in Davey's mind.

"Watch me," Davey muttered, folding his arms and stretching out his legs. There was nothing left to do but wait for morning.

Something scuttled across Davey's leg, and he jerked awake. A squirrel scampered up a tree and out of sight.

Davey rubbed his head. He had not thought that he would fall asleep. He stretched his legs before him and his hands above his head.

If I had slept under a tree, I would've become part of the root system.

Davey smiled at his mother's voice and the image of her exasperation that came to mind.

He stumbled upright and into standing position. Looking around, he stretched once more.

Nothing in particular stood out about the section of woods he was in. Not that that was surprising. All trees and plants looked the same to him.

Do you even have eyes, sire? Drew snidely remarked.

Davey examined the area around him, but could not tell from where he had come. Looking to the skies gave him no help. The clouds had partly cleared, and the sun was peeking out from behind them.

Worry grew inside his chest. How was he supposed to get back to the campsite and find everyone if he did not even know in which direction the campsite lay?

Clenching and unclenching his fists, he supposed that some ground looked more trodden down than the other areas and decided that he must have come from that way.

It was obvious.

He would be at the campsite in minutes.

The sun had moved a quarter way across the sky before Davey paused for a break. He had no water, no food, and no clue where he was going. Food and water he could find if he dedicated some effort to the task, but he also had no patience for that.

He took out his sword and stabbed it into the ground, pushing away Drew's complaints about dulling the blade.

This was impossible.

This was possible.

This was impossible.

He could not just stand here.

This was impossible.

Stubbornly, he crossed his arms, giving into his frustration for a few more minutes. Finally, he angrily snatched the sword out of the ground and stashed it back in the scabbard.

Just as he was about to walk away, he realised that he was hearing voices outside of his head.

"...toothwort...once a day..."

A voice wavered in and out of Davey's hearing until it stabilized.

"...my grandfather once used it to cure a wart he had. Supposedly. We are not quite sure if that was what had stopped it or not."

Drew wandered into sight, scanning the ground, Gabrielle's mother coming up behind him. Drew looked up. Without missing a beat, he announced, "And over there is an idiot!"

Davey raised his eyebrows in surprise and exasperation. Glaring at Drew, he addressed Gabrielle's mother. "Madam Marie, it is good to see you made it out."

"What am I, chopped chimera?" Drew interjected.

"Thank you." Marie nodded vigorously twice, abruptly stopping. "We have not seen Gabrielle, my husband, or the princess yet. Have you?"

Davey shook his head. "We'll find them soon," he assured her and himself.

"Tis what he says when searching for his socks," Drew remarked. Turning back to Davey, "We went back to the campsite."

"Good," Davey said. "I was heading there myself. Was anybody else there?"

Drew shook his head. "Sire, next time you are heading somewhere, I would suggest traveling toward the place. The campsite is that way." He pointed toward where the two of them had come from.

Davey ignored him. "Did you grab any supplies?"

"'Twas all gone."

"Do you have any idea where the others are?" Davey asked.

"None, which somehow is still more than you have."

Davey rubbed his eyes. "Why did you have to be the first person I found?"

"The first person you found?" Drew asked indignantly. "You are the second person I found! You have nothing to do with it. You just exist to be found by me."

"Where are we going to go?" Davey ignored him again.

"The opposite direction of whatever you would have chosen," Drew immediately stated.

"I thought you said you didn't know where the others are?" Davey asked as Drew started walking, and Davey begrudgingly fell in line behind Marie.

"I don't," Drew replied, "but you are as much of a woodsman as I am a swordsman so asking you where to go in the woods is like asking a rock how to fly. The same amount of brain activity occurs, and if you follow the advice, you end up dead."

Davey grunted. "At least your insults lengthen and grow wilder. I was starting to get bored hearing about my smelly socks."

"I apologise about those." Drew lazily waved his hand. "I do wash them for you quite often, but I forget that your distinctive odor fouls them quicker than others' feet."

"Do try not to subject madam Marie to hours of your prattle," Davey ordered, grimacing as the words kept rolling off his squire's tongue.

"I was just trying to save her from hours of yours."

Davey snapped his mouth shut and dedicated himself to not saying another word. Drew was just trying to goad him into an argument. He knew it.

"How did you two meet each other?" Marie asked.

"He was nothing before I met him," Drew began without hesitation.

"I found him in the stocks," Davey interrupted.

"You did not 'find me' in the stocks," Drew argued. "I strategically placed myself there in order for you to see me and then believe that you found me."

"What were you doing in the stocks?" Marie laughed.

"Enjoying the sunshine. Twas a beautiful day."

"He had filched a potato from a vendor."

"I had not!" Drew insisted. "He framed me!"

"We have been over this!" Davey rolled his eyes. "Why would he frame you for stealing a potato?"

"Ask him!" Drew threw back. "Furthermore, why would he frame me for stealing a potato and then throw that potato at me? That made little sense and a lot of pain."

Davey attempted to return to the story. "I saw Drew in the stocks. Did not think anything of it, but then the fellow, who is getting pounded with rotten fruit, calls out to me that he is grateful at least that he does not smell as bad as my socks."

"From . . . from the stocks," Marie confirmed.

"From the stocks, dripping in moldy tomato juice and rotten cabbage—"

"How can you be dripping in rotten cabbage?" Drew interrupted.

"How can you be moronic enough to call a prince's socks smelly?"

"Tis more moronic to say someone was 'dripping in cabbage'."

"I *was* a moron and only twelve at the time," Davey continued, "so I thought that the fool was funny and had courage. I recognize it as idiocy now. After his time in the stocks was up—"

"Because he could not have let me out early."

"—I offered him a job as my squire, or manservant, or jester, or lazy good-for-nothing, depending on what mood he is in."

"Is lazy good-for-nothing an actual job title?" Drew asked.

"Tis the actual title of the unemployed."

"But I am not unemployed."

"Give it a few minutes."

"You two have been together since then?" Marie asked.

"Indeed."

"Unfortunately.

"Seven very long years," Davey informed her.

"Mmh, good job, sire," Drew said. "I did not expect you to get the math right the first time."

Davey could not help some of his frustration slipping through. "Do you ever stop?"

"Tis only a little teasing. I should suppose that you are above actually being bothered by such childish pranks," Drew told him highly.

"Childish is correct."

"Come now, sire. Are you really not gentlemanly enough to stand a few harmless laughs?"

"You do more than a few."

"Is it more than you can handle? If you feel overwhelmed, just say so, sire, and I will restrict my gaiety."

If Davey did not hate it when people ground their teeth, he would have sheared away several layers of bone already.

"Dragon," Drew warned suddenly, tone devoid of jest. "Stay still. He is close."

The light atmosphere disappeared immediately.

Davey grimaced. He hated running and hiding, but he hated sitting and waiting even more.

He did not lower his eyes, keeping them fixed upon Marie's back, but he did not raise them either.

Marie's hair was light brown, incredibly straight compared to Gabrielle's twisting tendrils. Her hands were still, but the tips of her fingers moved infinitesimal amounts back and forth, almost like she was unconsciously reminding herself that they still worked.

A sudden odd, almost whistle-like sound caught his attention. He looked up to see something scaly diving right at them.

"Run!" he and Drew yelled at the same time.

Davey hesitated momentarily, wondering if he should grab Marie, but she was already running to the left. Knowing he had probably wasted too much time by taking just that second, Davey threw himself to the right, drawing his sword as he did so.

Something heavy landed on him, knocking him completely to the ground. Davey grunted as all the air was forced out of him. He felt immense pressure on his ribs, which ached painfully. He had almost forgotten that they were broken just a few days before and that the following day he had barely rested.

The roots and rocks digging into his stomach surely did not help. His arms were splayed out in front of him, his sword loosely held in one hand. He tightened his grip and brought the sword a little closer, hoping that the act would eventually do more than just calm his nerves. He felt hot breath upon the back of his neck as he fruitlessly tried to push himself up.

The beast took a deep breath.

"Hey! You salamander-skinned, overgrown reptile! I wash those clothes, and I don't appreciate the dirt you're getting on them!"

Davey would have smiled had he not been in the process of being suffocated.

A deafening roar was let loose right over Davey's head. His ears rang with the sound. A quiet *thunk* that Davey could barely hear and an even louder roar a second later assured him that, while Davey might not have his armor, Drew still had his knives.

The pressure had lifted from Davey with the roar, so he flipped around, sword out and ready, but the dragon was pursuing Drew now, breathing fire at a blazing tree that Davey assumed Drew to be behind.

Davey came to his knees and then to his feet. He could hear his father scolding him, telling him that that was an old man's way of getting up, he was showing his opponent weakness, but Davey was too sore and the dragon too distracted for Davey to care.

He briefly scanned the surroundings, spotting nothing of

interest except Marie standing hesitatingly in front of some trees, on her toes, ready to help but unsure of how.

"Marie!" Davey yelled to her, waving her farther into the trees with his hand.

Luckily, Marie seemed more eager to comply than Gabrielle and disappeared into the woods.

The dragon roared another time.

Davey gritted his teeth. Did it have to do that?

He ran forward with his sword lifted, the hilt warm in his hand. He slashed at the beast's back haunches. The sword sliced through the scales with little depth.

The tail swished at Davey, and he ducked, stabbing the sword into a lower section of the dragon's legs.

A huge gust of wind and more roars sounded as the dragon flapped its wings.

Davey raised his hand to cover his eyes from the debris the dragon was kicking up. He smelled the dark earth and could taste the grit of the ground in his mouth. Blinking, he raised his sword as he raised his head, the dragon flying higher, then leaning forward to fire upon them. Drew was still somewhere in the woods, so Davey shielded himself alone. His sword did not warm as it blocked the flames.

He felt a wave of unexpected gratefulness for the enchantment on the sword. He had not even known it existed until Drew pointed it out to him, yet that feature had saved his life many times over.

"Get away from him, David!"

Davey barely heard Drew's shout. He could fight this dragon.

Indeed, you could fight it, just not win.

Davey shook his head. Drew was just a few feet from him. He no longer needed to hear the squire in his head as well.

That you should be so lucky to have me twice over.

The dragon stopped its fiery breath, inhaled, and began again, drawing nearer as if hoping proximity would force Davey to be burnt to a crisp.

Davey reluctantly backed away from the dragon, the fire growing less and less. When Davey thought he could make it, he swung around and darted towards the trees, his back becoming momentarily seared.

He heard the dragon take a quick breath and blow hard and fast. Davey dodged behind a trunk and brought his hands across the front of his body, watching the flames flick around the edges of the tree. Knowing he could not stay there, he pushed off the tree, faced the burning log, and stepped backwards, sword in front of him to protect from further fire.

The dragon stopped spewing flames and came forward, barely going around the burning tree and felling some small trees right in front of itself.

Davey saw the trees coming, the tops reaching towards him. The beast breathed fire again as the tops fell.

Davey raised his sword, unable to turn and run from the trees, still trying to walk backwards as fire blocked his front vision. One of the trees, burning leaves all over it, came to Davey's right. He dodged left, his foot getting caught in a hole and tripping him. He fell on his side, sword awkwardly raised in front of him. Another tree suddenly appeared from the other side, heading straight for Davey.

Davey curled up, trying to avoid the burning log. A sudden gust of wind blew over him, two equally sudden thumps sounding, the small tree falling just one or two inches beside Davey instead of on top of him. Davey glanced in shock at the burning wood just two inches from his face, the heat giving him the feeling of a sunburn. He leaned forward more, twisting his foot out of the hole, and looked up.

The dragon was coming towards him.

Hurriedly taking a few steps back, Davey watched as the dragon fell to the earth. Knocked unconscious by its own burning tree.

Davey surveyed the scene, almost not believing his eyes. The smaller trees that had almost fallen on him were like kindling compared to the large one that had fallen on the beast, but Davey could still not believe his luck that the tree would hit the dragon just right and with enough force to knock it unconscious.

Why could he not be this lucky when playing poker with the knights?

The heat from the fire warmed him on all sides. Stepping over burning bits of brush and the roots he had been stumbling over earlier, Davey picked his way around the trees and dragon and to where Drew stood, arms folded, tapping his foot. Marie was coming up from behind him.

Drew greeted him, "I hope you realise that you are one very lucky idiot."

"One alive idiot," Davey corrected him.

"At least we agree on the idiot part."

Davey sighed.

A sharp crack.

Drew dropped to the ground.

"Drew—"

A sharp pain at the top of his head.

It throbbed.

Boom. Boom. Boom.

It was like a giant, flat anvil was pounding from the inside of his skull, right where his temples were. It had its own rhythm, an overpowering beat that drowned out Davey's heartbeat. All he could hear, all he could feel, was the painful drum.

Then there were little pokes, soft little pokes, like small children's hands but much stronger. They were all over his back, pressing gently for a few seconds then disappearing, at least twenty always on him. His head rolled back.

Boom. Boom. Boom.

The anvil continued its chorus.

The pounding too painful, his mind too disoriented, Davey could not yet bring himself to care or even to open his eyes.

This was awful.

Boom.

Something fell across his chest, across his legs, tightening slowly, but not painfully. The beating, the pounding, that was painful, but not the strips of pressure. They were manageable.

He began to recognize a quiet mumbling, like the babble of voices during a feast when one stood in a corner and focused on none, the sound of all washing over him.

The wind rushed across his face, cooling it. His stomach lightened with a swooping sensation.

Thunk.

Davey's eyes snapped open as his body jerked to a halt, gravity pulling him towards the earth. Ropes kept him from falling.

Blinking in the bright sun, Davey noticed that he was hanging about twenty-five feet in the air. Beneath him, a sea of white lay broken up by the sprouts of stunted trees. They were in a clearing of sorts, other trees of heights equal to his only at the edges of the break in the forest.

Now that he was hanging from instead of lying upon the pole, he could tell that his arms were uncomfortably tied behind and above his back. His fingertips could touch the flat top of the pole, but the ropes were expertly tied into smooth grooves so that he could not slip his hands free. The sun hung roughly in the same position he remembered it being in although it could have been a day or even a week later.

Thunk.

His head snapped to his left as another pole and body thudded into place.

Drew, unconscious.

Peering down on the other side of Drew, Davey saw one more pole, the white dots crowding around the beam and what he assumed was another person.

"Drew," Davey hissed, then realised that the white dots below probably could not hear him. Besides, what did he care if they heard?

Tis what makes you an eavesdropper's dream.

"Shut up," Davey muttered. "Drew!" he called a bit louder. His apprehension robbed the humour from the irony of his words.

Drew continued dangling limply, not responding to Davey's addresses or the sudden burst of jumbled noise from below. A third pole came swinging up, a third *thunk* sounding.

Twas Timothy, Gabrielle's father.

Timothy peered around, straining against the bonds and then shifting as he took in their considerable height. His head twisted to get a clear look all around, eyes falling upon Davey. He nodded as if they were two acquaintances passing each other on the street.

Davey nodded back.

Timothy examined the ground for a moment, then turned back to Davey, inspecting him critically.

"Do you have any sharp objects?" Timothy asked.

Davey readjusted his legs. He had not yet thought about that.

"My sword is gone, as are the few daggers I carry. Drew usually carries more than an inspector finds, but . . ." Davey let his voice trail off and gestured with his head towards Drew.

"What are those things?" he asked Timothy.

"Gnomes." Timothy surprised him with an answer.

"How do you know?" Davey asked.

"Marie told me what had happened. We followed them here. I was taken."

"Is Marie all right?"

"Yes. They did not get her."

"The gnomes?"

"Yes."

Davey felt like he was pushing an unwieldy stone up a steep hill.

"What do they want?"

"To have fun."

Davey gave Timothy an odd look, but then remembered what Drew had said earlier when he was explaining the "firebugs" as Drew had colloquially called the red gnomes. The gnomes existed to have their version of "fun", but their version of fun often led to others' deaths. Vaguely, Davey remembered Drew expounding upon the subject with Timothy, but it was Drew. Davey had not listened.

"What else do you know about these gnomes?" Davey tried to make the question very open-ended.

"They are sky gnomes. They catch beasts or humans by hitting them with fast, small pebbles near critical zones, then raise them on poles for the rocs to take."

Davey adjusted his body again and tried to think if he had anything else that was even semi-sharp on him.

"Have you seen Gabrielle?" Timothy asked.

Davey looked sharply at him. They were tied to poles twenty-five feet into the air, waiting for nearly certain death to swoop and snatch them up, yet the other man's concern was for his daughter.

"No," Davey said. "You have not either?"

Timothy shook his head. "Have you seen any dragons?"

"Not since last night," Davey replied.

"Your father hates dragons."

Davey's attention snapped back to Timothy with the non-sequitur.

"Yes," Davey said at last although it had not been a question.

Treading carefully on instinct, Davey continued, "Dragons have always hated humans, and it is my father's duty to make sure that they stay in dragon territory. Of course, sometimes the beasts cross over, and my father does his best to discourage that and prevent it from happening."

Davey thought of when Dannie was captured, the fear his parents and he had felt, the disbelief. It had been years since dragons had roamed that far into human territory.

"How will your father respond to the princess being taken?" Timothy acutely asked.

"He will bring back the border control. Due to a lack of activity, the patrol was disbanded about six months ago. He will more greatly enforce the laws against magic as well, making sure the kingdom is clean," Davey responded, wondering if Timothy was just trying to distract him from their situation.

"What will you do?"

Davey frowned. "I will do as he asks, whether it be border control or some other measure."

"Would you take the same measures that your father is taking?"

Davey did not understand why Timothy was asking him these questions. The timing was odd, and Timothy should not have even been asking.

Tis none of the people's business to know what the king's business is, his father would say.

Yet Davey had always disagreed with this sentiment. He wanted to know what his father was planning and thinking about all the time, but his father had only allowed certain things and decisions to be explained or even told to Davey.

To a point, he understood this. He had been a child and should not have heard much of what his father was discussing, but it had always irked him not to know. As an adult, his father shared almost everything with him, instructing him how to rule. Davey saw the benefit from their collaboration, how both he and his father grew from that. What was so different between that and sharing his plans or ideas with the people?

"I would also reinstitute border patrol," Davey said, but then went quiet, thinking.

Tsk, tsk, tsk. There you go again.

"My uncle," Davey began, ignoring Drew's voice in his head, "has always said that one spark can start a fire. I would prefer to not let this incident, however worrisome, be the spark that starts another war. By no means am I comfortable with magic in Aradin, but I see little value in causing a stir when there is no harm being done and no magic being seen."

Timothy's face was impassive. "Uncle? I did not think that the king had a brother."

"He does not," Davey assured him, more relaxed with the sudden turn to an easier topic. "My uncle is my mother's brother."

Two black dots on the horizon caught his eye. He peered at them as they grew larger, then shook his head disgustedly.

Dragon, roc, some other odd creature that Drew knew all the habits of, it did not matter. They were stuck.

"Do you see them?" Davey asked Timothy.

"Yes."

They waited in silence as the dots grew, Davey soon realizing that they were, indeed, rocs.

Timothy started shifting on the pole again, moving as much as he could to get loose.

Davey thought that it would not matter much even if he did. What was Timothy going to do if he got free? Drop to his death? Most likely, he would receive a broken leg, and he would land injured and unarmed in the midst of the sky gnomes.

Granted, Davey had looked for a sharp object to get loose, and he probably would have had to drop to the ground, too.

He twisted his hands nervously and started to move about as well. The chances of getting free were slim, and he would not be able to leave Drew. Wood slivers pressed uncomfortably into Davey's back as he slid about regardless. The hard chips nearly pierced his clothing. He grasped the top of the pole and tried to pull himself up, but the ropes were tight and unyielding.

He could see the tremendous rocs clearly, their speed slow and dominated by glides. Tugging at the ropes, not paying attention to the ground far below him, he continued to fruitlessly attempt to free himself.

Valencia.

What if Valencia appeared?

Loathing the hope inside his chest, Davey twisted around both ways to check for another flying dot or, preferably, a very close flying Valencia.

All he saw were the rocs. They were so close that the first and smaller of the two was opening its claws to take them.

The smaller roc went for Timothy, but was clumsy, the claws hitting Timothy's head and body several times. Timothy's head snapped back.

He slumped forward, unconscious.

The bigger roc circled, cawing once to indicate its frustration.

The smaller roc squawked back. It finally pried Timothy from the pole, leaving the pole entirely intact and stumbling back into the air.

Squawking once more at the smaller roc, the other beast swooped towards Drew and Davey.

Davey watched fearfully, and then oddly gratefully, as the beast simply snapped the top of the pole with Drew attached, then headed for Davey.

Davey winced automatically as the claws closed around him and the pole, the enormous, hard talons gripping him firmly and unmovably. The pressure did not suffocate, though.

A resounding "snap" rang out, and Davey's legs swung wildly as the pole was broken in two.

While his body looked intact, Davey was pretty sure that he had left his stomach where the remainder of the pole still stood. As the roc rose higher, Davey watched the ground grow farther and farther away, his heart beating erratically. Wind whipped against his face, and he felt a slight chill settle into his bones despite the sun and nice temperatures.

He decided suddenly that he hated heights. With ill-disguised jealousy, he looked over at Drew, limp and unaware.

Ha, ha! Drew laughed at him.

Davey shook his head and looked away, then shook his head and closed his eyes, hoping that he would not get sick.

After what seemed like forever, the claws loosened, dropping Davey in a free fall, still attached to the pole. Davey endured just a few seconds of the world spinning before he smashed against a web of branches. Twigs protruded into his skin, breaking through in many places. He could not stifle his shout.

Davey heard one more crash of pole on wood, then the birds settled into the nest, talking raucously to one another.

He was facing downward, into the nest, and could not see anything that was going on above him. Trying to shift his hands and body, he found himself just as stuck as before although now more painfully so.

One of the rocs made an especially loud noise, and Davey winced as it hit his eardrums.

Something gripped him and flipped him over. The sticks dragged through his body. Another shout Davey could not stop.

Then, he was staring into the face of a ridiculously large and ugly bird.

The giant roc stared back, squawked one final time, and struck.

XVI

Like an Animal

Gabrielle breathed heavily through her snout. She could see the rocs carrying Drew and Davey in the distance, but was having trouble gaining speed quickly enough. She wished to fly higher and use the currents more effectively, but the last thing she needed was another confrontation with a dragon.

They were almost to roc territory.

Then the rocs were there.

They landed at the edge of the territory, dropping three parcels of roughly the same size into a nest. Drew and Davey had probably met up with Danielle, and all three had been captured.

She flapped hard again and again and again, feeling tiredness quickly creep into her wings. Technically, she had told Jesalyn that she would practice being in both forms, but she had really only been focusing on fighting as a human and using her magic. Now she regretted that decision. Regardless, she doubted that she could have built up much stamina in the handful of days since she had met Jesalyn.

Gabrielle's shoulder blades ached even more than before, especially near her recently broken bone, but she was so close to the rocs.

The larger roc stood up tall and moved one of the people with its claw.

A terrible roar ripped through the air, rattling ear drums.

The rocs screeched in reply, clawing at their heads like dogs.

Gabrielle roared again, breathing fire on the rocs and smashing into them head-on.

Perhaps she would not be distracting, ducking, and avoiding.

She immediately tried to back out, regretting her decision. There were three people in this nest, which made this fight especially dangerous for them, and once within the embrace of the rocs' wings, Gabrielle realised how truly miniscule she was even in dragon form. Flurries of feathers swirled around her as she clawed and bit at everything that moved. She flapped her wings at the same time, attempting to retreat. It was like the inverse version of her dream of playing with the girls, braiding hair, white feathers gently floating down. Here they were snapping and slashing, raking feathers and stabbing scales, black feathers with droplets of blood swirling haphazardly and violently round all and to the ground far below.

Gabrielle changed tactics, digging into the roc ferociously.

Warm blood splashed around her snout. Blood-smeared feathers matted her body as she ripped through the screeching bird. For a moment, she ignored the younger one attacking her from behind.

After what felt to her a flurry of assaults on the roc, the larger bird fell out of the nest and spiraled to the ground, wings scraping the sides on the canyon. The roc landed with a loud, sickening *crack*. It was dead before the last feathers fluttered after it.

Hearing the smaller roc coming at her from behind another time, Gabrielle turned and launched herself upward, tearing through the bird as she had Benjamin.

She was going to be sick.

She brought the roc down as she fell back to the nest, flinging it over the side and on top of the other one, the second one landing with a quieter *thump*.

She whipped back around, anticipating another fight, scanning the area. Another roc some nests over cawed, but saw Gabrielle and decided not to investigate.

Gabrielle turned her attention back to the nest. She shook her head once in surprise, not expecting her father.

Davey and Drew were still tied, though, so she reached down and cut Davey's bindings, scraping the wood of the pole. She did the same for Drew. Without saying a word, she flew out of the nest, into the woods.

She landed among the trees and changed, quickly walking close to a trunk as she did so in case prying eyes were present. This time, the shift appeared quickly though twas still rough. Her skin was sticky and smeared with blood, bits of the giant feathers still clinging to her. Blood also covered her face, moving with Gabrielle as she wrinkled her forehead in disgust. She did not think she was squeamish. She had eaten a raw rabbit just that day.

"Elgh," she complained. There was no way she could help Davey carry Drew and her father down from the roc nest looking like this. They just might notice something a bit off.

Besides, she should have grabbed them while she was in draconic form. Gabrielle grimaced and steeled herself for another change.

"Gabrielle!"

Gabrielle turned at her mother's shout.

". . . Gabrielle." Gabrielle's mother repeated her name, now wearing the same face of disgust Gabrielle had.

Gabrielle moved her hands in front of her like she was trying to explain, but then just threw them up into the air. "Twas the rocs' fault."

Her mother raised an eyebrow and took a step back. "I would suggest washing up."

Gabrielle giggled. It turned into great laughs, then great pains. She winced and groaned. Cuts and bruises and scratches. More throbbing in her back.

"Sana," she muttered, the pain lessening.

She glanced at her mother.

Seeing Gabrielle's look, her mother smiled gently, eyes soft and . . . proud.

"I believe there is a pond close by," Gabrielle said. "I'm going to wash up before going into the nests to see if I can help Davey. Drew and Father are unconscious. Why are you here?"

"Why am I here?" her mother asked indignantly.

"Twas not what I meant," Gabrielle immediately said, raising both her eyebrows, amused by her mother's amusement.

Her mother smiled. "I was with the prince and Drew before they got captured by the gnomes. I escaped being captured. Then I caught up with your father who insisted on trying to rescue them and got himself captured in the process. I was not happy with that man. You will not guess who I met next."

"Dannie?"

"Not quite," Jesalyn said.

Surprised, Gabrielle squinted past her mother, more into the woods.

"You are a sight," Jesalyn commented wryly, a small bag hanging at her side. "Your match with the rocs was truly astounding."

"I believe there is a pond—" Gabrielle began.

"There is no need," Jesalyn interrupted her gently, raising her hand. "Limpidare."

Gabrielle had the sudden sensation of a large, warm cloth being draped over every part of her body, the feathers and blood seeming to soak up into this invisible cloth and disappear. A moment later, Gabrielle rubbed her hands across her arms, feeling cleaner than she had since leaving her parent's tavern.

"Thanks," she said gratefully, savoring the cleanliness.

"The spell only takes off much of the dirtiness, but does nothing for smell, so you still need to wash soon," Jesalyn told her.

Gabrielle sniffed, made a face, and nodded, grinning. "What are you doing here? What I mean is—"

"Tis all right," Jesalyn assured her, nodding and smiling. "We have kept watch over your group since you left, just checking in every once and a while. When you came closer to Havene, we decided that one of us should join you in order to ensure a safe journey back to human territory. Your journey out is more treacherous than your journey in. The dragons know ye are here and are anticipating a fight from ye."

Gabrielle nodded in agreement. "How did you get here so fast?"

"There are a few 'special' shortcuts hidden throughout the island," Jesalyn informed her, smiling. "They're hidden well and few and far between, but valuable in a pinch."

Gabrielle was about to respond, but then looked to roc nests. "Are we going to—"

She stopped.

"We'll help them," Jesalyn said.

Gabrielle felt her shoulders relax. A tenseness stayed in the air. She looked away from the rocs' nest and back at Jesalyn.

The older woman had her chin lifted, her arms clasped in front of her, and her shoulders straight. She waited until Gabrielle's attention was fully upon her before speaking. "Despite the prince's distaste for magic, he will not refuse it when it can be used to save his friend and your father's life."

When Jesalyn paused, Gabrielle gave a slight nod, guilt curdling in her stomach.

"That is good for us then." As Gabrielle's mother spoke, she shifted closer to Gabrielle, shoulders as rigid as Jesalyn's. "Good that the prince will allow magic to be used to save lives."

Jesalyn cast her eyes to the rocs' nest as she resumed speaking. "His and his friends' lives, yes."

She looked back to them, expression still blank, tone expressionless. "We can journey up to the nest, and I will awaken them with magic. Climbing down with them conscious should be much easier than the alternative."

A moment of silence, in which Gabrielle was deciding how to respond to this new Jesalyn.

Then Jesalyn exhaled, looked to the side of them, and laughed once quietly. Her gaze returned to Gabrielle and her mother, and she inclined her head. "Forgive me. I did not mean—well, I did. But that was unkind. And unfair."

When the silence stretched a moment too long again, Gabrielle looked to her mother, but her mother was watching her. Gabrielle hurriedly bowed her head towards Jesalyn. "'Tis forgotten."

Jesalyn nodded, her lips a thin but upturned line.

Gabrielle's mother gave a slow, low sigh.

Jesalyn's smile smoothed though it still stayed fairly rigid. "Marie," she said. "I believe it would be best if you stayed here for the moment."

Gabrielle hid her astonishment at her mother's pose— hand on hip and face turned slightly away from Jesalyn. After another short, stilted moment, Gabrielle's mother folded her arms instead and nodded. "Very well."

Gabrielle's mother turned to Gabrielle, a small but genuine smile appearing, the edges of it tight. "Stay safe."

Gabrielle agreed, returning the hug her mother offered and not mentioning how she doubted any part of their endeavor was safe.

When Jesalyn walked past her and towards the base of the cliff and the dead birds, Gabrielle turned and followed. In favor of also continuing past the tenseness of the prior conversation, Gabrielle preoccupied herself during the short walk by speculating on how they would scale the steep rock walls.

When they were almost directly below the nests, Jesalyn held up a hand to stop Gabrielle, then reached upwards and whispered, "Funem."

At first, nothing seemed to happen, then a long, twisting tendril of rope came into view as it coiled its way down to them. As it unfurled right in front of them, Gabrielle saw that it was not rope, but thin, pliable wood.

Jesalyn turned to Gabrielle, eyes wary. "Regardless of my words, I do believe it would be best if you went up first."

Gabrielle accepted the statement. She grasped the wood and began the arduous climb. The wood was stiffer than she expected and threatened with splinters, but Gabrielle supposed that this was preferable to having a slick stick that was impossible to hold. She had her feet against the cliff and was just walking up it as if on solid ground, though, of course, she was not.

Her muscles began burning almost immediately. Gabrielle gritted her teeth and told herself that they were not hurting that badly, but the more cynical side of her reasoning reminded her that she had just flown at top speed for a distance, fought with two rocs, had not even completely healed herself, and now was expecting her body to put up with scaling a cliff by pulling herself up by a thin wooden log. Expectations might exceed reality. She reached another hand forward, shaking and sweating, intensely grateful for the dryness of the wood, almost wishing for a splinter to remind her that things could always get worse.

The climb only lasted around five minutes, maybe a little less or a little more, but Gabrielle was exhausted by the time she reached the top. She pulled her way on top of a log, into the nest, and plopped down heavily, breathing hard, learning that she had muscles—twitching, aching muscles—where she thought there had been none before. Inspecting the base of the wooden rope, Gabrielle saw that it was attached seamlessly to the large log making up part of the roc's nest, as if the wooden rope had grown out of the log.

Jesalyn followed just a moment later, red-faced but not as weary as Gabrielle despite her age.

Gabrielle stumbled to her feet upon Jesalyn's arrival, awkwardly snatching at the twigs around her to steady herself. Internally sighing when Jesalyn wordlessly gestured upward, Gabrielle began making a scratchy and uncomfortable way through the branches, up through the nest and towards Prince David's voice.

"... You're such a big lump and completely useless. I think I should just leave you here. Yes, believe it or not I was actually thinking. Shut up or I *will* hang you from that tree. . . ."

"Prince David?" Gabrielle said, not really calling out to him, for she had not known she was going to speak until she did.

"Gabrielle?" he yelled back after a moment's hesitation. "Gabs!"

She thrust her hand through another hole that was too

small for her, breaking off twigs and creating a pathway, hearing more branches snap to the side and slightly above her. A moment later, Prince David was there, clearing away the branches with her and pulling her to the top of the nest and to her feet.

"Gabs," he said once more, almost coming forward.

She looked quickly to the side, and he took a step away.

"Are they all right?" she asked.

Drew was twitching, mumbling, and moving about a small bit, only half attached to the pole, but her father . . . her father lay quieter, nearly unmoving.

Gabrielle felt her heart flutter nervously and then suspiciously go missing.

His blonde hair was completely askew, his eyes closed tightly and not twitching. He lay as he had fallen, his arms stretched above his head, face laying upon the branches, one leg draped over the other in an odd, unseemly position.

"He's alive," Prince David assured her. "He's out cold but still breathing."

Her lungs released a big breath of air she had not realised she was holding.

Prince David's eyes darted to where Gabrielle had come from.

Rising out of the hole, Jesalyn gracefully got to her feet, wiping her hands on her clothing as if dusting off flour.

"Where are they?" Jesalyn asked promptly, seemingly oblivious to Prince David's look of shock and sudden reach for his absent sword. Seeing Drew and Gabrielle's father, Jesalyn walked around Prince David and over to Drew. Slowly, she placed a hand on his cheek and murmured something Gabrielle could not hear.

Drew's eyes shot open, and he tried to sit up.

Jesalyn quickly pushed him back down. "Drew," she told him evenly.

He nodded, eyes blinking rapidly.

"Are you injured anywhere?"

He shook his head.

Jesalyn moved on to Gabrielle's father, him awakening with less flourish. "Are you hurt?" she asked Gabrielle's father as Drew clambered to his feet and readjusted his clothing.

"Yes, madam," Gabrielle's father replied.

Gabrielle hurried over to them as he pulled up his shirt on the side to reveal several deep stab wounds from the twigs.

"Gabrielle," her father sighed when he saw her, dropping his shirt back down and reaching for her.

Gabrielle fell to her knees to meet him in a hug.

"Would you like me to heal you?" Jesalyn offered.

Gabrielle's father nodded. He pulled his shirt back up and watched closely as Jesalyn, saying "sano", healed the cuts in his side.

Jesalyn rose, Gabrielle joining her a minute later and helping her father rise as well. He was still a bit unsteady on his feet.

"Are you well enough to climb down?" Jesalyn asked Drew, observing him as he more fell than climbed into the hole they had created.

"We shall find out, shall we not?" Drew grinned.

Jesalyn shook her head reprovingly. Turning to Prince

David, she said, "Would you like me to heal your wounds, your highness?"

Prince David stared at her, his hands slowly moving to touch the places were blood leaked from wounds on his front.

Jesalyn continued, tone even. "Tis an arduous climb down."

"If you want," Drew yelled from somewhere in the nest. "Once she heals you, and you climb down, I can reopen the wounds."

Prince David's jaw tightened, but he didn't say anything.

After a long minute, he finally said, "I would be grateful. Madam Jesalyn."

Jesalyn reached out her hand, but did not place it on Prince David as she had for Drew and Gabrielle's father. "Sano," she firmly stated.

Prince David's back immediately straightened and his stature became stronger.

Jesalyn's eyes gleamed. She stepped out of the way and gestured Prince David through the hole. "Your highness," she allowed.

"No," Prince David demurred, motioning for her to go first. "You may go first, Madam Jesalyn."

Jesalyn tilted her head in acknowledgement, eyes flicking to Gabrielle's before she slid into the gap.

Prince David turned to Gabrielle's father and Gabrielle, suddenly looking nervous, then oddly determined. He came forward and helped her father through the hole, holding onto her father's hand as he descended.

Gabrielle suddenly realised how old her father was compared to Jesalyn or even her mother. They were twelve years apart.

As her father descended, Gabrielle did not bother to wait for Prince David to insist she go first, simply swung herself around and began climbing down.

"I can't move. My foot is stuck," Prince David said, tugging his leg.

Gabrielle looked up, and seeing him struggle with his leg a mere foot or so from the gap, she climbed back up and leaned over to see if she could untangle it.

Prince David leaned over as well, fighting with the branches entwining his leg. His hands always seemed to be where her hands should have been, and their hands collided and slowed each other down greatly until their work quickly came to a standstill.

Frustrated and concerned a roc would reappear, Gabrielle snapped, "This would be a lot easier if you kept your hands out of the way, sir!" She glared up at him, then grimaced and looked away.

"Are you calling me a royal pain?" A smile played at the edges of his lips, his eyes dark and serious.

"You! You're—!" Realizing twas no accident, she leaned over, intending to shove his shoulder.

She stopped.

Instead, she asked, "Would you like to descend first, sire?"

Prince David frowned, glancing away before catching her gaze and holding it.

Brown with flecks of blue.

Human.

"I'm sorry I lied." His hands clenched as he spoke. "I'm sorry I'm not who you thought I was, but I am as much the person who journeyed with you as I am the prince. It is not fair to hold that against me."

Gabrielle pressed her lips together and looked away. As apologies go, Prince David's wasn't the best, yet she knew enough of his character to not doubt his words. Her anger over the deception had been short-lived, truly.

Her fear about his hatred of magic, however, was as strong as ever.

When he was a squire, she had the chance of perhaps seeing a change in those beliefs. She had much less hope for that change in the prince.

Though perhaps that twas part of the unfairness he spoke of.

Perhaps she was a little too concerned, though, a little too paranoid. What if she just told him? He appeared not to harm those who were not harming others, and surely, she would fall into that category?

Then she remembered the events of earlier that week, when they had met Victoria, Ruby, and Heather for the first time, the young dragons who would have done them no harm, at least once they had been spoken to.

He was passionate. He was rash. He would act.

And even if he did not care himself, even if he kept her secret, then it would also be his burden to bear, his deception to perpetuate.

And it would take a single moment of doubt, a single word from him to a confidant, and she would be executed.

"Gabs . . ."

"I am no longer angry about that."

Prince David gazed at her for a moment. Then he closed his eyes and sighed. "There is a however."

Gabrielle could not help but bring a hand up to cover her mouth. But she, too, had lied, and her deception was more insidious.

Changelings were more dangerous than dragons, for one never saw them coming.

She took a stuttered breath. "But I thought you a squire. I thought . . . there's no trust—"

Hypocrite.

She took another breath. "I'm sorry. I— I can't."

He could not see the real problem. He did not know.

She shook her head. "I am so sorry."

She turned away, unwilling—unable—to bear the conversation longer.

"Gabs—"

"Sire, please. Let it be."

"At least . . . at least call me Davey."

She nodded.

They descended.

XVII

<hr>

Oh, Bother

Although her arms shook the entire time they climbed down, Gabrielle still found herself looking towards where she knew her mother to be and often checking the nests nearby. Now that Valencia had been absent for some time, the rocs were getting braver. One glided down to examine the carcasses at the bottom of the ravine. It pecked at its brothers' flesh.

Everyone was in the forest already, so Gabrielle and Davey hid near the base of the cliff before dashing for the woods when they thought the way safest.

The roc saw and hopped towards them. It dove into a short swoop.

Davey threw himself and Gabrielle to the ground right before the beast's claws touched them.

Gabrielle landed roughly on the rocks, scraping her hands and other exposed areas.

Davey shielded her as its talons whooshed less than a foot over their heads. Scrambling to his feet, Davey helped Gabrielle to hers, and they sprinted the rest of the way to the forest, close and fast enough to reach it before the creature dove again.

"Is everyone all right?" Davey asked, scanning each person.

Gabrielle looked at the rest of their group as well, and her stomach dropped. "Has anyone seen Danielle?" she asked.

No one said anything.

"Well," Gabrielle tried to convey a light tone. "She could not have gotten far."

"I could scry her," Jesalyn said. "You mentioned a pond. If the water is still enough, that would be a good surface to use."

A roc screeched loudly.

All of them ducked and turned, gathering closer together and retreating deeper into the forest.

Two rocs were rising from the corpses and another from its nest. They were trying to gain altitude though they were not having much success.

Gabrielle twisted around to look behind her.

"Tis the emerald green dragon!" she said.

The dragon gracefully wove between the rocs, neatly missing their beaks and claws, and swooped low to the ground to drop someone a mere foot above the earth. Then the dragon flew back up and began antagonizing the rocs, breathing fire while staying a good distance away, drawing the rocs away from the edge of the forest as Danielle ran towards the woods. As soon as she was beneath the green cover, the emerald dragon twisted around the rocs once more and made a straight shot away from the nests, losing the birds without much trouble.

"Dannie," Davey sighed, Drew's hand on his wrist no doubt the only thing that had kept him from running out to his sister.

"Why was it carrying you?" Davey asked the question only half-interestedly.

"He had found me in the woods and wanted to help," Danielle said. "Twas easy to find you once Valencia attacked the rocs."

"How did he know about that?" Gabrielle asked.

"It could be heard for many miles." Danielle smiled. "Apparently rocs do not die quietly, and Valencia has quite a roar when she puts her mind to it."

Gabrielle was suddenly worried that she was blushing. She reminded herself that whatever Valencia did was little concern to her.

"Are we going to continue traveling out of dragon territory?" Gabrielle's mother asked suddenly.

"Yes," Davey assured her. "We are only about three days from the border."

"There is a quicker way, sire," Jesalyn said softly, drawing everyone's attention.

"What way is that?" Davey asked politely, but stiffly.

"You could take a tunnel to Havene and then proceed towards human territory from there," Jesalyn suggested. "Tis much quicker and safer than taking your original route."

"If there is such a tunnel nearby, why did you not mention it while we were leaving Havene?" Davey asked.

"You would not have been as receptive to the idea."

Davey did not move, hand resting where his sword used to be.

"Your highness," Gabrielle's father finally spoke after several moments of quiet, "I realise you may believe it is safer to do otherwise, but I am taking my family to Havene."

Not expecting this firm statement from her father, Gabrielle was nonetheless pleased.

Davey did not seem to know how to take the declaration. He asked, "Why do you believe the underground route is better?"

"Fewer creatures will attempt to kill you there."

Davey's eyes flicked to Jesalyn.

Gabrielle's gut grew heavy. She forced herself not to look away from the prince.

Davey's eyes dropped to the ground. He stared for a long minute.

At long last, "If it would not bother you any, would you be willing to let us join your family?"

"Tis no bother," her father replied.

"Is your offer still open, Jesalyn?" Gabrielle's mother spoke.

"Of course," Jesalyn smiled. "There are two tunnel heads nearby, one leading to the sky gnomes, the other to Havene. If we take the one to Havene, we'll be there before night completely falls."

"Tis lucky there is a tunnel between here and the sky gnomes," Davey commented.

"Tis not luck," Drew shot back. Continuing on dryly, "I do not believe it would have taken many successes by the sky gnomes before that particular tunnel was created."

"The tunnel head," Jesalyn almost interrupted Drew,

beginning to walk towards the ravine, "is at the base of the cliffs, hidden as all entrances to Havene are."

They all followed her as she tracked the tree line along the entrance to the ravine, easily skirting the open areas.

"Once someone finds an entrance to Havene," Davey asked, "are they able to find it again?"

"If they can identify the correct area from the surroundings. Sorcerers can see the entrances no better than humans can, but sorcerers can sense the magic. However, tis easiest to memorize where the entrances are," Jesalyn said.

"Then Havene only keeps out those who do not know where the entrances are, not those who dislike magic," David clarified.

Gabrielle's shoulders tensed.

"Havene was created to dissuade those who abhor magic from entering. The all-encompassing presence of magic in the holes and tunnels should be enough to dissuade most. However, you are correct in implying that someone who is determined to get into Havene should have little trouble. Any person who seeks a sorcerer's help should be able to find one."

Jesalyn had taken on a tone similar to her husband's. And to Drew's, when he spoke of fauna and flora. The knots in Gabrielle's stomach loosened as amusement crept in.

Jesalyn continued, "Nevertheless, one of the lesser-known features of Havene's tunnel is that when ten or more beings in less than a half hour pass through the rock barriers in the holes, the exit of the tunnel in Havene glows bright red. This is just an extra precaution should some raiding company or smuggling group get the idea that Havene is a good place to secretly set up operations or even attack."

Jesalyn's tone stayed light.

Gabrielle slowly let her fingers uncurl.

Seemingly unconcerned, Jesalyn stepped through the rock of the ravine's wall and disappeared completely.

Drew followed without hesitation, then Davey with a pause, then Danielle, Gabrielle, and her parents.

The tunnel looked like the same one Gabrielle and the two men had traversed through before, glowing blue spheres gently lighting the way, the ground packed and solid.

Confidently striding forward, Jesalyn led them through the nearly unchanging scene.

"What is Havene?" Danielle asked.

Jesalyn paused, casting her a glance before kindly laughing once and continuing on. "Tis a village created for those with magic."

"Why was it made and hidden?"

"Havene was made as a place for those with magic during the time when magic was just beginning to be taboo. As the world grew increasingly hostile to sorcerers, the people of Havene withdrew more until it was hidden by more than just magic."

"People stopped believing in it," Danielle concluded.

"Yes," Jesalyn agreed, "and the sorcerers of Havene are grateful for that. We are able to blend in when elsewhere on the island. Not that many ever leave."

"Why do some leave?"

Jesalyn momentarily paused. After a few terse seconds,

she assured Danielle, "I'm going to answer. I'm just thinking of how.

"Some . . . some argue that the people of Havene need to hide and continue the secrecy of Havene because of the danger this world poses to sorcerers. Sorcerers are liked by neither humans nor dragons. Others accuse the people of Havene of . . . retreating from the world, pretending that it does not exist. Those in the latter category are more likely to leave. Although many return disillusioned, I know of a few sorcerers who are still out in the world having built up a life outside of Havene, but most who leave Havene venture out only as merchants. It is probable that there are other sorcerers outside of Havene who have never been there before, they're just not practicing sorcerers and are unlikely to know that Havene exists."

"What do you think?"

"What do I think?" Jesalyn repeated Danielle's question, confused.

"What do you think about Havene retreating and staying hidden? About those who venture out?" Danielle clarified.

Jesalyn went quiet again.

"I think that I respect those who are brave enough to leave Havene, but I also respect those who earnestly desire just to live with their families in relative peace and security."

Now it was Danielle's turn to be quiet for a minute or so.

Only a minute or so, though. "How big is the village?"

"Tis large enough. We have taverns and a few shops."

"What is it Havene like?"

"Like any other village, I suppose, except that we have no inns and that many of the inhabitants are sorcerers."

"What difference does being a sorcerer make, and are not all villagers in Havene sorcerers?"

"Being a sorcerer means that you do tasks a little differently than someone without magic, and no, not all villagers in Havene are sorcerers." Jesalyn explained the continuum of magic Jonathon had described, using very similar language.

"If Havene was made for those with magic, then are not also changelings welcomed there?" Danielle clarified.

Gabrielle could not help the silent shiver that automatically slid down her back.

Completely naturally, Jesalyn replied, "Indeed, they are. In fact, at one time there were a good number of changelings in Havene. However, as relations between dragons and humans broke down further, changelings were often called away to help their families whether draconic or human. The number of changelings has continued shrinking in Havene, finally dwindling away to almost none."

"But there are some changelings in Havene?" Danielle unknowingly asked Gabrielle's question for her.

"None that are currently changing. However, sorcerers are more likely to produce changelings than humans due to their magic. While a changeling born in Havene is uncommon, tis not unheard of. Those around the age of five are closely watched for any signs of being a changeling."

Hope fluttered in Gabrielle's chest. She had not imagined that another changeling could be born not of a line of changelings, but she should have realised such believing, as she had, that she had been borne of two humans.

"What happens if a changeling is born human to dragons

or born dragon to humans?" Danielle asked. "I mean, if you know."

"A changeling born dragon to humans usually is killed unless the parents isolate themselves until the child is grown or abandon the child near dragon territory to be found. Many dragons, but not all, would take the child to a brood to grow."

"What about the dragons that would not take them to a brood?"

"Those few would be dragons who realise that the child is probably a changeling and . . ."

"Would kill the changeling?" Danielle asked quietly.

"Yes," Jesalyn paused only briefly. "A changeling born human to dragons would also be killed unless the parents took extraordinary measures, the same measures human parents have with a draconic changeling."

Gabrielle tried to force her body to stay relaxed. Her shoulders refused to obey.

"But what does a dragon—" Danielle said in a rush. She cut herself off and let out a frustrated sigh.

"You may ask. I'll answer to the best of my ability," Jesalyn assured her.

"What does a dragon mother feed a human baby?" Danielle asked emotively.

Jesalyn laughed. Smiling, she explained, "Tis a valid question. A dragon mother can feed a baby changeling cow's milk although tis rumored that the healthiest children are those that are fed cow's milk along with certain crushed roots and herbs."

"How do they get the cow's milk?"

"Now that is a question for dragons," Jesalyn chuckled. "I would not suppose it to be easy, but tis possible."

"How do you know?"

"We have stories from years and years ago, most going far before this current king, your father, was born."

Danielle nodded, thinking. Then . . . "What do the houses look like in Havene?"

Jesalyn answered, and Danielle continued asking questions about Havene, the shops, the crops they grew, their entertainment. Jesalyn's words appeared true. Aside from a few customs that differed from that outside of Havene, it sounded like any other village.

At long last, the tunnel brightened, and the way was devoid of glowing spheres.

Jesalyn turned, smiling, seemingly unable to help herself, and announced proudly, "Welcome to Havene."

Gabrielle had to admit, the picturesque village she had seen earlier was even more beautiful as the sun gently sunk below the horizon, casting stunning pink stripes against a deep magenta-hued backdrop, eventually melding into a savory, velvety, bronze orange. It connected seamlessly to a light blue that gradually darkened until so rich and deep that one longed to reach up and dip their hands into it, collecting the color because the sky seemed too saturated with all the breath-taking hues.

Jesalyn led them through several streets and around houses, voices and laughter coming from a few. Almost everyone in the town was inside, eating supper or settling down for the night. With a start, Gabrielle recognized the house they were approaching as Jesalyn's home. The new perspective on the town had her a bit disoriented. Gazing up towards whence they had come the time prior, she scanned the area, believing that to be the exit from the other tunnel, but could determine nothing.

"We should have enough room for everyone," Jesalyn commented as she reached for her door.

It swung open before she touched it, a young man with a mop of bright blonde hair and a wide grin behind it.

"Jaxon!" Jesalyn yelled, immediately reaching forward to grab him in a tight hug. Her next words were quite muffled, but somewhere along the lines of "I thought . . . home . . . tomorrow."

"I wasn't," Jaxon replied, hugging Jesalyn back, eyes gleaming with wicked humour as he examined their group, "but I met some poor, lost soul who's also trying to find his way here. I took one look at him and knew he'd have no success."

Jesalyn abruptly pulled away from Jaxon, grabbing his arms. "Mateo?"

"Indeed, that does sound like the pitiful lad's name."

Jesalyn swatted him on the arm, then pushed past him, calling out Mateo's name and then hugging someone Gabrielle could only see the limbs of. Jaxon watched, bemused, but then turned back to their troupe. Holding the door open a little wider, he gestured them inside.

Davey went first, then Danielle.

As Danielle passed, Jaxon inclined his chest, gently grabbed her hand, and kissed it. "M'lady," he greeted her.

Danielle's eyebrows rose, and she leaned back.

Gabrielle caught a glimpse of Davey's face and let herself smile.

Drew went next, but Jaxon placed a hand on Drew's chest as he entered.

Drew stopped.

Jaxon leaned forward, sniffed, seemed to consider something, then motioned for Drew to continue forward, saying, "Mum was planning on cleaning the house tomorrow anyway."

From inside the house, Davey snorted.

Drew's hands curled into fists, but he did not say a word and just entered the home.

Just as Drew got completely inside, Jaxon's eyes went to Gabrielle's, calm and serious. Without a word, he stepped to the side of the open door, out of sight from any inside, and bowed.

Gabrielle just stared.

"I'd prefer to close the door before all of the warmth of the fire escapes, Valencia."

Gabrielle started forward suddenly, almost tumbling to the ground in her haste. She half noticed Jaxon swallowing a smile as she stumbled through the doorway, her parents and then Jaxon following. The door shut behind him.

The room was full of activity and the babble of voices. Jonathon was loudly engaging Mateo and Drew. Sitting in her rocking chair, Bernadette quietly and confidentially spoke to Danielle. Jesalyn bustled about getting the table set, and Davey . . . well . . . he stood near the entrance and looked lost.

"Dear!" Jonathon called to Jesalyn. "Why do you not sit down and enjoy yourself?"

"Dear," Jesalyn told Jonathon with a slight edge to her

voice, "why do you not sit down and enjoy yourself while I prepare all of this."

"I'm not sure if that is a hint or a threat," Mateo commented, opening a cupboard to grab some plates.

"Either way it means work," Jaxon noted, rooting around for a knife and starting to chop potatoes. However, though he walked away after only one slice, the knife continued cutting potatoes by itself. "You look like a fellow who needs some lessons in efficiency," he said as he sidled up to Drew, draping his arm over Drew's frame. "That," Jaxon pointed at the knife, "is what efficiency looks like. Take a good, hard look. Someday, you may come close to having a tenth of that efficiency."

Gabrielle felt her own eyebrows rise. Davey did not snort this time, but Gabrielle saw him earnestly attempting to wipe the smirk off his face.

"Jaxon," Jesalyn reprimanded him sharply, "he is our guest."

"Of course, Mother, I was simply giving the poor, young lad some advice." Jaxon patted Drew on the back.

"Forgive my sons," Jesalyn said, the edge to her voice still present. "Unfortunately, their humour often leads them to single out and *harass* one of the guests anytime they are home, and guests are present. I apologise for their behavior."

"A fully grown man and you still need Mum to apologise for you," Jaxon tsked as he took out a stack of bowls. "I think perhaps we ought to have a little talk later."

Mateo adjusted his course slightly, conspicuously and

purposefully hip chucking Jaxon, causing the bowls to go flying into the air.

Almost immediately, the bowls halted in their arcs, slowing down to a stand-still, then floated gracefully towards the table and onto each plate already set. Jesalyn had her hand raised and was directing them. The bowls were set in less than three seconds, but Mateo and Jaxon wisely used that short time to compose shameful expressions.

"Enough."

"Yes, Mother," the men agreed simultaneously, seriousness fading away almost as soon as the last syllable was pronounced, Mateo's grin the quickest although Jaxon had trouble choking down his smile.

Jesalyn shook her head. "Sometimes I think that tis better to get silence from ye than agreement. Enough potatoes, Jaxon."

Jaxon waved his hand, and the knife stopped cutting. The potatoes careened into the pot on the fire, and the knife came much too close for coincidence as it streaked past Mateo to its proper place.

"She really wanted a girl," Bernadette commented from the corner, speaking to a smiling Danielle but also talking plenty loud enough for everyone to hear. "I agreed."

"Mother!" Jesalyn exclaimed.

"What, dear? I even told you that we should do the old ritual—"

"That ritual doesn't work," Jesalyn sighed.

"You mean you would have done the ritual had it worked?" Jaxon asked.

"And you would have been just as much trouble anyways,"

Jesalyn continued, tacking on a glare when she saw Mateo's grin.

"Mother," Jaxon began.

"Not another word," Jesalyn warned, finger coming up to point at him. "Remember, we still have to figure out where everyone will be sleeping tonight."

"I was just going to tell you that I love you and ask what else you needed done," Jaxon defended himself with innocent, wide eyes.

"I will believe it when I see it."

"I love you, Mum. What else do you need done?" Mateo promptly said.

Jesalyn appraised him for only a second, then took him up on the unwilling offer. "We shall need more water for everyone, ten buckets. No, twelve. Will you go draw some from the well?"

Mateo's mouth opened. "Mum—"

"Yes, dear?" Jesalyn's voice definitely contained a warning this time.

Mateo swallowed his protest. "Nothing."

Jaxon was snickering and commented as Mateo walked past him, "I knew you were a poor soul the moment I saw you."

"Will you help him, Jaxon?" Jesalyn instructed.

It was Mateo's turn to snicker as Jaxon replied, "Yes, Mother."

The two walked out together, the sounds of a scuffle commencing as soon as the door shut.

Gabrielle turned to face a wall and examine the cupboards, uninterestedly considering them with a hand over her mouth.

"We like to blame a crazy great uncle on my father's side for their behavior," Jonathon informed them as Jesalyn threw a few spices into the pot and then disappeared into another room. Bernadette began talking with Danielle again. Jonathon, Davey, Gabrielle, and her parents formed a sort of pod at one end of the room.

"Tis done in jest," Gabrielle's mother offered.

"Indeed," Jonathon agreed.

Gabrielle sidled past them to Jesalyn. "Do you honestly need any help?"

"Honestly?" Jesalyn turned and grinned at her. "No, you can rest, dear. Take a bath. I would love to force the boys to get more water."

"I'll wash tonight," Gabrielle insisted. "Besides, I don't mind work."

"I know, which makes me all the more unwilling to give you anything to do. Nevertheless, if you would like to follow me, I just realised that I would love some help getting more chairs."

Gabrielle nodded and followed Jesalyn around the house, gathering odd chairs from rooms until they had searched for and found enough for the group that night. Mateo and Jaxon had returned by the time they were done, and everyone was starting to settle down.

Jesalyn served the meal, any attempts to aid her being shot down, and chatter bounced merrily around the room. Mateo and Jaxon had somehow succeeded in getting Drew to sit in between them, and they each kept putting more soup into his bowl, proclaiming that he definitely looked like he needed sustenance to build up his dainty frame. They prodded and poked him until Gabrielle was positive that Davey no longer cared that they were sorcerers and was going to award both brothers medals.

Finally, Jesalyn spoke up again, reprimanding her sons. "Please, boys. Leave him alone for a little while." She did not sound convinced that her words would do any good.

"Tis only a little teasing," Davey interjected suddenly. He had been uncommonly quiet throughout the meal, keeping a watch mostly on Danielle and Gabrielle's family alternatively and smiling at Jaxon and Mateo's harassment of Drew.

"Well, yes," Jesalyn hesitantly agreed.

Davey looked at Drew, eyebrows raised, clearly trying to hold back a triumphant look. "Well, tis only a little teasing. I should suppose that Drew is above actually being bothered by such childish pranks. Come now, Drew, are you really not gentlemanly enough to stand a few harmless laughs?"

Gabrielle's mother started quietly laughing, shaking her head at Gabrielle's questioning look.

"Tis more than a few," Drew replied stiffly.

"Tis more than you can handle? If so, just say the word, and we can ask the boys to restrain their gaiety."

Glaring at Davey, Drew smiled painfully. "I'm well, thank you."

"I'm glad," Davey told him grinning. He turned to Jaxon and Mateo. "Please continue making Drew feel welcome. You heard him. He doesn't mind."

Jaxon and Mateo looked at each other and grinned wickedly.

Gabrielle's mother finally got control of her amusement.

"What was that?" Gabrielle asked her.

Her mother shook her head, exchanging an amused look with . . . Davey?

"Oh . . . nothing." Her mother smiled even more broadly.

Gabrielle looked to Davey, but he was suddenly enraptured by his soup. She let it go.

While Mateo, Jaxon, Drew, and Davey "discussed" together, Gabrielle learned that Jonathon was an avid reader like her father, and the two of them conversed much of the night. Danielle had taken a shine to Bernadette and Bernadette to her, so they monopolized each other for the most part. Jesalyn, Marie, and Gabrielle formed a conversation group as well although all of the conversations in the room crossed over each other at some point.

Late into the night, Gabrielle asked Jesalyn what Jaxon and Mateo did for a living. Jesalyn called across the table to them and repeated the question. Jaxon immediately responded with "vendor of intelligence" and told Drew that he highly recommended his services to him. Mateo said juggler and juggled a potato right into Drew's bowl, splashing the soup all over Drew's front.

"As a side job," Mateo happily continued, speaking around Drew's aura of anger, "I travel outside of Havene and trade goods."

"I do the same," Jaxon added, "except I specialize more in food, herbs, and roots while Mateo trades products such as clothing and metalwork."

"We lost our weapons today," Drew said.

Gabrielle considered this brave considering that he had not been able to say a word without the brothers turning it into a joke.

"Someone trusted you with a knife?" Mateo asked, shocked.

"We'll resupply you in the morning," Jesalyn assured him, ignoring her son.

"Is there any possibility of getting our weapons back?" Davey asked.

"No. The sky gnomes don't use the weapons, and the redcaps usually don't travel that far. However, some dragons collect human artifacts, so I'd be surprised if your weapons were anywhere near the sky gnomes still."

"Could you scry them?" Davey asked, shifting uncomfortably.

Jesalyn still spoke calmly. "It takes much magic to scry objects. Having seen your weapons only once, the likelihood of me being able to scry them is low. You'd also have to then go get the weapons, which is not advisable."

"I understand. Thank you." Davey's hand rested on his empty sheath.

The loss of the enchanted sword was not ideal, Gabrielle knew, but she could not help but feel a small spike of satisfaction. She swallowed it along with another spoonful of stew.

The conversations were lighter during the remainder of the night. Sleeping arrangements were discussed, Jesalyn initially grouping Jaxon, Mateo, and Drew together before saying, "No! Absolutely not! Jaxon and Mateo, you sleep together by yourselves!"

At Jesalyn and Jonathon's persistent insistence, their own room was given to Gabrielle's parents, her parents requesting that Gabrielle sleep with them, Danielle requesting that she join their family. Davey protested slightly at this, but Danielle was firm after securing the blessing of Gabrielle's parents.

Jesalyn laughed and said that her house had not been this full since all the boys were home. Every room was at capacity except for the kitchen and dining room area.

As Jesalyn spread out blankets, Gabrielle asked about Jesalyn's third son. Jesalyn told her that he also traveled outside of Havene although came home much less often than Mateo and Jaxon did.

"He has built up a life outside of Havene while my other boys simple travel between the two places," she explained.

Gabrielle tried to imagine what would cause a sorcerer to choose to find a way to make a living, marry, and raise children outside of the safety of Havene as they put the finishing touches on the makeshift sleeping areas.

Although Danielle exchanged some whispers with Gabrielle, Gabrielle fell asleep quickly that night, body aching from the strenuous day. When she awoke, her muscles burned still, bones cracking with every movement. The sun barely peeped in through the window, and snores filled the room. Sitting up slowly and with a grimace, Gabrielle raised her head and then got to her feet, the ground suddenly too uncomfortable to sleep upon.

Gabrielle exited the room and headed towards the kitchen. Faintly, she could hear voices issuing from it. Drew sat at the table with Jesalyn, steaming mugs in their hands. A fire crackled in the hearth.

"Morning, Gabrielle," Drew smiled at her, both hands around his mug, leaning slightly over the table.

Gabrielle smiled. "Good morning."

"Tea?" Jesalyn offered.

Gabrielle shook her head. "But perhaps a little water?"

"Indeed," Jesalyn agreed. As she poured a cup for Gabrielle, "Would you like to take a walk with me?"

Gabrielle nodded, pleased by the simple request she could easily fulfill, even if her body wished to be lying in her bed in Seron.

Jesalyn gave the cup to Gabrielle, slung her bag from yesterday over her shoulder, and walked out the front door. Gabrielle followed close behind.

The chill from last night had continued into the morning. While the grass had no frost on it, the dew was heavy and cold. Large droplets clung to dark green strands upon the chilled ground. Gabrielle shivered and wished she had asked for shoes before leaving. The air was cold enough to be crisp, stinging the flesh. It was as if nature and winter had collaborated to create yet another foretelling of the season. Sunlight filtered through the morning air in the same bright, crisp manner. Each breath brimmed with the invigorating mixture of chill and sunrays.

Gabrielle walked beside Jesalyn, Gabrielle choosing to revel in the cold instead of hiding from it, letting every step she took become stronger and firmer.

Just after a minute or two, once the house had gone out of view due to other buildings, Jesalyn stopped and opened her bag, pulling out the spell book she had given Gabrielle earlier. She held it up for Gabrielle's brief examination, then slipped it back into the bag and gave the bag to Gabrielle.

Gabrielle took it with a grateful nod, and the two started walking again.

They enjoyed the peaceful morning, hearing little but the squawking of roosters, cooing of birds, and the occasional laugh or shout from an early rising child. After about ten minutes, Jesalyn turned back towards the house, taking a different route home.

Gabrielle's feet tingled fiercely from the cold of the damp grass. Her feet were thoroughly soaked. She was fairly certain there was more water on top of her foot than remaining in her cup.

She finally decided to break the quiet.

"Jesalyn?"

"Yes?"

"Jaxon knows who I am."

Jesalyn looked to Gabrielle, unconcerned, slightly smiling. "All magic leaves a trace. The stronger the magic, the stronger the trace. One can become attuned to recognizing magic. Jaxon, and the rest of my family, recognize the magic in you."

"Ye all know what I am?"

"Yes."

Gabrielle fell silent. She had always wanted someone to tell, but this had not been a choice.

"They'll tell none, Gabrielle," Jesalyn assured her.

"He also knew *who* I was, though, I mean."

"You did not expect him to know you're Valencia?"

Gabrielle looked to her sharply.

Jesalyn merely smiled calmly again. "A changeling arrives in Havene, traveling to dragon territory with the prince and his friend. Suddenly, an unknown dragon appears and helps the prince and his friend. For those who know both those facts, the evidence is not difficult to connect."

"Do you think anyone else shall make the connection?"

"Does anyone else know you are a changeling?" Jesalyn questioned.

"Some of the dragons suspected," Gabrielle admitted. "I—I accidently killed one of them, Benjamin."

Jesalyn took Gabrielle's hand and lightly squeezed.

"All I can say is this, the more time you spend in dragon territory, the more likely it is someone will make the connection. That being said, you could resume the form of Valencia every day for years and have no one discover you, or you could never do so again and have a person reason it to be so. I do not think I need to tell you this, but your very existence puts you in danger."

Gabrielle nodded.

"Keep your chin up," Jesalyn advised, tightening her grip on Gabrielle's hand. "You can't always change others or the circumstances, but you'll always have your choices."

"Missus Jesalyn!" a familiar voice called.

Gabrielle automatically grinned, Jesalyn doing the same.

Running up from behind them, wearing only a pair of trousers and his wide, bright eyes, Felipe raced towards them, coming to a halt a second before colliding.

"How are you, Mr. Felipe?" Jesalyn asked him.

"Can I come over? Please? Please?"

"Ask your mother"—he started running away—"but wait until she is up!" Jesalyn tried to quietly call to him.

He wildly waved a hand in the air, but Gabrielle could not tell if this was in agreement or parting.

Jesalyn shared an amused look with Gabrielle.

By the time they got back to the house, most of the others

were up and moving. Jesalyn got a towel for their feet, then allowed Gabrielle to help make breakfast while the men, with the exception of Gabrielle's father, replenished their weaponry. Gabrielle was inordinately pleased when Davey stopped Jonathon from putting away the weapons and protested that they had yet to find a knife for Gabrielle to carry, but she was even more pleased when they found out Drew had already set one aside for her.

Once Davey and Drew were satisfied, Davey offered to eventually somehow pay for the two swords and eight daggers Jonathon had given them, one dagger going to Gabrielle, one to Dannie, one to her father, and five to Drew. However, Jonathon insisted that no payment was necessary. Davey couldn't figure out how to respond to that, but Dannie simply hugged him and said thanks.

After breakfast, during which an excited and overeager Felipe arrived, it was time to leave. Jesalyn had packed a few bags for them, insisting as Jonathon had on no payment and even giving them enough coin for a night or two at an inn and food.

Gabrielle hugged Jesalyn this time, whispering her thanks and squeezing tightly.

Jesalyn hugged Gabrielle back, pulling away after a moment and nodding once, slowly.

Drew had forgotten a bag back in the house, so he and Jesalyn went back to get it while the others finished last minute checks outside.

Jonathon would lead Gabrielle's family, Davey, Danielle, and Drew through a tunnel out of Havene, and because time was no longer a great concern, they planned to stop at

Apude, the village nearest to dragon territory. The journey there would take only a day, and Jonathon would leave them as they left Apude.

After Apude was Seron, only another day and a half of travel though Davey was considering leaving early and traveling in the dark to make it in one day. Seron would be where their group officially disbanded. Davey, Danielle, and Drew would go on to the city of Aradin. Gabrielle and her parents would return to the tavern and inn. In all, Seron was only two days away.

Gabrielle wished that didn't make her so disappointed.

"Are we ready?" Jonathon asked at long last as the final few activities and checks finished.

"I believe ye are," Jesalyn replied to Jonathon, coming forward and pecking him on the cheek. "Be careful and return home."

"I always do," Jonathon grinned.

"Keep those who need a little extra help safe, Dad," Jaxon directed, eyes on Drew.

"You be careful as well," Jonathon told Jaxon. "I do not wish to return safely only to learn that one of my sons has started the town on fire or stolen Madam Marchetti's cat."

"We only did that once," Mateo protested.

"Indeed, and we were even able to get the flames out before anything important burned," Jaxon added.

"Ye laugh," Jesalyn told their group, "but ye do not understand what they have done in the past."

"The past is not so interesting," Jaxon commented. "Everything's already known! Indeed, the future tis where I am at. Who knows what'll go wrong there?"

Gabrielle pursed her lips, considering disagreeing, but it had only been a flippant remark.

"I'm ready, too!" Felipe piped up.

Everyone turned to look at the little boy, water canteen over his shoulder, a stick supposedly doubling as a dagger or sword in his hand.

Jonathon and Jesalyn exchanged glances.

"Mr. Felipe," Jonathon said slowly, going down to his knees to better speak with Felipe. Felipe looked honoured. "I appreciate your offer, but I need you here, staying with your mother and my wife."

"She has them," Felipe reminded Jonathon, pointing at Jaxon and Mateo.

"Tis what I am worried about," Jonathon said. "I need someone to watch them, too, and who will watch your mother?"

"But I want to come with you, Mr. Jonathon!"

"I know, but I really need you to stay here," Mr. Jonathon told him again, placing both hands on Felipe's shoulders. Felipe tugged gently but did not draw completely away. "I need someone to stay and watch over Havene while I am gone. It needs to be somebody brave and strong."

"I'm brave and strong, but I want to come with you, Mr. Jonathon!" Felipe insisted.

"Here." Jonathon tried guiding Felipe towards the house. "How about we have a short talk—"

"No!" Felipe cried, pulling away from Jonathon while also swinging a small, clenched fist.

Jonathon picked up Felipe and held the crying, writhing boy in his arms.

"I wanna come with you!" Felipe sobbed.

Jonathon looked to Jesalyn and then walked into the house carrying the distraught and screaming Felipe.

"He shall be just a few minutes," Jesalyn told them.

No one really said anything. They were out of time for real questions and goodbyes would have to wait until Jonathon returned.

Mateo and Jaxon began making plans with each other using quick eye movements and supposedly innocuous hand gestures, but their mother noticed them before they could act.

Felipe stormed out of the house, refusing to look at any of them, and ran to an outer wall of the home where he angrily kicked rocks. Jonathon followed slowly, his face appearing more aged than before.

"Thank you for your help," Davey formally stated as Jonathon returned. "We are grateful for your generous aid."

"Indeed," Jesalyn murmured. "Good to luck to you, Prince David. Thy father rules a kingdom divided, and I doubt such shall change before tis your turn."

Davey nodded once.

"Goodbye, Madam Jesalyn, Berna, Mateo, Jaxon!" Dannie told each of them in turn.

Gabrielle suspected that she would have liberally handed out hugs, but that Dannie wisely chose to refrain from such while her brother was present.

Gabrielle and her father nodded and murmured their goodbyes and gratitude. Marie determinedly told Jesalyn and Jonathon. "Thank you for all you have done for us. I cannot tell you how much your help has meant to our family."

Jesalyn smiled. "Twas a pleasure. Ye are welcome here anytime."

Gabrielle came forward for one more hug, and Timothy shook hands with Jesalyn.

"We shall be saying the same to you when we part ways," Marie assured Jonathon.

With a few more waves and goodbyes, their group officially started off, Jonathon leading the way to the tunnel with the softly glowing blue spheres. Behind them, Gabrielle could no longer see Felipe sullenly kicking rocks against Jonathon and Jesalyn's house. She knew his little heart would heal, but could not help but feel a pang of guilt for being the cause of some of his strife. If they were not taking Jonathon with them, Felipe would not have been so eager to join them.

Few words were exchanged as they walked through the tunnel. Danielle seemed too preoccupied with their leaving Havene to ask questions, and Gabrielle believed Drew was just glad to finally be away from Mateo and Jaxon.

When they reached the end of the tunnel, another muddy hole waited for them there. Jonathon dried a strip of ground for them to walk to the stairs without getting their shoes wet and unnecessarily dirty. Gabrielle appreciated the gesture.

The stairs were a ridiculously easy climb compared to the ravine yesterday. Everyone except Gabrielle's father was able to simply walk up the uneven ledges. The bag Gabrielle was carrying, which was the satchel Jesalyn had given her that morning, had not left Gabrielle's side, but it was so small and light that it bothered Gabrielle none.

Once above ground, Jonathon continued to lead them.

"How do you know how to get to Apude?" Davey asked. "I

did not believe that you left Havene?" This time, his tone was not the slightest bit accusatory, just openly curious.

Gabrielle wondered how many times he had mentally practiced the words.

"Apude is slightly southwest of here, closer to south than west. Tis a straight shot from here, for there are no roads. We make our own paths."

They walked in silence again for some time. All were tired from their journeys. Gabrielle took pleasure in speculating what spells were in the book Jesalyn had given her.

Her neck prickled.

"There's a dragon," she immediately informed everyone, glancing skyward, but not seeing one.

"See it," Drew murmured. "Tis too low and close to move."

Gabrielle did not bother to continue searching for the dragon, simply put her head down and hoped. She noticed the grass entwined around the twigs and the two edible mushrooms near her feet for only a moment. Her mind disregarded the sight to consider the dragon and the possibilities he or she brought. They had not yet successfully fought off a dragon. Her breathing slowed, and she closed her eyes, hoping that they would fail to catch the dragon's attention.

"Tis gone," Drew announced.

Gabrielle opened her eyes, confused, the prickling had lessened, but was still present. She scanned the area, nerves on edge. What if another dragon surprised them as Decius had? Blending into the trees with unnerving ease? The skies offered no answers. The trees . . .

Gabrielle sharply inhaled.

Davey heard, turned, and saw. He drew his sword.

Gabrielle looked—panicked—at Davey. This was one fight she did not want to see. This was one fight that she could not win.

Heather, Ruby, and Victoria were there.

Davey stepped forward despite the fact that his sword was no longer made of dragon's claw nor enchanted.

Ruby coiled downward like a spring despite the fact that Davey had little trouble challenging them last time. Victoria warily followed suit on the large branch they were all perched on. Heather was struggling just to maintain an air of calmness and did not follow her sister's lead.

"Davey!" Gabrielle said suddenly.

Davey held out a hand behind him, indicating that he had this and that she should get let him focus.

Gabrielle took a deep, stuttered breath, then walked forward.

Davey whipped his arm out to stop her, but she simply ducked it and stepped underneath. He grabbed her wrist, sword still out in front of him. "What are you doing?!" he asked through gritted teeth.

Gabrielle swung around, back to the girls, facing Davey head-on. "The first thing you do is bring out your sword. Twas not always that way."

Davey's eyes widened in surprise.

Gabrielle's stomach twisted and turned, roiling while disconcertedly still. She felt as if one of her legs was twitching madly, muscle spasming at two-hundred beats per minute, and she worried that her voice would give away the all-encompassing, mind-numbing fear she felt.

She tried to turn towards the girls. Davey's grip on her

wrist stopped the movement, and she sent a pointed look towards it, wondering how nobody could see through her façade.

To her surprise and relief, he released her without further comment or argument.

She faced them.

"I believe you told me that you were Victoria," Gabrielle spoke directly to Victoria, hoping that Davey and Drew would not remember specifically if Victoria had told Gabrielle her name while Gabrielle was in human form. She could not remember herself.

"Yeah," Victoria nodded, wary, but coming out of the crouched position a small amount.

"What are your names?" Gabrielle asked Ruby and Heather.

"Ruby," Ruby snapped.

"Heather," Heather gulped.

"I'm Gabrielle. These are my parents, Davey, Drew, and Jonathon. We are just heading out of dragon territory. What are you doing today?"

Gabrielle wanted to leave the "today" off, but figured that would sound too aggressive. While she wanted to reprimand the three for getting anywhere near humans, she decided that the action would be too much like Valencia for her to say anything. Besides, she was not supposed to know that they would be in trouble for traveling this far from the brood— never mind interacting with humans.

Victoria shifted, uncomfortable with the question, but Ruby did not hesitate to reply. Raising her chin, she said, "Why's that your business?"

"I'm just being polite," Gabrielle chastised her. "There is

no need for rudeness here. If you do not wish to tell us of your business, that's your business, but tis not necessary for you to respond like that."

Now Ruby shifted uncomfortably.

"We just wanted to see you!" Heather blurted out.

"Heather!" Ruby snapped.

"What? Come on, Ruby! Last time they fought us and I told you it wasn't a good idea to come but you really wanted to see humans again!"

With a sudden intake of air, life returned to Gabrielle's mind. They had wanted to see her as in the human, not her as in Valencia.

"Victoria did, too!" Ruby argued. "And you thought it was a good idea until we actually decided to do it."

"Mother said not to go this far from the brood!" Heather reminded Ruby.

"Yeah, and you think Mother would have let us see humans even if they were right outside the brood? Get real, Heather."

"I am real!"

"All right," Gabrielle interrupted soothingly. "How about this. You have seen your humans, even interacted with them. Perhaps you can even make it back to the brood without your mother knowing that you left. Not that I am condoning such action"—Gabrielle glared pointedly at the three girls—"but you may escape further punishment if you return now."

"I think we should fight you," Ruby declared. "Dragons are supposed to fight humans."

Gabrielle's heart slowly drifted downwards.

"Valencia wouldn't," Heather piped up.

Ruby glared at her sister.

"She's right, Ruby," Victoria pointed out, not sounding convinced either way, but Ruby still glared at her as well.

"Well, *I'm* not Valencia," Ruby cuttingly said.

"Mom's right. You're sassy," Heather observed.

"Better sassy than Heather."

"Hey!"

"Think!" Victoria interrupted them.

Both of the other girls turned and made faces at Victoria. Gabrielle agreed that it wasn't the best, most random word, but Victoria's method had, temporarily, succeeded again.

"I think—" Victoria stopped, drawing herself inward. Then she puffed out her chest and looked towards Gabrielle. "What's your name?"

"Gabrielle."

"I think . . . Gabrielle . . . is right. Somewhat."

Victoria paused, obviously considering each word carefully before speaking.

"I don't want to get into any more trouble because both our mothers are already super mad at us, and I don't think Valencia would do anything either. Yes, Ruby, we are not Valencia, but I like Valencia, and I don't think . . . I don't think she's always wrong in what she does." Victoria took a deep breath. "We said we'd come here to see humans and we did. We even talked to them, but now I think we should at least not fight them."

After a moment's pause, Victoria tacked on, "And not only because we all know that if we survive our mothers will kill us."

Ruby peered at Gabrielle.

Meeting Ruby's gaze, Gabrielle kept a steady, unassuming expression. If it came to a fight, she did not know who would win. Davey had been proficient before, but now his sword was of regular metal. Perhaps Drew would blind the girls.

The thought alone almost made Gabrielle cry.

"I won't fight," Ruby admitted, muscles relaxing as she did such.

Gabrielle felt some of her own tension fade.

"Can we leave?" Heather pleaded.

"Yeah," Ruby reluctantly conceded, but she stopped herself from flying away and asked Davey and Danielle suspiciously, "Are you two the prince and princess?"

Davey opened his mouth, about to deny the charges, but Danielle answered before Davey could. "Yes! I'm Princess Danielle. This is my brother, Prince David."

"Princess Danielle and Prince David?" Heather asked in shock.

"Yes," Danielle affirmed.

Davey glowered at her, much as he had done to Sir Drew back at the tavern so long ago.

"Wow," Heather breathed. "Wait till I tell Mother."

"You can't tell Mother, Heather, else she'll know we spoke with humans!" Ruby reminded her sharply, flying upwards and beginning to depart.

"Well, I know!" Heather protested. Then, noticing her sister already gaining considerable speed, "Wait for me!"

She took off as well, leaving only Victoria sitting on the branch, thoughtfully considering Gabrielle.

"Why'd you talk to us?" Victoria asked.

Gabrielle did not look away, but she could not think of what to answer.

That was not entirely true, though. A multitude of answers sprung to mind, but there were few she could share without giving away too much or without indicating that there was much more to be said.

Not knowing what else to say, and now having an inkling of doubt regarding the dragon Thomas' apparent wisdom, she replied, "Why not?"

"Because we're dragons and you're humans. Ruby was right when she said dragons are supposed to fight humans."

"Then why didn't you?"

Victoria sucked in part of her snout, thinking. "Because I don't think what is right is right. You seem kind of nice and I don't like fighting even though I know that you have killed dragons—"

"We have not killed any dragons," Davey interrupted suddenly.

Victoria was taken aback by his unexpected words, and she was not young enough to even attempt to hide it.

"Haven't you?" she asked.

"None," Davey said. "We have fought when necessary to maintain our lives, and unfortunately, that has made us quick to draw our swords. Gabrielle was correct that we have become too quick to rely on our swords instead of our words. I apologise, and I assure you that we have killed no dragons."

"I thought all humans killed dragons," Victoria mused.

"Do all dragons kill humans?" Gabrielle questioned.

"Of course not!" Victoria replied.

"Neither do all humans kill dragons," Gabrielle stated.

Victoria appeared to chew on this, unsure of how the thought tasted.

Gabrielle continued, "Perhaps humans and dragons are more alike than you think."

"Maybe," Victoria shrugged. Then she glanced at the sky, Heather and Ruby already out of sight. "I better go join them."

Gabrielle nodded. "Good luck."

Victoria cocked her head. She grinned. "Thank you. Good luck to you, too."

She flew away.

Gabrielle stood there for a moment, then walked back into the group, doing her best to ignore the others.

After a moment of quiet, Jonathon nodded and started leading the group again. Unsure of how she felt herself, Gabrielle was grateful when they started walking.

The day had already faded into early afternoon before they stopped for some rest. Davey called it this time, warily watching Gabrielle's father down much of the water and lean wearily against a tree. Gabrielle sat crisscross on the ground, back against the same tree. Groaning quietly, her father sank down next to her, letting out a sigh as he reached the earth.

"Tired, old man?" Gabrielle's mother asked playfully, standing next to Gabrielle's father, her hand lovingly resting on his head.

"Not of you," he replied, taking her hand and kissing it.

Gabrielle smiled before looking away.

Drew was lying flat on the ground in an open area, arms and legs spread as a chicken about to be dressed, eyes closed.

Jonathon stood over him and looked down. "Comfortable?" he asked.

"Indeed," Drew replied, cracking one eye open and grinning. "Much more comfortable than I was on the floor last night. Some greedy, inconsiderate person did not wish to share the blankets."

"Ah!" Davey cried. "He speaks! I thought we had finally silenced you for good! Got a little taste of your own medicine back in Havene, did you not?"

Gabrielle stifled a giggle at Davey's unusual enthusiasm.

"I don't know what you're talking about." Drew closed his eyes again.

"Of course not," Davey agreed with him. "My mistake. I guess I'm just used to your griping."

"I feel sorry for you," Drew said, unable to pretend that he had not heard Davey. "I only have to put up with you most of the time, but you have to put up with you all of the time."

"You just cannot accept what you serve," Davey said promptly.

Drew opened his mouth to respond, froze for a split second, then deftly rolled to his feet. "Raiders."

Davey and the others did not move immediately, and Gabrielle could suddenly hear them, grass rustling quietly beneath their feet, a twig breaking and ringing out, sudden silence.

Then everyone realised what everyone else knew, and they attacked.

XVIII

Sorcery

Fifteen to sixteen men rushed at them in a half semi-circle, only about thirty feet away. Davey ran forward, swinging the new sword. Drew came at them as well, palming two knives. Gabrielle pulled her own knife out of the bag Jesalyn had given her. She spared a moment to distractedly note that she had to find some way to store the weapon on her person.

Jonathon stood firmly in front of Gabrielle and her parents. "Clypeumle," he said, and the air glimmered, like a compressed, up close heat wave, but the effect was gone after just a few seconds.

Davey injured the first two men with one arc. Drew threw one of his knives and hit a man in the shoulder. Behind her, Gabrielle's father groaned, and she turned to help him stand.

Seeing that Davey was the more preeminent threat, most of the remaining men congregated around him. He was barely able to fend the multitude of them off, constantly striving to rove around them and use their own persons as his shield although he did manage to seriously injure another.

Drew was there as well, throwing another knife and killing the first man he had hit. Only then did Drew draw his sword, but he seemed to be barely able to hold his own when two were attacking him at once. One near miss made Gabrielle certain that he was going to die, but Drew threw himself to the left at the last minute, leaving his side exposed.

The other man who had not struck at Drew stood above and behind him. The man raised his sword.

Gabrielle's body grew heavy, and her breathing slowed. Though her father was now on his feet, there was no way for her to get to Drew in time to help him. Gabrielle could not wait. Gabrielle could not hesitate. She raised her hand.

"Funem," Jonathon firmly stated, and a wooden rope grew into existence. However, the branch did not whip out randomly, but wrapped itself around the man's waist and yanked him, spinning wildly, back to the tree. Jonathon sent Gabrielle a look, then stepped forward himself.

Gabrielle decided to cover her parents if the need arose and watched Jonathon proceed to repeat the spell on the remaining raiders. One by one, the raiders were pulled to trees, random branches sprouting long and low. A few minutes later and all were bound tightly against the trunks.

Davey turned solemn eyes upon Jonathon. "Thank you," the prince stated, nodding once.

A small voice in Gabrielle whispered *hypocrite.*

She tried to ignore it.

A wet, inhaling sound issued through the woods. One of

the men, though ten feet away from Jonathon, spat at him. "Sorcerer!" the man hissed, his scraggly beard partially hiding his scars. "Disgusting!"

Jonathon's face hardened, but he did not reply.

The man continued anyway. "You're dead when I get out."

All of the raiders who were still conscious were glaring at Jonathon, some fearfully. Only a single, cleanshaven man lacked any aggression, his terror too great.

Suddenly, the wooden ropes unfurled, each and every one retreating to the trees whence they had come. A few of the raiders lifted their hands as if they could not believe their luck, but then Jonathon raised his own hands and began chanting words that Gabrielle caught but could not hold. The air shimmered as it had before, but with translucent brushes of color as well, all various shades of red and brown. Gabrielle watched Jonathon in awe and fear as his voice rose in volume incrementally.

Then his chanting stopped just as suddenly as it had begun. He lowered his hands.

Nobody breathed.

The raider who had spat at Jonathon examined himself, flipping his hands back and forth, testing his legs. Seeing no sign of injury, he laughed uproariously. The other men quickly joined him.

Gabrielle glanced at Jonathon, but his expression had not changed. Looking at their group, Gabrielle saw Drew's face as stony as Jonathon's, but Davey's was graver still. It was as if Davey were fighting some instinct or urge inside so badly that he just shut down his thoughts for a moment, emotions dead. Gabrielle's parents were gripping each other's hands in unbidden shock, wonder, and fear. Gabrielle felt the same. She felt her lack of understanding acutely, and it was uncomfortable. It was frightening.

The outspoken raider picked up a sword one of the others had dropped, grinning. He wiped the dirt of the blade onto his pants. Quickly, the laughter died down as the other raiders did the same.

"I would suggest not proceeding," Jonathon calmly stated, reminding Gabrielle suddenly of his wife.

Gabrielle wondered if this seemingly innate calmness was in all sorcerers, but then remembered Jaxon and Mateo and rejected the thought.

"Why not?" The same raider spoke. He wiped his mouth with the back of his hand, grinning with his sword firmly gripped. "Are you going to speak some more? Wave your hands? You can't even fight like a man."

"You can't," Jonathon said, folding his hands in front of himself. "Should you attempt to take up a sword in attack, the only flesh you break will be your own."

The man snorted, but worry flickered across a few faces behind him.

"I'll take my chances," he said and strode towards Jonathon.

Davey took a stiff step forward, but Jonathon stopped him with a gesture before refolding his hands.

The raider's leader took two more steps and swung at Jonathon, Jonathon never unfolding his hands nor moving his legs.

The raider inclined his hand back at the last minute, so the blade missed Jonathon completely. However, the sword did not stop, and Gabrielle watched, horrified, as the blade continued until it had buried itself in the man's opposing shoulder, sinking deep into the flesh, nearly severing the limb.

She squeezed her eyes shut against the image.

That did nothing about the man's screaming.

He suddenly screamed louder, and there was a thump.

Gabrielle opened her eyes to see him on the ground, cowering as Jonathon took another step forward, hands held out again.

Gabrielle opened her mouth. To protest? To tell him to stop? She could not believe her eyes.

"Nildolor," Jonathon unflinchingly said.

The screaming stopped.

The raider's breathing was staggered from his alarm, his eyes wide with terror, but it seemed that his pain was diminished. Carefully, gazing at the raider, Jonathon lowered himself to the ground until he was crouching just two feet away from the other man. "I can heal you if you wish. Be aware that if you do not receive a healing in the next few hours, the chances of you surviving the week are slim."

His breathing becoming quieter and steadier, though still jagged, the raider simply stared at Jonathon.

The still, tense atmosphere tied Gabrielle's stomach into knots.

"Will you let me heal you?"

The raider still did not reply, but Jonathon came forward after another minute anyway with an awkward, crouched step. The raider flinched, and Jonathon paused. However, the pause lasted but a moment. Continuing forward, Jonathon came right beside the man and lay his hand over the raider's arm.

The raider watched unblinkingly.

"You are lucky," Jonathon told the raider. "Had the sword gone in deeper or higher, I would have neither the magic nor knowledge to heal you." Jonathon leaned in a little closer to the man's wound, then muttered, "Sano." The flesh healed partially and the bleeding slowed. "Percuro. Medum. Panace."

Each spell seemed to heal the wound a little bit differently, percuro leaving the injury looking fresh, but washed clean and ready for wrapping, medum knitting together the depths of the cut, panace re-growing the skin over top of the injury.

"Tis all I can do without my books," Jonathon told the man. "Keep your arm rested. Do not raise it up above your shoulders nor lift anything heavy. Your body will feel tired for the rest of the day. Don't fight it. Your wound was grievous, and your entire body needs time to recuperate. The spells saved you, but you need to heal the rest of the way."

Jonathon looked into the man's eyes for one second more, then stood up. "Also, I would suggest not using your sword."

Gabrielle did not realise that Jonathon had dropped the bag he had been carrying until he walked back towards her to pick it up. He swung it over his shoulder and turned towards Davey. "Should we resume our journey?"

Davey looked at him for a second, then nodded once, and Jonathon strolled away from the still raiders in the direction they had been heading in earlier.

With a grim look on his face, Davey followed. Drew sheathed his sword and retrieved his daggers as Danielle, Gabrielle, and her parents followed Jonathon and Davey.

Gabrielle noticed that Davey did not put away his sword but continued carrying it as they walked.

After some time, Gabrielle realised that her stomach was growling. They had stopped to rest, and it had been unspoken but assumed that they would eat as well. Nevertheless, with the raiders attacking and Jonathon's magic, everyone had forgotten about food. Gabrielle did not wish to disrupt the quiet that their group maintained, but knew that if she was hungry, then Drew was close to famished. Jesalyn had packed them a few loaves for their journey. While she did not carry any food, her mother did.

Continuing to walk forward as she did so, Gabrielle twisted around quickly and motioned for her mother to hand her the bag she was carrying. Gabrielle's mother made a questioning expression, but handed Gabrielle the bag without speaking. Digging into it, Gabrielle found the loaves and pulled out three, turning back around to hold up the bread to show her mother and give the bag back. Her mom nodded, and Gabrielle unwrapped the loaves from the cloths that covered them and broke the bread up for everyone in their group. She passed out chunks to silent nods of thanks.

"You just saved my life," Drew told her seriously as he took the large piece that she offered him. "Just a few more minutes, and I would've died of hunger."

"I thought you'd already died," Davey informed him. "You never go this long without speaking."

"Bestowing words of wisdom on you."

"Squandering air," Davey retorted.

"You have also been subdued, your highness," Jonathon

stated, cool eyes glancing back at Davey and his unsheathed sword.

Davey did not comment.

Jonathon continued, "I find that if there is something distressing dwelling on my mind, leaving it unspoken causes it to fester."

"Those men back there," Davey began, stopping for a moment. He resumed. "They could do nothing more, yet you cursed them."

"I disagree," Jonathon replied. "They were entirely correct in saying that the branches would not hold them forever. If I had left them in such a state, they would have continued to be a threat to those passing through the area and, yes, a threat especially to myself and other sorcerers. Instead of killing them, I found an alternative way to inhibit them from threatening others. What would you have done?"

"Regardless of what I would have done, you took it upon yourself to act as the men's prison maker and guard."

"Is stopping a man from attacking others with a sword a prison?"

"'Tis to some," Davey replied evenly, "and there are multiple circumstances when attacking with a sword, such as to defend or during war, is necessary. What will these men do then?"

"Other ways are available to protect oneself."

"And during war? And what of the fact that you had no right to take that ability"—Davey stumbled at Jonathon's sharp look—"away from them?"

"I shall trade one question for another. What right does a king have to take away the abilities or rights of his people?"

The air, which had certainly not been light before, became even thicker.

"The people trade some of their rights for protection. Tis necessary. If everyone had every right to do everything, then others would be at risk. Thus, we limit rights in order to protect them," Davey spoke slowly, assured of his words.

"Who has given the king this power?"

"The people."

"Am I one of those people?" Jonathon questioned.

"Ye—" Davey stopped speaking.

"If I am one of those people, then the king tries to kill those he is sworn to protect. If I am not one of those people, then the king tries to kill those he has no business dealing with."

"My father protects the people," Davey argued, "and he sees magic as a threat." Davey's back further tensed as he said the words.

Gabrielle glanced towards the ground, remembering the sword, the healing, the question of scrying. Part of her hoped Jonathon wouldn't bring it up.

Part of her desperately wished he would.

"Your father protects only those he considers people. He does not consider those with magic to be people," Jonathon returned coolly.

Davey seemed to want to say more, his jaw tight and clenched.

Jonathon noticed. "Do not hold back your words on my account. Stand up for your father."

"There is not peace between our peoples—"

"Now we are two different peoples?" Jonathon asked, mockingly surprised.

Davey sucked in a deep breath.

Gabrielle clenched and unclenched her fists, surprised by both men.

"You asked—" Davey took a moment to collect his thoughts. "You asked what gave my father the right to take away people's rights. I answered. Rights are the price of protection. Now you will answer my question. What gives you the right to take those men's rights away?"

"Because no one asked whether I wanted my rights taken," Jonathon answered coldly, "and no one gives me protection after taking them."

"That does not mean that you are outside the law," Drew interjected, unexpectedly jumping into the conversation. "That does not mean that you are outside of Aradin and all of its people."

"Aradin has wanted nothing to do with sorcerers or any magic. What right do they have to expect sorcerers to—"

"They do not," Drew interrupted. "Not one person on Aradin has any right to expect anything except hatred from sorcerers, but retreating completely isn't going to bring any resolution."

"We shouldn't have to put forth more work to earn what we already deserve—"

"Marion!" someone screamed in an incredibly high-pitched voice. "I'm gonna kill you!"

Jonathon starting running. Davey and Drew followed close behind, all heading towards the voice.

Gabrielle made to start running, but then remembered her father. She fell back and grabbed his hand, stopping him from going after them. "They shall handle it fine," she assured him, setting the pace a little faster than they had been going but still very manageable.

"I made it to dragon territory just fine, Gabrielle." Her father frowned as he spoke.

"I know," Gabrielle said, raising her eyebrows. "Do you think I doubt you?"

"Are you asking the cynical or optimistic side?"

Gabrielle smiled.

"I did not know you could retort so well, Mister Timothy," Danielle commented, also smiling.

"Tis seldom he does such, but it never fails to sting someone," Gabrielle's mother answered for him.

Neither additional screams nor threats were heard. They also heard neither fight nor scuffle. Soon enough, the three men came into view, seemingly standing alone in the middle of the woods. Then Gabrielle noticed two little pairs of bare feet among the men's boots.

Hearing them approach, Drew turned around and called out, "Our murderer tis Anthony, a bloodthirsty, seven-year-old savage with a longing for revenge."

"What did Marion do?" Gabrielle's mother called back as Davey and Jonathon turned and moved to the side, granting them a view of two barefoot children.

Anthony pointed a finger at Marion and accused, "She called me a carrot!"

Marion rocked back and forth on her heels, nervously eyeing all of them.

"We figured that we had better wait until the rest of you got here before we dragged the ferocious, vegetable-calling criminal home," Drew commented cheerily.

"Yeah!" Anthony's smile grew.

Gabrielle's heart melted as the little girl's lip began to quiver. She stepped forward to help, but Davey beat her to it. He kneeled beside Marion as she began to cry.

"He's only teasing," Davey told her, but soothingly, taking her hands in his and holding them gently. "We are going to take you back to the village and make sure your parents know where you are. No one is in trouble."

Marion stared at Davey, then wrapped her hands around his neck and held on.

Davey was not expecting this, and his foot snapped forward for balance. He adjusted quickly and hesitatingly wrapped his arms around Marion's small frame, then hugged her tightly, whispering something in her ear as Marion buried her face, snot and all, into his chest. Davey stood up after a minute, taking Marion with him as he did. She kept her face buried but allowed him to readjust her, so he was carrying her with one arm, the bag he had on the other shoulder. As he turned, his eyes caught Gabrielle's, and she realised suddenly that she was unconsciously smiling.

She tried to stop and was pleased when Anthony began to protest.

"Do I get to be carried?" Anthony whined.

"Indeed!" Drew replied indignantly. "Upon the shoulders. Let's go!"

Anthony ran to Drew and the two of them awkwardly got Anthony sitting upon Drew's shoulders. Anthony wobbled back and forth as Drew rose.

"Are you sure that is safe, Drew?" Gabrielle asked.

"Absolutely!" Drew replied cheerily. "I've never gotten hurt from this!"

Despite herself, Gabrielle laughed.

"How does the ground look from up there?" Drew "called" to Anthony.

"Like I'm the king of the island!" Anthony yelled back, throwing his hands into the air.

"Hands on the Drew! Hands on the Drew!" Drew grabbed Anthony's legs firmly.

Anthony giggled and put his hands underneath Drew's chin, his head resting on top of Drew's. Drew continued entertaining Anthony all the way to the village, which was just another twenty minutes away. By the time they arrived in Apude, Drew was sweating profusely, most likely because he had walked twice as far as the rest of them in his efforts to play with Anthony.

Apude looked much like Seron did, some wooden houses, a forge, a tavern and inn, but there were fewer shops and fewer people. Gabrielle supposed this was probably due to their even closer proximity to dragon territory.

Davey and Drew went into the tavern and inn with Marion and Anthony, Drew coming back out with the children after just a moment, pushing Marion and Anthony forward. He explained that this tavern and inn was not quite like the one Gabrielle's parents ran. Davey came back a few minutes later with two rooms for the night and information on the children's parents.

Their father was outside his forge, pounding on a thin piece of metal, fiery sparks flying. He was just as dirty as his children, soot smeared across a sweaty face and arms, sleeves rolled up as far as they could go. When he saw them coming, he laid down his hammer and the metal, eyeing them as they approached. "What do you want?" he called out when they were still ten feet away.

Davey stopped. He had taken Marion's hand again as they had walked to the forge. "We are looking for their parents," he gestured towards Marion and Anthony.

"Their mother done herself in. That'd be just me," the blacksmith grunted. "Where'd you find them?"

"In the woods," Davey said curtly. "A good twenty minutes from the village."

"You can leave them here," he grunted again, picking up the chunk of metal with tongs and going back into the forge.

Davey frowned. "Stay here," he instructed Marion and Anthony, then he strode inside the shop whence the working of the bellows could be heard. Shortly after Davey entered the forge, the bellows stopped and voices started though the words could not be understood.

As the voices' volumes rose, Gabrielle sat on the ground.

"Come on!" she told Anthony and Marion excitedly. The two of them uncertainly sat down beside her, their crossed legs forming a triangle. "I'm going to play a game. Would you like to join us?" Gabrielle asked her parents, Drew, and Danielle.

"Of course!" Danielle sat down in between Anthony and Gabrielle.

"Would not miss it for the world, or even dinner." Drew fit himself in on the other side of Gabrielle, so the siblings stayed together.

Gabrielle calmly explained a hand-clapping game, doing

her best to ignore the voices from the forge. They had just started to play a terrible first round, Drew breaking more rules than Anthony, a true feat, when Davey came back out of the forge, and the bellows started up even more fiercely than before. As Gabrielle started to get to her feet, Davey gestured for her to stay put and encouraged another round. They played the game twice more, then disbanded, the sun beginning to brush the horizon.

Davey did not say anything, just led the way back to the tavern and inn. He picked Marion up before they entered the tavern, hugging her closely and quickly weaving through the crowd to the stairs. Drew tried to pick Anthony up, but Anthony wanted to run everywhere. Snatching him by the hand, Drew restrained him for a moment. Gabrielle bent down and quickly whispered that she thought that she could beat him to the stairs. Anthony ran off, but in the right direction. Gabrielle was glad that she, too, got to hurry through the crowd as she raced after him.

Davey awaited them at the first step of the stairs. The rest of their troupe did not take long to arrive, and they ascended the stairs at a good pace. The floor above the commotion was significantly quieter.

Davey led them down the hall a short ways, then finally spoke. "We have two rooms for the night, across from each other. Mister Timothy, your family will have a room. I'm afraid that I assumed my sister would pretend to be in your family again for a night. Is that all right with you?"

"Yes," Gabrielle's father agreed.

"Dannie?"

"Wonderful!"

"The rest of us will be in the other room." Davey crouched down again to talk to Marion and Anthony. "Your father has agreed to let you come home with us. Would you like that?"

Gabrielle supposed it was good that her surprise stopped her from speaking. She felt her mother and father shift next to her. Her mother hummed lightly.

"Yeah!" Anthony yelled.

Prince David smiled, not shocked by Anthony's response, eyes going to Marion.

Marion wrapped her arms around herself. "We need to leave?" she asked softly.

"No," the prince told her, hand coming up to touch her shoulder lightly, "but you can come with us if you want. We have a place for you to stay and food for you to eat. It is in a village a little bit bigger than this but a really pretty place."

Gabrielle noticed her fists were clenched and forced herself to relax. Her parents and she lived far from Aradin. Twas likely that the crown provided support for orphans—though Marion and Anthony were not such.

At least, the crown must provide adequate care if the prince was promising it.

Marion shifted back and forth. "Can I stay with you?"

"Yes," Davey said without hesitating.

Her fists clenched again.

"Okay," Marion agreed softly.

"Do you want to stay with Drew and me tonight or with Gabs and her family?"

"With you," Marion decided immediately.

Prince David nodded.

"Sir—"

"I would like to be with you tonight, in fact," Danielle said before Gabrielle's father could finish his objection. Danielle smiled at her brother. "Twas pleasant to spend time with Gabrielle and her family, but perhaps we should share a room tonight as well." She looked to Marion. "Is it all right if I join ye?"

Marion looked between Princess Danielle and Prince David.

Gabrielle felt a laugh crawling up her throat. Clearly, it had been a long week if such was her response to the situation.

"Perhaps, sire," Gabrielle's mother began, "it would be best for you, your servant, and Mister Jonathan to select a room, and we shall go in the other."

The confusion on Prince David's face would have been humorous, Gabrielle thought, if it weren't so distressing.

"That leaves your room to be quite crowded," he said, visibly counting their numbers.

Gabrielle's father inclined his head. "I would be willing to join your room as well, if you would permit me."

Prince David gestured towards Marion, still not understanding. "She—"

"My lord." Drew placed a hand on the prince's arm. "Perhaps we should settle first for the night and discuss sleeping arrangements then. The bags are easily moved between rooms."

The prince frowned at this, but he did not argue further. Jonathon began walking towards him while Drew tugged at his arm, both herding Prince David to the room behind them. Gabrielle's father moved forward as well, as if they were corralling a wayward rooster or wandering hog.

Gabrielle's mother spoke to Marion in quiet tones, complimenting her hair and gently guiding her into the other room. Dannie picked up Anthony, who, though he still fidgeted restlessly, had let out a great yawn.

Upon entering their room, Gabrielle disbelievingly huffed. Her mother muttered under her breath. Dust thickly coated most surfaces except the bed, which was unmade. Gabrielle wrinkled her nose and tried even harder not to think about the smells of the tavern, which had an awfully sour tinge to them.

"Ah," Drew said, standing at the doorframe to the room. "We seem to have been given rooms in similar states."

"Wonderful," Gabrielle's mother said flatly, nearly glaring at the dust. Gabrielle resisted the urge to do the same. Then— "Anthony, don't touch that."

Drew stifled a laugh. "Perhaps ye would like to take the children outside—"

Gabrielle's mother was already shaking her head. "I would not like to take them through this establishment again, not since they have to return."

"We can clean one room and then return to the other," Gabrielle said, watching Anthony as he inched closer to the single, tilted table that was the only furniture in the room besides the bed.

Gabrielle's mother nodded. "I will stay here with the children."

"Can we not just ask for different blankets?" Prince David hovered behind Drew.

After a moment, Drew began laughing. He gestured

towards Gabrielle and her mother. "You truly are mother and daughter!"

Gabrielle startled, turning towards her mother.

Gabrielle's mother smiled, her own surprise fleeing, and touched Gabrielle's cheek. "Our expressions, love."

"Oh." Gabrielle involuntarily smiled, no doubt mirroring her mother again, as pleasure filled her.

"Ye looked the same." Prince David shifted as he spoke. His uncomfortableness was unsurprising to Gabrielle given she knew what she had thought and could only imagine her expression at the prince's suggestion—at many of his recent suggestions.

Jonathon came up behind the prince, and Drew came forward, and then Gabrielle's father appeared behind them, and it was soon decided that too many hands spoiled the stew. Jonathon planned to visit the traveling herbal vendor he saw before they closed and agreed to have Gabrielle's father accompany him, so he was not alone. However, then Drew insisted on buying a meal though Gabrielle's father suggested he only buy it if he were granted access to their kitchens, and then to look for evidence of sawdust being added to the bread and rolls or otherwise unusable organs being slipped into the soup or—

—at which point it was decided that Gabrielle's father would buy the meal, if the kitchens were satisfactory, and Drew would accompany Jonathon. Dannie eagerly volunteered to watch the children, and Gabrielle's mother, casting a wary eye over the sixteen-year-old princess, said that she would assist Dannie.

That left Gabrielle and Prince David to clean the rooms.

Gabrielle's father frowned at this, but Gabrielle squeezed his hand and kissed him on the cheek in silent assurance that such was fine.

As Drew made several loud remarks about the thinness of the walls and then tested what sounds they muffled with a giggling Anthony, her father's shoulders eased, and he quietly left to inspect the kitchens.

Soon, their group was divided, and Gabrielle entered the other room with Prince David on her heels. She paused at the entrance to take stock. If they overturned the bed, they could use the blanket from such to wipe the dust from other surfaces and then to cover the few obscene drawings Gabrielle could already spot from the doorway. They had brought only a few light blankets from Havene with them, but such would still be a great improvement.

Gabrielle strode towards the bed and began stripping it, coughing as a veritable cloud of dust rose. "Do they ever use these rooms?" she muttered to herself.

"Not much from the sound of it," Davey told her, eyes squinted against the particles. "The tavern part of this establishment gets used often, but when I asked if they had any vacancies, they laughed, said I could have all the rooms if I wanted."

"I do not suppose that they would get much traffic through here," Gabrielle commented. That, and her parents probably took whatever business they could have had. Music started up from below, the floor vibrating from the cheers. Gabrielle only paid brief attention to it, though. "Are you really going to take Anthony and Marion back with you?"

Davey looked up at her. "Yes."

Gabrielle picked up the pillow and beat it with one hand, more dust flying into the air. She did not know what words had been exchanged in the forge, and she could barely imagine what could have been said to cause such a reaction in Davey and such a concession by their father. She wanted to know if Marion and Anthony would be staying with the prince as he had promised or, the more likely scenario, if he was going to find someone to watch them. Whatever provisions or system in place at the city of Aradin could hardly compare to what he told Marion.

Gabrielle realised her teeth were cutting into her lips and she stopped, shaking another blanket and the thoughts from her mind. They still had another day to Seron, and the topic would surely come up then.

The room took only a few more minutes to clean, then they switched rooms with Gabrielle's mother, Dannie, and the children. The second room took a shorter amount of time to tidy up, having already done it once before.

Clapping her hands firmly to get the dust off of them now, Gabrielle surveyed the room. Content with the job they had done on the two rooms, tiredness crept upon her. She looked over the room again but was thinking of her parent's inn in Seron, of the music they occasionally played there. Subconsciously, she began swaying to the melody, remembering how her father used to dance with her. Catching sight of Davey watching her, she explained with a small smile on her face.

"My father would dance with me when I was younger. He would place my feet upon his and dance me all over the floor. I would never stay there, though. He'd swing me up and between his legs and throw me into the air." She paused for a minute, imagining such once more. "While I started by standing on his feet, I invariably ended by clinging around his neck."

"That sounds . . . nice," Davey said.

"Did you ever dance with your parents?" Gabrielle asked him suddenly, smiling contently. Night often loosened her inhibitions.

"No."

"No? Who taught you to dance?"

"Nobody, I guess. We don't really dance." Davey shifted as he explained. "Whenever there are feasts or whatnot, everyone eats and enjoys the festivities, but you do not dance. Tis not considered something . . ." He trailed off as he remembered Gabrielle before him.

"Tis not considered something for nobles and royals to do?" Gabrielle finished wryly for him.

"Aye," he grimaced as he admitted it.

Gabrielle felt the wonderful intoxicants of a long day and wistfulness steal her reason. "Would you like to learn?"

"To dance?"

"Of course."

"You . . . want to teach me?"

"If you wish," Gabrielle stated plainly, seeing the little girl peek out from behind the bed post, spotting the father roaring and scooping her up, viewing a young boy who had never had the pleasure of uncomfortably placing his small, bare feet atop the humongous ridges of a father or mother and then struggling to stay near those islands of safety as the tune began.

"I . . . I'd love to."

Gabrielle stepped confidently forward, grabbing his right hand and placing it on her waist, taking his left hand and leaving it hang in midair. She set her left hand on his arm and grasped his left hand with her right. Below, the music and stomping continued at a fast pace, cheers and hollers ringing out occasionally. Gabrielle closed her eyes and listened to the music, feeling the beat, instinctively knowing that to try and dance with Davey on this first song would result in utter failure.

"Wait a moment . . . perhaps . . ." Gabrielle reorganized their hands so she was grasping his waist and he was holding her elbow.

"Are you sure this is how it is done?" Davey questioned uncertainly.

"Tis not. You be a little big to stand on my feet, though, so I think it best for me to lead during the first song." She closed her eyes again and listened as the fast-paced jamboree terminated in an exaggerated flourish, some of the resounding yelps rattling the floorboards beneath their feet. The crowd below quieted fractionally, and a slower, though still lively, tune picked up. Gabrielle counted in her head, memorizing the pattern they would use.

"Follow my steps," she instructed, gripping his hand and side firmly and stepping to the side. "One two three–"

Davey collided into her and nearly sent her sprawling to the floor. He caught her quickly.

"Sorry!" he said immediately, face going red.

"Tis fine," Gabrielle said smiling. She shook off his hands, readjusted their positions and began again. "One two three. One two three. One two three. One two three . . ."

She counted to the rhythm past when the words blended together and no longer made sense, to the point where eventually she regressed into metronomic mumbling, then just bobbing her head.

Davey stumbled in his attempts to keep up with her, stepping on her toes until she was sure they were simply veined pulp hanging off the edge of her foot, but she did not complain. He was getting better.

The song ended, and a faster one began.

"Now you lead," Gabrielle instructed, knowing that her toes were going to take another beating.

"I lead?" His eyes widened.

"You get so nervous," Gabrielle stated, still feeling oddly detached from her normal reserve. "In dragon territory, you neither hesitated nor feared."

"I feared," Davey corrected her, meeting her eyes straight on with clear irises. "I feared and I worried and I was assured many times over that we were going to die, and twas all my fault."

"You never showed it."

"I'm not supposed to. I'm not supposed to fear or get nervous. I—" He hesitated, then took a breath and continued, "I will be king someday and cannot be seen as weak or indecisive."

"You believe tis foolishness not to fear a dragon."

"Yes, but tis even greater foolishness to let the fear paralyze you, to fear so much you cannot act," Davey spoke firmly, eyes determined.

Gabrielle's gaze drifted to where they clasped hands. It was hard to imagine this young man before her, this Davey, as becoming king someday. He seemed too young, too normal, too . . . human. Kings were larger than life. They towered over the average person in stature and dominance, in all things. They were horrendously evil or unbelievably good.

Davey . . . wasn't.

And, Gabrielle thought, for all his talk of courage, bravery with a sword differed from bravery with words. With laws. With promises. With the reality of the kingdom his father ruled.

"Are we going to dance or not?" she asked him suddenly, pulling herself out of her thoughts, sealing them away for a later date.

Davey nodded, a little more confident than before, and slowly began. He did not move with the rhythm, stepping much slower than the beat required.

Gabrielle guided him gently, and she carefully thought of nothing but the music and their feet slowly trekking a winding, unclear path across the dusty floor.

XIX

Another Mistake

The door crashed open.

"Sire!" Drew yelled in surprise.

Davey jumped back from Gabrielle.

"Knock!" he said. "Knock!"

There were supposed to be other words in this command for Drew to ask before entering a room, but they wouldn't come.

"Who's there?" Drew asked.

Davey turned around and faced away from the door, face in his hands.

"I, um . . . I think, um . . . I need to go to the other room." Gabrielle pushed past Drew.

"Gabs!" Danielle bumped into her in the hallway, the platter of food Danielle carried wobbling precariously.

"Gabs," Danielle said again with an undertone and grin as she saw Gabrielle's red face.

Davey groaned.

"Let me help you!" Gabrielle nearly spilled the platter in her haste to get the door open for Danielle. Then the door was open, and Gabrielle ducked her head and escaped into the other room.

Danielle raised her eyebrows at Drew, who only laughed. She disappeared into the other room as well.

Drew entered the one with Davey, a slightly smaller tray of food in his hands.

Davey tried to avoid looking directly at him.

"Would you like to talk about it, sire?"

"Shut it, Drew."

"What happened to politeness?"

"Please shut it, Drew."

It was Drew's turn to roll his eyes.

Davey eventually looked at him, face still shining, and ate some of the food Drew was already digging into.

Davey did not know what to think. She had made her position clear, but did not the dancing throw that into question? He had ignored this fact by concentrating on where his feet were supposed to be although the dancing had not been difficult.

Gabrielle had surprised him earlier today as well. He had not expected her to talk to the dragons. She had gone past him determinedly. She had succeeded and stopped the fight before it had begun. She had been right.

Davey had not always drawn his sword as quickly as he had today. He had felt a surge of panic at the sight of the dragons and reached for the weapon. Talking had not even crossed his mind.

"Where are the children going to go?" Drew interrupted his thoughts.

"With us," Davey said immediately although it took a moment for his brain to catch up to the situation.

"Yes"—Drew smiled—"but where will they go with us when we get back to the castle?"

"There are plenty of rooms."

"You're not their father," Drew reminded him.

"I know," Davey said seriously, staring at Drew. "I saw their father. You saw their father. If you had been in that forge with me, you would understand why I pressed to take them to the city."

"Their home is here," Drew countered.

"With a father who does not care for them and no mother? Their grandparents and other family members are dead or uncaring. The father told me he feeds them and clothes them and assured me that they could learn the rest on their own. That's not how it is supposed to be."

"Yes, but you are not their father."

"I. Know. Once they are more settled, I will look for a family willing to take them in, but I could not leave them here."

"Will you really look for a family for them?" Drew questioned.

"Yes."

"Were you planning on doing that before I started talking to you right now?"

Davey opened his mouth, but no words came out, his eyes wandering the room suddenly.

Drew chuckled darkly.

Davey took another bite of the almost finished meal.

"You're welcome, by the way," Drew stated.

"For what?" Davey asked.

"For setting it up so you could look *so* considerate and *so* kind while comforting Marion today—ow!" Drew rubbed his arm where Davey had punched him.

"Twas for making her cry," Davey justified the blow.

"I did not make her cry!" Drew protested.

"You just took credit for it. Do you ever even listen to yourself?"

"Nah." Drew grinned. "It wastes too much time."

Davey shook his head. "You never cease to amaze."

"Thank you, sire."

"Twas not a compliment. Admit it, you just were not paying enough attention to Marion to realise she was crying."

"Neither were you!" Drew accused. "You were too busy looking at . . . something else," Drew changed his words at the last second upon Davey's glare, but could not resist smirking. "*Ow!*" Drew said again as Davey thumped him on the arm once more. "I think I need a raise."

"I think I need a muzzle."

"You could have just said earmuffs, but, no, you go straight to muzzle."

"Then nobody has to hear you speak."

Drew folded his arms and raised his eyebrows, waiting.

Davey raised his eyebrows as well although he thought he would only look stupid crossing his arms.

"Advice on what?" he asked at last, unwillingly curious.

"About you and"—Drew grinned and jerked his head towards the door—"Gabrielle."

"I don't need your advice."

Drew did not budge, continuing to stare at Davey.

Davey rubbed the hilt of his sword. He shrugged suddenly, leaning back and splaying out. "All right," he said, "I might as well hear your advice, so I know exactly what not to do."

Drew grinned. Then his expression softened, and he became serious. "Be her friend. Don't expect anything back and be her friend. You both could use one."

Davey looked at Drew, covering his frown. Twas good advice, he would think, from the man who always managed to step up to the occasion.

"She needs a friend more than you, of course, because, you know . . . you have me."

Davey rolled his eyes. Stepping up, indeed.

"Be her friend," Drew repeated one more time.

The room fell silent. Davey glanced at Drew, questioning, Drew doing the same at Davey. Then there was a single scream, and the sound of chaos.

What had she been thinking?

Her face was red, and her parents and Dannie were smiling. Marion and Anthony were wonderfully oblivious as they snatched bites of their meals.

Gabrielle did not say anything to anyone as she sat silently trying to eat her food. While never as ravenous as Drew, she had been hungry before the door had banged open.

Marion had already finished her plate and noticed Gabrielle not touching hers, so she sidled up next to Gabrielle until

Gabrielle simply put the meal to the side and let the little girl clamber into her lap. Her light brown hair a mess, Marion curled up on Gabrielle, eyes closed and breathing light and soft. Gabrielle hugged the girl close, breathing in her earthy scent and feeling the persistent beat of her heart. Perhaps they would try to bathe the children before settling down. The night was still young enough, and such filth could not be conducive to their health.

She wished that all of them could be in Seron.

Her stomach betrayed the worry she felt when she considered what awaited the children. Even if Davey fulfilled his word and took them to the castle, life in Aradin would be drastically different from how they lived here, from how anyone lived here. At least in Seron they would be in a village roughly the same size. She had never been to a city but knew how overwhelmed she had felt as a little girl when the king's army had come to defend the border, and she had seen only a portion of the soldiers. How would Anthony and Marion adjust?

Gabrielle held back a sigh, tightening her grip on Marion. She was tired. Since she had left Seron how many days ago, it seemed to be almost nonstop activity. The unexpected was the anticipated, and a dragon lurked behind every tree.

Once they got back to Seron, the normalcy and stability of life there would return. Her journey would be over. Their journey would be over. Gabrielle wished that they were already at Seron, giving these children the beginnings of consistency, and she wished that Seron would never be reached.

Gabrielle leaned back, studying Marion's face. She would

turn into a lovely young lady. Gabrielle smiled. She sounded like her mother.

The room fell silent. Uneasily, she glanced at the floor.

Someone screamed.

Marion clutched Gabrielle.

The silence gave way to yelling and crashing and bellowing voices and sobbing cries, and Marion trembled in Gabrielle's hands.

Gabrielle stood, clasping Marion to her chest as two pair of feet thundered past their room and down the stairs, Davey and Drew. She desperately wished Marion had not climbed into her lap. Their room stood still as they all warily watched each other and listened keenly to the happenings downstairs. The uproar only seemed to tick up a notch when Davey and Drew's footsteps reached the actual tavern floor.

Gabrielle's father took a step forward.

"Father," Gabrielle said.

He looked to her, and she shook her head slightly, pleadingly. Her father had never broken up a bar fight. The bar fights in their village lasted a single punch before the others in the town stopped it. Below, the entire village brawled.

Gabrielle's mother took her father's hand, grasping it tightly.

Her father's lips thinned, but he stayed.

Gabrielle hugged Marion close. "Everything is going to be all right," she whispered in the little girl's ear.

Then she saw the smoke.

Tendrils twisted through the cracks between the rattling boards, wispy curls weaving a warning as they rose to the ceiling. Gabrielle's eyes met her father's.

In a moment, he was scooping up Anthony with a grunt while Gabrielle's mother and Danielle grabbed the bags in the room. Gabrielle helped by taking two bags as well.

Disregarding the bags on her own back, Danielle held out her hands, offering to take Anthony, but Gabrielle's father shook his head and led the way out the door and to the stairs. With equal parts trepidation and urgency, they hurried down them. Gabrielle's father paused as the main floor came into view.

Tables and chairs were flipped or in ruins. Fire hungrily ate the wooden planks of one such piling, licking the equally wooden floor and liking its taste. A few men seemed to be feeding the bedlam. They carried pitchforks and clubs and other weapons and terrorized those in the room. Davey and Drew were confronting three such men, a wall of panicked people at their backs complicating maneuvers and making three men the limit of what they could handle. Other people scrambled into corners and ran across open spaces and in general tried to reach the door, but a tall, proud man with a scraggly beard stood there, watching the pandemonium, a splitting maul in his one good hand.

It was the leader of the raiders.

Gabrielle looked over those in the madness again and recognized familiar faces, all from the raiding party.

One of the raiders threw another table onto the fire. From somewhere in the turmoil, presumably the owner started pleading for the men to stop. Those who did not confront the men were approached by the raiders and then declared too near. Some fought back, but the tankards and clenched fists they brought to the fight were no match against the majority of the weapons.

A raider bearing two carving knives caught sight of their group huddling at the foot of the stairs, and his eyes lit up.

Gabrielle's gut lurched.

"Danielle." Gabrielle turned to her and gave her Marion, who resisted for only a moment before abruptly switching to cling to Danielle.

"Gabrielle," her father protested, still holding Anthony.

Gabrielle did not pay any attention, taking her own knife out, letting the bags slip to the floor, eyes on the raider.

He grinned as he watched her.

She needed to keep the knife close to her body. Keep her body behind her knife. She needed to move and move and move because there was no other way she could win the fight. Keep her head on straight and not panic. She needed to breathe.

He was three feet away. Two.

He attacked.

Gabrielle effortlessly evaded his slash, stepping around and outside his reach. He needed to be away from her family. Luckily, he turned to follow her, determination settling over his features. He came at her again, and Gabrielle dodged it. Seeing an opening, she forcefully hit him with her shoulder, hoping to get him unbalanced.

He didn't even stumble.

"Afraid to use it, aren't you?" he asked righteously, eyes flicking to her knife.

She had used a knife before. She had killed a man with one before.

She had killed a dragon without one.

Her hand tightened around the slick handle, heart beating faster. Still, he wasn't wrong.

But she could trap him as Jonathon had done.

She kept one eye on her family as she moved around the man. Her father cautiously led them around the edges of the room. Anthony had wiggled his way out of her father's arms and was hanging onto his hand.

More confidently than ever, the raider lunged at her.

Gabrielle sidestepped again, but he had been expecting this and slashed with his other knife. Sharp pain stung in a strip near her stomach. Wincing, she was almost distracted enough to miss the raider's proceeding strike. Her instincts helped her dodge it, and she grabbed his arm and pulled him forward, plan abruptly coming together in her mind.

Focusing briefly on the floorboards where she estimated the man to step, she imagined them breaking without opening completely. Struggling to keep her desperation at bay, she pushed him there.

He stumbled onto the boards and began turning around.

Gabrielle grimaced and glared at the floor.

The wood gave way.

The raider tumbled all the way through the ground into the tavern's cellar. Splintered pieces of wood lined the edge of the drop, and floorboards leaned precariously into the hole.

Gabrielle pressed her lips together. That occurrence was . . . possible . . . without magical interference. She just had to act like it wasn't her doing.

The board underneath her bent even more towards the

hole. She scrambled back from the edge and the hole that, most assuredly, could have occurred naturally.

A strong, short whistle halted everyone. Gabrielle turned to the door. The leader of the raiders stood in front of Jonathon, head cocked.

"You know, there's a lot that don't count as a weapon." The leader hefted his splitting maul higher, making a point.

"Did you not learn?" Jonathon evenly asked.

"Yeah." The raider jerked his head in an approximation of a nod. "Never attack a sorcerer without having something he don't want to lose."

From the corner of the tavern closest to the entrance, keeping his back to the crowds and his eyes on Jonathon, the youngest of the raiders stepped out, back bent, hand steady—knife against Felipe.

Jonathon lurched forward.

The leader held out his hand and tsked. The young raider pressed the knife tighter against Felipe. Felipe whimpered.

"We wouldn't want no one to get hurt, now do we?" the leader asked in mock sympathy.

Jonathon's face tightened more.

"We found this little one in the woods right after our little meeting. Said he knows you. We didn't want him to get hurt, see? We had to bring him here."

"What do you want." Jonathon said flatly.

The leader of the raiders did not speak for a moment, then spat, "An island free of sorcerers." He swung his splitting maul at Jonathon, but Gabrielle was distracted by Felipe's cry. Too fast for her to move, too fast for her to blink, the youngest raider used the knife.

The raider flew all the way backwards, into the bar at the other end of the room, barely missing one or two bystanders.

Felipe stood by himself for a moment, hands reaching for his throat. Then he fell slowly, horrifically.

She was stuck in thick, clogging air, unable to move quickly, unable to breathe.

He was supposed to fall to the floor knees first. He was supposed to clutch the wound.

He crumpled.

He lay still as Gabrielle easily turned his slight body over. His wide, wondering eyes were open, surprise and fright upon his visage, his small arms and thin legs askew.

A sudden, sharp pain in her right shoulder heaved her forward. It burned without spreading. She snapped back around with vicious force, hitting the raider with her fist and magic, feeling the powerful crack and hearing him smack against the floor on the other side of her. She reached behind her back with her other hand and pulled the knife out of her shoulder. It clattered to the ground.

Drew appeared, lifting her elbow.

Jonathon was there, kneeling by Felipe.

Gabrielle leaned forward, but Drew was tugging her back, towards the door, and Jonathon was cradling Felipe in his arms and standing.

Then they were outside.

They were standing in the light of a waning gibbous, the fire and tumult behind the door that swung closed at their backs.

Drew pulled her along. Jonathon was there. Davey was

there. There were her parents and Danielle and Anthony and Marie.

They were walking, nearly running. Running in the near darkness away from the light. Behind them they could hear the yelling.

The raiders were behind them. They were running in the darkness.

"Wait," Drew quietly stated. He turned to Jonathon.

"He's—" Jonathon choked on the word.

"Just to be doubly sure," Drew softly said. He gripped Felipe's arm. He touched Felipe's chest. He placed his fingers against Felipe's lips.

He walked away.

They were running in the darkness.

The night was thick.

They stopped running. They must have stopped running. She was lying on the ground. The ground felt like ground, but different, and the air tasted like it should, but not.

Her mother lay down next to her. She felt her father's hand on her arm. She turned into their warmth.

The night was quiet, except for Jonathon.

Gabrielle closed her eyes and tried to sleep.

XX

Where Dying is Still a Possibility

"Up!" a voice barked.

Gabrielle wearily blinked, eyes opening slowly, joints stiff. Her father groaned, and her mother shifted beside her.

"Sir Michael—" Davey began.

"Up! By the king's orders, you must rise," the voice interrupted.

Gabrielle put her hands on the ground to raise herself up. A sharp pain lit in her right shoulder. She fell back with a gasp.

"Gabs—"

"Do not move!"

"She's hurt, Sir Michael," Davey firmly stated.

"Here," a new voice implored. A hand came into Gabrielle's line of vision. She grimaced while looking up.

A knight of the king stood before her though she should not assume such. His calloused hand matched his well-worn armour and rugged, young face.

She took his hand, and he came closer to help her to her feet.

Two knights and their squires stood before them, the other knight's sword out and ready.

"What's going on, Sir Michael?" Davey demanded.

"We are instructed by King Germaine to take the prince and any of his traveling companions back to base camp," Sir Michael answered stiffly.

Davey's face betrayed a sudden look of panic. He covered it quickly. "These people—"

"We must take the prince and his companions back to base camp," Sir Michael repeated.

"Sir Michael—"

"The king was adamant, sire."

"They . . ." Davey was struggling to speak, regret filling his face. He licked his lips and let out in one breath, "None of them knew that I was disobeying my father's orders. Any part in this they took was borne out of my deception, and I take full responsibility."

"The king predicted you would say that," the other knight regretfully said. "He made it explicitly clear that nothing said or done should stop us from bringing everyone with you back to base camp."

"Base camp?" Danielle asked.

"I am glad to see that you are safe, Princess Danielle." Sir Michael bowed.

"I'm glad to see all of you as well." Danielle smiled, the

cheerfulness sliding off her face awfully quick. "What base camp?"

"Because of their overt act of aggression, the king has decided to declare war on the dragons."

Muscles tensing, Gabrielle winced as needles shot through her shoulder wound.

"War?" Danielle asked incredulously. "Surely when he sees I have returned safely he will disband whatever men he has gathered?"

"Such an aggressive act cannot be forgiven lightly, your highness," Sir Michael explained stoically. "We must bring you to the king."

The silent astonishment of their group continued.

". . . Will you please come, your highness?" the other knight asked Davey quietly.

Davey did not speak right away, a stricken look upon his face. Finally, a soft, "Of course."

"We will take your bags and weapons." Sir Michael gestured to his squire.

Sir Michael's squire went around to each of them, collecting bags until he looked severely overladen. The other squire came forward to help, only taking three smaller sized bags. The unknown knight also took a bag himself before Sir Michael's squire could snatch it up. Gabrielle noticed the unknown knight's own squire shaking his head as he saw such.

Once the bags were collected, Sir Michael motioned for the unknown knight to take the lead while he circled around their group to the back, Sir Michael's own overladen squire following him.

"What happened?" the unknown knight asked gently, eyes on Felipe.

"Raiders," Jonathon said, adjusting the boy in his arms.

"I'm sorry," the knight said, seeming genuine. Then he turned and began leading the way, sending a glance back at Gabrielle. His squire fell back to walk beside her.

The squire nodded once at Gabrielle's shoulder. "Once we get back to camp, we'll have someone look at that. Will you be fine until then?"

Gabrielle wondered if anything would happen if she said no. "Yes, thank you."

The squire nodded and then fell back a touch farther in the group.

"Just how angry is the king, Lucas?" Drew said. Gabrielle guessed he was speaking to the squire.

"Remember when you two disappeared to defend Galog?" Lucas asked.

"That bad?"

"Worse."

"They really had no clue."

"It won't matter this time," Lucas said. "He wants to make an example of them. He made it clear that anyone caught helping the prince would be punished according to the laws."

"And how will the prince be punished?" Drew asked cynically.

"Disobeying a direct order of the king? Tis worthy of capital punishment, but I doubt the king thinks his son would look any better with his head chopped off."

"And what of his companions?"

At his silence, Gabrielle closed her eyes for a moment despite the terrain.

Drew laughed quietly. "In that case, perhaps I shall tell him what exactly I think of his new robes."

"Good thinking," Lucas agreed, "then perhaps he shall have you all set on fire before executing you."

"I did tell Davey this would end in a fiery death," Drew commented lightly.

"Oh, don't be a weeping willy." An edge stayed to Lucas' near joking tone. "You know very well that they'll will fight tooth and nail before letting any of you die."

"Yes, knowing my life is in Davey's hands brings me great comfort," Drew remarked.

Lucas grunted his acknowledgement.

Drew hummed thoughtfully.

"What?" Lucas asked.

"I wonder if Davey's judgement would improve without his head."

Another knight of the king came into view some distance away. Spotting their group, he called out to them, then did the same behind himself. Two more knights came into view, and all three knights of the king and their squires approached.

"The princess?" the nearest knight of the king yelled.

"Safe," Sir Michael declared.

The newest knight was close enough that Gabrielle could now see his crinkly smile around a beard sprinkled with gray hairs. The squire at his side had a sword of his own, but was also carrying a water canteen and a bag. He looked to be about Davey's age and just as fit, and he scrutinized their group with a quiet alertness.

"Were they all with the prince?" The pepper-bearded knight's eyes roamed their group.

"Unfortunately," the first unknown knight answered.

The pepper-bearded knight spoke to them, "I apologize for your worry. Unfortunately, there is little I can say to assuage your fears. I can't imagine your confusion and concerns. While I can make no promises, let me at least introduce myself and those who will be escorting you back to base camp.

"I am Sir Nicholas. This is my squire, Bentley," he gestured toward the squire at his side. Motioning to the unknown knight of the king who had been leading their group, he continued, "If you do not already know, this is Sir Asher and his squire Lucas. Behind you is Sir Michael and his squire Bryson."

Sir Nicholas gave them a small grin as a lively knight and his squire came up on his left side. "Please don't worry if you do not remember our names. This is Sir Alexander and his squire Samuel and still coming is Sir Jeremiah and his squire . . ."

"Xavier," Bentley supplied.

"Thank you, Bentley." Sir Nicholas nodded. "Xavier just began working for Sir Jeremiah around last week, I believe?"

"Yes, sir," Bentley agreed.

"What are your names?" Sir Nicholas asked them, grin gone but eyes still gentle.

They shared their names in turn, and Gabrielle was surprised at the comfort, albeit small, that rose in her during the exchange.

"It is a pleasure to meet you all although, of course, I wish the circumstances were different," Sir Nicholas told them, his eyes going back to Jonathon and Felipe once they had all spoken. "I am sure you have some story to tell, but it must wait until we reach base camp. We must take you there, but if you need anything on our trip, do not be afraid to ask."

Sir Jeremiah and Xavier had reached them. Sir Nicholas gestured to either side of their group and a knight of the king and his squire each took a side. Sir Asher and Lucas, the men who had originally been leading their group, now let Sir Nicholas choose the path.

They walked in silence this time, Lucas and Drew not exchanging any more words, and the atmosphere, though lightened by Sir Nicholas, stayed tense. As they drew nearer to base camp, more knights as well as members of the cavalry, archers, and swordsmen appeared, many of whom called out a greeting to Princess Danielle. Many faces dropped as they scanned the rest of their group.

Sickness and guilt roiled in her. Her parents would have been safe had she stayed at home.

"The princess?" another knight of the king asked.

"Safe," Sir Nicholas answered. "Where is the king?"

"He is journeying here as we speak."

"Send a messenger informing him of these events," Sir Nicholas instructed.

"Yes, Sir Nicholas. These people, were they traveling with the prince?"

"Yes."

"If you recall what the king—"

"I do recall what the king instructed, Sir Robert, and I have every intention to fulfill his commands. However, they carry the dead among them. We shall let them bury their dead first before constraining them further."

"Yes, sir." Sir Robert clenched his jaw with the words.

Sir Nicholas turned back to their group. Speaking directly to Jonathon, "You have the opportunity to bury the boy now. You may not get it again."

Jonathon's eyes rested upon Felipe for a moment. He nodded once slowly.

"Bentley, please get two shovels. Sir Robert and Elias can dig the boy's grave. What was his name?" Sir Nicholas asked Jonathon.

"Felipe."

"He was a beautiful boy."

"Yes."

"Sirs Robert, Asher, and Alexander will accompany you in the woods," Sir Nicholas informed their group and the knights at the same time. "Bentley will meet up with you."

They set off again, Sir Asher and Lucas leading the way, but their journey was only about two minutes into the forest. Bentley arrived with two shovels just as they stopped in a small clearing, so small it could barely be classified such.

"Elias," Bentley said, handing one shovel to Sir Robert's squire, a boy who could not have been any older than fifteen.

"Sir Robert." Bentley tried to hand the other shovel to Sir Robert, but the knight of the king waved his hand.

"I believe you would use it better than I," Sir Robert told Bentley.

Bentley scowled but did not say anything, just retracted his hand and started helping Elias dig.

"He would use it for a better purpose," Lucas whispered to Drew.

Somehow, the squires had found themselves together again.

"And what purpose would that be?" Drew asked quietly, smile in his voice.

"Hopefully to bash Sir Robert's head in."

Gabrielle's eyes widened with Lucas' words.

"Have I told you how much I have missed you?" Drew whispered amusedly to Lucas.

"No, and please do not. I hear that enough from Cecilia."

"You really should take a day off," Drew advised, laughter in his voice.

"Last time I did that the idiot nearly got himself killed."

"I have the same problem."

"Want to commiserate?" Lucas asked softly.

"I would like nothing better, except perhaps to see that better use of the shovel."

Gabrielle closed her eyes, not knowing if she was trying not to laugh or cry.

"What really happened to him?" Lucas wondered.

"Raider," Drew told him, his sadness evident. "He was quicker than we expected."

"What was going on? How did the raider even get close?" Lucas pried.

Gabrielle's heart quickened. She glanced nervously at Jonathon.

"We fought a group of raiders. Felipe tried to follow us without our knowledge. The raiders got ahold of him. They came back to us and killed him."

"How old was he?"

"Five. He had his birthday about two weeks ago."

They fell silent.

The pile of dirt grew.

Gabrielle's right shoulder throbbed, but only slightly. She could feel that it was not nearly as bad as the night before. She should have healed herself or had Jonathon do so when she had the chance. Now she needed to get it wrapped up before anyone noticed how quickly it was healing. While the stab wound was deep, it would still only take three or four days to heal completely. Already, she would probably have to argue in favor of letting her father or mother wrap the injury. Anyone else would notice the wound looking peculiarly well.

By the time the hole was deep enough, Elias and Bentley were slick with sweat. They moved away from the hole, and Jonathon came forward without direction, placing Felipe into the ground. He deliberately positioned Felipe's legs crossed and his arms bent at odd angles. Standing up, Jonathon explained, "Tis how he sleeps. His mother thinks it a wonder he does not wake up with broken bones or twisted ankles."

His voice caught.

Bentley and Elias waited.

"May I?" Jonathon asked, motioning towards Bentley's shovel.

Bentley eagerly handed it over, looking like he was about to make a comment, but thought better of it and said nothing.

Jonathon began shoveling dirt back in the hole.

Davey came up from behind Gabrielle and silently took Elias' shovel.

Together, they buried the child.

The walk back to camp was subdued. Upon reaching the tents, Sir Michael appeared and ordered Bryson to whisk Princess Danielle away.

"They come with me." Danielle held Marion and Anthony's hands.

"The king ordered—"

"The king ordered the prince's companions to be taken wherever you are going. These children are my companions, not Davey's," Danielle interrupted Sir Michael and spoke with a force Gabrielle had not known she could muster.

Sir Michael did not argue, only nodded with a tight smile. Bryson led Danielle, Anthony, and Marion towards the center of the camp while Sir Michael took the rest of their group a minute walk along the edge, stopping by a large tree that had chains linked all the way around it, manacles fastened every foot and a half or so. He guided them towards it and went one by one, snapping the chains on their wrists, Davey protesting for their sake again, Sir Asher watching, Sir Michael unmoved.

Gabrielle resisted the instinct to lower her head when Sir Michael came to her. She had helped two men find their way to dragon territory. That was not illegal. She would find no shame in that act.

The metallic clang sounded, and the heavy weight of the cold metal fell upon her wrists. Sir Michael caught her eyes but could not hold them. Gabrielle wondered if he could see the fear in them.

She twisted her arms, feeling the rough material rub against her skin.

"At least we have some time together," Gabrielle's mother told her, trying to smile.

Gabrielle did not even make an attempt. "I am so sorry."

"For what?" her mother quietly and incredulously asked as Sir Michael left, leaving Sir Asher watching them from a tent fifteen feet away.

"If I had not insisted on going to dragon territory then we would not be in this mess."

"We," Drew started, "have been attacked by redcaps, nearly drowned by kelpies, carried by rocs, starved by a prince, assaulted by dragons, almost ran over by karkadans, bruised, battered, broken, hit, punched, kicked, and flung"—he took a deep breath—"and only when we are sitting peacefully next to a tree do you regret wanting to come to dragon territory."

Gabrielle somehow had the strength to giggle.

From Gabrielle's right, her mother turned to her and solemnly stated, "You are never leaving the house again."

Gabrielle sincerely hoped her mother was exaggerating.

"Nothing fazes you, does it?" Davey asked Drew, who was to Davey's right.

"Other than your stupidity? I told you we were going to die."

"We are not going to die."

"Right, I told you everyone but you was going to die."

After a moment, Davey said, "I was wrong to involve anyone else. I am sorry. My father gets angry, but he's fair. He will see that you have been deceived in this."

Gabrielle wondered who he was trying to convince.

Lucas hurried towards them, carrying some strips of linen

and a medicine kit, coming around the tent Sir Asher sat at the back of.

Gabrielle shifted nervously.

Lucas kneeled next to her, confident hands opening the kit and placing the strips of linen where they would not get soiled. "May I?" he asked, pointing at her shoulder.

Gabrielle could see no reason to resist, so she nodded.

"I am a fast healer, and the wound was clean," she told him as he pulled back the clothing, grabbing his knife after only a second or two to cut the top of the cloth. Trying to be nonchalant, Gabrielle looked down at the injury at an awkward angle. The wound was situated more on her back, so she complied with Lucas' gentle tug and leaned forward. She pressed her lips together and sucked them in slightly when she saw the injury or, more accurately, what was left of it.

Her skin was red and irritated, but a firm growth of tender, light brown skin had already formed. While her bloody clothing told of a wound days old, her body looked like it had been healing for weeks. Never had she healed this quickly.

Lucas met her eyes.

They did not speak for a very long moment.

"I'm sorry." He turned to Gabrielle's mother who was worriedly watching the exchange and had a wonderful view of Gabrielle's healing injury. "Who are you again?"

"Marie," Gabrielle's mom said quietly.

"And"—Lucas waved his hand about—"you know Gabrielle because . . ."

"I'm her mother."

Lucas nodded slowly. "I'll ask you to look away while I clean the wound and such. I don't want you to get worried.

I promise you it'll be looking as good as new sooner than you expect."

Her mother nodded and looked away, pressing her lips together as Gabrielle had done, face as white as a sheet.

"I'm unsure if I can make that same promise to you," Lucas told Gabrielle, eyes glinting. "You are a fast healer after all. You would know better than I when this injury of yours will be completely gone. However, I can give you some help to ward off infection and attempt to speed up the process even more."

Lucas' eyes glinted with amusement. "Tell me"—he started to clean the area around the wound with some of the cloth— "where are you from?"

"Seron."

"Have you lived there long?"

"My whole life. My parents own the inn and tavern in the town," Gabrielle said, speaking as quietly as her mother had done.

"And how did you get mixed up with the ruffians on the other side of this tree?" Lucas stopped cleaning the wound and picked a few prepared herbs out of the kit.

"They needed a guide, and I volunteered."

"A guide through dragon territory?"

"To dragon territory!" Drew corrected. "We're not complete idiots. At first, we tried to convince her not to come along, too!"

"I tried," Davey spoke up. "You liked the idea."

"I didn't like the idea," Drew argued. "I told her we would die awful deaths and that our chances of success were ridiculously small."

"The size of a stunted midget," Gabrielle recalled.

"A stunted midget?" Lucas asked incredulously, placing the herbs on Gabrielle's shoulder and beginning to slowly wrap a clean strip of linen to hold them in place.

"Yes," Gabrielle said, swallowing her fear and continuing, "Drew said that their chances of success were as small as a stunted midget."

"Now that's just mean," Lucas said.

"Find me a stunted midget, and I'll apologize," Drew challenged him.

"I can't. I just look right over them when searching for the little fellas."

Drew barked out a laugh. "You are truly horrible."

"You make me grateful for Drew," Davey said.

"I'm sorry. What did you say?" Drew asked.

"I said shut up, or I'll run you through."

Lucas chuckled as he wrapped the cloth around one more time. His actions were complicated by the manacles on Gabrielle's wrists. Bringing the end of the strip to the top, he tucked it into the prior wrappings, then dug into his kit, pulling out a needle and thread.

"I'm no seamstress, but I can make two stitches somewhat close to each other."

"Her wound needs stitches?" Davey exclaimed.

Lucas raised his eyebrows.

"No!" Drew berated Davey. "If her wound needed stitches, he would have started many minutes ago. He probably had to cut the top of her shirt to get to the wound, and now he's offering to sew it back up."

Lucas tried to swallow his grin. "You know, for an idiot,

you can sound pretty discerning at times," he spoke loudly to Drew.

"I like to mix it up every so often. Keeps things lively."

"I thought that was what you went into dragon territory for," Lucas said.

"Nah, we went into dragon territory to die," Drew said lightly.

"Having failed at even that, you come back and must ask the king to finish the job for you?"

"Indeed, but I am sure Davey will still screw it up somehow."

"Thank you, Drew. If I manage to complicate your plans and not get you killed, you don't have to thank me."

"Was I planning on doing such?"

"Were they like this all the way to dragon territory?" Lucas asked Gabrielle.

Gabrielle mustered a small smile. "They kept things lively."

"What of you?" Lucas asked Gabrielle's mother. "How did you get drawn into this mess?"

"We went after Gabrielle," her mother told him.

Lucas paused and looked up. "All the way into dragon territory?"

"Beyond the river," Drew called from the other side of the tree.

Lucas' eyes fell upon Marie again, but then went back to Gabrielle. "You have truly amazing parents."

"Do you have any children?" Gabrielle's mother asked him.

"Three," Lucas told her. "Gregory, Hailey, and Chrysanthemum."

"Chrysanthemum?" Gabrielle's father asked.

"Timothy!" Gabrielle's mom rebuked. To Lucas, "He meant it as a compliment."

Lucas smiled. "That's the usual reaction. My wife decided to let Greg and Hailey name our third child. They were only four and three at the time, so of course, I supported the idea. Naturally, the first flower they saw would be the name of the baby. We're just lucky they didn't spot an agapanthus or the like.

"Where are you from?" Lucas asked Jonathon. He was almost done sewing Gabrielle's shift.

"Seron as well," Jonathon told him. "My family lives outside of the village itself, though."

Lucas nodded and finished tying off the thread. "Tis not beautiful."

"Tis wonderful," Gabrielle told him. She waited until their eyes met. "Thank you."

Lucas nodded again, wry smile upon his face. "Anytime. Easiest wound I've ever had to clean." He packed the kit and stood. "I did not clean that wound for nothing," he told her, eyes somber. "There still is a good chance the king will abstain from capital punishment, so long as the king does not suspect you are anything more than villagers who wanted to help a knight of the king. Try to keep your ears clean."

Gabrielle nodded her agreement.

Lucas turned and walked away.

"Seems we have more company," Jonathon murmured to Gabrielle. Two knights and their squires were approaching with their confiscated bags. "What are those knights' names again?"

"Sir Alexander and Sir Robert. Their squires are Elias and . . . I cannot recall."

"Tis all right. Thank you," Jonathon told her.

When the knights and squires had reached the area in between Sir Asher and the tree, Elias and the other squire unceremoniously dumped the bags upon the ground.

"We need to search your bags," Sir Robert informed them disinterestedly. "In front of you, it seems, according to Sir Nicholas' order."

He nudged one of the bags. "Well?" he asked Elias, turning away without waiting for a response.

Elias glared at Sir Robert, but bent down and started opening the bag. The other squire began helping, and Sir Asher joined in as well. They shifted through clothing, half-heartedly examined a few pots, and dug through a medicine kit Jesalyn had lent them.

Then Gabrielle remembered the spell book. It was in the bag next in line for Elias to search.

Trying not to show her fear, she shifted uncomfortably on the ground, eyes drawn to Jonathon. He noticed and cocked his head slightly. Gabrielle leaned towards Elias, trying not to be obvious. Then Jonathon understood. Gabrielle wondered if Jesalyn had told him or if he was just guessing.

The wind picked up, causing Gabrielle's hair to dart to the side and a crouching and unstable Elias to nearly fall over. Elias leaned forward, placing his hand upon the ground, then seemed to think the effort was too much and just sat down. He reached for Gabrielle's bag.

A tree branch snapped suddenly from behind them. All

three knights and two squires looked up, peering into the woods. No one spoke.

"Tis too near to be a dragon," Davey commented.

Gabrielle could imagine him rolling his eyes. She wished he would shut up.

The prince continued, "A twig that close means that we would have seen the dragon by now. They're not that small."

"Then how come they've snuck up on you so many times?" Drew asked.

"You're with me every time, so why don't you say?"

"Am I allowed to answer without having a death threat as a response?"

Elias opened Gabrielle's bag and froze, spotting the book. He reached in and pulled it out, pausing perhaps when he noticed the lack of a title. He flipped through a few pages before closing it again. "Is this yours, your highness?" he called to Davey, waving the book in the air.

Gabrielle tried to sink into the tree.

Noticing that Davey could not see the book, Elias stood to walk it to the prince.

"Tis a book," Jonathon said curtly.

"A book?" Drew laughed. "Tis certainly not Davey's!"

Then Gabrielle understood.

Elias did not know how to read.

"Tis mine," she admitted suddenly.

"You read?" Elias asked, confused.

"Yes," Gabrielle said. "Don't you?"

Elias looked down at the book, eyes widening slightly. "Of course," he lied. "I haven't read this one, though. What's it about?"

"Tis a history book." Gabrielle tried not to wince as she scrambled for words and an honest face.

"Oh," Elias said. "I think I read something like that a while ago. Is it any good?"

Gabrielle gave a noncommittal shrug.

Elias put the book back.

Gabrielle let out the breath she had been holding. Her eyes slid to Jonathon, and he glanced at her, offering a small smile but otherwise not acknowledging the incident. Gabrielle realised that was probably wise and looked away, watching the men search the rest of the bags with a much lighter heart.

"Greetings!" a young voice called from the forest.

Gabrielle turned her head, but could not get a glimpse of their visitor.

"Greetings," Sir Robert called out solemnly though he could not have been much older than whoever was coming. "Who are you, and what business do you have here?"

"I'm Ian. This is Gavin," Ian nervously introduced himself and Gavin. "We wish to become knights."

Sir Robert snorted. "To become knights you must do something worthy of honor. We might be able to find an empty squire spot or a stable hand opening that needs filling. You can do something useful while you wait."

"I would like to protect villagers from dragons," Ian responded. "How can I help with that?"

"Like I said," Sir Robert repeated shortly, "to become knights you must do something worthy of honor."

"Is not protecting villagers from dragons worthy of honor?"

"Come back when you have done something worthy of honor," Sir Robert told him.

Sirs Asher and Alexander did not seem pleased by this response, and Sir Asher was opening his mouth to speak when the other traveler spoke up.

"How about protecting dragons from villagers?"

"Excuse me?" Robert questioned unbelievingly.

"If you don't believe that protecting villagers from dragons is honorable, then perhaps we should protect dragons from villagers."

Gabrielle tried not to smile.

"Who are you?" Sir Robert demanded.

"Gavin. You are?"

"Sir Robert."

"Glad to know your name, Robert. I believe knowing the names of dragon protectors would be advised."

"I do not protect dragons, and it is *Sir* Robert."

"My apologies, Robert."

"I'm Asher," Sir Asher quickly said, coming up next to Sir Robert and placing a hand on his shoulder. "My squire is"— he looked behind himself—"not here."

"He would be if you kept a better eye on him," Sir Robert snapped.

Sir Asher shrugged. "His name is Lucas. I can introduce you later."

"You do not introduce squires."

"I shall have Lucas introduce himself later. Over here is Sir Alexander and his brother Samuel. Elias is Sir Robert's squire."

"He's not quit yet?"

Elias snorted.

"Shut up," Sir Robert barked at him.

"Elias, will you please finish searching the last three bags and then store them in the camp?" Sir Asher asked.

"Of course, sir." Elias bowed slightly to Sir Asher and went back to the bags.

"I am certain you misunderstood Sir Robert, Gavin. Protecting villagers from dragons certainly is worthy of honor. Simply, you cannot be called a knight until you have done such in a manner worthy of honor."

"And what of protecting dragons from villagers?" Gavin asked.

"Not honorable, assuredly." Sir Asher smiled slightly. "Are you good with a sword?"

"Yes," Ian stated promptly.

Sir Asher nodded, taking the boy's response with a grain of salt. "Are you, Gavin?"

"Never used one."

"Yet you want to become a knight?"

"Where does it say a knight must use a sword? This young man was telling me that a knight is simply someone dedicated to serving the peoples with integrity."

"A knight of king—"

"Is that," Sir Asher interrupted Sir Robert. "Usually, we say a knight of the king is dedicated to serving the king, kingdom, and peoples in every possible way with all gentlemanly respect and integrity."

"Oh," Gavin said, "perhaps not then. Good luck, Ian."

"Excuse me!" Sir Robert sounded almost genuinely offended.

Gabrielle finally noticed her neck prickling.

"Dragon," she whispered.

Sir Robert drew his sword. "You insult me. You insult the king—"

"It would appear you have your priorities sorted."

Jonathon's face was tense. He leaned down and whispered in Gabrielle's ear, "Do not act unless you must."

"Dragon!" Sir Asher yelled, unsheathing his own sword.

Sir Alexander visibly swallowed and did the same.

A roar split the air.

Sir Robert took a few steps back, sword out in front of him.

"Samuel! Get the keys, and get them out!" Sir Asher said.

Sir Alexander took a step towards Gabrielle and the others around the tree.

"No!" Sir Asher commanded him. "Go the other way. Lead the dragon away from them!"

Gabrielle wondered if Sir Asher realised that the dragon could understand him just fine. Then she wondered if she knew the dragon. She nearly sighed at that.

Branches broke, and Ian shouted. While she had not yet seen the boy, she pictured an older Felipe charging recklessly into battle against a dragon.

"It's heading towards them!" Sir Robert shouted. All but he were out of sight as the knights and squires tried to fight the dragon.

Gabrielle tensed. The dragon needed neither claw nor tooth to kill. He or she could simply breathe fire, and Davey and Drew would be the first burnt to a crisp. Lifting up her hands, she realised that they could swing the chain around the tree, so the men were no longer facing the dragon, not that Davey or Drew would ever agree to that.

"Jonathon," she spoke fast and low, "can we move around the tree, so we are facing the dragon?"

He grinned and replied quietly, "That is the first time I have ever heard of someone wanting to face a dragon."

"We shall have to do so quickly, for Davey and Drew will protest."

"Tell your parents."

Gabrielle turned and informed them in a few short words of the plan. The dragon roared again as she nodded to Jonathon, and he yelled, "Go!"

So fast did the chains whip around that the manacles nearly broke through Gabrielle's skin. She regained her balance quickly and tugged as well. They were three quarters of the way around already, fire blazing in front of her, when Davey realised what was going on.

"What are you doing?" Davey shouted.

She could just see him digging his feet into the ground. Gritting her teeth, she pulled at the chains, but nothing budged.

"Kick him," she whispered to Jonathon.

Jonathon grinned, looking like one of his sons.

"Ow!"

They lurched forward, Davey and Drew now completely on the other side of the tree.

She could barely hear Davey's shouts over the dragon's roar.

This was a dragon she did not recognize, the scales an almost translucent green, though the fire reflected upon him danced in warm rays of color across his cool shaded body. He had lit up several of the trees around them, but had failed to hit their tree yet. This seemed to be due mainly to Sir Asher, Ian, and Gavin. Sir Alexander stood slightly off to the side and between them and the dragon, perhaps a line of last defense.

Sir Asher was trying to engage the dragon in actual combat, but was failing miserably, his sword just glancing off with every slash. Though his attacks were an effective distraction, he would most certainly have been killed had not Ian and Gavin also been weaving around the dragon with their choice of respective weapons, a sword and stones.

Gabrielle watched, tense and waiting. She stole a single glance at Jonathon and found him the same. He did not seem to be doing any magic, just observing and looking for an opportunity. Perhaps he was worried that he would upset the balance between human and dragon. At the moment, the two sides seemed evenly matched.

Someone stepped in front of her.

Davey crouched to look her in the eyes. "That was incredibly insane."

Gabrielle let out a quick breath and smile. "Idiocy and insanity. We are really rolling sevens."

Davey smiled.

"Excuse me," Drew said, shoving the back of his head into Davey's face and bending down to unlock Gabrielle's manacles.

Fuming, Davey moved his head away and stepped to the side.

"Oh," Drew said, standing up after only a moment, Gabrielle's manacles already unlocked. "Was I in your way, sire?"

Davey smacked him on the back of the head.

Drew grinned mischievously at Gabrielle. He turned to Jonathon. "Hmm." He shifted the key back and forth in his hand.

"Unlock the chains." Jonathon emphasized the four syllables.

Drew grinned again and did so.

Davey had already run closer to the dragon. He spoke with Sir Alexander for a mere moment, and then Sir Alexander was giving Davey his sword and running back towards them. "I am here to take you to safety."

"Could you just show it to us on a map? I'm sure we could find our way," Drew said.

"You're hilarious!" Sir Alexander said, grinning. Then he abruptly stopped smiling. "Walk."

"I'd much prefer to run."

Samuel came up to them, breathing hard. "Swords," he gasped, throwing them on the ground.

"You're out of shape," Sir Alexander told his brother, selecting a sword from the small pile.

"Oh, yeah?" Samuel asked, red-faced and grabbing a sword of his own. "Least I'm better at fighting a dragon!" He tried to raise his voice, but lost the breath and simply stated it. Then he began racing towards the dragon.

Drew also chose a sword and went after them although

not at the breakneck speed they were running at. The dragon was close enough that Drew reached it quickly anyway.

Gabrielle wondered if she should start worrying that the knights and squires would trip over each other in their efforts to battle the dragon.

Without a weapon from dragon's claw, there was little chance of the humans winning the fight. Perhaps they could distract the dragon until he wearied enough from their efforts and simply flew away.

Turning around to face her parents, she saw that a few more men had gathered by the tents but did not intervene. She was about to ask if they were going to retreat to the tents themselves when another roar sounded.

The dragon flapped his wings a few times, encouraging the fires. Then he took a few steps and leapt into the air. Roaring, he soared over Gabrielle's head, towards the tents, breathing fire upon them.

The gathered crowd scrambled to evacuate the area. A few prepared archers launched arrows at the dragon. After a few lucky ones hit his snout, he flew up and around, going back over Gabrielle's head, back to dragon territory.

He was gone.

The camp was not much quieter without him. One or two people had caught on fire and were furiously trying to take off their clothes or douse the flames in their hair with dirt. Flaming tents ejected swordsmen, cavalry, and archers, all of whom poured into the area between the tent entrances and continued panicking about the fire. Some threw hand-fuls of dirt onto the fire. Others called insistently for order, creating more commotion. The fringes of the crowd fanned out, but did not seem to be able to pull themselves away from the commotion, wanting to help yet only making the tumult worse.

Gabrielle noticed someone walking slowly and calmly towards the crowd, an obvious act in this chaos. Davey was nearing the crowd steadily, but patiently, and those on the edge grew quiet and somehow made room for him to pass through. Spreading, the silence slowly fell upon the crowd like a rug gently lowered to the floor by an edge.

By the time Davey was thirty feet into the tents, the popping of flames and occasional crack of wood supports breaking were the only sounds. Davey climbed onto a barrel that was outside one of the tents, giving him about four feet of height above the knights, squires, swordsmen, archers, cavalry, and occasional cook and washerwoman. He surveyed the scene quietly then spoke calmly and loudly.

"Everyone must leave this area. Knights and archers, collect buckets and find a water source. Swordsmen and cavalry, line up from a knight to the camp area. Squires, use wet cloth and dirt to try and put out the fire. Everyone else go to where help is needed. If the dragon returns, the same men will fight it while the rest of you continue to put out the fire."

As soon as Davey finished speaking, the crowds spilled out of the tented area. Gabrielle wondered if she should look for Danielle, Anthony, and Marion or help with the fire.

Deciding that Danielle had an army to help her, she and her parents joined a water line. The amount of people soon became overwhelming to Gabrielle, but she focused on her task and tried to ignore the others all around her. She supposed that, in time, one might get used to it.

As they passed buckets, she learned from those around her that they were simply at the head branch of the gathered army. The king had been organizing the other battalion units, but was planning on returning to head the attack soon which is why he was on his way when they had been arrested.

In spite of her carefulness, the water in the buckets eventually slopped down her front, and she slowly but surely got soaked. Her shoulder began to ache again. Quietly, she whispered a healing spell. The wound was already obviously healing by magic.

Gabrielle reached for another bucket from her mother, but Gabrielle's mother only raised her empty hands. Looking down the line, Gabrielle saw an unorganized group of people wandering back towards the tents, the line ahead of them also dispersing. "Fire's out!" a swordsman yelled excitedly.

Both Gabrielle and her mother turned to face the other direction. Twas difficult to see the camp, but they could no longer hear nor see the fire though lazy smoke still drifted into the early afternoon sky. Twas only early afternoon. The sudden efficiency of the people amazed her.

"Where do we go?" Gabrielle's mother asked as a few cheers broke out and more people milled past them, all relieved and many laughing.

"We should leave," Gabrielle's father said at once.

Gabrielle studied her parents' faces. They seemed as reluctant as she did to just leave. What were they to do, though? They certainly could not stop the king's decision to go to war. Staying here would only endanger them further. If she was being honest, she just didn't want to leave Danielle and Anthony and Marion and Davey and Drew and Jonathon though Jonathon might already be gone. She certainly did not want to leave without even saying goodbye.

What about her spell book? Most likely, it was still somewhere in the camp. If it was found, it surely would garner the king's – and the prince's – attention. It would be a leap, but a small one, to connect Gabrielle's book to the spell book. At the very least, it would spur an inquiry, and that was definitely undesired. Perhaps then, for the sake of the book, they should stay a little bit longer, just to get it back and ensure their family would be left alone.

Except staying here was dangerous. They were wanted for the crime of helping the prince save the princess. Anger surged within her.

Gabrielle took a deep breath, focusing on a meaningless point of space between her parents. Such emotion would not help.

"Tis dangerous, Marie," her father reminded.

"I know," her mother agreed.

"We're not safe."

"Tis the meaning of dangerous, my dear."

"My . . . book is still in the camp," Gabrielle told them hesitantly.

Her parents looked at her blankly.

She briefly closed her eyes. "Tis a spell book," she whispered.

"From where?" Her father somehow kept his voice even.

"Jesalyn gave it to me," Gabrielle said. "Elias found it, but could not read it. If it is left here, though, eventually someone who can read will discover it."

"It may not lead back to us," her mother said.

"No," her father conceded, "but knowing as everyone who searched our bags does that Gabrielle owned a book, our family would come under scrutiny. It would only take the prince or one of his 'traveling companions' to identify the bag as Gabrielle's, and the king would have us all executed."

Gabrielle's mother sighed and nodded.

They would get the book.

Her father inclined his head and gently grasped her mother's hand. "We'll be all right. We'll get through this."

Gabrielle felt another strong wave of guilt. "I am so sorr—"

Her father pulled her into a hug, her mother joining in. The three of them stood there, noiselessly swaying in the stragglers that finished the dismembered troupe heading towards the tents.

Gabrielle thought back to Lucas' words. Her innkeeping and peaceful tavern-master parents had sailed the sea, traveled to dragon territory, fought a chimera (however unsuccessfully), fell off a cliff, slept in a dragon's cave, had been chased by karkadans, survived a surprise attack by dragons, were captured by gnomes, carried by rocs, and arrested and chained by knights of king. Arguably, all of that was entirely her fault, yet her father cut off her apology to hug her, then kiss her on the forehead and say, "I love you."

Yes, her parents were a smidge astounding.

XXI

In Which Everything is Wrapped up with a Hint of More

"Gabs!" Danielle's voice carried across the tented area.

Upon hearing Danielle, Gabrielle paused searching with her parents for the bags and stood on her tiptoes to scan the surroundings for any sight of the princess.

Anthony whipped out from between two tents, giggling fiercely and racing as fast as his little legs could carry him. He collapsed in a heap at Gabrielle's feet.

Smiling, Gabrielle picked up the little boy and held him in her arms as Marion and Danielle followed close behind in Anthony's tracks.

"Whew!" Danielle gasped. "You guys are one hard group to find!"

The swordsmen passing by sent bemused glances at the princess with rolled up sleeves and hiked up skirt.

"We are looking for our bags," Gabrielle explained. "Do you know where they are?"

"No, but I know someone who will! Can I steal her for a moment Marie and Timothy, sir?" Danielle grabbed her hand.

"I have Anthony," Gabrielle reminded Danielle, smiling. "Besides, we'd rather not lose each other."

Danielle let go of Gabrielle's hand and pointed towards the top of a large tent that peeked out over the rest. "We can regroup there. Please?"

"Go ahead." Gabrielle's mother smiled.

Danielle yanked Gabrielle's arm. "Come on, Gabs!"

"Go! Go! Go!" Anthony yelled.

Gabrielle plunged into the bustle after Danielle, closely tailing her and Marion. They wove in between tents and around people, dodged hurrying squires, and ducked strolling knights. A spark of excitement lit inside of Gabrielle. Nobody knew who she was. For a moment, the anonymity was relaxing.

"Lucas!"

Their game abruptly ended.

Lucas turned and scanned them, a grin appearing almost immediately. "Yes, your highness?"

"We are looking for"—Danielle dropped her voice—"the bags."

Anthony and Marion giggled.

Danielle scratched the side of her mouth, theatrically covering it. "Do you think you know where they might be?"

Lucas leaned in towards Danielle and then a little lower, including Marion more. "If I do recall, those bags were moved to the tent to the right of the king's after the fire. Do you know where the king's tent is?"

"It's the big one!" Anthony told him excitedly, pointing in the wrong direction.

"Exactly!" Lucas said. "It is the really big one that is taller than all the others. Think you can find it?"

"Yes!" Anthony cheered.

"Thank you, Lucas," Danielle said. Turning back to Marion, "Are you ready? Let's go!"

Danielle and Marion took off again.

Gabrielle looked to Lucas.

"Go! Go! Go!" Anthony reminded her.

Gabrielle nodded at Lucas and broke eye contact. She began to chase after Danielle.

Her hesitation to leave Lucas left her greatly behind. She had to pay much more attention as she tried to find her way to the king's tent. As far as she had heard, the king still had not arrived. Hopefully, her luck would hold until her family had gotten the book.

She took a few wrong turns, so by the time she had reached the king's tent, her parents, Danielle, and Marion were all standing and talking calmly out in front of it.

Gabrielle wiped some of the sweat off her face. The day still spoke of the oncoming winter, yet her running had left her winded and perspiring.

"Tis in here, Gabs," Danielle brightly said, gesturing towards the tent to the right. "Anthony." Danielle held out a hand for him.

Gabrielle set him down, and he ran towards Danielle.

Stepping into the tent slightly muffled the sounds of the base camp around her. The atmosphere was quieter, reserved, but the air was also stuffier and smelled of damp parchment and leather. Something shifted and moved about behind a crate. Gabrielle crept up to the box slowly.

"Gabs!" Davey hit his head upon another crate poking out slightly above him as he spoke. He grunted. Then his eyes darted to her, and he straightened. He spread his arms wide. "I assume you are looking for your bags?"

Gabrielle gave him a small smile. "Yes."

Davey nodded. "I know where it is."

He scrambled over the crate instead of walking around it. He nearly tumbled to the ground, but then jumped to his feet and headed towards the corner near the door. He turned around with the small satchel in his hand. "Your bag." He gestured behind himself. "The other bags are here, too."

Gabrielle's heart pounded. She shoved her worry down. "Thank you."

As she reached for it, he pulled it out of her reach, grinning. "What's in it?"

Gabrielle forced another smile, wondering if the sudden twitching she felt in her leg was visible. "You already know. They had to search everything."

Davey gripped the bag tightly, then offered it to her. His eyes darkened and chin lowered. "Do you want help getting out of here? Sir Michael does not budge on the rules, but there are others in the camp who can make you and your family disappear, go back to Seron with no trouble. You are still not known well enough to be found easily, and your finding can be made much more difficult."

The bag waited in between them.

Perhaps they could just disappear, but if they left and were found, what would the punishment be then? Double or nothing? Davey seemed so confident in his ability to help them not be found, but she had also known his confidence that his father would be fair. If he was so confident in his father's fairness, then why this offer?

He just wanted the best for them. She knew that. It was in every action he took. His intentions did not justify, but she understood.

She hesitantly reached out and took the bag from Davey.

"I was only teasing about keeping it from you, Gabrielle," Davey told her.

"I know." She bit her lip, then remembered again that she was not alone. "Davey, I think this should be a decision made by my parents and myself, for it affects all of us."

"I understand," Davey said, nodding. "Do you—"

The tent flap flew open, nearly hitting Davey.

"So sorry, your highness!" a swordsman with a bright red beard apologized. "Th—th—the king, sire, the king is here. He requests your presence, and the presence of your traveling companions."

Davey's eyes flickered to Gabrielle. "Where is the king?" Davey asked.

"Here."

A well-built man with a short, dark brown beard and a cleanshaven head stood at the entrance to the tent. His fine armour gleamed and bore a kneeling red dragon with two crossed black swords behind it—the crest of Aradin.

King Germaine's frown deepened when he saw Davey. "Follow me," he said and left the tent.

Davey shot a glance at Gabrielle, but Gabrielle could not decipher anything before they were walking out as well.

King Germaine stood outside his tent, a small crowd before him.

The king began without a prelude. "I have returned and heard immediately about the bravery and skills of Ian and Gavin. You have come here today searching for knighthood, and the opportunity presented itself much sooner than it has for anyone else. You took your chance and succeeded, demonstrating for all in the camp your bravery in facing the dragon, your manners in protecting those in danger, and your abilities in fighting the beast, whether it was with a sword or without."

His eyes, looking almost amused, flicked to the man Gabrielle assumed was Gavin.

"Normally, you would be knighted with great ceremony in the city of Aradin, but due to the great eagerness on your part"—a younger man, most likely Ian, blushed and looked to the ground—"it is my honour to knight you today. Your accomplishment is especially impressive considering that this is, by far, the shortest amount of time it has ever taken someone to be knighted since expressing the desire.

"Ian"—he beckoned the incredibly young man forth—"kneel."

Ian came forward and nearly fell with his eagerness and disbelief, but managed to land roughly on one knee.

King Germaine did not change his expression, just drew his jewel-encrusted sword and rested it upon Ian's right shoulder. "Ian, do you swear to serve the king, this kingdom, and the peoples with all gentlemanly respect and integrity. If so, say 'yes, with all my abilities'."

"Y— yes, with all m-my abilities."

King Germaine brought the sword to Ian's left shoulder. "Ian, do you swear to serve the king, this kingdom, and the peoples with all gentlemanly respect and integrity. If so, say 'yes, with all my heart'."

"Yes, with all m-my heart."

King Germaine laid the sword, blade flat, against the crown of Ian's head. "Ian, do you swear to serve the king, this kingdom, and the peoples with all gentlemanly respect and integrity. If so, say 'yes, with all my mind'."

"Yes, with all my mind."

"By the power vested in me, I proclaim you a knight of the king. Rise, Sir Ian, and fulfill your vows."

Ian kept his head low and rose slowly to his feet, swallowing several times. He lifted his head, then bowed. "Thank you, your majesty." Straightening, he proudly walked back to his place by Gavin, unable to contain his bright smile.

"Gavin." King Germaine called him forward.

"I wish to serve the peoples," Gavin told him.

"So you shall," King Germaine said, eyes appraising Gavin. "Tell me, young man, why do you wish to be a knight?"

"I don't."

Gabrielle pursed her lips. At the very least, Gavin could have waited until after the king had dealt with Gabrielle and her family before souring the king's disposition.

Gavin continued, "I wish to serve the peoples. If being a knight would help me do such, then I'll become a knight, but I see no purpose in being a knight if it doesn't help me serve the peoples."

The air was uncomfortably hot, and Gabrielle rubbed the back of her neck uneasily.

King Germaine examined Gavin, taking in his old, ratty clothes, his ruff beard, his disheveled brown hair and scuffed hands. "Why do you wish to protect the people?"

Gavin did not lower his eyes at all nor dampen his gaze. "The peoples need protection."

"You speak wisely, young man. I promise you, being a knight will help you protect the people."

"The peoples come first," Gavin stated.

"Naturally," the king agreed.

"Then I pledge with all my abilities, all my heart, and all my mind to serve the peoples with the utmost respect and integrity."

Did his boldness have no limits?

King Germaine studied Gavin a final time. "Come forward, Gavin, and let the sword rest upon you as a testament to your pledge."

To Gabrielle's relief, Gavin did such, kneeling before the king and receiving the sword upon both shoulders and his head. "By the power vested in me, I proclaim you a knight of the king. Rise, Sir Gavin, and fulfill your vows."

"With pleasure." Gavin stood and bowed as Ian had done, but more boldly, more confidently, and he returned to his spot grimmer than he had left.

"The second order of business concerns my son. To our

. . . great . . . surprise, he has chosen to disobey a direct order again."

"I request a council—"

"Denied." King Germaine cut him off curtly. "You have requested council before, and I have listened. However, still you continue to disregard my words."

"I listen carefully to your words. You have told me to serve the peoples and have integrity—"

"And respect," his father reminded him, "yet you fail to respect my commands."

"I respect your words and your—"

"Not my commands. You have trampled upon them once again with nary a thought of the consequences."

"I take full responsibility—"

"Denied." King Germaine interrupted him again. "You take full responsibility, but the punishment fails to enact a response. You portray a frightening lack of concern over your own welfare."

"Are we not pledged to put the needs of the peoples—"

"The needs of the kingdom, David. You forget the needs of the kingdom. The needs of the kingdom include a king who has an heir and an heir who is able to preserve himself."

"Yes, but of what worth is an heir if he does not protect the peoples—"

"An heir is worth much, and I would caution against such a tone."

"What about the needs of your other child? What about the needs of your daughter?"

"You lack prudence and understanding—"

"I understand that if I had not acted, you would be warring right now with the dragons," Davey interrupted.

"We *are* warring with the dragons," his father coldly said.

"We could not even kill one dragon today, Father, with all the knights, with all the swordsmen—"

"Enough."

"If you bring a war when we are unprepared you bring disaster—"

"I said enough."

Chills ran up and down Gabrielle's spine. Gabrielle had wondered about Gavin's limits. She had not realised that Davey had none.

A deep, stuttered breath interrupted the thick silence though an evident effort was made to stifle the sound.

King Germaine glanced at his daughter, and his entire demeanor changed. His shoulders sank. His eyes mellowed.

"Danielle," the king sighed. "I am exceedingly glad to see that you are safe and sound." He held out a hand and gestured her forward.

Danielle straightened slightly, leaving the children behind her, and approached him with no hesitation. "Father," she bowed, speaking softly, "tis good to be safe and sound."

"The ordeal you have gone through is unimaginable." King Germaine took her hand.

Princess Danielle kept her head bowed but lifted her hand to kiss his. "I am ever so glad to be home. I am thankful for my brother's bravery but also for my father's wisdom."

King Germaine's face twitched, his expression darkening.

"I am glad you understand such although I do not know whether to call it bravery or stupidity."

The crowd rustled. Gabrielle's own cheeks flamed, but she bit her tongue.

Danielle shook her head, gripping the king's hand tighter. "I've spent many nights with the dragons, my lord. They are fearsome beasts and not to be trifled with. Their roars shook the ground and with a single hand they brought down castle stones. Their bodies are so large they cannot fit between the trees of a dense forest, and to walk in a tunnel or down a hall is unimaginable. Every time one came close, I had to raise my eyes and tip my head to view it fully."

King Germaine nodded while scowling. "They are dangerous foes, but my army has beat them before. We shall do so again."

Danielle gave a small smile. "An army would fight them, but your son has shamed them. Even with their strength and ferocity, he traveled alone through their very own territory and back out without being harmed. Two dragons, however, were blinded, both through my brother's cleverness and skill."

Shock flickered across the king's face. He looked to the prince. "Is this true, David?"

"Yes, sire," the prince answered.

Drew's face remained impassive.

Princess Danielle laughed gently, kissing her father on his hand again. "To think they planned to draw ye out to kill! How mortifying David's safe travels must be!"

King Germaine let out a light, nearly indiscernible breath,

amusement and resignation suddenly warring upon his face. "How mortifying, indeed."

Danielle met his gaze. "Their desperation overpowered them no doubt. To start a battle they could not win? To fight a war they would only lose? And their wounds compared to ours are nothing to boast of."

"Yes," King Germaine muttered. His eyes went to Gabrielle and her parents.

Gabrielle tried to shrink into the ground.

Her mother grasped her hand, her head also bowed, though her eyes still looked up.

"How mortifying," the king repeated, his attention returning to Princess Danielle.

Neither said anything for a moment.

King Germaine lifted Danielle's hand and kissed it for the first time. "And I see your imprisonment has changed you little."

"To your relief?" Danielle lightly asked, hand tracing a pattern on the back of the king's.

Davey's relation became evident as a slight smirk quirked up the corner of the king's mouth. "Of course."

King Germaine pulled his shoulders back, rising higher though he had not taken a step. "Yes, we have struck a great blow to the dragons this day by thwarting their attempts to destabilize the kingdom, by proving once again the strength and intelligence of Aradin against the vicious beasts."

His tone had adopted a lulling tilt, just as Gabrielle's father's tone did while reading a passage.

"We have overcome them through our prince alone while the princess bore imprisonment. Today we have won a victory. Tomorrow, we shall return home, safe in the knowledge that Aradin has once again overcome magic and the beasts that horde it, and tonight, we shall celebrate."

A moment of silence, then Lucas whooped, and the ones closest joined in, the cheers growing in volume and excitement.

King Germaine leaned close and whispered into Danielle's ear.

Danielle turned to smirk at Davey and said though it seemed only mouthed because of the noise, "He does."

Her father said something else, and then Danielle was approaching Gabrielle and her parents. The princess stopped before them with sparkling eyes. She bumped Gabrielle on the arm, grinning.

"And that's why you never catch flies with Davey."

Gabrielle ran her hands along the worn bed stand in her room, the fading carvings familiar beneath her fingertips. Her feet traced the dear scratches upon the wooden floor, toes etching out the intimate curves. Savoring the shutters, she opened the window and gazed upon the memorized view. Fields of potatoes and vegetables, rowdy stables and pecking hens, the sun peacefully setting, though not as brilliantly as at Havene.

Mr. Henry walked across the back woods, head still low, but his stride steady. He had helped the tavern and inn greatly while Gabrielle's parents were gone and planned on continuing the trend when the fields could do without him.

Her parents knew she was a changeling.

Gabrielle smiled as the thought interrupted her again. She

had never thought the statement would bring her so much relief. Her parents knew.

She was a changeling.

Perhaps twas not simply her parents knowing that brought her such relief. The word, while still lethal, did not seem as ugly as before. It rang, not with elegance, but perhaps with potential.

She was a changeling.

Gabrielle smiled and leaned upon the sill, contemplating the events of the past few days. The army had begun disbanding the next day as promised. Danielle had surprised her, and not only with the king but also with her dealings with Gabrielle's parents.

They fired her.

Her parents had decided that they wanted Gabrielle to go onto new and different things though Gabrielle noted twas primarily her mother speaking, so they no longer wanted her to work as the barmaid. When Gabrielle had asked what she could possibly do, they explained that there just so happened to be an opening for a maidservant in the palace – a hand-maiden for the princess. Gabrielle could not help but laugh. Then she realised that her parents were serious.

She had wanted to go, desperately, but to leave her parents? Leave her home? Seron was all she had ever known. She had planned to grow old here, imagined herself as the aging "taverness", grandchildren scurrying about. Her father had always talked half-heartedly about formal education, but she had preoccupied herself with learning from him when time allowed, not that time often did. Seron had offered plenty of preoccupation. Seron had offered her all she ever wanted. All she ever needed.

However, even she had to admit that there was a new, different satisfaction she now held from journeying to dragon territory, and she did not know if she would get the chance to leave Seron again.

That, and Danielle had smiled at her and asked to be friends, and Gabrielle, for all that she failed to remember, saw Mackenzie. Twas the grain that broke the millstone.

She was moving to Aradin.

Her fingers followed the grooves in the sill.

They were leaving tomorrow. Danielle had been able to set the timing due to the army being large and slow to disassemble. Jonathon had left almost immediately. Davey had left two days ago. While no punishment had been placed upon him, from the sound of the duties King Germaine had assigned him, no punishment was necessary. Danielle had shrugged and smiled when Gabrielle pointed this out.

"He did disobey the king's command," she told her, grinning mischievously. "I'm just glad he hasn't remarked upon the children yet."

Marion and Anthony were coming with them. Danielle had assured Gabrielle that her father would just assume that the children belonged to a servant.

Gabrielle had voiced her doubts about this lasting long, with which Danielle agreed.

"But it shall last long enough that he no longer will care to change it," Danielle said. "Mother may be a slightly different problem, but I believe we can win her over by slowly exposing her to them."

It was then that Gabrielle remarked how expertly Danielle used what she knew about people. Even though the words came out naturally softened, the implication sat like a heavy stone between them.

Gabrielle shook off the memory and smiled again. She was moving to Aradin.

She was leaving behind all she knew for a friend and a hope and . . . change. Perhaps not the change that Thomas envisioned. Perhaps not the change that she was starting to hope the peoples in this kingdom would undergo. Twas change nonetheless.

She felt a deep conviction she could not explain. She felt this conviction, and she desperately wanted to live up to it. Indeed, she could sway neither her feeling nor her hope that this was a beginning.

Indeed, twas only the beginning.